Canon

CW00803006

Cwm Woods

The Manor

Beddows' House

Post Office

k Lion

New Bungalows

River Wye

hool

N

W   ℰ

S

OF APPLES AND SERPENTS

Of Apples and Serpents

Mike Knight

Illustrations and dust jacket design by the author

Cappella Archive
Book on Demand Limited Editions

Cappella Archive
Foley Terrace : Great Malvern : England
www.cappella.demon.co.uk

Reset impression printed : July 2001

British Library Cataloguing–in–Publication Data
A catalogue record for this book is
available from the British Library

ISBN 0-9525308-6-4

*Typeset in ten point Cappella Baskerville and printed on
Five Seasons paper from John Purcell of London.*

DEDICATION

To Judy

Thank you for your patience and support while I spent many hours with my new-found friends, the people of Lower Kings Canon. Many thanks and all my love.

THE MAIN CHARACTERS

Miss Acton	*Headmistress of the village school*
Frank Beddows	*Tom's grandfather and one of the `Young Farmers'*
Ken Beddows	*Tom's father*
Mrs Beddows	*Tom's mother*
Tom Beddows	*The main character*
Jane Beddows	*Tom's young sister*
Peter Beddows	*Tom's young brother*
Sarah Beddows	*Tom's daughter*
Steve Bufton	*A farmer dealing in second hand tractors*
Mr Cargill	*The firm's solicitor*
Matthew Davies	*Transport Manager at Jones Road Haulage Ltd.*
Edith	*A maid at The Big House*
Edward	*A `Young Farmer'*
Dai Evans	*Proprietor of a building restoration company*
Jean Evans	*A cleaner at the Big House*
Sam Evans	*Jean's husband and a lorry driver for Jones Road Haulage Ltd.*
Bob Gregory	*Chris's father*
Chris Gregory	*A boy of Tom's age, who grew up in Gorston*
Jennifer Gregory	*Chris's sister*
Goggles	*Chris's friend*
Gran	*Chris's grandmother*
Major Hudson	*Lord of the Manor*
Mrs Hudson	*The Major's wife*
Penelope Hudson	*The Major's daughter*
Miss Henworth	*A school teacher*
Brian Jones	*Tom's `enemy'*
Pierre Le Brun	*A French builder*
Roger Meddows	*Manager of the Farm Supplies Centre*
Melanie	*A secretary at the cider plant*
Nellie Partridge	*The object of Frank's dreams*
David Peters	*An unscrupulous car dealer*
Paul	*Jane's boyfriend*
Roberts	*A supermarket manager*
Mike Sturgess	*Farm manager on the estate*
Angela Sturgess	*Mike's daughter*
Doctor Sherwood	*The village doctor*
Susan Sherwood	*The doctor's daughter*
Trevor	*A garage mechanic*
Walter	*An old estate worker*

The Black Lion

Chapter One

In the days when cattle were taken on foot along the drovers' roads to market, the Old Black Lion had been a watering hole for both livestock and men. It has hardly changed in five hundred years and the drovers would still feel at home if they saw it today. It stands on the Welsh border; a black and white, half-timbered building under a lichen-covered roof.

A gnarled wisteria clambers over the building, dangling its mauve tresses against the timbers, and bees hum amongst the flowers, making their contribution to the lazy sounds of summer. The porch leans at a crazy angle as it always has done, because that is the way it was built by the rough hands of carpenters so many years ago.

The inside is cool and seems dark after the bright sunlight and it takes a while for the eyes to adjust to the low light. A group of men sit on stools around the massive stone fireplace in which there is no fire burning, as the landlord does not light it until October. Each patron of this inn has his own stool and, if he sits outside in the summer, he risks losing his place near the fire when the cold winds blow in January.

Only a few brave souls sit on benches in the sun. Copper kettles, ladles, and plaques, glow in the red light from the wall lamps. On the walls hang old sporting prints of pheasant shoots and fox hunting. Chalk marks are drawn on the flagstones —to keep away the evil spirits, say the old men. The ceiling is low and supported by heavy black beams, ravaged by time.

A young couple drove into the car park, parked close to the front door and went into the bar. "A pint and a dry white wine, please landlord," said the man. He picked up the drinks and joined his wife at a table by the window. An elderly man with white hair and a pint of cider sat at the next table.

He was smoking a pipe and he looked up from his newspaper, mumbled an incoherent greeting, and returned his gaze to the back page. The couple looked around the pub. When they first entered it had seemed dark and gloomy but, now that their eyes had adjusted to the low light, it seemed bright and cosy.

"Nice pub this," said the young man, in the direction of the next table.

"Aye, it suits me," was the response and once again he returned his gaze to the newspaper.

The young man continued, "I should think it's very old isn't it?"

The local folded his newspaper and joined them at their table, "It certainly is and it could tell you a tale or two." He nodded towards the door and asked, "Did you see that man leaving just as you arrived? He must have been getting into his car when you came in."

The young woman replied, "We saw a car going out, but I didn't notice the driver. Why?"

"It was Mr Chris Gregory. He lives in the village and he's one of the richest men in the country. He owns Gregory's Country Cider, you know."

"Really?"

"He is, and this pub could tell a tale about him; a tale of hatred, success, failure, mass-murder by poisoning, and do you know, people come in here and say this is a sleepy little village and don't think anything ever happens here. Hah! if only they knew."

"You're fascinating me. Did you say mass-murder by poisoning? I think that I remember it. Wasn't the case known as the Cider Poisonings? The worst case ever."

The old man smoothed his strands of grey hair and said, "That's right, dozens of 'em, and the newspapers and television were full of it. All young people and they died a terrible agonizing death. The poisoner used to come in this pub and sit here. He probably planned all the details at this very table." He emptied his tankard and slid it towards the young man, "Would you like to hear the story?"

The couple glanced at each other and the man said, "Yes, please, we're on holiday and we've got plenty of time. It sounds very fascinating."

The old man sat in silence and then nodded towards his tankard.

In response to an elbow in the ribs from his wife, the young man abruptly stood up and said, "Oh, would you like another?"

When he returned with his cider, the old man took a drink and said, "I'm glad you've got plenty of time and nothing better to do, because it's a long story and I expect we'll need a few of these." He tapped the side of his tankard and winked at the girl.

They sat in silence while he took another drink. All they could hear was the steady tick of the grandfather clock.

He put down his tankard and wiped his mouth on the back of his hand, "Ah, good cider that." Then, with the young couple leaning forward in anticipation, he took a deep breath and began his story.

There was a twenty-first birthday party somewhere in London. It was in a large house in a suburban street and there was plenty of drink flowing. On the kitchen table there were bottles of wine and spirits and stacked on the floor were cases of beer and cider. The cider was Tom Beddows' Country Cider and, while the music thumped out from the big speakers in the lounge and the dancers stamped and gyrated, there was a constant procession into the kitchen of young people refilling their glasses.

The cider was popular as the dancers were becoming hot and thirsty as the evening went on and the cider was an excellent thirst-quencher, but after the party many of them became ill. The next day they began to act as if they were drunk; slurred speech, staggering and falling over, then terrible pain.

Sally Broderick, a pretty girl with a bright future, was one of the victims and her mother found her lying on the bedroom floor, doubled up in pain and covered in vomit. "Jack!" called her mother, "Come quick. It's Sally."

She was taken off to hospital by ambulance and her parents sat by the bed, watching her sweating and writhing about in agony.

"For God's sake!" shouted her father, can't you do anything for her?"

The nurse shook her head slowly and said, "Doctor is on his way and he'll have a word with you as soon as he gets here."

The doctor took them aside and explained that she had been given pain-killers but she was not responding to them. At first they thought it was food poisoning; something she ate at the party perhaps, but now they didn't know what it was.

"Quite honestly, I'm afraid we have no idea what the problem is, but we're doing tests and hope to have an answer soon."

He scratched behind his ear and said, "It's strange, because we've got a lot of similar cases all from last night's party, so that gives us a clue where to start looking, but it's all pointing to some sort of poisoning. The police are investigating now."

He was interrupted by a scream from Sally's bed. They rushed over and she was violently kicking and screaming. The nurses tried to calm her but she gave a final scream and lay still.

Sally Broderick had become the first victim of a poison that had been put into the cider and in the next few hours another twenty or thirty died, all in a terrible agony which the drugs could not alleviate. The owner of the cider company, Tom Beddows, was arrested as all the evidence seemed to point at him."

The old man paused to empty his tankard and slid it across to the couple. When it was replenished he continued with his story, "I expect you're a bit puzzled what all this has got to do with Chris Gregory, the man who left as you arrived."

The young man ran his hands over the table and said, "Yes, and you say the poisoning was all planned at this table?"

"Yes, it was, but it's a long and complicated story and to get to the bottom of it we have to go back a few years to nineteen forty-eight.

In 1948 the Inn looked exactly the same. Even the pictures and the chalk marks hadn't changed. The summer of that year was long and hot; the sort we dream about as we grow older and memories become rosy. The sounds and perfumes of summer were on the air but inside the Old Black Lion in Lower Kings Canon all was quiet, save for the ticking of the grandfather clock and the occasional laughter from a few people playing quoits in the top bar.

"Four more pints over here!" came a shout from the chimney corner and an old gentleman creaked to an almost vertical position and collected the pewter tankards from his three companions.

"Right you are, Frank," replied the landlord. The tankards were filled with cider and the old man made his way back to the fireplace with the drinks on a blue tray. In spite of his faltering progress, not a drop was spilt. Frank was eighty-five and his friends were of similar age; known affectionately as 'The Young Farmers' by the other locals, many a mischievous plot had been hatched around the fireplace by those old men.

Frank's face was wrinkled, the lines around his eyes emphasising the wicked twinkle. Although the weather was warm, he wore a tattered raincoat tied around the middle with twine and his boots were worn and dusty.

When he returned to the fireplace and carefully put down the tray, the old man nearest to the wall began to shake and then let out an uncontrollable burst of giggling.

"What's up with you? You old bugger," said Frank as he hovered over the table. Then his eyes fell upon a pair of ladies' panties resting on his stool.

"They dropped out of your pocket when you stood up to get the cider," said George solemnly.

"You old bugger!" exclaimed Frank, as he picked them up and made a show of noisily blowing his nose on them. "You put 'em there when I went up to the bar. Mind you, I've got a few of these back home that I've collected over the years."

"I'll hang them up behind the bar," said the landlord, "That'll set a few tongues wagging."

The Young Farmers settled down with their tankards, talking about the old days; the incident of the panties inspiring many exaggerated and often told tales of past conquests in hay-barns, dairies and cornfields.

It was the proud boast of these men that not one of them had missed a day sitting around the fire for as long as they could remember. The conversation ebbed and flowed as the grandfather clock continued to tick, just as it had done for a hundred and fifty years.

"Hey, Les, there's a little lad tapping at the window," came a voice from one of the quoits players in the top bar.

The landlord breathed vigorously on a glass and scrutinized it against the light with screwed up eyes. "That'll be young Tom and I reckons you're in big trouble, Frank."

Frank fumbled inside his raincoat and produced a watch from his waistcoat pocket. "Aye, I'll be in trouble and no mistake. I'm late for dinner and I expect young Tom's bin sent to find me."

"I wouldn't like to be in your shoes," grinned George, between puffs of his pipe.

Frank downed the last inch of his cider. "I'm not frightened of her —much," he added with a wink and went out into the sunshine.

"Come on, Granddad," said the fair haired boy. "Mum says you're to come right away or your dinner'll be cold."

"Alright, young man, let's go. What've we got anyway?"

"Rabbit stew."

"Oh, yes, that'll be the rabbit I caught in Cwm woods; a nice plump one she was. I'll show you how to catch 'em when you're a bit older. When I was a lad, I used to go into those woods and bag twenty or thirty a night. I never got found out, you know, but I had a few near misses."

The old man kicked at a stone lying in the road and continued, "I used to sell them out the back of the pub for sixpence each. My Mum and Dad were glad of the money, I can tell you. Those rabbits kept us from starving."

He bent down to pluck a piece of grass which he proceeded to chew on and Tom looked up at his grandfather and said, "Oh, yes, Granddad, I'd like to learn how to do it. Will you show me tonight? Will you Granddad?"

"Why not, young lad? Fair play, I was no older than you when I started."

He looked down at his grandson as they walked along the lane between the fragrant hedgerows. The boy wore a tweed jacket that was too big and had leather patches sewn on the elbows. His grey flannel trousers came down to just below the knees and his socks had dropped, to hang in folds over his sandals. His freckled face looked up at the old man with obvious affection as he skipped along beside him.

"Look out, Tom, here's the boss," said Frank. As they neared a small red-brick house at a bend in the lane, a female figure stood at the garden gate gesticulating wildly. She shouted, "I told you to be home at one o'clock and it's half past two. I've had the stew on the range for so long it'll be dried up like old boots!"

Frank was not intimidated. "Hold your tongue, woman. It'll be all the better for stewing."

The three went through the door into the cosy little house. A delicious aroma met them as they walked into the kitchen and Tom's mother organized them round the table and ladled generous helpings of the steaming stew. His father, Ken Beddows, broke chunks of crusty bread and handed them round and the meal was eaten with very little conversation. Also at the table sat Tom's younger brother and sister, Pete and Jane. Usually boisterous children, they ate quietly, well aware of the effect of Frank's late arrival on their mother's mood.

Tom's father eventually broke the silence. "Well done, Dad, you haven't lost your touch. A good rabbit that."

"Aye, and I'll be showing the lad how to do it tonight," replied the old man, with a sly wink at Tom.

Mrs Beddows noisily collected the plates and cutlery and placed them on the draining board. "Well, you make sure you don't get caught. That Major Hudson can be right nasty when he catches poachers and we don't want our little lad branded a criminal. It doesn't matter about you. Everyone knows you're one anyway."

"I ain't never been caught yet in seventy years and I don't intend starting now."

"Well, just you make sure."

Ken tapped out his pipe on the range and refilled it. He leaned back in his chair and slowly blew smoke up to the ceiling. After a long silence he said, "Who was down the pub today Dad?"

"Oh, the usual crowd."

"I expect you've been up to your pranks again. You old boys will get yourselves into trouble one of these days, you know."

Frank grinned at his son and said, "Just harmless fun."

As Mrs Beddows washed the dishes, the two smallest children went into the back garden to play and the men sat either side of the range, watching the flickering flames.

After a while, Mrs Beddows called out, "Hey, Tom look at the time. You've got your jobs to do."

Frank looked across the table at Tom, who was reading the *Beano*. "Come on, Tom, get your jobs done and then we'll go up to Cwm Woods and see what we can catch for tomorrow's dinner."

Tom did not need to be persuaded. He did his jobs quite happily, realizing that everyone in the family had to pull their weight, and he was soon getting in the wood that his father had cut to feed the kitchen range. Although it was a hot summer, the range had to be kept alight for the cooking. Fuel was also needed for the boiler, so getting in the wood was a vital, all year-round job. He felt proud that such a responsibility was entrusted to him and he worked hard at the task without complaining.

He had to collect the wood from the shed, where it had been neatly stacked. It was mainly ash and oak and he'd learned to recognize the different types by their texture and smell, particularly liking the fragrance of freshly split oak. He threw the logs into a wheelbarrow and wheeled it into the house, skilfully negotiating the sharp turn through the door. They were stacked by the cast iron range in a tidy pile and he soon had enough to last his mother for several days.

The house was owned by Major Hudson, who lived in the Big House, as the locals called it and he owned a large estate with tied cottages. He was the main employer in the village, often referred to as the Squire, and his ancestors had held the title of Lord of the Manor of Kings Canon for generations. Ken Beddows paid him rent for the house and the two small paddocks that went with it.

In one of the paddocks was a chicken house with nesting boxes and a pop hole at one end, and it was Tom's job to feed the chickens and collect the eggs. Lifting the lids, he found seven brown eggs nestling in the straw. He'd collected eggs for as long as he could remember but he was always excited when he found them. His heart would skip a beat when he discovered the round treasures in the straw.

The few hens produced enough eggs for the family in the summer months and, when they were laying well, there was a surplus to sell in the village. As well as feeding the hens, he had to let them out in the morning and shut them in at night. Each morning, he would open the pop-hole and stand back as, one by one, they hopped out and pecked at the corn which he'd scattered on the ground.

The magnificent Rhode Island Red cock was usually the first out, followed by the hens. Their bright eyes would dart about, looking for the best grains before any of the others could pounce on them. Their combs and wattles were red as it was summer and they were in lay. They spent the day free-ranging around the fields before putting themselves to bed at dusk, when Tom would shut the pop-hole to keep them safe from foxes, who are always on the lookout for an unwary hen.

Not all of them laid in the nesting boxes which had been provided for them and Tom would have to search for nests in the hedgerows. One hen in particular, whom he called Henrietta, refused to lay in the house, and her eggs were to be found under a forsythia bush. Another hen had not come home at dusk the previous night and Tom found her under a pile of logs in the far corner of the paddock.

She was broody and sitting on thirteen eggs. She had raised broods of chicks every summer for years and she sat tight on her eggs as he approached and ruffled her feathers, clucking aggress- ively. Tom had just finished attending to his flock, when Frank called from the kitchen window.

"Have you finished your jobs yet?"

He'd forgotten for a moment that he was going rabbitting and a wave of excitement swept over him.

"Coming, Granddad," he called, as he went scampering into the house.

Before long they were walking down the lane towards the Cwm Woods.

"I think Mum was a bit cross with us for coming poaching," said Tom.

"No, lad, she's worried in case we get caught. It's against the law, you know, is poaching and if Major Hudson catches us, he could get the police onto us and then we'd be in trouble, but the trick is not to get caught."

He stopped to lift a bramble for the boy to pass under and said, "Some folks say its thieving, but it ain't. It happens in the country and it always has done. Taking a few rabbits ain't thieving. Anyways," he added with a grin, "we're doing him a favour because the little beggars eats his grass and young corn. We cut across the fields here, less chance of being seen. The only person we're likely to see between here and the woods is Mike Sturgess, the Farm Manager, and he'll most likely be down the pub, it being Saturday night."

The lane from which the two furtive figures had turned was lit by the evening sun. The buzz of insects was on the air and a cuckoo sounded in the distance. Either side of the narrow lane were clouds of cow parsley, standing taller than the boy and making the lane seem narrower as they leaned over towards the centre.

Every so often a straggling bramble would snatch at their clothes and Frank would stop and hold it up for his grandson. The excitement of the adventure heightened Tom's perception and he was acutely aware of the different smells on the warm evening air. He'd been waiting for this evening for a long time and he was relishing every minute of it.

They had climbed the style and were following the hedgerow around the cornfield. The corn was still green, but quite high, and the occasional partridge or startled pheasant would rise noisily from under their feet, making the boy's heart pound. As they passed under some oak trees, a flock of wood pigeon rose and wheeled away, grey against the clear blue sky.

The two didn't speak as they headed towards the cover of the woods and, as they drew nearer, the old man touched Tom's arm and said, "This is the place to catch 'em. They have their burrows just a few yards inside the wood under the bracken. They spend most of the day in there and come out at dusk to feed on the grass in the field."

The shadows were beginning to lengthen and the light was becoming more golden. The dark trees of Cwm Woods were changing to orange in the evening light.

"Quiet now, you can see them over there," whispered Frank.

There were a dozen or so rabbits with their heads down nibbling at the grass; their fur also taking on the golden hues of the evening light.

"How many are there, Granddad?" whispered Tom, breathlessly.

"Well now," chuckled Frank, "What you have to do is count their ears and divide by two. About twelve I think. Look, when they leave their burrows to feed at dusk, they use the same paths through the undergrowth. If you hunt around you'll find them."

They quietly separated the grasses and Frank took a few lengths of wire from his coat pocket. Each one had a loop at the end and he put the end through the loop to make a noose and fastened it to a tree root, with the noose spanning the tunnel in the grass.

"Now, watch carefully. You have to get the noose the right size, about like this. Too big and the little buggers will go right through, too small and they'll get suspicious and go the other way."

He fixed all six wires and whispered, "They'll be caught when they comes back from feeding. All we have to do now is go home and come back at first light to see what we've caught."

Then he scratched his head thoughtfully and said, "Do you want to learn how to catch pheasants?"

"Oh, yes please, Granddad."

"Right, we'll go a different way home round the side of the wood. Major Hudson's got some pheasants over yonder."

Frank glanced at the sky and began to walk briskly along the edge of the wood. "Come on. We'll have to be quick before it gets dark."

He led his grandson through the gate and into the wood where the undergrowth was thick and at first it was hard going. Tom was impressed with the agility with which his eighty-five year old grandfather moved through the woodland. Around the house he seemed to be stiff and slow, but in the woods he was rejuvenated and had no difficulty moving through the most difficult conditions.

They came to a clearing and the going became easier as they followed a path. The light was fading and the air heavy with the sweet smell of honeysuckle. The ghostly white shape of a barn owl glided silently past them and disappeared into the shadows.

At the next clearing, Frank stopped and produced a handkerchief wrapped round something bulky, tied in a knot. He knelt down on the grass and winking in conspiratorial fashion, sprinkled the contents on the ground.

Tom gazed at the old man and asked, "What're you doing, Granddad?"

"Catching pheasants."

"How does that catch pheasants?"

Frank winked again and said, "These are some raisins I'm putting down for them as a special treat."

"Do pheasants like raisins?"

"Aye, they like these," chuckled the old man, "They've been soaked in rum. I've had them soaking for a week or more. The pheasants are roosting now and they won't feed until dawn. Then they'll eat the raisins and fall down drunk and then you and me'll come along and pick them up. Clever ain't it?"

The wide-eyed boy was incredulous but he believed his grandfather, because he realized that there wasn't much he didn't know about poaching. The old man slowly rolled himself a cigarette and lit it as he led the way back home.

"Come on, lad, or we'll be late for supper," he said, without taking the cigarette from his mouth.

A heavy silence had descended on the woods as darkness had fallen. The only sound they could hear was the distant grunting of a hedgehog. They headed home at a brisk pace and, just as they were about to emerge from the dark and silent woods, Tom stopped abruptly as his arm was grabbed and held tightly.

"Shush, lad!" hissed Frank, "Stay here."

He crept stealthily towards a young ash tree, while Tom held his breath and strained his eyes in the gloom to see what was happening. He could see the glow from the cigarette dimly lighting Frank's face and he could make out his dark form amongst the trees. He felt his heart pounding and wanted to swallow hard, but didn't dare in case it made too much noise in the silent woods. He had no idea what his grandfather was doing but he was spell-bound by the tension and drama.

Suddenly, the silence was shattered by a blood-curdling screech, followed by a violent flapping and silence again. Tom could feel his heart pounding against his ribs and he strained his ears and eyes to discover what was happening.

"Come and see, Tom. He's a beauty," came a voice from the darkness.

Frank was holding a cock pheasant, which had been roosting on a low branch until the sharp eyes of the old poacher had spotted him. He'd been grabbed from his perch and killed with a swift twist of the neck. Frank held it tight against his chest as it flapped again for a few moments. Then all was silent.

"You'll get a better look at him when we're out of these trees."

In the open field there was sufficient light left to see the bird. It was now still, with its broken neck hanging over Frank's arm. In the fading light the boy could make out the scarlet around the eye, the iridescent blue and green of the head and neck and the long tail feathers. He felt a pang of compassion for the lovely creature which had met such a violent end. His grandfather sensed what he was feeling and noticed a tear glistening in the boy's eye.

"He didn't feel anything, you know," said the old man, tenderly putting an arm around the boy. "Better to be finished like this than to be shot and crippled or torn to pieces by a fox, and I'll tell you something else as well. He'll taste good when he's roasted next Sunday with some home-cured bacon and some of your mum's roast taters."

Tom tried to reply, but no sound came as Frank put the pheasant inside his coat and they headed for home, keeping a wary eye open for the gamekeeper.

At home, Mrs Beddows had served up supper for the two youngsters and got them into bed. They didn't want to go, as it was such a light evening, and it had been hard work getting them upstairs, but now they were in bed and the parents had the evening to themselves.

She was sitting by the kitchen range opposite her husband, who dozed in his armchair. The radio was on; a comedy with Arthur Askey, but she was only half listening as most of her attention was on the back door. She was waiting for the sound of the latch while she knitted. When the door opened, she tapped Ken's arm. "They're back, Ken," she said softly, with obvious relief.

By this time, Tom had come to terms with the murder he'd witnessed and was very satisfied with the evening's work. He could hardly wait for the morning to come, so that he could go and see what they had caught. He grinned to himself as his youthful imagination saw a picture of drunken pheasants staggering about in the woods, wearing party hats and giggling in the bracken.

Mrs Beddows was pleased to see them safely back, but there had not been much risk as Major Hudson rarely went into his woods, and none of the estate workers were any threat, because they all knew Frank and would turn a blind eye if they saw him up to his nefarious activities.

The only real threat was Mike Sturgess, the farm manager. He was an ambitious man, quite capable of reporting poachers to gain favour in his employer's eyes. He knew all about Frank, but had never managed to get the better of him. He'd often tried, but had always been outwitted by the wily old man, who knew the woods better than he did. After all, he'd been walking about in them for eighty years. His father had taught him how to catch rabbits when he was younger than Tom.

While the couple had been having their adventures in the woods, Mike Sturgess was in the pub with his wife and quite unaware that one of the pheasants in his care had come to a violent end at the hands of Frank Beddows. There was an empty stool by the fireplace and the other Young Farmers knew why.

Next morning Tom arrived, breathless, in the woods, twenty yards ahead of the old man. He'd been up before day-break, got his jobs done in record time and had set out bursting with excitement. It didn't take Frank long to get ready either. He never shaved on Sundays and he wasn't keen on washing. His last bath was when he had to go into hospital for a minor operation, a year earlier.

"Washing ain't good for you," he would say. "It gets rid of all your natural oils and if they don't like me the way I am, they'll bloody well have to put up with me."

It promised to be another beautiful day. The early mist was clearing and the sun was beginning to dry up the overnight dew. The dawn chorus had been in good voice at first light and, to Tom, there was an exhilarating promise in the air.

Frank had put on his poacher's coat, a long shapeless garment with capacious pockets sewn in. The pockets would take a lot of game without altering the coat's shape. Most local people knew what he was up to whenever they saw him in that coat.

Tom had run most of the way and reached the snares first. He slowed down as he got near and, peering round an ash tree, he saw that the first snare was empty. It had been disturbed but had not caught a rabbit. They had better luck with the second one; a rabbit lay on its back with the wire noose tight around its neck. The other four also had rabbits in them and when Frank arrived he soon had them tucked in his big pockets, and then they were off to see if the rum-soaked raisins had done their job.

At the clearing, Tom was disappointed to find nothing.

"Hang on," hissed Frank, "Listen."

A faint flapping noise was coming from some bushes and they saw a hen pheasant caught in the undergrowth, weakly flapping her wings and struggling to get to her feet.

"She's had one over the eight," grinned Frank. He swiftly dealt with the bird and stowed it in his pocket. Almost immediately, Tom spotted a fine cock bird walking in circles with one wing drooping. He was a magnificent specimen, with the early morning sun bringing the colour in his plumage to life.

Tom ran towards him calling out, "I'll get him, Granddad," but as soon as the boy moved, it took flight. It clucked noisily and with whirring wings flew at full speed into a tree trunk, falling into a clump of nettles.

"Rub a dock leaf on those stings. That'll make 'em better," said Frank, as Tom had stung his hands and arms retrieving the bird.

At the house, a delicious aroma of frying bacon met them as they returned along the lane. Frank scratched his stubbly chin and then putting his finger in the air he turned to Tom. "Smell that," he said. "Now that's what I call living. The sun is up and it's going to be a beautiful day. I've got pockets full of game to keep us in dinners and your Mum has cooked us some of that home-cured bacon for breakfast. Just smell it. What more could you want out of life?"

He heaved a sigh, when a shrill voice came from the open kitchen window. "Get that game out of sight!"

The rewards of their efforts were soon hidden in the barn. Many years ago, Frank had constructed a false wall at one end of the barn and the family were sworn to secrecy. It had never been needed, but Frank had said, "It's better to be safe than sorry."

When the game was hung in the cupboard behind the false wall, it was undetectable.

"You never know who might come sniffing about the place," he said as he closed the false panel.

Hay—making

Chapter Two

Frank used his bread to mop up the last of his egg and, leaning back in his chair, began to roll himself a cigarette from his battered tin box. He kept his Old Holborn tobacco in a tin which he'd used for fifty years. The design had rubbed off long ago and it was now brown and dented, but it was one of his most treasured possessions. He ran his tongue along the paper and thoughtfully stuck it together. Then he looked across the table and said, "Hey, Ken, I see they're hay- making at Westwood Farm. Isn't it about time the Major's was cut, while it holds good?"

Ken worked as a labourer on the estate and had done since leaving school. "Aye," he replied, "I think you're right. I was telling Mike Sturgess only yesterday. I said we ought to start today, but he wants to hang on for a day or two. I reckon he'll come unstuck one of these years. He's always later than everyone else and he had a drop of rain on it last year, but he got away with it, the lucky bugger."

The old man took a spill from under his chair and carefully lit his cigarette from the range. The loose paper on the end flared up alarmingly and then reduced to a glow as he drew on it. Closing his tin box with a snap and putting it back in his pocket, he said, "If you take my advice, you'll cut it today, because I don't think this weather will hold for much longer. The wood pigeons are roosting lower in the trees. That's always a sign the weather's on the turn. They know."

"Don't be daft, Dad," replied Ken, grinning, "You've just made that up. I never know what you'll come out with next. Pigeons roosting lower indeed."

Ken didn't always fall for his father's homespun wisdom, but he did trust his instinct for weather forecasting, as he was usually right. He said, "It's not up to me. I just do as I'm told, but I'll be seeing Mike in church and I'll have a word with him." He gave a sigh and continued, "But I don't know why we worry about it every year. It's not our problem. He's the one who's paid to worry about it."

"I know, but I hate to see good hay go to waste. You see if you can get him moving."

Tom listened to the conversation with mounting excitement. He considered Christmas and hay-making to be the two best times of the year, though since yesterday he'd added poaching to his list.

By mid-morning Frank was to be found in the pub, sitting by the fireplace and enjoying a pint of cider with his friends. The pub was busy because on Sunday mornings people drove out from Hereford and swelled the numbers to the point where it was standing room only, and it was a struggle to get to the bar. The rest of the Beddows family in their Sunday best were walking to the church.

Peals of bells echoed all around the village and over the sunlit fields as they made their way down the lane to the church of Saint Peter's. It was a small medieval building surrounded by ancient yew trees, which had been sheared into cylindrical shapes and formed an avenue from the lych gate to the church door.

The trees cast welcome cool shadows in the church yard because, although it was early in the day, the sun was hot and Tom was feeling uncomfortable in his scratchy Sunday suit.

He walked through the gate and along the avenue, resplendent in his polished shoes and his hair plastered down with his father's Brylcreem. His face was pink from his mother's vigorous efforts with soap and flannel. He hated going to church. His suit had long trousers and he was not used to them. For the rest of the week, he wore the grey trousers that came down to just below his knees, and the long trousers of his Sunday suit felt strange against his legs and made him walk with a stiff-legged action.

The only thing that made church-going worthwhile was the prospect of seeing Angela. She was Mike Sturgess's daughter and

Tom thought she was pretty. She was the same age as him and in his class at school. Both children were nine years old and, although Tom generally didn't have much time for girls, he had a soft spot for her and blushed whenever she came near. He regarded most girls with contempt, because they didn't play the same sort of games as him and they often told tales to the teacher.

She was different though and frequently appeared in his day dreams as a damsel in distress, imprisoned in a tower by the wicked Baron Brian; a classmate whom Tom disliked. Tom would appear in shining armour, riding a white charger, and rescue her from the castle. He'd read a story like that in one of his fairy-tale books and it had made a lasting impression on him.

He stood in church between his parents with his young brother and sister. Old Frank rarely accompanied them. He only went to church on special occasions and always muttered something about being good enough without having to go to church every Sunday to be made better and, besides, he didn't hold with all that hymn-singing and praying, and you couldn't get cider in church.

The family were happy with the arrangement, because when he did attend he usually disgraced them in some way, and they felt more comfortable with his sitting in the Old Black Lion, rather than next to them. The last time he went, he'd made a rude remark about Mrs Edmunds' new hat. She had never forgiven him and hadn't spoken to any of the Beddows family since.

As Tom stood with his family, Angela came in and stood in the same row on the other side of the aisle. He felt the colour rise in his cheeks and a prickly heat under his collar. She was standing between her parents and wore a green dress with yellow flowers printed on it. Her blonde hair was tied back with ribbon and Tom thought she looked very pretty in her new dress. He usually joined in with the singing of the first verse and then his attention would stray.

Being smaller than the adults, he couldn't see much when they were standing up. If he looked ahead he could only see people's backs. The men, mostly wore dark suits but the women wore hats in a variety of shapes and colours. His gaze alighted on the roof of the building. It was wooden, with stone groins between the panels, and at each junction was a boss carved into a grotesque head.

The carvings fascinated him and he knew every one intimately. Long after he had grown out of childhood, he could close his eyes and recall the details of every head. Each one reminded him of someone and the one directly overhead reminded him of Miss Acton, his teacher, with its long nose, piercing eyes and mean little mouth.

The church had Norman origins and the main structure was built in the thirteenth century. The stained glass windows were of a later date and depicted scenes from the life of Christ. Tom was equally familiar with every detail of the windows. He had plenty of time to study them as the singing droned away in the background and his attention wandered from windows to carved heads and from carved heads to ladies hats.

He sat down automatically when the congregation did and the vicar's voice droned over his head. The vicar, an elderly white haired man, stood in the pulpit reading from his prepared text in a dull monotone. He occasionally lost his place and panicked, stuttering, desperately trying to find it again.

Tom never understood the sermon, so he never listened, and his young sister, Jane, began to fidget and turn around to look at those in the row behind.

A gentle tap from Mrs Beddows' foot stopped her fidgeting and Tom's thoughts returned to Angela. By leaning forward discreetly and looking to the left, he was able to catch her eye as she moved forward of the row of adults. She smiled and he tried hard not to blush. Then she leaned back again and was gone, leaving only a row of dark suits.

After the service, the vicar stood in the doorway shaking hands with everyone as they left and the congregation gathered in small groups outside the porch. It was an opportunity to exchange gossip and keep up to date with village news. After the cool of the church, the heat outside was oppressive and Tom managed to loosen his tie without being noticed by his mother.

Swifts darted over their heads, flying in and out of their nests in the porch roof and in the distance the sun transformed the river Wye into a shimmering silver ribbon. A heat-haze obscured the details of the Brecon Beacons to the west, where they rose up above the valley as a flat blue backdrop to a checkerboard pattern of fields and hedgerows gradually fading into the distant haze.

Tom's father took the opportunity of speaking to Mike Sturgess, who was engaged in conversation with the fat lady who'd recently moved into the Old Smithy.

Ken coughed politely to gain his attention and said, "Excuse me, Mike, can I have a word?" and added, "I'm sorry to interrupt you, Mrs Davies. I only want a quick word."

She smiled and drifted off to join another group by the elm tree.

"Before you speak, I know what you're going to say," said the farm manager. "It's time we cut the hay. I expect the old boy has been talking to you, like he does every year. I don't know why he doesn't just apply for my job and be done with it."

"Well, I think he's right. The weather can't stay like this forever and he reckons it's going to rain soon so we ought to get cutting."

As the two men talked, Tom and Angela kept their gaze down on their shoes; embarrassed and not knowing what to say to each other.

"Well, no time like the present," said Mike, looking at the sky through narrowed eyes. "Not a cloud to be seen. Let's go for it." Then, looking across at the embarrassed Tom, "Can you send your boy to tell the lads. Tell them we're starting as soon as they've had their dinner. There's five here we can tell now and the others all live near each other, so it won't take them long to get ready."

Tom was sent on his errand and he felt sure that in Angela's eyes he was a hero for being entrusted with this urgent mission. Hay-making was one of the most important events in the farming year and it was his responsibility to muster the troops.

"Well, Tom, it's up to you now. The whole operation depends on you. Don't let them down," he said to himself, after he'd changed into his working clothes and was on his bike heading for the workers' cottages below the Big House. His news was greeted with much swearing, as the men didn't relish the prospect of sweating and grunting in the sun, but they had been half expecting it and understood that the work had to be done as soon as possible.

Soon after lunch, fifteen men assembled at the gate of Tinker's Field. Five fields were to be mown and Tinker's was the biggest, about eleven acres. Most of the farms in the area were beginning the post-war mechanization, but it had not yet caught up with Major

Hudson's estate. He was a man who looked back to the 'good old days' and did not have much interest in developing the estate, so he was lagging behind his neighbours.

While they had invested in modern machinery to reduce labour, on this estate hay–making was still done as it had been for centuries with scythe, rake, and pitchfork. The Major had recently bought a new Fordson Major tractor and a plough to go on the back of it, but that was the full extent of his mechanization programme. His hay was still made and got in by man–power and horse–power.

Each one of the hay-making team gathered at the gate had a scythe and a sharpening stone hanging from his belt, as it was essential to maintain a sharp cutting edge. Tom was not allowed to use a scythe, so there was nothing for him to do at this stage, but he stood around with the men, feeling important. It was good hay-making weather but too hot to work comfortably.

There was much grumbling and cursing as they lined up along one side of the lush field and spaced themselves evenly. Some were giving their scythes a last minute sharpening as they waited and looked across the vast sea of green, receding into the distance to a line of trees at the edge of Cwm Woods. The herbage in the hay meadows had not seen a plough for a hundred years and they were fragrant with the scent of the flowers which had been allowed to flourish.

"I should be picking my strawberries now," grumbled Tom Pugh.

"I'm hot before I start," moaned Jack Price, mopping the sweat from his neck. "You could pour most of me out of my boots and we haven't even started yet."

The men stood still, waiting for the signal. A covey of partridge got up and wheeled away over the hedge towards Kings Tump.

"Okay, boys," called Mike and the mowing began. The leading man moved forward swinging his scythe and felling curved swathes of grass. The razor-sharp edge hissed as it sliced through. As he cleared a space, the second man began to swing in line behind him. The remaining men followed, one by one, forming a crescent of swinging scythes, each man keeping well clear of the other. The field seemed enormous to Tom, but the grass was cut with surprising speed. After an hour of steady work, more than half of it was cut and the sweet scent of new mown hay filled the warm air.

"Keep going boys," shouted Mike. "We'll stop when this field's finished."

The work continued and occasionally a man would stop to freshen up the edge of his blade and mop his sweat but then worked more quickly to catch up and resume his place in the perfect curve of men spreading across the meadow.

Tom sat on the gate, chewing a piece of grass and swinging his legs. A fly was annoying him and he swatted at it with a length of elder branch. He looked across the field, watching the progress. His father was halfway along the line, swinging with a steady rhythm and sweating profusely.

He wore a red scarf around his neck to catch the sweat. His hands were used to work and the hardened skin was standing up to the effort, but the constant twisting was taking its toll on muscles that he did not normally use.

Ken was beginning to feel the strain. His trousers were rubbing him in his sweaty groin and he was looking forward to stopping for a break at the other side of the eleven acres. The first man was almost there, so it wouldn't be long now.

He looked over his shoulder and said, "They do this by machine at Westwood Farm, you know. One man in a tractor and one of those mowers on the back would have finished this and two more fields by now."

"I know," came the reply, "and they've only got two men working on the farm. Think of that when you next get your pay."

"Aye," said Ken, and he put his head down to finish the last few yards.

As each man finished, they put down their scythe and flopped onto the ground.

"Look at that," said one of the men, gazing back across the vast area of fallen grass, "Just look at that. There's nothing quite like it. It's hard work, but it's a beautiful sight to see when you get to the other side. Makes you feel you've done something good."

As they neared the other side, Tom picked up the two heavy bags and trudged over the cut grass. He kicked it up as he went and released more of the heavy perfume. His timing was perfect, arriving just as they had finished, and a cheer went up as he put the bags down.

"Here's the most important man in the field; the cider man."

The men gathered round and flagons of cider were handed out.

"Nothing like a drop of cider for hay-making. Just the job," said Walter, wiping his droopy moustache. "In the old days, cider was part of our wages at hay-making and harvest. We used to have as much as we could drink and we drank until it came out of our ears. This is tidy stuff. Who's is it?"

"Jack Hargreaves from Eardisley," replied Ken, "It'll put hairs on your chest that will."

"Can I have some, Dad?" asked Tom, "It's thirsty weather."

"No, it's too strong for you. It'll blow your head off. If you're thirsty, go and get some water from the stream. It's cool and clean and much better for a lad of your age."

"Oh, give him some," said Walter, "He's a Herefordshire lad and I reckons he deserves it after dragging those bottles over here. I was weaned on cider and it never done me no harm."

"I'm not so sure about that," came a voice from the back of the group.

Ken gave a nod and Tom took a deep draft of the cool, dry cider.

"That'll do. It's not pop, you know!" exclaimed Ken, grabbing at the bottle.

It tasted good and he'd worked up a thirst in the hot sun. The cider was sharp and fruity and he thought it was a pity his Dad wouldn't let him have any more. The men stretched out in the shade of an oak, pulling off their boots and wriggling their toes.

"Weather looks set fine," said Walter, between puffs of his pipe, "We should be alright again this year."

The sky was deep blue, with not a cloud to be seen from Hereford in the east to the Brecon Beacons in the west. Two buzzards were wheeling and mewing on their outstretched motionless wings.

Tom lay with his head on the grass, watching the birds glide against the blue sky. They rose high, twisting and turning on the warm air currents. The men's conversation became a distant drone, rather like the vicar's sermons, blending with the murmur of insects, and his eyelids became heavy and began to close. He drifted into a blissful sleep.

When he awoke, he was alone under the tree and getting

unsteadily to his feet he peered over the hedge and saw that the workers had almost completed the next field. There wasn't anything useful he could do now, so he collected the empty bottles and slowly wandered home, feeling as if he'd done a good day's work.

Hay takes several days to make and has to be spread out to dry in the sun. It is turned and teased with rakes and must be thoroughly dry before it is brought in, otherwise it could go mouldy and be useless, or even heat up and spontaneously ignite. Tom helped with the turning and the next few days were spent toiling in the sun, with a knotted handkerchief on his head at his mother's insistence. They turned the hay with their hay rakes and spread it out to dry.

It was a good hay-making summer and a fine crop was made. After four days of turning, Mike walked around the fields and rubbed samples between his fingers. Then he smelled it and declared it ready.

"Yes, we can get it in," he announced, and soon three hay carts came trundling along the lane, rattling and rumbling on the sun baked ruts. The carts which turned into the gateway were pulled by powerful horses.

"Whooh there," called Walter, pulling on the reins. The cart came to a standstill in the field and he jumped down, followed by Tom, who'd been helping to harness the horses at the Manor House. Walter taught him a lot and he knew just what to do. Walter was one of the few people left in the area who regularly worked with heavy horses and he'd made an effort to teach Tom all he knew. Tom liked him, as he treated him like an adult, whereas the other farm workers tended to tease him.

He was sixty-five and always held a yellowing clay pipe between his teeth. He had gaps between his teeth and the pipe just fitted in one of them and stayed there, whether it was lit or not. He had a heavy moustache, like the ones seen on Victorian men posing stiffly in old sepia photographs. Few people knew if he had hair, because he was never seen without his trilby. His corduroy trousers were baggy and tied beneath the knees with twine.

Walter supervised the entry of the other carts with much shouting and waving and then the men set about throwing on the hay. It was Tom's job to stay on a cart and arrange the loose hay as it was thrown up to him. He felt more and more important as he rose higher. How he wished that Angela could have been there to see him; muscles rippling, swinging his pitchfork with the men. The carts had timber frames at each end so that the hay could be piled high and soon a huge pile was stacked on the first cart.

The journeys back to the farm became treasured memories for him. He lay back in the sweet smelling hay and Walter flicked the reins, "Walk on," he called, and the horse began the slow progress across the field and down the lane towards the barn at Home Farm.

Tom looked up at the sky and the branches slowly moved across his field of vision, causing a flickering effect from the sun. Alternate shadows and sunlight rippled over him. He listened to the soporific clip clop, the creaking of wood and leather, and the chinking of harness. The lazy sounds formed a background for the main instrument of the orchestra, Walter's mouth organ. As he drove, he played sad and haunting tunes.

Tom was impressed by his ability and marvelled at the beauty of the music coming from such a rough old man. It was the loveliest music he'd ever heard, but what was so remarkable was that he managed to play without taking the pipe from his mouth. The sounds blended into what Tom thought was perfect music. It was a magical experience and he never forgot it for as long as he lived.

It was nearly dusk before all the hay was stacked in the barn and Mike Sturgess produced large quantities of cider.

"Courtesy of the Major," he declared and the men sat in the barn, telling tales and jokes as the light faded and the warm evening turned to night. Walter enthralled them with tales of his childhood.

As the men sat around in the hay, Walter told them about cider-making on the farms where he grew up. He told of how the poor cottagers crushed the fruit by hand but at the Big House they could afford a horse-powered circular mill. It was made of stone and had a vertical grindstone which was pushed around a channel. When he was a boy, the apples, which had been left to mature in straw covered heaps, were loaded into the centre of the mill and the young Walter knocked the apples into the trough with his stick.

"I used to throw a bucket of water in the trough to stop the pulp getting too sticky and at the end of the day it smelled lovely. The pulp was pressed and the juice was a thick, dark brown and I can smell it now. Beautiful it was; the finest smell in the world. The

Squire and his family used to get the best cider and the squeezed pulp was mixed with water and pressed a second time. That was what made the cider for the likes of us, but we could drink as much as we liked and it wasn't bad. It was called 'small cider' but we knew it as 'ciderkin' and it was part of our wages."

Walter took another deep draft of cider and, grinning, said, "When the pulp was finished with, we used to feed it to the livestock. It was reckoned to be good for 'em and come cider-making time there used to be a lot of drunk pigs about the place. They used to walk in circles and fall over. Aye, the chickens used to get drunk as well and they fell off their perches. I can remember we used to put bullock's blood in the cask to make it clear and, on the farm down our lane, they put beetroot in to give it good colour, but it was 'orrible cider, sour, with a nasty kick, 'squeal-pig' we used to call that stuff."

The story that remained in Tom's mind was of Walter's going into the cider cellar and sucking the cider out of the barrels with a long straw. He described nearly coming to a premature end when he fell into a vat. Luckily his little sister saw him fall and raised the alarm. He was dragged out by his feet, close to drowning, and held upside down with cider pouring out of him.

"That's why I've got such a lovely complexion," he grinned. "It would've been a lovely way to go though. I'll tell you something, boys, that was the best cider you're ever likely to taste. Fair play, it was famous in these parts. Hey, Tom, it was your great-grandfather who made it and, by God, it was good stuff. If someone could make cider like it today, they'd make a fortune and no mistake. He re-lit his pipe and blew a cloud of smoke, "Aye, they'd make a fortune."

Chapter Three

Chris Gregory grew up in Gorston, a grimy industrial town in the heart of the Black Country, only seventy miles from Lower Kings Canon on the map but a world away in every other respect. He was the same age as Tom, a cheerful boy with dark curly hair, and a pupil at Gorston Primary School. It was a very different school to Lower Kings Canon Primary; larger, with seven teachers and a headmistress.

It was built just before the war in a street of terraced houses called Foundry Road. The houses were of brick, which had blackened from the industrial grime in the air, and halfway along was a pub called The Colliers Rest, a shabby building with peeling paint on the window frames and frosted glass windows engraved with Snug, Public Bar and Smoke Room. Chris Gregory lived in a terraced house in Jubilee Terrace; a small house with an entry at the side leading to a back yard with just enough room to hang a washing line.

A rag and bone man's horse and cart rumbled on the cobbles. The cart was draped with clothes and festooned with balloons. The clothes hung over the side, right down to the ground, and the reds and yellows of the balloons were almost the only touches of colour in the dreary street. The man called out,

"Ayyyyyy Ole Aggs. Ayyyyyy Ole Agggs!" The call echoed round the street and everyone knew that the strange cry meant "Any Old Rags. Any Old Rags!"

As he drove down the street, children brought out old clothes and in return he gave them a balloon or a goldfish in a jam jar.

The cart passed a group of children playing football and they carried on with their game, quite oblivious of him. The driver flinched and jerked his head to one side as the ball rocketed over his shoulder and hit the wall, close to a window. It bounced off and dropped back into the road, where it was pounced upon and kicked back into play by a small boy.

"That was a close one!" shouted Chris, kicking the ball at the makeshift goal posts painted on a wall. He was usually to be found either playing football or riding his bike around the maze of identical streets. He also spent much time on the canal towpath, fishing, or just mooching about with his friends. The area was

criss-crossed with a system of oily canals, which had been constructed during the industrial revolution.

At one time, they had been the arteries of local industry,
transporting the life blood of raw materials, coal, and finished
goods, but now they had fallen into disuse. Some barges still used
the overgrown waterways, chugging lazily along with five or six coal
laden barges in tow, or pulled by a horse on the towpath.

Before the war, a unique culture existed, a society of people who
lived and worked on the canals and lived a separate life from the
rest of us. That way of life was by now almost extinguished and only
a few gained their living from the waterways, though they left a rich
folk history for historians to study in years to come. Now the canals
held a fascination for children and the towpath was their favourite
playground.

One winter, a coal barge had sprung a leak and sunk and, as the
canal was not very deep, the top part was protruding above the
surface. Before the barge and its cargo could be salvaged, the
children from the surrounding streets had been sent with old prams
and wheel barrows to collect the coal.

Anything with wheels was utilized and Chris and his sister had
used a rickety cart on pram wheels and made several trips. It was a
curious sight to see the streets full of blackened children, pushing an
assortment of wheeled containers loaded with coal. The streets were
slippery with the brown slush of melted snow and they slithered
about as they struggled to push their loads up the hill.

In hard winters the canal froze over and the children could ride
their bikes on it, skidding and sliding with squeals of delight. Chris
and his friends were drawn to the old waterways like moths to a
flame.

"Are you coming down the cut with us?" called one of the boys,
on the other side of the street.

"Yep," replied Chris, kicking the ball at the goal and running to
his bike.

He rode with his two friends down Foundry Road and into
Roberts Avenue, past the derelict nail factory and onto the
wasteland purple with willow herb. They pulled aside a length of
corrugated iron to gain access to the canal bank. The boys were
usually drawn to a bend in the canal near a brick bridge, with a plate

declaring that this was Bridge No. 73. It was a place far from the eyes of adults and one of the most exciting bridges on their stretch of canal. However, the broad pipe running alongside was their main attraction, because it presented a challenge to the boys.

"Go on, Chris, it's your turn," said the spotty boy and Chris leaned his bike against the wall and climbed onto the pipe. The challenge was to walk the whole length of the slippery pipe without falling into the water. It was covered in slime, making it difficult to balance. He negotiated the barbed wire on the iron frame put there to stop small boys climbing onto the pipe, stretched out his arms and looking straight ahead made his way towards the other side.

Halfway across, his passage was made more difficult by the need to dodge stones thrown by his companions. He ducked to avoid a well aimed missile thrown by Spotty and, when he felt he was losing his balance, he made a dash for it, swaying alarmingly but making it to the safety of the other end. He clung on to the bars of the iron frame to get his breath back.

"Phew, I thought I was a gonner then," he panted, "Ay, Spotty, why did you throw stones? You nearly had me in the cut."

Spotty laughed, "That was the idea," and he threw a clod of turf which hit the wall and showered Chris with soil.

"Ugh, that's gone down my neck." He spat out some soil and scrambling down he said, "I'll get you for that. Just you wait."

Spotty was on his bike and pedalling furiously before Chris reached the bottom, but when Chris called, "Alright, pax!" he braked violently, sending a shower of grit into the water.

"What shall we do now?" asked Goggles, a small boy in National Health glasses which were held together with sticking plaster. He had protruding teeth and receding chin and his hair was short and spiky. It stood up like a sweep's brush in spite of liberal quantities of hair cream.

"I know," said Spotty, "let's go down to the lock."

The lock was another of the places which fascinated the boys and they mounted their bikes and raced along the towpath, zig-zagging between each other and skidding on the bends. The lock in their eyes was an adventure playground, with steps to run up and down, beams on which to swing, and enticing machinery with water pouring through gaps in the slimy gates. There was a long drop to the bottom and a constant gushing noise made by the water forcing its way through gaps in the timber gate.

"I know," said Chris, "I've got a spanner in my saddle bag that'll fit that nut. Let's see if we can undo it."

The boys set to winding up the sluice with their spanner and jumped up and down with glee when the water began to escape through the sluice, first as a dribble, and then a torrent. They sat on the oak beam and swung their legs while they watched the cataract.

"Good isn't it?" said Spotty.

"Yeah," replied Goggles, "but my brother says you shouldn't do this because it empties the basin when the top gates are open."

"Augh! What does your brother know about it anyway?"

"My brother's got an O Level in Art and his friend's Dad is a teacher, so he knows."

"Get out," responded Spotty, "Anyone can see there's loads of water in the cut and opening that little hole isn't gonna make any difference is it?"

Goggles was unconvinced because he had a great deal of faith in his big brother. They watched the water pouring through the sluice and gurgling into the next section of the waterway.

Goggles pushed his glasses back up his nose and slowly said, "Erm, I think, you ought to turn round and see what I can see. I told you so," he added triumphantly.

The boys turned and saw with horror that the basin was almost drained and an expanse of evil-smelling mud stretched away into the distance, with bicycle frames and prams protruding from it. At their feet two gasping fish splashed in an inch of water.

"Oooh, now we're for it," said Chris, with a sharp intake of breath.

"I hope it starts to rain soon," said Spotty hopefully.

Chris looked at the mud in dismay, "If the Inspector comes along here we'll be in trouble."

"He'll have to catch us first," said Goggles, jumping on his bike.

The other two reached for theirs and, as they skidded off, Chris's pedal caught in the spokes of one of the other wheels and he was thrown out of his saddle into the mud. It was soft and stagnant and he disappeared completely before resurfacing, black, slimy, and smelly. He wiped as much as he could from his eyes, before squelching to the crumbling edge of the canal and pulling himself out. Mud oozed into a pool at his feet and looking down he realized that he'd lost a shoe.

Goggles sat astride his bike, grinning broadly, "Your Dad's gonna give you hell when you get home. Those were your new shoes. Your Mum told you not to scratch them."

They left a black trail to Chris's house and Goggles was right, Mr Gregory was not pleased to see his son in that state. "Stand there. Don't move!" he demanded and, pushing a hose pipe through the kitchen window, he connected it to the tap and hosed him down.

"It's freezing! Stop it!" he squealed, but his father played the hose on him until he was reasonably clean. The hose was turned off and he stood shivering as the last of the muddy water swirled away down the drain.

His father shouted, "Now take everything off and put it in the wash house. Then you can go in and have a bath and don't think that I've finished with you, because I haven't!"

The other two boys sat on their bicycles behind the back wall, giggling with their hands over their mouths. When it went quiet, they cycled down the alley with tyres skidding onto the cobbles of Foundry Road and pedalled away between the grimy terraced houses.

Chris's father worked in a factory a short bicycle ride away from Jubilee Terrace. The factory made nuts and bolts and it was his job to collect them as they came off the machines and take them on a trolley to another part of the factory, where they were treated in a bath of chemicals, the fumes from which took his breath away and made his eyes sting. Bob Gregory had a perpetual smell about him, as did all the other factory workers, and everyone knew where he worked by the characteristic odour.

When he came home from work, which could be at any time of night or day because he worked a shift system, he had a bath and scrubbed his hands, but it did not remove the smell. When he went to the Smoke Room in The Colliers Rest it was still detectable, a metallic smell, like damp rusty nails, and the smell lingered in the bars of the pub because most of the customers worked at the factory.

They spent their evenings playing dominoes, reading the *Express and Star* —the local newspaper—or just sitting. It was a dull pub, with faded floral wall paper rubbed through to the plaster where the plastic chair backs contacted it. The walls were hung with brass plates and the only picture was a print of Constable's *Haywain*, the colours of which had long ago faded to blue. On the floor was a patterned linoleum, worn through in places to the floor boards.

Chris had an older sister, Jennifer, who'd left school and was working in the office at Garringtons, a big factory which was the main employer in the area. It was a foundry and the Drop Hammer, or the big 'Drop Ommer' as the locals called it, was heard all day and night. It never stopped; a slow rhythmic thump, which shook the houses two streets away. The factory walls were dirty and the surface of the bricks was eaten away by the acid in the air. Some of the walls still had traces of wartime camouflage.

When Chris left the Primary School, he passed the eleven plus exam and went to the local Grammar School for boys, a building sandwiched between the railway cuttings and a factory. He never discovered what the factory produced, but it was obviously busy and made a lot of noise. The railway was also noisy and as the track was used for shunting there was an incessant clattering from the trucks. When they moved off there was a clack, clack, clack, clack, clack all the way down the line, and the fumes from the steam engines hung on the air.

He was often reprimanded for letting his concentration lapse during lessons. When his attention was caught by the shunting locomotives outside the maths room window, the teacher would say, "I know it's fascinating, Gregory, but I assure you those train drivers wish they'd concentrated at school and obtained some qualifications to give them a better job. Keep your mind on your work, or you'll end up doing a dead-end job too."

The Headmaster was a unique character, an old-fashioned teacher, who wore a mortar board and high stiff collar which left red marks on his neck. He was always in a shabby black suit and his gown, which he used for cleaning the black board, hung in shreds from his shoulders; the chalk dust following him in a cloud wherever he went. He had a moustache stained yellow with nicotine and he lived on the other side of the playing field in a house which he shared with numerous cats.

The house had been condemned as unfit for human habitation, but he continued to live there, walking a plank laid across the floor joists to get to his bed and lighting his cigarettes with shreds of paper torn from the walls. He ruled the School with terror and his voice boomed around the corridors, "You blasted little apes!" frightening boys and staff alike.

He was a clever man and a world expert on chess problems. Chess was on the School curriculum for everyone. Every boy had to learn the game and the chess lesson took up an entire afternoon each week. He had a large chess board, which he stood up at the front of the class room, with symbols that could be moved around to teach the moves. On one occasion he moved the pieces and said, "Now, boys, what should White do now?"

There was silence while the boys studied the board and eventually Chris summoned the courage to put his hand in the air.

"Yes, boy?"

"Nothing, Sir."

"What do you mean?"

"Well, nothing, Sir, because it's Black's move."

Ezzy Kemping, as he was known by the boys, went purple and shouted, "You cheeky little brat. I'm going to thrash you for your cheek!" Then he looked at the board and said in a gentler voice, "You are quite right boy. Here's a penny," and he groped in his pocket and threw the coin across the room to him.

The Headmaster rewarded boys with pennies and it was considered to be the greatest honour he could bestow. That was the only time that Chris ever received one.

The Head's wrath could be terrible. He once gave a stick of chalk to a small boy and asked him to draw 'Pi' on the black board. Instead of drawing the mathematical symbol, he put out his tongue in concentration and in all innocence produced a commendable picture of an apple pie with crinkled crust and steam coming from it. The head's wrath had to be seen to be believed.

"Come here, Smith," he shouted and dragged him out of the room. The rest of the class, in unison, counted the cane's swishes; one, two, three, four; getting up to six before the unfortunate tear-stained boy was led back in by the ear.

When asked in a History lesson to write an imaginary letter from a Roman centurion based in Britain to his parents in Rome, the same boy wrote,

> *Dear Mum and Dad*
> *I am having a lovely time in Britain. I wish you were here.*
> *The weather is not bad but the food is very boring.*
> *I am fed up with having tins of baked beans every day.*
> *Love from Adrian.*

Once again the poor child was not trying to be cheeky, but he suffered the same fate in the Headmaster's study.

Although Ezzy ruled his school by terror, his pupils in later years remembered him with great affection. The old Headmaster had founded the School as a young man and his life had been dedicated to the welfare of the boys who passed through his hands. Many owed a great debt to him and Chris was a pupil at the School in the year in which he reluctantly retired.

The day his career finished was one of the most touching that Chris had experienced in his young life. The Headmaster had called for a special assembly to give his last address and at the appointed time a violent thunder storm broke and it was difficult to hear him above the din.

It seemed as if the Gods were angry that the old Headmaster had to go and, with one flash and roll of thunder, the electricity supply was cut and he could not read his notes. Boys and staff watched, spellbound by the drama, as the Head Boy with great resourcefulness produced a lighted candle, which he placed on the lectern. The speech continued with the Head's face lit by the flickering candle and a dramatic shadow was cast on the wall behind him.

The Headmaster finished his last assembly and, slowly stretching his hand, he snuffed out the candle. "Very appropriate," he declared, as the flame died and he turned and left his school hall for the last time.

In later years, Chris retained unpleasant memories of standing on cold football pitches every Wednesday afternoon. It was required that the boys supported the School team and it was a terrible offence if anyone was caught sneaking through the gap in the railings to escape the suffering. He had to stand, stamping his feet on the frozen ground, willing the final whistle to blow.

There were frequent fogs in the winter but the games still went on, even though visibility was limited to only a few yards. When he took the yellow scarf from his mouth and nose, there would be a black mark from the filtered dirt in the air.

The only way to escape the Wednesday misery was to volunteer for a cross-country run. Goggles had also passed the eleven plus and attended the same school and the two boys went along to the Sports Master. "Please, Sir, can we go on a run?" they asked.

"This is better than watching that stupid football," panted Goggles.

"Yeh," replied Chris, pulling up his shorts, which kept slipping down as they were too big now that the elastic had stretched.

Behind the railway line was an industrial wasteland, 'the country' as the Sports Master called it, and that was where the cross-country runs took place. The smell of the sewage beds pervaded the air and through the centre of the area ran a stream, the river Theme. When the level dropped in the summer, the boys were amused to see that the overhanging branches were hung with condoms.

The rest of the pack were ahead of the two boys and Goggles slowed to a walk. "I've got the stitch," he complained. He held his stomach and doubled up with pain. So the cross-country run became a cross-country walk and they followed the banks of the stream and climbed the stepping bridge over the railway. On the other side were brick arches supporting a viaduct and as they passed a voice called to them.

"Hey, Gregory—Williamson!"

The voice came from one of the arches and they found it belonged to Cotterill, the school bully, who was treated with great respect by the smaller boys. He was in his running kit but he never got further than the viaduct, because he used the arches as his smoking room. The two boys went under the arch and strained their eyes to make him out in the gloom. They could see the glow from his cigarette and, as their eyes became accustomed to the low light, they discerned the figure of Cotterill, sitting in an old armchair and blowing smoke rings from his Woodbine.

"Here, have a Woody," he said, offering a white paper bag. They both declined, with a shake of the head.

"Have a drag of this one then."

Again they shook their heads. "Not men enough, huh?" he

continued. "I come here every Wednesday for a fag and a cough. Tattey Head thinks I'm flogging my guts out running about like the other clots, but I wait in here for an hour, have a few fags, and then run back. I pant a bit as I go through the gates to make it look good though." He drew self-consciously on his cigarette. "It beats watching those idiots kicking a ball about any day. Give me a fag any time."

Cotterill was not a popular boy; a bully, constantly boasting about his exploits with girls, or tarts, as he called them. He obtained the money to buy his cigarettes by threatening the meek boys in the first year and Chris and Goggles were careful not to say anything to upset him, because they knew that he could be very nasty.

They listened to his boasts for a while and then, after their encounter, they walked the rest of the way down the railway tracks to the empty warehouse, along the stream and back to school. The rest of the runners, including Cotterill, were getting changed when they arrived fifteen minutes after the others and they had to endure jeers, but they still thought it was better than standing on a frosty football pitch all afternoon.

These were the surroundings in which Chris Gregory went to school and grew up. He was of the same generation as Tom, but they had very different backgrounds and ways of life.

Chapter Four

In Lower Kings Canon, summer was coming to an end and a dark cloud was beginning to fill Tom's horizon. He made efforts to dispel it by keeping himself occupied on the small-holding and exploring in the woods. Even poaching expeditions with his grandfather failed to lift the gloom, as the prospect of returning to school after the summer holidays came closer to reality.

"At least I'll see Angela," he thought, and then he brightened a little, but when his mother announced that he was being driven into Hereford in the old Austin, the cloud reappeared. He was taken to buy some new school trousers from the outfitters near the Cathedral. Buying school uniform was a sure sign of impending misery and the black cloud now refused to disperse.

The trousers that were bought were rough and scratchy like his Sunday suit and his mood sank even lower as school started on the following day and he became resigned to the tyranny of the dreaded Miss Acton. School began in early September and the summer of freedom and hay-making with Walter was over. Ahead lay months of despair until he was set free again at Christmas.

Lower Kings Canon Primary was near the Old Black Lion, along a lane between some cottages. An area of waste ground separated the pub car park from the School which was a red-brick Victorian building with a playground area to one side. It had a tiled roof, in the centre of which was a clock tower surmounted by a weather vane. Thirty-two children attended the School, which was presided over by the formidable Miss Acton.

Most of the pupils were terrified of her. Under her arm she carried a cane with a curved handle and just one glance from her steely grey eyes was enough to quell the most rebellious spirit. She looked very much like the carving in the church roof, which Tom studied so intently each Sunday, and her grey hair was tied in a tight bun. She glared at the children through steel framed glasses with thick lenses and she usually wore a bright red blazer, the vividness of which emphasised her fearful image.

She had been in the same school since she started her career and had taught most of her pupil's parents. Tom's mother and father had both been taught by her and they had fond memories, though he couldn't understand why. She had the best interests of the children at heart, in spite of her fearsome appearance, but in Tom's view her aim was to make their lives as miserable as possible.

He dragged himself reluctantly to school on the first day. His new trousers felt uncomfortable and he was aware of the tightness of the tie that his mother had insisted he wore. He hadn't worn one since last term, so it felt strange, and he was particularly aggrieved because hardly any of the other boys had to wear one.

"It makes you look smart," his mother had said, and Frank had sent him off to school with, "Go on, son, learn your lessons and get somewhere in life. You don't want to end up an old poacher like me do you?"

His steps became slower as he turned the pub corner. The landlord was in the porch, shaking a rug. "Hello, young Tom. First day is it? Happiest days of your life they are," and then he disappeared into the building. Tom could never understand why adults insisted that school days were the happiest. He detested school.

As he passed the pub, the school bell began to ring and he broke into a run because he did not want to face Miss Acton's wrath on the first day back. The children were excited at being back and were chatting noisily in the playground about the things they had been doing in the holidays. Some boys were kicking a cap belonging to a very frightened new boy. He was in tears and quite convinced that he was not going to enjoy school.

Suddenly, with earth-stopping drama, Miss Acton materialized at the top of the steps. She glared down, white-faced, red-jacketed, with the cane under her arm. It seemed as if the birds had stopped singing and the sun had gone in. The children were stunned into silence. The brave ones gazed back at her, but the more timid looked at their feet and shuffled uneasily, not daring to look her in the eye. The three new pupils were terrified and one began to sniff and sob in the silence. The child whose cap had been kicked around was more convinced than ever that he was not going to enjoy school.

With one snap of the fingers, two queues were formed. The newcomers looked bewildered and then joined on the end of a line. A second snap rang out and the line filed noiselessly up the steps and through the doors, followed when it was clear by the second line.

The newcomers came to an abrupt halt as the cane was thrust into the chest of the first child.

He was a small, red-haired boy, shabbily dressed in a crumpled shirt and a baggy jacket that was obviously home-made. The other two children bumped into him as he came to a sudden standstill. The Headmistress poked him in the chest and glared down her nose through narrowed eyes. As the terrified child looked up, she put her head on one side and lifted his face a little higher with the cane.

"And what is your name, boy?"

He opened his mouth but no sound came.

"Speak up!"

"Paul, Missus," the sharpness of her voice shocking him into speech.

He flinched when the cane came down with a crack on the side of the door.

"You do not call me Missus. I am Miss to you," and then in a slightly kinder tone, "Now, Paul who?"

"Paul Lloyd, Missus, er, Miss," he added hastily, flinching in anticipation of the cane cracking again.

"And is your father called Thomas?"

"My Mum calls him Tom, Miss."

She smiled and said. "Yes, I thought so, Tom Lloyd."

She leaned back and squinted at him again with her head on one side. "You look like your father. I taught him when he was your age and I can remember him on his first day. He stood here looking frightened, just like you."

She put her face close to his, "Are you frightened, boy?"

"No, Miss," replied the boy, fighting back the tears.

"Quite right boy. There's nothing to be frightened of. You see if you can be as good a pupil as your father was. Work hard and do as you as you're told and I'm sure you'll like it here, alright?"

"Yes, Miss," he replied, brightening a little.

"Run along now and join the others in the classroom with the green door. Miss Henworth will be your teacher. You two as well. You go with him."

Miss Acton taught the pupils in the top class and Tom was sitting with the rest of the class, whispering excitedly on the wooden benches. In front of each bench was a desk with a hinged lid and a hole containing an ink well, surrounded by blue stains.

When the Headmistress entered, the children were instantly silenced and when she snapped her fingers it was the signal to chant in unison.

"Good-Mor-ning-Miss-Ac-ton."

The room had tall windows, which were too high to allow a view of the outside world. Apart from the desks, there was a tall cupboard, the teacher's desk, and a blackboard and easel. Otherwise the room was bare. On one wall were faded National Savings posters of trees and fungi.

A boy called Brian Jones had been first into the classroom and so was able to choose the best desk. By general agreement it was the one at the back near the radiator, where one could duck down and not be seen by the teacher, and in winter the radiator was useful for warming cold feet. Brian was one of the boys who had been tormenting the new boy by kicking his cap around the playground.

Tom noted with dismay that not only had Brian laid claim to the best desk but he was sitting next to Angela. Both boys were fond of her and there was bitter rivalry for her affections. It is said that 'All is fair in love and war' and Brian certainly was not averse to dirty tricks. He was a nasty little boy, who devoted much energy to getting Tom into trouble and he was a master of the art.

His father owned Westwood Farm and ran a road haulage company called Jones Haulage Ltd. The family was well off and their son was developing into an arrogant big bully. He was a constant cause of trouble and delighted in harming others, particularly Tom, and he seemed to have a gift for not being found out. His plans were well thought out and cunning.

On one occasion, he stole a spinning top from a little girl and hid it in Tom's desk while the pupils were in the playground. When the girl went crying to Miss Acton, the desks were searched and the top was found hidden under a book. Tom protested his innocence but had six strokes of the cane across each hand. Miss Acton did not believe in doing things by halves and when she caned a child, she put all her effort into it. The pain was excruciating and red wheals were raised across his hands.

"Let that be a lesson to you!" she shrieked, "I will not tolerate sneaky little thieves in my school."

The punishment was administered in front of the class and he returned to his desk, desperately trying not to cry. He lost the struggle and the tears welled up and ran down his cheeks, not because of the pain, but because of the overwhelming feeling of injustice. He had not taken the top and he knew that Brian had done it, but now he had to suffer the pain and humiliation. Angela would think he was a thief and that thought made him cry all the more.

Through the mist of tears, he could see Brian smirking with smug satisfaction and he could see Angela, watching him with a look of horror. He felt sure that Miss Acton would never believe him as she had a high opinion of Brian and did not think that he was capable of anything wicked.

When Tom had got home that day, news of the day's events had somehow got there before him and when his father came home, he had to suffer six lashes of a heavy belt across his backside; when he gave his explanation, he had six more lashes for lying.

The next day, Brian sniggered as he went into the classroom, "What did your Dad say when he found out?" he enquired, "I bet he wasn't pleased."

It was clear to Tom that Brian had made sure his father found out.

He hated school. He hated it because he was afraid of Miss Acton. He hated it because of Brian and he hated it because the high windows imprisoned him and blocked his view of the countryside and his beloved Cwm Woods in the distance.

The term dragged on towards Christmas. The only bright spots were the walks home with Angela as far as the Post Office on the corner, where they went their separate ways. He enjoyed the walks, in spite of the taunts from some of the pupils.

"Look at the lovers," they shouted, "Go on, have a kiss."

One day, he summoned up the courage to say something which had been burning inside him for a long time. As they drew near to the corner, talking about school and the Christmas play which they were rehearsing, he stopped abruptly and blurted out, "When we're grown up, will you marry me?"

She blushed and said nothing.

Now that he had taken the plunge, he became more courageous.

"Will you?" he asked, with growing confidence.

Again the response was nothing but a shy giggle.

He felt in his pocket and said, "I made this for you," and took out a piece of wood, wider at one end than the other.

"What is it?"

"A love–spoon."

"A what?"

"A love–spoon," he repeated proudly.

She took the wood and looked at it from all angles, turning it over in her hand. After a while she asked, "What's a love–spoon?"

"It's a thing that men carve for their ladies to show that they love them," replied the boy, now bursting with confidence.

"Why?"

"They just do, that's all."

"How do you know?"

"My Granddad told me that you should get a piece of wood and carve it into the shape of a spoon, to show the lady that you want to marry her, and that's what I've done," he added proudly. He tapped the spoon with his forefinger and said, "I got the wood out of my Dad's woodshed."

She studied it intently, and said, "It doesn't look much like a spoon to me," but, when she saw the disappointment register on Tom's flushed face, she quickly said, "It's very nice and I think you are clever."

"Will you marry me then?"

Her reply was drowned by the rumble of a tractor and the hooting of its horn. Tom turned to see Walter waving from the driving seat of a blue Fordson Major tractor as he drove up the road.

"Hello, Tom!" he shouted, without taking the pipe from his mouth. Tom waved back and, as the noise died away leaving the smell of diesel fumes on the air, he

"I said yes."

They looked at each other for several seconds and then he gave her a timid kiss on the cheek, "Smashing," he said with a broad grin and scampered off down the lane, calling over his shoulder, "See you at school tomorrow."

That evening, while Frank was leaning on the paddock gate

smoking a cigarette, Tom went up to him and said, "Granddad—can you keep a secret?"

"Aye, lad, I'm good at keeping secrets".

Tom looked over his shoulder and lowering his voice to a conspiratorial whisper said, "I've got a girl friend, and her name's Angela."

Frank looked at his grandson with pride, "Well done, lad. Is she pretty?"

Tom was now feeling very grown up and able to talk of grown-up matters, man to man.

"She's the prettiest girl I've ever seen and she says she'll marry me."

Frank shook him by the hand and said, "There's nice. Congratulations."

The two leaned on the gate in the twilight and Frank rolled another cigarette. Turning his back to the breeze, he lit it with both hands cupped round the match and the glow lit up his wrinkled face. Tom watched the glow die down and said, "I saw Walter today, driving that new tractor. He passed me when I was coming out of school."

"Walter, driving a tractor?" said Frank in surprise, "I didn't know the old bugger could drive. He's good with horses mind, fair play, but I thought he was too old a dog to learn new tricks."

He turned up his collar against the east wind which was pulling the yellow leaves from the willow tree and swirling them round in playful spirals. "There's a nip in the air tonight," he said, "Walter lived on the farm next to me when he was a boy and his Dad was a good pal of my Dad. He got blown to bits in the great war, poor bugger. Nobody could plough like him though. His furrows were the tidiest you'd see anywheres and he won all the ploughing contests. What a waste of a good bloke."

He sighed and drew deeply on his cigarette, "I know a lot more who went that way too. I hope it's a thing you never have to live through. A lot of good boys was killed in the war. Aye, he could plough well, could Walter's Dad."

"I know. He was telling me about it the other day when I was helping him with the hedging, and he's told me that your Dad made the best cider for miles around. Is that right?"

"The very best. Folks used to come from all over the place to buy it and it won all the prizes in the big show every year. He reckoned it was his secret recipe which made it so good."

"What was special about it?"

"I'm buggered if I know. He used to put all sorts in it which made it a bit different."

He pulled his cap down lower and said, "I reckons I've got his recipe somewhere upstairs. I'm sure I have come to think of it. He gave it to me before he died and said it might come in useful one day, but I never did anything with it. I don't think I've even looked at it since that day. I'll dig it out and give it to you. My old Dad would like to think it'd been handed down in the family."

Then as the wind began to bite harder, they made their way into the kitchen and warmed their toes on the range.

Chapter Five

In Gorston there was a nip in the air. Summer was giving way to autumn and the workers cycled home with their lights on, their breath condensing in clouds under the street lights. The big 'Ommer' continued to thump its way through the inexorable shifts and when the blast furnace at the steel works was opened, the fearsome glow lit up the night air, turning the sky orange.

Gorston people were not as aware of the seasons as those in Lower Kings Canon. It did not matter much. As far as Bob Gregory was concerned, it was either cold or warm, or wet or dry, for cycling to work, and that was the extent of his interest in the seasons.

There was excitement at number seven Jubilee Terrace because Chris had joined the Scouts. They met in a hut on the edge of the waste ground every Wednesday evening and at that night's meeting plans had been unveiled for a weekend's canoeing on the river Wye. It was a new experience for him, never having canoed before.

He had hardly ever left Gorston in his young life, except for a caravan holiday in Great Yarmouth and a day trip to Aberystwyth. His father could not afford holidays and he was not a great believer in them, so Chris's experience of life outside his home town was limited.

To him, the Scouts represented a big adventure because they did exciting things like making camp fires on the waste land and midnight walks round the town. The prospect of canoeing on a river with his scouting pals and being away from home, filled him with the same excitement that Tom felt when he went poaching on that beautiful summer's evening. They were going to sleep under canvas and cook their own food on a camp fire.

His mother made him some sandwiches to sustain him on the journey and his father gave him a half crown. "You don't have to spend it all at once," he said, ruffling his son's hair.

"Corr, thanks, Dad," said Chris, carefully putting the coin into his pocket.

They waited, stamping their feet and blowing on their hands. The coach picked them up before it was light from the corner of Bessemer Street and the rucksacks were stowed in the luggage compartment. By dawn, they had left behind the claustrophobic streets and as the coach sped into the countryside, the chill mists began to lift. He cleared a circle on the hazy window to look at the fields, which had appeared as the grey light of dawn gave way to the morning glow. The mist still hung over the ploughed fields and the bare branches stood proud, like the rigging of sailing ships on the grey seas. Smoke from the chimneys rose high into the still air and it was another world to Chris, and a great adventure.

When they had boarded the coach, there had been a rush to get on the back seat and the lucky ones started a sing-song. They began with *Ten Green Bottles Hanging on the Wall*, hesitantly at first, and then more strongly as the rows further forward joined in. Before long, they were all singing lustily as the bus headed west towards the Welsh border.

They arrived at Glasbury and his adventure gathered momentum. He stood on the shingle river bank by the Glasbury scout hut. The river was bigger than he had expected, as he was used to the river Theme, the stream which ran through the School cross-country course. The Wye was wide and sparkled in the weak winter sun. To the right he could see the misty silhouettes of the Brecon Beacons through the open branches of the beech trees.

"This is great isn't it, Goggles?"

"What is?"

"All this."

"It's alright, I suppose."

The adventure impressed Goggles less than Chris, but the weekend was a success and most of the boys enjoyed it. Chris got through the whole weekend without falling in, which was an achievement, because many of the boys overturned and were tipped into the icy water.

The instructor had shown them the basic canoeing techniques on dry land before they took to the water and then they had been downstream as far as the Whitney toll-bridge, stopping at Hay-on-Wye to buy fish and chips. After the first day, they did more advanced things and went upstream towards Builth Wells and found some rough water, where they practised white-water techniques.

The highlight of the holiday was a torch-lit supper round the camp fire. It was a bitterly cold night and the boys sat as close to the fire as they dared. Chris's trousers felt as if they were about to ignite, so he shuffled further away from the fire. When a fresh log was thrown on, a column of sparks was sent up into the frosty air and, as he raised his head to follow them, he saw the bright full moon with a halo of light forming in the ice crystals.

When the fire died down, they cooked sausages on the embers. They impaled them on a long stick and held them over the heat. Chris's sausages were overdone. He'd never cooked anything before and was unsure how long to give them.

Goggles pushed his glasses further up his nose and squinted at Chris's culinary efforts. "You're burning yours," he declared, with the air of an experienced chef.

"No, I'm not, they'll be smashing."

"They're not supposed to be that black. Hold them further away from the fire."

Chris's sausages were put into rolls and he ate them with relish. The black, crusty objects were to him the most delicious things he'd ever eaten.

He took another bite and leaned back, studying the night sky, and nudged Goggles in the ribs. "When I grow up, I'm going to live in the country," he announced.

Goggles blew on his hot sausage and thought for a while. Eventually he took a bite and with a full mouth mumbled, "I don't like it."

"Why not?"

"I just don't. It's too empty, nothing in it but fields and trees and wild animals."

Chris looked into the flames and said. "I think it's great, better than in the picture books."

And so Chris Gregory had his first taste of country life and, when he arrived home and alighted from the bus, he looked around his shabby surroundings and for the first time experienced dissatisfaction with his way of life. It had never occurred to him before to even think about it. Gorston was where he lived and all he had known up to now, but his weekend with the scouts had opened up new horizons and it proved to be a weekend in his life that he never forgot; an experience that had a profound effect on him.

Chapter Six

At Lower Kings Canon Primary School, the term continued to drag on and Tom and Brian remained enemies, but Tom had the satisfaction of knowing that Angela had promised to marry him when they were grown up. The Christmas play was uppermost in every one's minds and preparations gathered pace as the end of term approached. The play was the same every year; written by Miss Acton on the theme of the Christmas story.

Tom always played a shepherd in a dressing gown and on his head was a tea towel, tied around with an old tie. He wore a beard which tickled him under the nose and kept slipping down. It smelled of mothballs and he had to wear it every year. Even when he played one of the wise men he had to wear the same beard, much to his disgust. He carried his father's crook and the only lines he had to say were "Let us follow that bright star in the east."

Angela had the starring role as Mary and had a large part to learn. Tom was relieved to discover that the part of Joseph was to be played by the Blacksmith's son. He would have found it hard to bear if Brian had got the role. He was the Archangel Gabriel, wearing a halo and a set of giant cardboard wings that kept getting caught up in the curtains.

In rehearsals of the last scene, the cast had to face the audience and sing *While Shepherds Watched their Flocks by Night* and Brian kept pulling Tom's head-dress down, prompting Miss Acton to shriek, "Thomas Beddows, if you don't keep your head-dress on properly, I'll give you the part of the donkey."

The play was performed on the last evening of term and most of the village turned out to see it. It had cost sixpence to go in and everyone considered it money well spent. There was little entertainment in the village and to many the school play was the high-light of the year and helped to put them in the festive mood.

Frank did not consider it money well spent. He would have preferred to be in the pub with the other 'Young Farmers', but he had been coerced into putting on his suit and tie and coming along to watch his grandson's performance.

"Highway Robbers," he muttered, as he parted with his sixpence at the door, but even he warmed to the Christmas atmosphere and clapped enthusiastically as the cast took their final bow. "Well done,

Tom!" he shouted at the top of his voice, earning a kick on the ankle from Mrs Beddows.

Miss Acton made her traditional speech when the play had finished, but between Mr and Mrs Beddows was an empty seat. Even as the Headmistress began to speak, Frank was ordering a pint of cider in the bar of the Old Black Lion.

"How come you're all dressed up like a dog's dinner tonight?" came a voice from near the fireplace.

"I've been courting Nellie Partridge," replied Frank.

Nellie Partridge was the butcher's wife; a young beauty, and to the Young Farmers she was a goddess. Scarcely a day went by without Nellie's name coming up in the fireplace conversation.

"Get away with you," said Edward from the stool closest to the fire.

"Aye, I have, and she says I can squeeze her dumplings whenever I'm in her shop. Best dumplings in Herefordshire she's got too."

None of the gang believed him, but the rest of the evening was spent in elaborating the story of his evening with Nellie Partridge. His imaginary affair became written into the repertoire of the fireside conversation for years to come.

Christmas was approaching and Tom was free of his prison for a few weeks. The Beddows family was busy preparing for the festive season.

Tom and his young brother and sister had taken an old pram into Cwm Woods and cut holly and mistletoe. It was a good year for berries and they found some beautiful specimens near the place where the drunken pheasants had been caught.

Ken had brought in a Christmas tree from the estate and was splitting some dry elm logs which he'd been saving since the summer. "Nothing like dry elm for giving out the heat on Christmas Day," he said, as he swung the axe. "It'll warm our toes while we're eating the mince pies."

In the outhouse, Mrs Beddows was plucking the goose which had been fattening on barley meal. Ken had killed it that morning and, as she plucked, wispy feathers floated around settling on her hair and shoulders. Every so often, one would settle on her nose and she would purse her lips and blow it away.

The tree had been decorated by the two youngest children. They dragged the cardboard box from the loft and with great excitement unwrapped the shiny decorations, climbing on chairs to hang the baubles from the branches.

After much discussion, a drunken Father Christmas had been put with great ceremony on the top-most branch. The children could not decide what to put on the top and had to choose between a star, a fairy, and the wobbly Father Christmas, and Father Christmas had won the debate this year. Ken put on the lights, which worked first time, and they all agreed when they stood back to admire it, that it was the best Christmas tree ever.

"Well, this is the first year that the lights have worked first go without all that fiddling about. It usually takes me hours to get the damned things working," said Ken.

On Christmas Eve, it began to snow. Large flakes as big as half-crowns drifted silently from the leaden skies, covering everything with several inches. The pub was decked with holly and in the porch was a large Christmas tree that Major Hudson had donated. Frank sat by the log fire with a sprig of mistletoe in his party hat.

"You never know your luck," he chuckled.

"Aye," said Edward, "Nellie Partridge might come in tonight."

"There's a few in here to practise on first," said Frank and began kissing the ladies in the lower bar. Squeals of embarrassment came from the reluctant recipients as he chased them round the bar.

"Give it a rest, Frank," called the landlord, "Some of these ladies have led sheltered lives. Being kissed by an international playboy like you could be too much for them."

Frank, who had cornered Mrs Edmunds under the case containing the stuffed pike, called back. "Get away with you, it'll be the best Christmas present they ever had!"

The evening was clear and starry and a sharp frost made the covering of snow crisp underfoot as the Beddows family —minus Frank—returned from the candle-lit Midnight Mass. A bright moon illuminated the village, reflecting from the snow and lighting the scene like daylight.

All was quiet, the blanket of snow muffling the sounds, and an eerie silence enveloped the village. Yellow lights shone from the windows and wood smoke from the chimneys went up into the starry sky in silent vertical columns. Occasionally, muffled laughter and singing came from the late revellers in the pub, punctuating the otherwise quiet village.

Christmas morning dawned bright and clear. Tom had hung one of his father's socks at the end of his bed. He was too old to believe in Father Christmas, but his mother had threatened him not to give the game away to Jane and Peter, so he went along with it all. Nevertheless, he was excited and woke long before it got light. He lay awake for what seemed an eternity, waiting for sufficient light to see his presents.

He felt a thrill as he delved inside the sock and found several small toys, a clockwork monkey, a tin fire engine, and a kit for making a model of The Golden Hind. In the bottom was an orange, some nuts, and a shiny new shilling. The lump at the very bottom turned out to be a pink sugar mouse, tied to a crumpled envelope. The envelope contained a note which read:

Dear Tom,
A Happy Christmas from Granddad.
Here is my Dad's special cider recipe which I told you about.
You might want to make some cider when you are grown up.
Keep it somewhere safe and don't lose it.

"Thanks, Granddad. I'll keep it safe for ever," he said, when Frank came into his room to see him open his presents.

After breakfast the grown-ups opened their presents.

"A new pinny, just what I wanted," cried Mrs Beddows and crossed the room to kiss her husband. She held the apron up against herself and gave a twirl to show it to advantage.

"I bought it at Jones' and I've got the receipt, in case you want to change it," said Ken.

"No, it's just what I'd have chosen for myself. It's lovely."

The two smallest children had a pile of toys which they unwrapped with squeals of delight. Their parents had been saving all year, putting spare pennies and threepenny bits in a jar on the top shelf.

Frank had a box of handkerchiefs from Mrs Beddows, "Don't you dare use them for anything else but blowing your nose. I'm tired of seeing those horrible stained things and I don't want to see any rabbit blood on them. See if you can keep them nice and white."

"There's tidy," he said and added them to his pile of socks.

Mrs Beddows had been up in the early hours to stoke up the range and put the goose in the oven. She wanted to get her jobs finished early, because they had been invited to the Big House for a drink before lunch and, after all the excitement of the present opening, they were spruced up and on their way to Major Hudson's in the Austin. It was not far to walk, but Ken thought there was more snow in the air so they took the car.

It was traditional for the Hudsons to invite the estate workers and their families to the house on Christmas morning. The tradition went back three generations and Christmas without the gathering at the Big House was unthinkable. A large section of the village was assembled in their best clothes and even Frank and Walter were in ties and suits. Walter was still wearing his trilby, but it was not considered to be a breach of etiquette, because no one expected to see him without it.

The Hudson's young daughter, Penelope, carried a tray of drinks which she served to the guests. She was the same age as Tom, but she went to a boarding school in Wiltshire and Tom did not see much of her. When they did meet on occasions such as these, he didn't take much notice because they moved in different social circles and she might as well have lived on another planet as far as he was concerned. She was from a different world; a world in which there was no room for Tom. She wore strange fashionable clothes and 'talked posh'.

When the Beddows family arrived, they were met at the door by the butler, given drinks, and shown into the glittering ball room. The biggest Christmas tree that Tom had ever seen stood at one end and the chandeliers were reflected in the gilt framed mirrors. A log fire was burning brightly and the air was filled with the smell of wood smoke and the sounds of excitement and gaiety.

The room was full of people, standing in groups talking noisily. The Major was a tall, slim man in a grey suit. He wore a yellow waistcoat and his greying hair was well-groomed. He was not from an aristocratic background, but he looked as if he were, He'd inherited the title of Lord of the Manor of Kings Canon with the house and the villagers believed him to be a genuine aristocrat. He greeted his guests with a warm smile and an outstretched hand.

"A very Happy Christmas to you. I am so glad you could make it," and "Can I get you another drink?" greeted them as they met.

"Please help yourselves to the food," said his wife.

"Now there's a real lady and gentleman," said Mrs Beddows in a reverent whisper as they moved away. "Just look at the ceiling and the furniture. Isn't it beautiful? Fancy having to dust those chandeliers. Though I suppose if you can afford to live in a place like this, you can afford to pay someone to do the dusting."

The others were too overawed to comment and just gazed around the ball room in silence.

The table was loaded with mince pies, sausage rolls, game pie, and all kinds of dishes that the Beddows family had not experienced before.

Frank was the first to make himself at home and quickly joined Walter at the table.

"Best thing about these mornings is the cider cake," said Walter, putting his pipe into his top pocket and helping himself to as much as he dared.

"Only one thing wrong with them," mumbled Frank through a mouthful of mince pie, "You can't get a decent drink here. Who wants to drink these tiddley little glasses of punch I'd like to know? What's in it anyway? There's a bit of oak tree floating in mine."

"It's what the posh folks drink, ain't it?" replied Walter, cutting himself another slice of cake, "What did you get for Christmas this year?"

"I had twelve handkerchiefs, four pairs of socks, and an ounce of Old Holborn—Oh, and a promise from Nellie Partridge."

"Well, that's better than I got—I got a card from my sister in Ludlow. That's all." He looked sadly round the room. "Look at all these people. They've got family and this is the time for them. Christmas isn't for the likes of me with no family, except Biddy in Ludlow, and I haven't seen her for years. No, I'm always glad when it's all over. It makes me feel lonely and it's the only time I do."

Frank did not respond but looked intently at him, slowly shaking his head and putting a comforting hand on his shoulder. Then he looked around and said, "Have you seen Nellie Partridge this morning?"

"Aye, Frank. I saw her just now, behind that settee with Jack Pugh from Pentre Farm. Going strong they were."

451

"Get away."

"Aye, it's true and as I was passing, I heard her say, "Corr! that's a big one.""

"Get away."

"Aye, bigger than Frank's," she said. "I don't know what she was talking about mind."

"I reckons she was talking about his sausage roll. It couldn't have been anything else if it was bigger."

Tom did not enjoy these occasions, because they went on for so long and he couldn't wait to get home and play with his presents. Even a glimpse of Angela across the room, failed to ignite any enthusiasm for the event. The adults talked about things that didn't interest him and the children had been threatened with dire consequences if they were not on their best behaviour. They stood like dummies, hardly daring to speak, but most of the adults enjoyed the Christmas morning gatherings.

There was a sense of occasion and an opportunity to meet friends in elegant surroundings that set the mood for Christmas Day. Christmas would not be the same without them. Walter came for the cider cake. Frank came in the hope that Nellie Partridge might be there, and Mrs Beddows came because she hoped that some of the elegance might rub off on her in some way and enrich her life. She felt as if she was moving in a higher social strata.

Tom was bored and his attention began to wander. The family portraits impressed him most. They were of the Major's ancestors and hung in heavy gilt frames on the oak panelling. Tom could see the family resemblance in them and the one that fascinated him most was over the piano; a full length portrait of a gentleman in hunting pink and white breeches. He had a pointed beard but otherwise he was a perfect replica of Major Hudson. It was almost as if he'd been painted in fancy dress, but the date in the corner, 1750, showed that it was a picture of someone who lived in this house a long time ago.

There was no doubt that the worlds of the Hudson's daughter Penelope and Tom Beddows were poles apart.

Chapter Seven

The Christmas of 1948 came and went in Lower Kings Canon, as did several subsequent Christmases, until Tom was to be found aged sixteen and working as a farm labourer on the estate. The Coronation of Queen Elizabeth II had passed, together with other national and world events, but life went on in the village as it always had done. The Coronation had made an impact on village routine. Celebrations marked the event and the village burst into colour with flags and bunting.

The School put on a pageant and a procession along the High Street with the children dressed up as past monarchs; the day culminating in a party in the School Hall. The Women's Institute organized a street party outside the Old Black Lion, which had been decorated with banners strung from the building, and tables had been set up in the centre of the road.

It had proved to be a memorable occasion, with plenty to eat and drink, and most of the villagers had entered into the spirit of the day and turned out in patriotic costume of red, white, and blue. Union Jack hats were everywhere and the revelries went on until well after dusk, when the adults moved into the pub to continue the celebrations when it got too dark.

Earlier in the day, they had watched the Coronation on a television in the School Hall. It was a flickering, snowy picture; the first television pictures that many had seen, and the hall rang to the cheers as the carriage moved down the Mall and the day's events unfolded.

Miss Acton made a patriotic speech, full of references to the start of a new exciting age for the nation. "We are entering a new era and from today we may call ourselves Elizabethans," she announced, in a voice trembling with emotion. "A beautiful young queen has been crowned Head of State. She rules over Great Britain and her Empire and long may she rule."

She ended with *God Save the Queen* and the entire village rose to its feet and shouted 'God save the Queen' followed by a rousing cheer.

Then she moved to the piano and played the *National Anthem* and they all joined in. It was a day to be remembered.

"How did they get those pictures into the School Hall?" asked Edward Morris as he sat near the fireplace with his friends.

"Buggered if I know," answered Frank, putting down his tankard.

"It's called television and they get the pictures down wires, like the telephone," said George, with a knowledgeable air.

"Don't be daft," replied Frank. "How can they do that?"

Another of the old men contributed to the conversation with "No, it doesn't. I heard that they come through the air and my lad's got a television, so he knows about these things."

The Young Farmers sat in silence for a while. The only sound being the tick of the grandfather clock.

"These scientists," said Frank, "they're messing about with things they don't understand. It's not natural." He took a sip from his cider and continued, "Sending pictures through the air. That's why the weather was so bad last winter. Stands to reason, if you sends pictures through the air, it's going to effect the weather, don't it?"

The old men solemnly nodded their heads in agreement and Frank, warming to his theme, added "That's why those winds knocked down the big oak in the back lane. We didn't get winds like that before they started sending pictures through the air and there ain't as many rabbits in Cwm Woods as there were when we were lads. I reckon it's got something to do with that as well."

Again the men nodded wisely and lifted their tankards for another drink. The inexorable march of technology was not impressing the regulars of the Old Black Lion.

Tom had been lucky enough to be taken to London to see the decorations. Dai, the Blacksmith, took his son Steve, because he wanted an excuse to go on a long journey in his new Morris Minor, and his son had persuaded him to take Tom. They both worked on the estate and had become good friends. Neither of them had been to London before, so it was an exciting trip.

They walked down The Mall looking up at the decorative arches surmounted by huge crowns and then they moved on to Trafalgar Square and down Whitehall to see Westminster Abbey and the Houses of Parliament. They stopped in Trafalgar Square to eat their sandwiches by the fountains and Dai took a photograph with his Brownie 127 camera of the two boys sitting under a bronze lion. When he eventually had the film developed, he stuck the fuzzy photograph in his family album and wrote underneath it, 'Lions by Landseer—Boys by Dai and Ken'.

Near the Abbey there was feverish activity as workmen erected stands for viewing the procession.

"It's big isn't it?" said Tom, giving a low whistle.

"What is?"

"London."

"Oh, yes. It's big alright."

"And so many people. What do you reckon they all do for a living?"

Steve thought for a while and then said, "Blowed if I know. I haven't seen a sheep since we arrived."

Tom continued to work on the estate and village life went on as usual. The Coronation had taken place and it had left an indelible mark on many memories. A pop singer called Elvis Presley could be heard constantly on the wireless and Teddy Boys were to be seen on the streets of Hereford. They stood on the street corners in their drape jackets and drainpipe trousers.

Tom read in the newspapers of damage done to cinemas by youngsters driven wild by the music of Bill Hailey and the Comets. They were getting up and dancing in the aisles, but all of this was another world to Tom as he went about his work on the farm and the seasons came and went.

Chapter Eight

Chris Gregory spent his formative years in Gorston. He had grown into a young man and on leaving school had been accepted as an apprentice toolmaker at Garringtons. In the factory, the big drop hammer sounded even louder and when it dropped the ground moved and he could feel the vibration in the pit of his stomach.

He was taught basic toolmaking skills at evening college in Wolverhampton and he worked in the factory for three years, but he was not happy. He did not like the dirt and noise. It was impossible to speak to anyone without shouting in their ear and what he was doing seemed pointless. He was a young man who felt he had a mission in life. He didn't know what it was, but he knew it was not this.

His father, Bob Gregory, still worked in the nuts and bolts factory, pushing his trolley backwards and forwards all his working hours. He made life tolerable by perfecting a mental disassociation with the work. The job required no mental effort, so he was free to wander in his own fantasy world. He occasionally communicated with his fellow workers but most of the time his mind was elsewhere.

He was looking forward to clocking off at the end of his shift, because he'd acquired a new pigeon and he was keen to get home and see how she had settled into the pigeon loft in the back yard. Bob was a keen pigeon fancier and a member of Gorston and District Pigeon Fanciers Club.

It was a well supported club, which met regularly and arranged races. The pigeons were taken in their baskets to venues many miles away and released, wheeling high into the sky before setting course for home. Their homing instincts took them back to their loft and the winning fancier was the one whose pigeon was first home.

It could be said that pigeon racing was popular in the area because their flights represented freedom to their owners, trapped as they were in uninspiring surroundings, but Bob did not indulge in such philosophy. He just knew that he liked pigeons and the shift seemed longer than usual because he was so keen to finish work and get to know his new acquisition.

When the factory hooter sounded, he clocked out and was soon cycling out of the factory gates, one amongst many, all on bicycles in a pack; weaving round the bollards and into the wet street; bells ringing and pedals whirring. It was foggy and he could only see a few yards ahead, before the grey world dissolved away. He leaned back to check his rear light and then the front one to make sure it was shining brightly. He pedalled through the murk, straining his eyes to make sense of faint grey shapes.

The fog muffled the sounds and all he could hear now that he was alone was the echo from the brick walls of his whirring chain. The weak glow from the street lights did nothing to help and, as he turned into Foundry Road, a grey shape loomed out of the fog. He looked up at the tall object and the next thing he remembered was lying in bed and a voice saying, "Nurse, call Mrs Gregory and tell her he's woken up."

His wife explained that he was in hospital after being knocked off his bicycle by a lorry. He put a hand to his throbbing head and felt a bandage and, looking down the bed, he saw that his right leg was in plaster, suspended by cords and pulleys.

"You were lucky, Bob. We thought we'd lost you," said Mrs Gregory, gently pulling the sheets up to his chin, "You were coming home from work and a steel works lorry came down the wrong side of the road and went straight into you. The police say he only had his sidelights on, so I don't suppose you saw him until it was too late. He was lost in the fog; didn't know where he was."

"I don't remember anything," he said, "but I know that I've got a hell of a headache and I feel a bit sick as well."

Bob stayed in hospital for several weeks and then he spent some time recuperating at home. He was on crutches for a long time and was never quite the same again, walking with a pronounced limp. He could not cope with physical work and his head injury had made him short-tempered. He also lost the ability to concentrate for long.

The Personnel Officer had tried to find him a light job in the plating shop but he couldn't cope with that either. He was summoned to the Personnel Office, where Mr Ellis sat behind the desk with his back to the window.

He was cleaning his glasses when Bob entered and he put them back on and peered at him through the thick lenses; so thick, that they resembled the bottoms of bottles and made his eyes appear tiny. Bob thought he looked like a pig.

"Well, Mr Gregory," began the officer, "What are we going to do with you?"

"What do you mean?" he snapped.

"Well, I'm told that you can't concentrate for long and you're upsetting everybody with your quick temper."

Bob looked startled, "I can cope. I hope you aren't suggesting that I should leave. I wouldn't get another job at my age and the dole isn't enough to live on."

"Yes, Mr Gregory, I am saying that it might be best for all of us if you left the firm but, before you get upset, let me tell you something." He pulled his chair closer to the desk and said, "It may surprise you to know that I have been doing some work behind the scenes on your behalf. "

"When you had your unfortunate accident which was the cause of all your problems, I made some enquiries and the firm has been negotiating with an insurance company. We didn't say anything to you, in case it all came to nothing and we didn't want to build up false hopes. The lorry driver was obviously in the wrong. He shouldn't have been driving on the wrong side of the road and he should've had his headlights on. Well, to cut a long story short, Mr Gregory, it looks as if you are going to get a tidy sum by way of compensation."

"Really. How much?"

"We're still negotiating to try and get the figure higher and we think there's a good chance of obtaining considerably more for you, taking into account your disabilities and your difficulties in earning a living. They have offered fifty thousand pounds, but we think we can do a lot better than that."

Bob gasped, and Mr Ellis continued, "Now, my advice to you would be to take early retirement. You could buy yourself a nice house in the country, away from all this mucky air, and have some left over to invest. You will also get a disability pension."

Bob took his hand and pumped it up and down, "Thank you, Mr Ellis, thank you."

Chris came home from the factory and, as he went upstairs to have a bath, his mother called up the stairs, "Chris, your Dad and I have something important we want to discuss with you when you've had your bath, so don't be long."

He could sense that this was a big moment as he went into the sitting room. His parents were holding hands, a thing they didn't normally do. His sister, Jen, was sitting expectantly in a chair by the fire.

"What's up then?" he enquired.

Jen answered, "I don't know. They wouldn't tell me until you arrived, but I can tell that it's something jolly exciting."

Mrs Gregory started the conversation. "You know that Dad had all that money for his compensation?"

Chris nodded.

"Well, we've been doing a lot of thinking about what to do with it and—"

Bob Gregory continued, "I don't need to work now, so we've invested the money and I'm going to retire."

"That's good isn't it?"

"Yes, it is, Son. It's great, but we wanted to have a word with you both to tell you that we're going to buy a little place in the country and we want you, Chris, to stay here and finish your training, and I don't think that you, Jen, would want to leave your job now you're doing so well. You can both live with Gran. She'd love to have you and her house is handy for the factory."

He paused to allow the information to be absorbed and then said, "I know this is a bit of a shock but I'm sure you'll come round to the idea. We've thought about it a lot and we don't want to leave you, but you can come and stay with us at weekends and we'll come to see you and Gran as often as we can."

When he finished speaking there was a silence, which Jen was the first to break. "Don't you two worry. We'll be fine at Gran's, so you go ahead and make your plans."

"Where are you going to live?" asked Chris.

Mrs Gregory beamed and said, "We've been to an estate agents and found a lovely modern bungalow in a village, a smashing black and white village in Herefordshire, just on the Welsh border and it has a nice friendly pub. We were coming back from Fishguard and we stopped off at a little pub for a drink and a meal. The locals were so friendly and there was a group of old men who sat by the fireplace and we haven't laughed so much in years —some of the things they came out with—they kept talking about a young lady called Nellie Partridge and the one old man said he'd squeezed her dumplings and

Anyway we liked the village. We had a walk round and looked at all the pretty gardens, real nosy we were," She barely paused for breath as she told her story, speaking more rapidly as she became excited, "It was so clean and lovely and we saw a bungalow with a nice front garden, not too big for your Dad to look after, and we went and looked through the windows, and we went to the agents and made an appointment to go inside, and it was lovely, central heating and a lovely kitchen looking onto the back garden." She paused for breath and, flushed with excitement, she held her husband's hand. They smiled at each other like young lovers.

And so Lower Kings Canon acquired two new residents. The bungalow was on the edge of the village in an area where several new houses had been built. It was within walking distance of the pub and post office and the Gregorys enthusiastically set about making it a home.

Back in Gorston, Chris and Jen moved in with Gran. She lived in one of the terraced houses in South Street and it was close enough to the factory for them to walk to work, but every time the drop hammer thumped down, the house shook. "I don't notice it now," said Gran, "I suppose you can get used to anything in time. Familiarity breeds contempt."

Granny Higginbotham was their maternal grandmother and had lived in there all her life; it was the house where she was born. Chris and Jen had always been fond of her and they were pleased to be staying there.

Granny Higginbotham's husband had been a nail maker, but he died before Chris had any clear memory of him. He just recalled him as a small bent man in a cloth cap. Any other details were too hazy, but Gran had clear memories and she took every opportunity of telling the youngsters all about him.

She was a grey-haired lady, always wearing a floral apron, and over her shoulders she usually had a cardigan. Her glasses were constantly sliding off her small nose and she had a habit of pushing them back up. She was well-known for quoting proverbs, though the chosen one was frequently inappropriate for the situation. Chris was astounded at the seemingly inexhaustible arsenal which she had at her disposal, some of which he'd never heard before.

"I saw you with your young lady yesterday," she said, standing at the sink drying a saucepan.

He blushed and said, "Oh, did you?"

"She looks pretty. What's her name?"

"Alice, and she works in the office with Jen. I'm taking her to the panto at Dudley Hippodrome tonight, Puss in Boots, and they say it's very good this year."

"That'll be nice. Make hay while the sun shines. You're only young once."

Alice was his first girlfriend. He was a shy boy and this was the first time he'd summoned the courage to ask a girl out, suffering agonies of indecision over where to take her. Should it be the pictures or maybe roller-skating? But he eventually settled on the theatre.

"It'll create a sense of occasion," he thought, "everyone goes to the pictures, but the theatre's a bit different. That should impress her."

They caught the trolley bus into Dudley and got there too early.

"Let's go and have a drink while we're waiting," he said, and they made their way through the chilly streets and found a pub. While she sat at a table, he squeezed his way through the crowd and went to the bar for the drinks.

"What are you drinking?" she asked.

"Double whisky," he proudly replied, "It's my tipple."

In fact it was the first time he had been in a pub and the first time he'd tried whisky. He thought it would impress her and make him look like a man of the world. "She'll think I'm grown up if I drink the hard stuff," he thought.

Instead of sipping it, he took a large gulp, as he'd seen the cowboys do in the Westerns. He struggled to look sophisticated but he was fighting back the tears and trying not to choke. He felt as if all eyes were on him and went red in the face.

"Excuse me," he croaked, eyes streaming, and he rushed to the toilet, coughing and gasping for air. He wiped the tears that were streaming down his face and, regaining his equanimity, returned and sat down, taking a sip of the drink which he treated with greater respect after that experience.

Queuing to go into the theatre, he felt light-headed and during the performance he closed his eyes and felt the building turning round. The children were shouting, "Oh, no, you didn't," and hissing at the wicked fairy but he didn't see any of it. He had planned to put his arm round Alice when the opportunity presented itself, but he was feeling too ill.

On the homeward bus journey, he fell asleep and was awakened by a sharp nudge in the ribs when they arrived at their stop. Walking back to Alice's house, she said, "Chris, I have never been out with a more boring boy. I've not enjoyed this date and I never want to see you again."

He tried to kiss her; a clumsy attempt and she pulled away, saying, "I mean it. I never want to go out with you again," and, with a toss of the head, she stalked down the alley.

So ended Chris's first attempt to woo a young lady.

"There are plenty more fish in the sea," said Gran when she heard about it, "Lots more pebbles on the beach."

It was a Wednesday and that was the day that Chris worked on the big press. A flat piece of steel was put on the bench and, with a thump, the press came down and formed a shape that was used in the manufacture of motor cars.

He worked on the machine all morning, making pressing after pressing, and just before his lunch break he put in the last piece. In the office window behind the press, he caught a glimpse of Alice.

She tossed a strand of hair from her eyes and reached for a piece of paper to put in her typewriter. He hesitated for a moment and then screamed in agony as the press came down on his hand. It felt as if his arm had been torn off and he slid from his seat and lay stretched out on the oily floor.

"Oh, my God! Look!" cried a female voice.

He passed out and when he awoke he was lying on his back in a hospital bed, his hand heavily bandaged. At the bedside sat Jen and Gran.

Jen said, "I've been on the phone to Mum and Dad and they'll be here soon. They left right away," She hesitated, and asked, "Have you been told yet?"

"Told what?"

She looked flustered and said, "Oh, nothing."

Bob Gregory stood by the bed and said, "There's something we have to tell you, Chris. I have to say it quick or I might lose the courage. There's no easy way to say this, so I'll just come right out with it. You've lost your hand, Son. The press smashed it to a pulp and the doctors had to cut it off."

Chapter Nine

February 1958 found Tom Beddows standing in the bitterly cold north wind. He stood in the churchyard, shivering as the wind cut through his clothes, and he felt the tears beginning to freeze on his cheeks. He was standing with a group of people who'd come to pay their last respects to his father, Ken.

His thoughts went back to a hot summer's day, when he'd stood almost on this same spot and listened to Mike Sturgess talking about hay-making. Now Mike and many villagers stood around his grave. Snow swept across the churchyard as the vicar said his words and the group stood in silence. Ken had been quite young when he suddenly died and the hospital had said it was a heart attack.

This was the first time that death had made itself felt in Tom's young life and he was finding it difficult to cope with. He'd always thought of death as something that happened to other families and the suddenness of the event had made it worse for him. Perhaps if his father had died after a long illness, he would have found it easier to come to terms with, but he had been a fit man and his death had come as a great shock.

Ken had been working on the farm the day he died and had to struggle with a boisterous cow, who was reluctant to go into her pen. The doctors said the strain of that might have triggered the attack, but he had a massive heart attack and died almost instantly.

Tom looked into the grave after the coffin had been lowered and, as when he'd been caned at school, the tears flowed and his body convulsed into violent sobs. He was vaguely aware of a comforting arm around his shoulders, but didn't notice whose it was. Nothing else in the world mattered at that moment but his aching emptiness and sense of loss.

In the church, he had not dared to look at the coffin in case he burst into sobbing but had concentrated on his hymn book. He had stared at the gold letters on the cover, unaware of the vicar's words or of anything around him. He stared so hard at the letters that his vision became unfocussed, but he was determined not to take his eyes off them in case he lost his self-control.

He slowly became aware that he was back at the house. He'd made his way from the church in a daze and could remember nothing of the walk. He mumbled a "thank you," as he absent-mindedly took a ham sandwich from a tray which passed before him and, looking across the room, he caught a glimpse of Frank wiping away a tear.

The sight of the old man looking so upset, caused a sob to shake his body, spilling the tea which had found its way into his hand but, as the mourners gathered in the kitchen, he regained his equilibrium enough to join in with conversations and even managed a joke with Walter to try and lift his spirits. The blackest day of Tom's young life wore on and he experienced utter despair.

When everyone had gone, the family got through the rest of the day wrapped in their own thoughts, hardly speaking to each other. The two youngest children stayed in their room, playing rock and roll records on their Dansette record player. Frank's stool in the pub stayed empty all day.

He sat by the range, distractedly whittling a piece of wood with his penknife, while Mrs Beddows cleaned the house, sobbing occasionally as her emotions got the better of her. "I shall miss him. He was a good man," she said.

Tom spent the rest of the day splitting wood in the back yard and swung the axe furiously as if to smash away the despair. He felt better as the wood split. Splitting wood was his job from now on.

The weeks went by and life got back to normal, but the sense of loss did not leave and he involved himself in the farm routine to try and blot it out.

"Hello, Tom. How're you doing?" came a cheery voice from behind the Post Office greetings card rack.

He looked up to see Brian Jones smiling at him and holding out his hand. The two young men lived in the same village but their paths rarely crossed. The animosity which Tom felt towards him had not dispersed over the years and the sight of his self-satisfied smile brought back bitter memories.

"Oh, hello, Brian," he responded, making an effort to sound friendly.

"I was sorry to hear about your father. It must have been a big shock, and so sudden too."

This awakened the despair that Tom had felt at the time of the death. He had still not really come to terms with the loss. The renewed feelings combined with his memories of Brian and a wave of loathing swept over him.

Brian went on, "I expect you're finding it hard to support your family now that you're the breadwinner aren't you?"

"Oh, I get by."

"What're you doing these days?" He turned over a can of baked beans and read the label, "Still labouring on the farm?"

"Y—es," answered Tom, cautiously, not sure if he had detected an unpleasant innuendo in the question.

Brian then confirmed his suspicions, "I'm the manager of Jones Road Haulage now and making a lot of money, and I mean a lot," he said, with added emphasis.

"There's nice," said Tom, hoping he sounded unimpressed, and then tried to change the subject, "That bacon looks good doesn't it?"

"I took over from Dad when he retired early. He knew he was leaving the business in safe hands."

He took out a cigar and lit it with a self conscious flourish. "I have these sent to me by a firm in St James's. That's in London, you know. Would you like one?"

Tom ignored the offer and then said, "I think I'll get some of that bacon as it looks so good."

"See you around, old friend. We must get together one of these days and have a chat over a pint." He threw a one pound note on the counter saying, "Keep the change, Mrs Price." He left the shop, blowing smoke from the corner of his mouth into Tom's face.

Since his father's death, Tom had the responsibility of supporting the family. His younger brother and sister were growing up and becoming expensive to look after. Frank brought his pension into the house, but it didn't go far, and he was finding it an unequal struggle on his labourer's pay packet.

Some extra money came in during the summer when the children and Mrs Beddows went fruit picking. They went to a fruit farm near Leominster and picked strawberries and blackcurrants, but the pay was meagre, and a day's toil made only a small difference to the family income.

"Every little helps." Tom would say as he put the coins into the biscuit tin on the top shelf.

The income received a small boost in the late summer when the apple harvest got under way, and there was always the hop picking, but for most of the time they had to rely on the wage which Tom collected working for Major Hudson.

He was a general farm worker but, now that he'd been working for a number of years, he'd been given responsibility for the sheep and spent most of his time tending to them. His busiest time was at lambing in the spring, when he was awake most nights helping with the difficult births. He got extra pay then, which made it seem worthwhile. He struggled on and he was no longer a boy, growing up quickly because of the extra responsibility his father's death had given him.

One evening, he was sitting by the fire with Frank, scrutinising the old man carefully.

"What do you keep staring at me like that for?" demanded Frank, irritably. "You've been staring at me since tea time. Have I grown another head or something?"

"Sorry, Granddad. I didn't know I was."

"Well, you was."

"I was just thinking, you're very quiet tonight."

"Well, I can be quiet can't I ? No law against it is there?"

"No, Granddad, but you aren't quiet very often."

Frank didn't answer but took out his tin box and rolled himself a floppy cigarette.

"What's the matter? Why aren't you down the pub tonight? You've hardly missed a night in years, except to go poaching."

"I don't have to go down the pub every night do I?" replied the old man, indignantly.

"You haven't been rabbitting for ages either and I can't remember the last time you asked me to go with you. We used to have some good times in the woods, you and me".

Frank picked up the *Hereford Times* and studied it, holding it up at an uncomfortable angle to hide his face.

Tom, undeterred, carried on the questioning, "Come on, Granddad. What is it?"

"Just a bit tired, that's all."

Tom emitted a long whistle and looked up at the ceiling in exasperation.

Mrs Beddows raised her head from the knitting and said, "You won't get any sense out of him, the stubborn old man."

All was then quiet, save for the fire's crackle and the ticking of the clock.

After a while, Mrs Beddows announced that she was going to bed and moved the kettle closer to the heat. "I'll just fill my hot water bottle."

Frank lowered the paper and looked at his grandson, who'd put his head back against the chair and closed his eyes.

Mrs Beddows said, "Goodnight, boys," and disappeared up the stairs.

Tom began to rise from his chair, saying, "I think I'll go as well. It'll be a hard day tomorrow on the hedging."

"Hang on, Tom, I've got something to tell you." There was no twinkle in his eyes as he fixed Tom with a steady stare.

Tom slowly nodded, "I knew there was something bothering you."

"Don't tell your mother this. I don't want her to know—yet," he added.

"'Know what?"

The old man scratched his head, "Sit down again, Tom," and after a brief silence, he said, "I won't be squeezing Nellie Partridge's dumplings no more."

"What!"

"I won't see another Christmas. I haven't been feeling well lately and I've been off my cider, so I went to see Doctor Sherwood and he did some tests."

"And?"

"Well, I went back this afternoon to get the results." He looked hard at Tom and said, "He told me I only have a few weeks to live."

Tom stared in disbelief.

"I'm telling you, I'm going to die Tom, and soon." He gave a little sob and rolled another cigarette.

All he could say was, "Are they sure?"

Frank nodded.

Tom did not sleep that night, but cried like a baby for a while and then lay awake, staring at the moonlight flooding in through the open curtains.

The mourners stood around Frank's grave. The other Young Farmers stood with their heads bowed. It was a big funeral, as Frank was well-known and well-liked.

"He had a good innings," murmured Walter, "but I shall miss the old bugger."

The sad and haunting melody from Walter's harmonica drifted across the silent churchyard as Frank was laid to rest.

The feeling of loss, which Tom had experienced at his father's death, was as nothing compared with what he felt now. There had been a special bond between grandson and grandfather and he could not grasp the idea that he would never see him again.

It was several weeks before he emerged from the house. He'd spent most of those weeks sitting in a chair staring at the flames in the range. He remained unshaven and unwashed and he emerged only to visit the Post Office and then returned to his chair.

Some days later, Mike Sturgess came visiting. "Are you ready to come back to work yet?" he asked.

Tom did not reply but stared at the flames.

"He's sat like that since Frank died," said Mrs Beddows.

Mike tried again, "I've come to see if you're ready to start work again. You've been off for some weeks now."

Once again there was no response, and his young sister sniffed and ran out of the room.

"Tom, old mate, the Major won't keep your job open for ever and if you don't come back soon, he'll sack you, and then how will you keep the family fed?"

Tom turned his head to look at him and spoke for the first time, "I'm not coming back."

"What!" exclaimed his mother.

Tom did not answer and turned back to stare at the fire.

The farm manager tried to make him see sense for a little longer and then, shrugging his shoulders, departed, leaving Tom poking at the fire and his mother weeping with her head in her hands.

Next morning, there was a knock on the door and Mrs Beddows opened it to find Major Hudson on the doorstep. He was standing with his back to the door, trying to straighten his umbrella in the rain. It had blown inside out in the fierce winds and as the door opened he turned and touched his hat.

"Good morning, Mrs Beddows," he said, "May I come in and talk to your son please?"

She nodded and stood back to allow him in. He stood, dripping on the lino, while she looked at him in bewilderment.

"Well, where is he?"

"Oh, I'm sorry, Sir. Here, let me take your coat. He's in the kitchen, through that door."

He slipped off his wet coat and she showed him in.

Tom did not turn when he entered but continued to stare at the fire. "Good morning, Sir," he said, without looking up.

The Major smiled and walked towards him, wiping his face with a large handkerchief. "Good morning, Tom. I've come to see if I can help you in any way."

"There's kind," said Tom, expressionlessly.

"Well, is there anything I can do to help?"

"No thanks."

"Well, why don't you come back to work and start earning some money?"

Tom gave the fire another poke, sending a shower of sparks up the chimney.

"Well?" said the Major expectantly.

"No, I don't feel like it. I don't want to do anything any more."

In the days that followed, several people called to try and talk him round. News had spread that Tom was sitting by the fire, with no interest in doing anything to support the family for which he was responsible.

"He just doesn't care any more. It's as if he's stopped living," said Mrs Beddows.

"Come on, Tom, snap out of it," pleaded Jack Powell, a fellow worker, "I can understand you being upset, because he was a nice old bloke and his loss came so soon after your Dad too. The old boy was special to you. He was to us all, but more so to you of course; but he was over ninety for God's Sake and we all have to die one day. You must have been expecting it any day at his age, so why are you sitting around like this?"

Tom said nothing but leaned back in his chair, drumming his fingers on the arm.

"You've not earned a penny in weeks, and winter's coming on.

What are your mother and the kids going to do?"

Tom slowly shook his head.

"Oh, this is bloody ridiculous. I was upset when my grandfather died and my mother died last year, but we've had to get over it—Answer me, man!"

He looked down at the surly young man in the armchair, sitting in front of a dead fire. He'd run out of fuel and could not be bothered to go and get any more. He looked a pathetic figure, unshaven and unwashed. His stubble had grown into an untidy beard and his hair was hanging over his collar. His eyes were expressionless and his face had taken on a pasty hue.

Jack turned on his heel saying, "I'm sorry, Mrs Beddows," and went out into the rain.

Jane Beddows was now a teenager and yearning for a social life outside the confines of the village. She had grown up in Lower Kings Canon and endured the regime of Miss Acton. After leaving the School at eleven, she'd gone to the secondary modern in the neighbouring town. She had tolerated it, but didn't enjoy her time there.

Tom had gone to the same school some years ahead of her, but it had made very little impression on his young life. He had counted the days until he could leave school and start working on the farm. Jane had some friends in Hereford and spent as much time in the city as she could. The atmosphere at home was oppressive, dominated as it was by the brooding presence of her elder brother.

She sat in a coffee bar in the centre of Hereford with her friend Sally. They went to the same school and had come in on the bus to look at the shops. She had no money to spend, but felt that she was keeping in touch with fashion by coming into Hereford. The Milano coffee bar was for young people and it had the ubiquitous juke box, which pumped out rock and roll.

Three of the youths standing around it were teddy boys and they posed self-consciously. The most outlandish of the three wore a pink jacket, with trousers so tight he could hardly bend his legs. He had a boot lace tie and shoes with thick crepe soles; his greasy hair falling forward over his forehead.

There was an all-pervading smell of coffee and the two girls sat at a table near the wall and drank coffee with froth on the top from transparent cups. Before leaving home, Sally had spent twenty minutes piling her hair into a beehive and spraying it with lacquer until it was stiff.

"It's young Jane, isn't it?" came a smooth voice from behind her, "Don't you remember me? I'm Brian Jones, owner of Jones Haulage Limited, and I went to school with your brother. Aren't you going to introduce me to your friend?"

"This is Sally."

"Hi, Honey," said Brian and he sat down in the vacant chair. He spoke in that manner because he'd recently seen an Elvis Presley film. Elvis spoke to the girls like that and Brian thought it was how a managing director of a leading haulage firm should speak. "I saw your brother the other day. I thought it was a tramp at first. He was shuffling along the High Street in his tatty clothes and his beard. I thought to myself, is that really my old friend Tom?"

He blew on his coffee and took a sip, looking at Jane over the cup. His voice became louder and he went on, "He's a disgrace to the village."

He put down his cup and lit a large cigar. Jane could feel the tears coming but she said nothing. She didn't know how to deal with the situation and was wishing that the earth would open up and swallow her. Her cheeks were burning and she looked down at her coffee to avoid Sally's gaze.

Brian puffed on his cigar. He was enjoying himself and just warming up. He took the cigar from his mouth and holding it up to his face, studied it intently and continued, "Sally, do you think you should be seen in public, talking to one of the Beddows family? They're a family of tramps and gypsies."

The girls looked uneasily round the coffee bar and saw that the couple at the next table were nudging each other and giggling.

"A nice girl like you should choose your friends more carefully, Sally." He looked at his watch, "Gosh, is that the time, and I have an appointment with an important client. See you around, Honey," and he left the coffee bar.

Jane looked at her friend and without speaking, rushed out, not waiting to put on her coat.

By the time she returned home she had regained her composure. The conversation had upset her badly, but on the bus she had time to think and was now determined not to let things get her down. She entered the kitchen to find Tom sitting in his chair, as usual.

"Where's Peter?" she asked.

"Out somewhere."

"Where's Mum?"

"Don't know."

She took off her wet coat and hung it on the door. "Perhaps she's nipped out to the Post Office," she mumbled, filling the kettle and putting it on the range. "You've let the fire go out again!" she shouted, stamping her foot in exasperation.

Tom shrugged his shoulders.

She stamped on the lino again and went out to get some wood from the shed. Struggling back with a large armful, she angrily kicked away his outstretched legs and got down on her knees to light the fire. "It's no use asking you to do it." She rolled up some newspaper and placed kindling on top. "I don't know what's going to become of us," she sobbed. "We've got no money and we're the laughing stock of the village."

Her resolution not to let things get her down was short-lived and she became more angry. "Why don't you shift yourself from that bloody chair?" she shouted, attempting to tip the armchair over and then sobbing with frustration when she couldn't move it.

She banged her fist on the hearth and scraped her knuckles. "Normal people don't behave in this way when someone dies, well not for so long anyway. They get over it. We all loved Dad and Granddad but we've got over it."

The screwed up newspaper flared as she applied the match and she put some more bits of wood on, before rubbing her hands together and pulling herself to her feet.

"I wish you could have heard the conversation I had with an old friend of yours this morning. He was right in everything he said and I hate you. I hate you." She paused and took a deep breath to calm herself down. "What did the doctor say today?"

Tom shrugged again.

"It's like talking to a brick wall." She looked around the room and said, "Did the Postman bring anything?"

He nodded towards the table. One letter lay there. It was addressed to Tom and had been opened. She looked at the signature first and saw that it was from Major Hudson, but she knew what it would say before she read it.

They had been evicted. The letter was apologetic but firm, expressing regrets, but making it clear that they could no longer stay in the house. Tom was sacked and the house was needed for the man who was taking his job. It ended with more apologies and his thanks for excellent work in the past.

She stared at the letter and read it through again, in the vain hope that she had misunderstood. "Have you seen this?" she demanded, waving the letter under his nose.

"Yes, I've read it."

"So you can speak then."

Tom said, "I'm sorry. Mum is upstairs in the bathroom. I'm very sorry."

The man in the dark suit handed Jane a cup of tea and said, "She must have got the pills from your brother. The doctor gave them to him this morning, apparently."

He took off his glasses, breathed on them and polished the lenses with his handkerchief. He held them up and looked at them against the light from the window. "I expect everything got too much for her, the poor woman. The letter must have been the last straw."

He went on, "But it's you and your brother Pete we must think of now. We'll have to find a nice new home for you, because your brother has had a breakdown and can't cope. He'll have to go to hospital for treatment but we'll make sure you are kept together, so you don't need to worry about that."

An involuntary sob shook her body.

The man said, "Try not to worry. Everyone in the office will do their best to make sure you are found somewhere where you'll both be happy."

In this tragic manner, the Beddows family broke up and within hours the little red-brick house at the end of the lane was locked and empty. The kitchen range, the heart of the house around which the adults sat and the children played, and where old Frank used to roll cigarettes from his precious tin box, was cold and dark. Jane and Peter were taken into council care and Tom went to Hereford hospital.

"Terrible isn't it?" observed the landlord of the Old Black Lion, wiping his moustache and putting his glass on the bar. The pub was almost empty and Selwyn from the top cottages was leaning on the bar discussing the day's events.

"You're right. It is," he replied, "You never know what's around the corner; what life is going to throw at you next."

The landlord refilled his glass and continued, "I knew Tom Beddows when he was a lad. A nice little lad he was and I can picture him now, tapping on that window to tell his Granddad that his dinner was ready."

"Old Frank, you mean?"

"Aye, that was him, a nice old boy and we all miss him."

"He used to sit over there by the fireplace, didn't he? We used to have some good evenings in here when Frank was alive and the old place don't seem the same without him."

The landlord looked at the fireplace and smiled, "Do you remember when he brought that bacon in and the old boys fried it on the fire and sold bacon sandwiches to the customers? I wasn't very pleased at the time because they were taking my trade, but I can see the funny side of it now."

"I remember, and I remember a lot of other things too. There was never a dull moment when he was around. They threw away the mould when they made him. He used to fancy a young woman called Nellie Partridge didn't he? He liked her dumplings, so he said." Selwyn paused for a drink and said, "He thought the world of his grandson though and Tom thought the world of him. It's terrible to think what has happened to Tom—terrible."

"Yes, they say he went off his head when Frank died so soon after Ken. His mother couldn't take any more when the Major evicted them and she did herself in, took an overdose."

"You don't say—well, well, well."

"Yes, she's hardly cold yet and the kids have been taken away to God knows where and Tom's been taken off to hospital.

Tom lay in his hospital bed looking around the ward. Nurses in green uniforms scurried about carrying trays of medicines and Tom was shocked into a sense of reality by his new surroundings. The strangeness and bustle around him had achieved what even his mother's death had failed to do. He began to take an interest in life.

He called out, "Hey, nurse!" and a young nurse came over to his bed.

"Hello, Mr Beddows," she smiled, "What can I do for you?"

"You can tell me why I'm in here."

Tom didn't like hospitals. He had been in this one before when he was a small boy. He'd had suspected appendicitis and had to be kept under observation. Although it had turned out to be a false alarm, the experience frightened him. At the time, he'd never been away from home before, and his friends had told him all about the horrible things they do to you in hospital. He developed a fear of them which had stayed with him ever since and even the smell of hospitals made him go weak at the knees.

He remembered how old Frank and his mother and father came to visit him and brought some grapes; the first he'd ever tasted. He smiled to himself as he recalled how Frank had eaten them at the bedside and left only a bag of stalks. Mrs Beddows had clipped his ear and made him go out and buy some more.

"You haven't been very well, Mr Beddows," said the nurse sweetly, "and you are here so that we can make you well again."

"There's nothing wrong with me!" he shouted and threw back the bedclothes.

"Doctor!" called the nurse and she gently pushed him back in and covered him up.

The doctor explained that he had to stay in hospital for his own good and would not be allowed out until he was better.

Fifteen minutes later, cars travelling along the Brecon Road passed a scruffy figure walking with a thumb in the air, hitching lifts. It was dark and raining heavily and he had no coat as he stumbled on the grass verge, shielding his eyes from the glare of oncoming headlights. Vehicles splashed him with muddy water as they forged through the deep puddles and he was forced to leap up the bank to avoid the deluges. He became soaked and cold as the water ran down inside his clothes.

He'd walked twelve miles before he got a lift. A pickup truck stopped and he ran forward to the vehicle, which stood with clouds of steam issuing from the exhaust. Headlights lit up the cloud but it was several seconds before it cleared and he could see the truck clearly. It waited, with its engine running, and he could see children clearing the mist from the windows and pulling faces at him through the rain lashed glass.

"Where do you want to go?" asked the driver.

"Lower Kings Canon please."

"Hop in," was the response, indicating the back of the open truck with his thumb, "No room inside, so you'll have to sit on the chickens. I can drop you off by the turning to Westwood Farm. That's as far as we're goin'."

"Fine thanks," said Tom, as he climbed up and found somewhere to crouch on the crates of live chickens.

The truck lurched off into the darkness, throwing him backwards, and he grabbed at the sides to steady himself. He curled up behind the cab to shelter from the rain and spray and the chickens pecked at his backside through the slats. He shifted his position to a crate containing less aggressive fowl and considered himself fortunate to have even this uncomfortable lift, because he'd walked a long way and was exhausted.

His old house was locked and boarded up, so he spent the rest of the night in the barn where his grandfather used to hide the game. He gave the secret hiding-place an affectionate pat as he took off his sodden clothes. He found an old jacket of his father's and even a pair of trousers that he used to wear when he worked on the Austin. The car stood at the other end of the barn, jacked up on blocks with most of the engine on the work bench.

He put on the dry clothes, hung his wet ones from a beam, and set about making himself comfortable in the sweet smelling hay. The perfume evoked memories of hay-making with Walter and, with a long drawn out sigh, he stretched out on his back and with his hands behind his head, stared up at the ancient beams which he could just make out in the darkness.

In the Old Black Lion there was a good log fire going and the old men sat around it talking about Nellie Partridge. Frank's place had been taken by another of the Young Farmers and at the bar the landlord was in conversation with Walter.

"Someone told me that they saw Tom Beddows tonight," said the landlord.

"He's been taken off to hospital this afternoon by all accounts, ain't he?"

"That's right, he was, but I'm only telling you what someone told me. They said they were coming back from Hereford and they saw him thumbing lifts. They said a truck had stopped and he was climbing in."

"Well, I'll be buggered," said Walter, pushing his trilby up on his forehead. "They must have let him out then."

The landlord refilled Walter's glass and passed it back to him. "Well, I was told he's got clinical depression, whatever that is."

"It means he's gone round the bend, a few sandwiches short of a picnic, playing without a full deck of cards, short of—"

"Alright, I get the picture," interrupted the landlord, "The poor chap."

"Aye, said Walter, "I wonder what'll become of him now."

Chapter Ten

Chris Gregory's wound had healed but he gave up working at the factory. He was frightened of the machines, breaking into a sweat when he got near one, and he decided that he didn't want to continue with his apprenticeship.

Gran said, "Well, boy, you don't have to work there if you don't want to. There are plenty of other ponds to swim in. Every cloud has a silver lining."

So he left Garringtons and started looking for a new job. After the dirt and noise of the factory, he decided that an outdoor job would suit him. He perused the jobs section in the *Express and Star* and found one working in the open air. On his first day, he took a deep breath and thought, "This is better than being in the factory, lots of fresh air, and it's not so dangerous."

He did up the top button of his jacket to keep out the driving rain and adjusted the canopy on his hot dog stand. He had a position outside the Gaumont cinema selling to the queues waiting to go in. The queues stretched along the pavement past his stand and the smell of frying onions tempted some to buy a hot dog. He could not understand why, because he thought they smelled disgusting and tasted even worse.

"Two hot dogs, Mister."

He looked over the edge of the counter and saw a small boy in a torn duffel coat looking up at him holding a half crown in his hand.

"With onions?"

"Yes, loads."

Chris put the Frankfurters in their rolls and dumped a generous portion of fried onions on top of them. "Help yourself to mustard or tomato sauce."

The boy stretched up and, taking the encrusted mustard tube, squeezed a yellow worm onto his sausages. When Chris held out his hand for the money, the boy took a bite and through his mouthful said, "Mister, when you were at school, were you good at sport?"

"Not bad. Why"

"Were you good at running?"

"Yes, I liked running. Why?"

"Because if you want your money you'll have to catch me first."

Chris made a lunge at the child, who clutched his hot dogs to his chest and dashed round the corner, leaving him banging on the counter in frustration. The child was the first customer in his new job.

"Not an auspicious start," said the supervisor, when he took the cart back to the depot at the end of his shift. The evening had started badly and got worse. It was a cold night and he was soaked to the skin. The smell of the cooking sausages had made him feel ill, and he hadn't done much business because when the cinema queues dispersed, the dark streets were empty.

The wind, which whistled round the corner, blew the onions from his bowl, and several times he had to chase down the street after his paper serviettes, which spiralled and dived just out of his reach. He performed something like an Indian war dance, as he tried to trap the fluttering paper with his feet. Huddled figures scurried past without giving him a second glance and at one time he thought he was going to be beaten up by some drunks, who jeered and threatened to turn his stall over.

"Give us a sausage, mate," said one, "or we'll put your stand on top of that roof."

When they began to rock the stand, it became clear that they were intent on trouble, and he decided that discretion was the better part of valour, as Gran would have said. He gave them a sausage each and they went away.

"Not a job with career prospects," he muttered to himself, as he finished work on his first evening.

The next evening, he was studying the jobs section again. He scribbled with his ball point on the paper's margin to get it working and, biting his lower lip, began to study each of the jobs that were on offer. Without qualifications or experience, his choice was limited, and he became more and more dejected as he found nothing for his biro to circle.

The months went by and he had a succession of jobs, none of which suited him and, as winter gave way to summer, he was again rustling the pages of the *Express and Star* and opening it at the jobs section.

Gran lowered her knitting and said, "Cheer up. Opportunity knocks. They're advertising for usherettes at the Gaumont."

"Don't be silly Gran. That's a job for girls—usherettes indeed."

"Oh, is it? Horses for courses," she replied, pushing her glasses up her nose and returning to the knitting.

"You're not much hel—" He paused in mid-sentence when an advertisement caught his eye, spreading a smile across his face.

Within a week, he was travelling to start his new job. It meant living away from Gran's for the summer and he alighted from the train at Skegness station and hauled his heavy bag over to the bus shelter.

"A sixpenny one please," he said to the bus conductor, and the bus wound its way through the Skegness streets, past the pier and headed north, along the coast road. The cold wind from the North Sea blew sand across the road as the bus made its way alongside the beach. He craned his neck to read the caption on a poster. *Skegness is so Bracing.* "It certainly is," he thought, watching an elderly couple struggling to walk in the strong wind. They had their heads down on their chests to keep the sand blast from their eyes.

His new job was that of kitchen porter at Butlins Holiday Camp. He was given a chalet in the staff quarters on the edge of the camp and then sent to the stores to collect his uniform; a set of blue overalls, made of stiff material and smelling of bacon fat even though it was fresh from the laundry. The holiday season was getting under way and the camp was full. He walked back to his chalet with the uniform under his arm, stepping aside as a redcoat ran past, blowing a kazoo. The man hurried along like the Pied Piper of Hamelin, followed by a horde of excited children. Everywhere that Chris went, he heard the public address system broadcasting incessant pop music and an advertisement for cigars, played *ad nauseam.*

"Tom Thumb, Tom Thumb, the ideal gift for men, Tom Thumb, Tom Thumb—"

"Ding dong, Radio Butlins calling. Campers may like to know that Uncle Bill's puppet show is starting in the tropical ballroom and there is a knobbly knees competition by the swimming pool. Come along, Dads and show 'em what you're made of, and don't forget the Glamorous Grans' contest, which is about to start in the Tropicana dance hall—Ding dong."

He reported for duty in the kitchens the next morning and the Supervisor, a Scotsman, wearing a supervisor's uniform of pale blue blazer, gave him a mop and bucket and set him to cleaning the floor. He moved about the kitchens, cleaning around the stainless steel catering equipment, while dining hall porters in their white jackets hurried in and out pushing trolleys loaded with plates.

"Hey, Gregory," called the Supervisor, "I've got a job for you."

He took him over to a large steaming vat. "It's full of bloody custard," he explained. "for the bleeding happy campers to put on their sodding apple pies. Now, when I tell you, I want you to clean it out, so clean that I want to see my bloody face in it. There's always a wee drop left in the bottom so you just open the tap like this to let it out." He turned on the tap and a gush of steaming custard poured out into the drain. "Don't worry about the bloody waste, there's often a lot left. Okay? Now get on with your mopping until I give you the nod."

Chris mopped the floor as the dining hall porters filled their jugs with custard and wheeled them on a trolley into the dining room. He'd never seen so much. "There must be hundreds of gallons," he thought.

"Okay, Gregory," called the supervisor, "When it's ready."

Chris remembered what he had been told and turned on the tap to empty the last dregs. He stood back, leaning on his mop, and waited for the yellow cataract to cease. The custard kept on coming and he pushed back his white hat and scratched his head. He did a little more mopping and returned to find it was still gushing out, a steaming torrent, splashing through the grid of the drain and gurgling down the gully.

"What a waste," he thought, but Jock had told him not to worry about it as there was often a lot left.

Eventually it slowed to a trickle and the trickle became a mere drip, so he climbed the step ladder and leaned inside to start his cleaning. He had to stretch right inside to reach the bottom and he scrubbed the sides with a stiff brush. As he scrubbed, he became aware of raised voices outside his little stainless steel world. The voices became agitated and angry and then he was grabbed by the legs and dragged into the outside world.

"Where's all the custard gone?" demanded a porter.

Chris looked bewildered as someone said, "It's all gone. There's none for second sitting."

The supervisor was called. "You bloody imbecile!" he shouted.

Chris thought he was going to hit him, as he protested that no one had told him there were two sittings.

The train headed across the flat Lincolnshire countryside, carrying Chris away from Skegness and back towards Gorston. Only the day before, the train had been carrying him in the opposite direction towards his new job. He stared disconsolately across the flat fields at the Boston Stump and thought, "Well, that job didn't last long, just three-quarters of an hour." Then he smiled and thought, "Well, at least they paid me ten shillings and I had a free breakfast. Ah well, back to the Express and Star."

"There's many a slip, twixt cup and lip," said Gran, as he arrived and dragged his bag into the little terraced house. "Everything comes to he who waits."

Chapter Eleven

Tom Beddows had only stayed in the barn for a few nights, because he had to leave when the new tenant took over, and he had now made his home in Cwm Woods. Some years ago, he'd built a shack for his brother Pete to play in; sturdily constructed of scrap materials and it was still standing. He busied himself repairing and enlarging the structure. It was situated deep in the woods and sheltered from the prevailing winds by a bank of brambles. He put a layer of turf on the metal roof, both for insulation and to hold the sheets of metal down, and he built turf against the plywood walls.

The result was surprisingly cosy. The remains of a charcoal burner's house was only a hundred yards away and he carried the old bricks to his new home and used them to build a chimney. He had no cement to bind them together, but used clay instead and lined the inside. It was a crude but effective chimney. When first lit, it smoked and filled the shack with dense, choking fumes, but it worked well when it dried. Throughout the winter, Tom didn't allow his fire to go out. He had plenty of fuel and ample time to gather it and anyone passing Cwm Woods in the winter saw his haze of smoke, perpetually drifting through the branches and over the bare trees.

The primitive shack became his home and the poaching skills which he'd gleaned from his grandfather became his lifeline. He was able to survive by catching game and he knew what could be safely eaten from the woods and what should be left alone. The smell of cooking mushrooms could often be detected drifting through the woods, as he became expert on cooking the various fungi which grew there.

Many of the fungi which grew on rotting tree stumps looked unpleasant, but he knew which ones made delicious and nourishing meals. Some of them were large and made a filling meal on their own without the addition of other ingredients, but other ingredients there were in plenty and Tom lived well.

He enjoyed the challenge of preparing ambitious meals and dined on roast pheasant, rabbit, hare, and wood pigeon, and delighted in baked trout, which he tickled from the nearby stream. There were berries and nuts, nettles, and numerous roots, and there were herbs, flowers, and fruits. His *piéce de resistance* was roast woodcock, stuffed with hazelnut and elderberry sauce and served with garlic mushrooms. He even made a good coffee from dried dandelion roots and as he became more settled he grew vegetables. He was careful to ensure that they were grown in rotation, so that he had fresh produce at most times of the year.

One day, two men in suits called on him while he was spit roasting a young rabbit.

"Are you Thomas Beddows?" asked the taller of the two.

They had been told that he was to be found in the woods and they had parked their car in a gateway, donned their wellington boots and had struggled through the undergrowth to find him. The smell of roast rabbit drifting through the trees, mingling with the smell of smoke from burning oak, had led them to him.

He was a wild-looking figure, standing in the clearing basting the rabbit. He had long unkempt hair and an untidy beard. His clothes were tattered and he had a small mongrel dog at this feet. The animal was a stray which had befriended him and the two were inseparable. It barked furiously when he heard the men making their way through the woods.

"What's it to you if I am?" was his answer to the man's question.

The two men looked around the clearing and one tapped the shack with his foot. The tall one said. "We are here to tell you, Mr Beddows, that you don't have to live in squalor like this."

Tom scratched his head, thoughtfully, "What do you mean?" He gave the spit another turn and fat dripped into the fire, flaring up, so that the men flinched and backed away.

"The government of this country go to a great deal of trouble and spend a lot of money to ensure that people such as your goodself do not starve. You are eligible for assistance and could collect money each week so that you do not have to live like this. Someone brought your plight to our attention and asked us to try and help and we thought that most probably you are unaware of the system, so we've come to help you. All you have to do is fill in a form and—"

Tom gave the spit another turn and raked at the embers to intensify the glow. "Forms, handouts, charity. Do I look as if I'm starving? Just smell that."

"But you don't have to do this," continued the man, "You can collect National Assistance while you remain unemployed."

Back at the car, the men leaned against the bonnet and took off their boots. "Well, we tried," said the one.

"Some people are beyond helping, but I don't think he needed to be so rude. I've never heard language like that before."

Tom lived from season to season in total isolation, his only companion being his dog. He made occasional trips to the village, but otherwise never left the woods. Major Hudson knew of his sitting tenant, but chose to ignore him and he remained undisturbed.

Winter made his life more difficult and some mornings he would awake to woods that were sparkling white with hoar frost and he had to break lumps of ice from the stream to melt for coffee and washing. His diet also became less varied as the growth in the woods rested until the spring, but his ingenuity and the knowledge obtained from old Frank helped him to survive in an environment where most would not. If things got really harsh, he would gather snails from under stones and produce acceptable and nourishing escargots with the addition of his dried wild garlic.

Shuffling past the village school one day on one of his rare excursions out of his woods, he heard a little girl call out, "Look at that old tramp."

A group of children came running up to the railings, shouting and jeering, "A tramp, a tramp. Look an old tramp."

Miss Acton had retired long ago and Miss Henworth was now the Headmistress. She came out to see what had caused all the commotion. "That's not an old tramp," she explained, "He's quite young and I remember him when he was a pupil here. Come away from the gate, you children."

As Tom moved on, he heard her say, "If you don't work hard at your lessons, you might end up like him."

One crisp autumn morning, while he was preparing a meal outside the shack, he heard a pack of fox hounds in full cry, their blood curdling howls echoing round the woodlands. The pack streamed through his clearing, scattering his possessions and pulling down his washing line. When the horses thundered through, Tom was on his hands and knees picking up the trampled washing. They scattered his things over a wider area and looking up he saw an attractive girl on a grey hunter. She was dressed in white breeches and black jacket. Her hair was tied up under her hat and she turned to look at him as she cantered past.

Their eyes met and a flash of recognition passed between the two. It was Penelope Hudson, the daughter of Major Hudson, who had been serving drinks at the Christmas party some years ago when he was a small boy. She was now a young woman, but had not really changed. He'd recognised her instantly and, although he looked very different, she'd seemed to recognise him.

Tom had created his own little world in the woods. He led an uncomplicated life and it was the simplicity that kept him there. Since his breakdown, he could not cope with the problems created by other people, so he shunned them and lived in isolation. His main preoccupation was food and in the winter it was food and warmth. He could go for months without seeing another human being and, because his life consisted of a succession of routines, each task became an important part of life itself.

He would take a long time over the preparation of a meal, taking a pride in doing everything well. A rabbit would be skinned slowly and neatly. It would be cut up and put into his pot with his meticulously prepared vegetables and herbs and every aspect of his life in the woods was done with extreme care. He had no worries and staying alive was what preoccupied him and all that was important to him.

In that manner life proceeded, with nothing to interfere with his chosen existence. He had everything he needed in the woods.

Chapter Twelve

Tom emerged from his shack, stretched and looked up at the sky. It was a clear, blue, autumn sky and it was a good year for colour in the trees, with the early sun catching the beech leaves on the other side of the clearing. Underfoot was a layer of crisp leaves. Last night's fire was still alive and the smoke was hanging in a distinct, horizontal layer in the still air.

The air was cold and sharp to the nostrils. It promised to be a beautiful day and he had a plump hen pheasant that he was going to cook later on. Several wood pigeons took to the air as he strolled across the clearing to wash in the stream. The cold water took his breath away as he splashed it on his face and round his neck, but it was invigorating.

After washing, he stood and took deep breaths of the crisp morning air, smiling as he looked up at the delicate tracery of branches and glowing leaves. He walked slowly back to the shack and busied himself with his routine, breakfasting on boiled eggs from the three hens that free-ranged and roosted at night in the tea chest which he had nailed in a tree.

The hens scratched about in the undergrowth, eating worms and seeds, and produced tasty eggs with deep orange yolks. After the boiled eggs, he had some of his dandelion coffee and, when he had finished breakfast, he sat and listened to the sounds of the woods. Summer had come to an end and autumn was hurrying along, but the woods were still full of bird song. It was as if they were having one last glorious effort before the onset of winter.

The thud of horses hooves came from the depths of the woods. It was a familiar sound because riders often used the bridle paths which criss-crossed the woods. The hoof beats stopped abruptly and Tom cupped a hand round one ear, straining to hear through the trees. He sensed that something was wrong for hoof beats to cease so suddenly, and he wondered if someone had fallen.

His dog pricked up his ears and barked furiously, so Tom put down his coffee and began to run in the direction of the last sounds he heard, disturbing rabbits as he went. They scampered off through the bracken, which was taking on the rusty hues of autumn, glowing in the shafts of morning sun coming through the trees.

He ran swiftly and beneath an oak the shafts of sunlight flickered on a grey horse, nervously pawing the ground and blowing hard through his nostrils. Tom cautiously went up to the animal and patted his neck. "Good boy," he murmured and tied the reins to a young ash tree. The little dog found the rider lying behind a fallen tree and Tom knew who it was before he got there, as he'd recognised the horse from when it had galloped through his clearing a few days previously.

Penelope Hudson lay face down in the bracken and Tom decided that it was all right to move her, as there seemed to be no injuries and she was beginning to come round. Trying to get up, she fainted, so he picked her up and carried her to his shack.

In the shack, she opened her eyes and looked at him, then panicked and tried to struggle to her feet.

"It's alright. You're safe and I don't think you're hurt, just a little cut on your chin which I've bathed. It looks as if you've sprained your ankle as well. Let's have a look at it."

Penelope looked at him with wide eyes and said, "You are Tom Beddows aren't you?"

"That's right," he replied, "but I don't think you should be talking just now. Try and rest for a while."

She smiled and said, "Daddy told me to keep away from you. He said there was a strange man living in the woods and I must never come near you. He said you are not normal and no one knew how you might react when you come into contact with people. Now here I am in your house and you're helping me."

She closed her eyes and put her head back on the straw. Then she suddenly opened them wide, "What about my horse? How's he?"

"Oh, he's fine, just hurt his fetlock a bit, but I've put a herb poultice on it and he'll be as good as new."

"Where is he?"

"Tied to a tree outside. He's fine. Don't worry."

"Well, thank you very much for helping me. Without your help I might still be lying out there and my horse might be lame."

She tried to get to her feet again, saying, "I had better be going home before Daddy starts worrying about me."

Tom gently pushed her back on the bed and said, "No, you must rest for a while before you go. Just lie quietly and I'll make you a nice coffee."

Penelope lay on the straw bed and, now that her eyes had become accustomed to the dark, she looked around and studied her new surroundings.

Tom put the kettle on the fire and sat down beside her, "It won't take long to boil as it's already hot."

He studied her as she gazed around his home and he thought she was very beautiful. "She's a real lady," he thought as he studied her profile.

She had high cheekbones and a small, finely-chiselled nose. Her eyes were large and blue, with a tantalising hint of a smile playing around them. He thought back to Christmas morning when he met her at the Big House. She was then only nine years old and home from boarding school for the Christmas holidays. She had grown into a beautiful woman.

As if there'd been telepathic communication, she said, "I met you when you were a small boy, one Christmas morning. Do you remember coming to our house with your Mum and Dad?"

"I remember it well," replied Tom, lifting the kettle lid to see if it was near to boiling. "I remember thinking what a real lady you were. You were from a different background to me. I went to the local school and you went to a posh boarding school. My Dad was a farm worker and yours was Lord of the Manor and you lived in a big house—still do. You live in a different world to me."

Penelope said nothing in reply but just fixed him with a blank stare.

After a while, she said, "Can I ask you something? I'm puzzled by you. I thought you were some sort of freak; a bearded hermit who lives in the woods and eats snails and berries. I thought you were a mad man in fact and when I meet you I discover that you are a normal man with a kind heart and a loving nature. I don't know what to make of you. You used to live a normal life and now you are living like this. Why?"

"Is that what you really thought, a mad man living on snails and berries?"

"Well, what am I supposed to think?"

"Ah, the kettle's boiling," said Tom and there was a lull in the conversation while she watched him make two cups of coffee.

She blew on it and took a sip. Then she said, "You're not going to answer my question are you?"

Tom shook his head and smiled at her.

"Do you think I'm very rude for talking like that?" she asked.

"No," he replied, "If the truth were told, I don't really know. I suppose you could call me a pretty mixed-up sort of bloke."

She put her hand on his for a moment and said, "I won't ask you any more questions," and then added, "How can I repay you for your kindness?"

"No need. You've already said 'thank you', and that's enough for me."

"Yes, but I would like to do more."

The little dog put his paws against Tom's leg and licked his hand.

"Anyone would have done the same. I didn't do anything special."

"It's not so much what you did, as the way you did it, and I want to do something to show my gratitude."

Tom patted the dog's head and shrugged his shoulders, "No need," he replied.

"Why don't you come to lunch tomorrow? I'm not offering you charity, because I know you don't need it, and I can see that you eat better than we do at the Manor, but I just want to say thank you."

He threw back his head and laughed out loud.

"What's the matter?"

"You can't be serious. Can you really imagine it? You having lunch in a magnificent manor house. The lady of the house lunching with the hermit from the woods; all hairy and ragged. I don't belong in a house like yours. I haven't got the clothes for it and I'd be like a fish out of water."

"I'm serious. We don't have to eat in the banqueting hall —unless you want to," she added, "We only eat in there on special occasions anyway. We can eat in my private suite and I'll cook it for you. It doesn't have to be a grand affair, just a simple lunch."

She paused and then said, "And I've just thought of something else too, which would be a good way of thanking you. Our farm manager, Mike Sturgess, is looking for helpers in the orchards, so why don't you come along tomorrow morning and earn yourself some money, and then I'll get your lunch. What do you say?"

Tom was amazed, after shunning company for so long, to hear himself saying, "Yes, thank you. I'll be there."

He enjoyed the morning. It was like the old days and he worked hard, picking the cider apples and tipping then into the waiting trailers. The Manor had extensive orchards and much labour was needed at this time of the year.

"Nice to see you again, lad," said Walter, dragging a sack of apples across the grass.

Tom had not seen him for a long time, but he hadn't changed. He still wore the same trilby and smoked his clay pipe. Walter stopped work for a moment and leaned on the tractor wheel. "Why don't you come down the pub one of these days and see your old pals again?"

"Aye, maybe," said Tom, though he had no intention of doing so. He lifted a sack up onto the trailer and Walter persisted with the conversation.

"Come on, lad," he said, "we need another trailer for this job, so will you come and help me to harness up Juno."

In the stables, the smell of the horses and leather brought back memories. Walter lit his pipe and between puffs, said, "Harness him for me, will you. You'll remember how to do it."

Before he'd finished speaking, Tom was sliding the collar and bridle over the horse's head. He didn't need to stand on a box any more and he soon had the other items of harness fitted. The ridge pad and britchen went on, followed by the crupper, the loop of leather that goes round the tail. He then led the big horse into the yard where he backed him between the cart's shafts and hooked the tugs onto the harness. Finally, he fastened the britchen chains and stood back to admire his work, like an artist standing back from his painting.

"Don't forget the belly chain," called Walter, "or the shafts will rise up with the weight of the apples. They're bloody heavy."

Walter walked round the horse, checking the fastenings, and said, "You've done a good job lad."

Tom spent the rest of the morning helping with the harvest and then strolled up the drive to meet Penelope.

"Hi, Tom," she called, from the top of the steps as he approached the main entrance. She led him through the reception hall and the state ballroom.

"That's where Frank and Walter stood, eating cider cake that

Christmas morning," he thought to himself as he passed the great oak table, "And that's where Dad stood, talking to Mr Davies."

She led him through the ballroom and into a small room. "We'll have our lunch in here," she explained, "Those big rooms are not very homely and they're expensive to keep warm."

It was a strange sight, Penelope on one side of the table, well dressed and immaculate, sitting opposite a ragged figure of a man with long hair and beard. During the meal, he put down his knife and fork to take some wine and said, "Do you know, I always thought you were a snob. You had posh friends and I never thought you would have time for the likes of me."

"I think you were right. I was a snob when I was a little girl and I'm ashamed of it now, but I expect it was the way I was brought up. I did look down on those who worked in the fields and lived in the cottages. I was led to believe that I was better than them," she took a sip of wine and continued, "But I've grown up, thank God and I'm not like that now."

"No, I can see you're not, but I suppose we all put people into pigeon holes. I thought you were snooty and because of my lifestyle and appearance, you had me tagged as a nut case."

"Maybe that's one of the things wrong with the world. I mean we all tend to judge a book by its cover and make instant judgements."

"Aye, my grandfather used to say, 'You can't judge a sausage by its skin.' so he was saying the same thing." He continued, "I thought you were better than me, living in this house and riding with the hunt and all that. I suppose I still do really."

"Nonsense!" she exclaimed, wagging a finger at him as if he were a naughty child. "I think you're a very nice man and I want to help, give you a leg up, if you know what I mean."

She pointed at a brown paper parcel in the corner and said, "I've looked out some things for you."

Tom frowned and looked at the parcel suspiciously, "What sort of things?"

"Oh, you know, tins of food, some of Daddy's old clothes that I think will fit you, and there's a bit of money too."

"No!" shouted Tom, jumping to his feet and knocking over a glass of wine.

The outburst startled her, "Please," she pleaded, "let me explain."

She laid a hand on his arm and gestured for him to sit down again. "Please," she repeated, "accept it in the spirit in which it's offered. Call it a gift. I'm just giving you something to say thank you, but I'm making it a practical gift which will help you. I don't want to insult you by offering charity."

She smiled at him but he did not return the smile.

"You are patronising me and treating me like a bloody child!" he shouted, "Maybe my first impressions were right. You are a snob and you see yourself as the aristocratic lady, dispensing largess to the needy. I bet you didn't think I knew words like patronising and largess."

He spat out the words with contempt, the colour rising in his face.

"You're quite wrong. If you don't want to be helped that's up to you, but there's no need to be so rude."

"I'm going," declared Tom and strode towards the door.

"And good riddance, and I hope I never see you again," was Penelope's parting shot as he slammed the door.

Chapter Thirteen

Tom was seething with anger as he walked back to his shack, furiously kicking up the fallen leaves as he went. He stopped at the edge of the clearing. There was smoke coming from his chimney, as if fresh fuel had been put on, and he knew that he'd let it die down before he left that morning. He crossed the clearing and got closer.

"Coffee, Tom?" came Penelope's voice. She had got there before him in the Land Rover and parked it on the other side of the wood. She held the cup out at arm's length. "Peace offering," she said, pretending to flinch, as if he was about to hit her.

He took the cup automatically and she gave him a kiss on the cheek. She took a deep breath and said, "I'm sorry Tom. I shouldn't have said those things and I shouldn't have offered you that parcel. I meant well, but I can see how it must have looked to you, and I'm very sorry. I'm a thoughtless pig and I hope you'll forgive me."

Tom thought for a moment and then said, "And I'm sorry too. I said things that I didn't mean."

"Are we friends again?" she asked, her eyes going misty.

He put down his cup and pulling her to him, kissed her on the lips. "Yes, we're friends again," he whispered.

The kiss occurred quite naturally, as if they were lovers making up after a tiff, rather than relative strangers from contrasting social backgrounds.

They drew apart, looking into each other's eyes, and then the spell was broken and awkwardness took over. Penelope looked away and, searching for something to say to break the silence, came up with, "Your coffee's going cold."

Tom picked up his cup and the moment of closeness had gone. They searched for small-talk to fill the awkward silences.

"Oh, I nearly forgot. I've got something for you," said Penelope suddenly.

"Not more charity," exclaimed Tom, holding up his hands in exaggerated horror.

"No, not this time. Follow me." She led him to the Land Rover. "It's not charity. It's your right," and she opened the back to reveal four sacks of cider apples. "It's a tradition that workers in the orchards get four sacks as well as their wages."

She smiled, and continued, "Now you'll be able to make some

97

apple sauce to go with your roast pheasant."

"Thanks," he replied, "but I've got a much better idea. I'm going to—" but she interrupted him.

"Hang on a minute, there's something else, before I forget." She climbed into the cab and slid back out with a brown envelope. "It's your wages."

"Thanks, that's the first wage packet I've had for a long time." He tucked it in his back pocket.

"What's the better idea you started to tell me about?"

"What?"

"You said you had a better idea; for the apples."

"Oh, yes. I'm going to make some cider with them."

"That's a good idea."

"Yes, I have a recipe in the shack somewhere that I'll dig out. My grandfather gave it to me some years ago. I was only a small boy and it was in my Christmas stocking one Christmas morning and I've kept it safe ever since."

"What a funny thing to have in your Christmas stocking," she teased.

"I suppose so. It was a recipe that my great grandfather used and it's said to make wonderful cider. Walter told me once that people came from miles around to taste it and I remember him saying that if anyone could make cider as good as that today, they'd make a fortune. Would you like to help me have a go?"

"Yes, it will be fun. Actually these apples are from the old cider orchards, so you should be able to make some good stuff. They are the old fashioned cider apples with names that always make me smile. One's called Foxwhelp and there's Joeby Crab. I think the funniest is Slack–my–Girdle."

"Slack–my–Girdle. That's a funny name and I've heard it before, and I've heard of the others. There's Lady's Finger too."

"Yes, there's some of those in there. I heard one of the men mention the name."

"That's good. When I was helping with the picking, Walter talked about all those names and they're what my great–grandfather used, so it should be just like his when we've made it. Come to think of it, he worked on the estate all his life and he probably got the apples from the same orchard; from the same trees in fact."

Chapter Fourteen

In Gorston, the autumn mist was hanging low on the oily water of the canal and Chris Gregory was sitting on the lock gates, absent mindedly throwing pebbles into the water. The surface was smooth and he morosely watched the ripples spread. He was not a happy young man, having spent years drifting from one dead-end job to another, and he was feeling dissatisfied with life.

He did not like the dirty town in which he had grown up and Gran was beginning to irritate him. She was becoming forgetful and everywhere she went she carried a duster and perpetually cleaned surfaces, lifting ornaments, dusting, and putting them back.

The process went on constantly and everywhere he sat she would lift his feet and put a cloth under them or put a cover on the chair behind his head. 'Cleanliness is next to Godliness', she would say.

It was getting him down and he was seriously considering what his next move should be. Should he go abroad? Jack, at the factory, had emigrated to Canada and sent him a picture post card of the Rockies, telling him what a wonderful life he was having. He once thought of getting a job in a Spanish bar, "I would meet lots of girls over there," but the more ideas he had, the more confused he became.

He pulled a hip flask from his back pocket and took a shot of whisky as he kicked a tin can into the water. Heaving a sigh, he got to his feet and taking another swig, wandering along the towpath, kicking grit into the water as he went. The chill north wind was tearing the yellow leaves from the alders and depositing them on the water and at a bend in the canal the surface was covered in a layer of leaves that seemed almost solid enough to walk on.

He got as far as the derelict steel works and looking at his watch, he said, "Opening time," and retraced his steps in the direction of The Colliers Rest.

It began to rain as he neared the pub and he walked briskly, arriving just in time to avoid a torrential downpour that ran down the dirty walls and gurgled into the drains. He stood in the doorway before entering, dabbing his face dry with his handkerchief and watching a flattened Players packet washing down the gutter, twisting and turning in the eddies.

There were no other customers in the bar and he got himself a pint of Banks' bitter and sat at one of the round tables. The bored barmaid incessantly wiped out ash trays and polished the bar top.

By the time he'd finished his fifth pint the bar had filled, but he didn't know any of the customers and, while they played darts and dominoes, he continued to stare into his glass, deep in thought.

He walked unsteadily into Gran's kitchen.

"You've been drinking again, haven't you?" she accused.

He sat down heavily, "Full marks for observation, Gran. Go to the top of the class, but you won't have to put up with it for much longer because I'm going."

"Going?" she echoed, "Going where?"

"Mum and Dad have always said there's room for me in their bungalow, so I'm going to live with them and see if I can get a job on a farm or something. There are plenty of farms round there and there's nothing to keep me here."

Gran thought for a moment and pushing her glasses up her nose said, "Look before you leap."

Chris sighed and said, "He who hesitates is lost."

He moved to Lower Kings Canon, installed himself in the back bedroom of the bungalow, and set about finding work. Within hours, he'd found himself a job as a gardener at the Manor House.

"But you don't know the first thing about gardening," said his father Bob, when he came home with the news.

"But I can learn and, in any case, I'm only an assistant. It just means that I have to pull up weeds and do some hoeing. I think I can cope with that, even with only one hand."

He settled into the job's routine and enjoyed the clean air, which was such a contrast to Gorston. The cough that had recurred constantly since he was a child had gone away and he felt that he'd made the right move.

However, his parents became increasingly concerned about his drinking. He usually had a bottle of spirits in his room and he was soon banned from the Old Black Lion for being drunk and disorderly. Since his first taste of whisky in the Dudley pub when he was young, he had grown to like it and become addicted.

"This is a nice, quiet country pub," said the landlord, "and you're welcome in here if you behave properly, but until you learn to do so, I'm afraid you'll have to drink elsewhere." So Chris took to walking the mile and a half to the Rising Sun, where the landlord was more tolerant of him.

"I think he has a drink problem," said his father, one day, "He's never without his hip flask and I've seen him knocking it back before breakfast. I think he's an alcoholic."

Mrs Gregory lowered her tea cup and said, "I haven't dared to think about it, but I think you're right. Oh, what can we do about it Bob? We've told him not to drink so much until we're blue in the face."

"I don't know."

Chris got bored with his gardening job because it didn't hold enough challenge and he became restless again. After work one day, he went for a walk through the village and next to the pub he saw an old, timbered house that was undergoing restoration. The roof had been taken off and the in-filling panels removed, leaving only the timber-frame stark against the sky. He stopped, fascinated by it and leaned on the gate while he took a drink from his hip flask. He looked up at the timber frames, putting his head on one side and squinting.

"I'll show you round if you're so interested," said a large man in a checked shirt, who appeared from behind a shed, "Are you interested in old houses?"

"Oh, yes, I should say so," he lied. He had never shown interest in old buildings in his life, but he found this one interesting.

The man took him inside and they stood and looked up at the oak beams. He waved an arm in their direction and said, "All done without a nail."

"What holds it together then?"

"Wooden pegs, that's all."

Chris put his hand on a beam and gently ran it along the timber. "How old is it?" he asked.

"It was built in about fourteen-twenty."

Chris's eyes widened, "That makes it getting on for six hundred years old."

"Yes, and the wood must have been a few hundred years old when it was used, so I expect that beam was a tree when William the Conqueror invaded the country."

Chris gave a long, low whistle and walked round the building, studying the way the beams were fitted together. "What are the marks carved on the joints?" he asked.

"Carpenter's marks. These old buildings were like do-it-yourself kits. They were made in a workshop and then transported by horse and cart to the site in sections. The owner then got a team of workers together and they assembled it themselves. These marks were carved to number the joints and show which bits fitted with which.

They could get the main structure, like this," he waved an arm again, "assembled in a few hours." Pointing at the beams, he continued, "They were put together in pieces joined with wooden pegs and then the sections were hoisted up into position. The timber was green, not seasoned like you might expect, so that when it dried the whole building tightened up together."

"And how did they cut these great big beams without any machinery?"

"With man-power in a saw pit."

"What's that?"

"A hole in the ground, and the tree was laid over it. Then one man was at the top on one end of a big saw and a second man in the pit on the other end, and they sawed; as simple as that. It was usually a boy, an apprentice sawyer, who was in the hole, and he was the one who got the sawdust in his eyes."

Chris walked around, fascinated by all that he saw. "It's so amazing that the timbers have lasted so long."

"They're as good as the day they were put in. My name is Dai by the way, Dai Evans. I run a firm specialising in the restoration of old houses, like this one, and there are a lot in Herefordshire to keep me busy."

He held out his hand and Chris shook it and said, "Chris Gregory, gardener at the Big House, not that I like the job very much."

And so another door opened. Dai Evans questioned him for a while and then offered him a job, "I need another pair of hands about the place, now that young Danny's left, so you've come along at just the right time. Oh God!" he exclaimed, clapping a hand over his mouth.

Chris put his arm behind his back, "No matter," he mumbled.

"I'm sorry, but I suppose you're used to that sort of thing by now. Anyway it doesn't matter about experience," he said. "we can train you up, just as long as you're adaptable and willing to work hard."

He enjoyed the work. It was challenging and he could see a future in it. Before long, he had developed new skills, such as using an adze as the old craftsmen did and he could be trusted to carry out small jobs unsupervised. At times, the lack of a hand was a problem but he developed skills to overcome his difficulties.

The restoration firm was asked to do a job on a timbered house next to the Post Office; Doctor Sherwood's house, a fifteenth century building, in a well-kept garden. They had been asked to solve the problem of rain coming through the panels on the south west elevation; the side that caught the prevailing winds. Rain was being driven through the edges of the panels. Chris was told to strip out the old panels and replace them with modern insulation while Dai attended to a job in Kington.

"I have to go and see about replacing some timbers in an old cottage, but I know I can trust you to do this on your own," said Dai.

Dr Sherwood had a daughter, Susan, and when Chris stopped for a break and was sitting on the floor of the empty room, she came in with a mug of tea.

"Oh, thank you," he said, getting to his feet, "just the thing for a thirsty worker. Thirsty work this."

He sat down again and she sat beside him. "By your accent," she said, "I can tell that you're not from round these parts."

"No, I live here now in the village. Only up the road really, but I grew up in a place called Gorston."

"Whereton?"

"Gorston. It's in the Black Country. Wolverhampton is the nearest big town that you will have heard of."

"So why are you living here?"

"I didn't get on there, so I joined my parents when they retired here." He took a drink of his tea and noticed her looking at his damaged hand. When he automatically lowered his mug and looked at his hand, she became flustered and blurted out,

"Oh, I am sorry, I didn't mean to—"

"That's alright. Don't worry about it."

"Is it rude to ask how you did it?"

"No," he replied, "I had an industrial accident. I used to work in a factory and I was on a press, a machine that stamps out shapes from pieces of steel. I wasn't concentrating and it came down on my hand, or the hand that I used to have," he added. "The machine had a guard on it, but I had been distracted and lifted the guard without realizing it. Stupid really."

"You poor chap. Did it hurt?"

Chris puffed out his chest and replied, "Oh, no, it was nothing," but then his grin faded and he said, "Well, to be absolutely truthful, it hurt like hell. It was smashed flat and I passed out with the pain. The pain got worse after the surgeons had operated and it felt as if my whole arm had been pulled out of its socket. It was terrible. The pain killers didn't seem to help at all and it still hurts sometimes, usually when the weather's damp and cold."

"It must have been awful for you. Does it stop you doing anything?"

He looked at her as she spoke. She had long blonde hair and blue eyes, which were large and child-like, and he gazed into them, forgetting everything for a moment, "Oh, pardon. What did you say?"

She smiled and repeated, "I asked if it stops you doing anything."

"No, not really. I've learned to adapt. Sometimes it can be a nuisance and I get depressed when it hurts. I think, why me? When I see a football crowd for example, I think, well none of those people have got my problem. Why am I the only one like this? But then I think again, it could be a lot worse. Just think how many people have lost whole limbs, but it doesn't stop me getting depressed from time to time."

"Yes, I can understand how you must feel."

"Can you?"

"Yes, but I'm stopping you working."

She began to stand up.

"No, don't go," he said, putting his good hand on her arm, " I'm enjoying talking to you."

She sank down to the floor again and they sat in silence until Chris asked, "Have you always lived here?"

"No, I used to live in Weobley and we came to live here some years ago, when Daddy took over the practice in the village."

"And do you like it?"

"Oh, yes. It's a nice place to live, quiet, friendly."

"It is, isn't it—I was thinking," he said, "Would you like to go out with me one evening? Maybe we could go for a drink or something."

"Fine. We could go to the Old Black Lion. That's a nice pub."

"No," said Chris hastily, thinking of his ban, "Let's try the Rising Sun."

"The Rising Sun it is then."

Their relationship flourished and within months they were married. Dr Sherwood had serious doubts about the wisdom of the match. He didn't take to Chris and thought that his daughter could do better. When he learned through a colleague of Chris's drinking problem, he became even more unhappy and tried to dissuade her from becoming involved, but it was too late.

"I suppose you know that your young man is an alcoholic. Have you any idea what misery that is going to cause you?"

"Yes, I know he likes a drink, Daddy."

"Likes a drink! It's not just a question of liking a drink. Lots of men like a drink. I like one myself but he has a serious drinking problem. He's already been banned from the Black Lion because he's disgraced himself in there and I think you're asking for trouble taking him on, and what prospects has he got? A chippy, that's all he is, a carpenter's mate, and he'll never be anything better."

"He's a craftsmen and I love him."

"A craftsman." He repeated contemptuously, "I am telling you my girl, if you marry that boy, you'll be making the biggest mistake of your life." He wagged a finger at her, "The biggest mistake of your life," he repeated with added emphasis.

The wedding took place in the village church and the reception was held at a hotel in Hay-on-Wye. Gran was a guest, wearing a mauve suit and big hat. "There's a crock of gold at the end of every rainbow," she said.

After the wedding, Chris moved out of the bungalow and into Dr Sherwood's house. They settled down to married life, but from the beginning Susan could hear her father's words echoing round her head and, although she would not admit it even to herself, she had serious worries. He'd been out on binges which had alarmed her and every evening he drank large quantities of whisky. She looked across the room at him as he took another drink and she bit her lip and heaved a sigh.

Court Farm

Chapter Fifteen

At the Old Black Lion, Brian Jones had parked his Jaguar outside the porch where it could be seen to the best advantage. It was carefully placed, so that those in the bar had a good view of it, and he was standing at the bar drinking a gin and tonic with a friend. He blew cigar smoke and discussed the subtleties of the haulage business in a loud voice.

"We're buying three new lorries next week," he said, "as business is booming."

"Really?" was his companion's response.

"Yes, we're getting a lot of business from Europe these days. That's where the future lies, you know, and I was in Paris last week doing a huge deal with some people over there. I drove a hard bargain and got them right where I wanted them." He looked round the bar to see who'd heard him.

His grey suited companion said, "At this rate, I think you'll end up a millionaire."

"You're right there. There's a big future in the haulage business and I've got what it takes to get things moving." He drew deeply on his cigar and, blowing smoke up to the ceiling, went on, "My father did the right thing, handing the firm over to me, because I've expanded the business and I have big plans for diversifying into other areas. That's the name of the game these days, divers-ification."

Sitting in the window overlooking the Wye Valley were two

young women. They sipped their sweet sherries and the dark girl absent mindedly popped salted peanuts into her mouth. Her blonde friend supported her head in both hands, engrossed in a glossy magazine. Brian cast frequent glances in their direction and lowering his voice, said, "I'm sure I know that blonde girl by the window."

The landlord replaced a bottle on the shelf and speaking over his shoulder, said, "You should do. You went to school with her."

"Angela Sturgess!" he exclaimed, "I thought I knew her."

The girl looked up from her book, startled to hear her name. "Hello, Brian," she responded, recognising him immediately.

Angela was the little girl who had been the object of both Tom's and Brian's affections at school and the recipient of his carved love-spoon. When she left the village school, she had passed the eleven plus exam and gone to the Grammar School in Kington and was now at university studying to be a vet. She had grown into an attractive woman and was back home for her holidays.

At school, Brian had got Tom and others into a great deal of trouble, but managed to get through his school career with a blameless record. He'd been a cunning child, who went to a great deal of effort to cover his tracks. Angela had no idea what an unpleasant character he used to be and still was. Many would say that he'd not improved, now that he was a young adult.

Since taking over his father's business, he'd become a successful business man. He had achieved his success, partly through good luck and partly by ruthless cunning. He was in the process of diversifying from haulage into other ventures, operating under the general title of *Jones International Ltd.*

Angela looked him up and down and was impressed. He and his companion went over to their table. "This is Malcolm, a business acquaintance of mine," he said, as he sat down, and then, "This is Angela, the prettiest girl ever to come out of Lower Kings Canon Primary School."

His charm and smooth manner had a big effect on her and she soon found herself accepting an invitation to dinner.

"Where are you going tonight, all dressed up like that?" asked Mike Sturgess of his daughter.

"I'm going out to dinner with someone I met, an old school friend."

"A boy, I presume?"

"Yep."

"Do I know him?"

"Sort of. It's Brian Jones, you know, of Jones Haulage."

"Oh, him."

"Yes, and he's taking me to Clunton Manor, to the new restaurant they've opened."

"Clunton Manor! That'll set him back a bob or two. It's the most expensive restaurant for miles."

"Yes, Dad, that's right," she replied, closing her hand bag and looking at herself sideways in the mirror. "How do I look?"

"You look beautiful. He can afford to take you there. They tell me he's making a fortune, so I think you ought to keep in with him," he grinned.

"I'm not going out with him for his money. I think he's a nice chap, well dressed and he knows how to treat a girl. He's good looking too, just like Elvis Presley."

"God, I hope he doesn't sing like him," he joked, kissing his daughter on the cheek. "Well, have a nice time, and don't be too late home." He stood watching, as she skipped down the path to the waiting car.

In Cwm Woods, Penelope used the back of her wrist to brush some hair from her eyes as she pounded the apples in the tin bath. She banged at them with a length of oak until they were pulp. "You didn't tell me it'd be this much work," she complained.

"You didn't ask," replied Tom.

"Very funny, and why don't you come over here and help anyway?"

"Because I'm doing the important bit."

"And what's that?"

"Finding out what to do next."

"You mean you're finding out what I have to do next, don't you?"

Tom grinned, "I'll come and help when I've read this. Give them a good bashing, because we have to get plenty of juice out of them. It's a pity we haven't got a proper press. It would make the job much easier."

"You don't need a press when you have a slave like me," she quipped, throwing more fruit into the bath.

"We need a dead rat now. That might be difficult, but I think a squirrel will do just as well. They're nearly the same aren't they."

"You are joking!"

"That's what it says here and I've heard of it before. I think it puts body into the cider and I want to stick rigidly to this recipe, because it's supposed to produce cider which is a bit special. I'll throw a rabbit in. I've got plenty of those and there are some other funny ingredients too, but I should be able to find them all."

Anyone passing through the woods that day would have seen two figures amongst the russet and gold trees, happily pounding apples and wrapping the pulp in hessian 'cheeses', as they are called; blocks of pulp wrapped in sacking. Tom rigged up an ingenious press to extract the juice.

He made a timber frame and with a rope and piece of timber made a tourniquet to exert pressure on the cheeses. As the juice trickled into the earthenware pot, the couple held each other and danced with delight. "It works. It works," echoed round the woods and the little dog, sensing an important occasion, joined in the merriment and barked at the sky.

"We just wait now and let nature do its work," said Tom, after the juice had been collected and put into a covered container in the shack. "I'll keep the fire going to make sure it's warm enough for it to work."

He helped Penelope out of her overalls.

"What are you grinning at?" she demanded.

"I was just thinking, that's the first time I've seen a posh girl from the Big House working hard and getting dirty."

"It is the first time. What would Daddy say if he saw me?"

"I expect he'd say, 'Have I spent all that money on your education to have you grovelling about with a hermit in the woods in a pair of dirty overalls?' That's what he'd say."

She tidied her hair and looked at him, puzzled, "You're still grinning. What's the matter now, for Heaven's sake?"

"I was thinking, Penelope, how much prettier you are like this than in Walter's old overalls."

"Thank you," she replied, "and let's get one thing straight, shall we. You keep calling me Penelope, but to friends and workmates I'm called Penny. Okay?"

"Okay, Penny."

The apple juice was left to ferment and mature and at the same time Tom and Penny's relationship matured. They became good friends and she was a frequent visitor to the shack. He cooked her meals and they spent hours talking over the table or wandering about, absorbed in their conversation and the sounds and perfumes of the woods. He had cut his hair and beard and looked much younger.

"Now I can see what you look like under all that hair. I knew you'd be handsome."

"What if I'd been ugly?"

"It wouldn't have made the slightest difference," she said, linking arms and resting her head on his shoulder.

The season changed from autumn to winter and their feet, which had crunched on dry leaves, now crunched on the crisp snow. One evening, Penny called for him in the Land Rover, as they had decided to go for a drink in the Old Black Lion.

She parked in the gateway and hooted the horn, whereupon Tom emerged from the bare trees, wrapped in a duffel coat with his scarf pulled up to his nose. She had the heater working and the cab was filled with warmth and expensive perfume.

"You smell wonderful tonight," said Tom.

"I think you sometimes forget that I'm a woman," she joked, "You usually see me dressed for the woods or for work on your cider project."

She put her hand on the gear lever and, looking over her shoulder, she said, "Let's go."

He put his hand on hers and softly said, "Not yet. Let's wait for a little while."

"Why?" she asked, turning off the engine.

"And the lights," said Tom, reaching for the switch.

In the silence, he felt sure that she could hear his heart pounding.

He swallowed hard and leaning closer kissed her on the cheek. She turned her head towards him and they kissed tenderly on the lips. Her immediate response was to run her hand up to the back of his neck and kiss him again; a long lingering kiss, with eyes closed.

Tom had only intended to kiss her, but the tenderness and the intoxicating perfume made him bolder, and he slowly undid her buttons and slid his hand inside, fumbling under her jumper and running his hand over her breasts. Becoming bolder still, he slid his hand inside her bra and cupped his hand over her soft breast. Her nipple was hard to his touch and she kissed him, sighing, "Yes," as she leaned against the door and pulled him on top of her.

Some time later —they had no idea of the time—Tom cleared a circle in the condensation and peered out of the windscreen. The white shape of a barn owl glided silently over the bonnet. He looked up at the sky and said, "It's a clear night."

Penny pulled him back to her again, "Come here," she said, kissing him again.

"Well," he whispered, "I suppose that makes us lovers now."

"I suppose it does," she smiled.

Winter turned into spring and spring into early summer and Tom stood in the clearing holding a glass of cider up to the light. "It looks good," he announced, "and it's been maturing for the recommended amount of time. Who's going to taste it?"

Penny held her glass up and turned it. She then put it to her nose and inhaled the bouquet, "It smells good too," she declared, " A lovely, sharp, appley smell. It brings back memories of that beautiful autumn when we were making it. You know, the smell of apples and wood smoke and the mist in the trees. Go on, you first."

"Very poetic, but the important thing is, what's it taste like?"

"I'm sure it will be lovely, Darling."

Tom smiled. "It might be horrible, of course." He held it up to the light again and studied the golden colour against the clear sky. "Well, here goes."

He took a deep breath and held it up to the light one last time, looking at it from all angles.

"Go on then. I can't stand the suspense."

He breathed deeply again and finally took a sip, followed by a deep draft. He looked at her, expressionlessly.

"Well?"

He drank down all that was left in the glass and shouted, "Wheeeeh. It's wonderful. It really is. You try it."

She too took a hesitant sip at first, followed by a longer drink, and said. "You're right. It is lovely."

They hugged each other and Tom shouted up at the sky, "Thank you for my Christmas present, Granddad!"

Penny finished her cider and, as she lifted the glass, she caught sight of a tear glistening in the corner of his eye.

"Walter was right," said Tom, "Let's take some to the boys up at the farm and see what they think of it."

The cider was a success and Penny had access to ample supplies of apples from the Home Farm orchards and was able to find more pots and containers. He was soon brewing it in larger quantities and word of his excellent cider spread through the village.

Once he was organized, he did a good trade as people sought him out, equipped with jars and barrels to be filled. He made a fruit press with a car jack that his father had used for the Austin and so was able to press the apples more effectively and in greater quantities to keep up with demand.

The familiar hooting of the Land Rover's horn sounded through the trees. "Hop in," said Penny, "I've got a surprise for you."

She drove him down the lane, round the far side of the woods and through the Dingle.

"Where are we going?"

"You'll find out round the next corner."

"She stopped near a stone cottage and switched off the engine. Tom jumped down into the road. "It's Jack Pugh's place isn't it?" he asked, opening the wooden gate, which broke off and fell to the ground.

"It used to be, but he died a year ago and it's been standing empty ever since."

He stepped back and stood with his hands on his hips, looking at the old cottage, "But why have we come here?"

"Follow me," was her reply and she took his hand and led him round the house to the rear where there was a courtyard surrounded by an extensive range of outbuildings. The main building was a dilapidated barn, with what appeared to be a sound roof. The wall timbers had been filled with white panels. Swallows swooped in and out of holes under the eaves and outside stood a cider press and big stone apple crusher.

It had a circular stone trough in which apples were placed and a circular stone which rolled round inside the trough to crush the fruit. A beam attached to the stone was intended to be hitched to a horse, which would walk round and round pulling the stone inside the trough. The surrounding cobbles had been worn smooth over the centuries by the hooves of the horses.

Tom walked round it, running his hand over the stone, "Are you going to tell me we can use this equipment to make our cider?" he asked, with mounting excitement.

"Yes, it's all arranged, my little surprise for you, and you had no idea, did you?"

Tom grinned and shook his head.

"I've been busy over the last few weeks making the arrangements."

"I thought you were being a bit mysterious and I should have guessed you were up to something." He walked round once more and said, "This will be perfect. Thank you, Darling."

Penny smiled and held both his hands. "Come here," she said, and took him to the end of the barn, "There's more."

He looked across the courtyard and high up on the wall was a painted sign. It was green and in gold letters, it read:

Tom Beddows' Country Cider and underneath in smaller letters *Naturally the Best*.

"It's all yours," she said, clapping her hands with excitement, "You can move in whenever you like. You can live in the house and run the business from the barns. You have plenty of space to expand as demand increases and," She linked her arm in his and continued, "before you start rushing about shouting 'It's charity!' I want to tell you that it's a business arrangement. Daddy owns all this and you can pay him a fair rent out of the profits."

Tom remained silent, staring at the sign.

"Well, say something," she demanded light-heartedly, "Do I get a reward?"

He took her in his arms, "What can I say? Thank you," he said, "Thank you."

She pulled away, flushed with excitement and said, "You haven't seen everything yet. Stay here for a moment and sit on the press. Don't move."

She walked across the courtyard and called again, "Don't follow me."

She went into the darkness of the barn and Tom did as he had been told and sat on the trough in the warm sunshine, swinging his legs and looking around his newly acquired empire. He leaned to one side, to get a better look at the sign and smiled to himself, slowly shaking his head in disbelief. He looked from the sign to the press and from the press to the barn, his mind in a whirlwind of activity.

"What are you doing in there?" he called in the direction of the barn, but there was no answer, so he continued to sit on the stone trough and watched the swallows, swooping and diving around the buildings.

He squinted up at the sun and then repeated his shout towards the barn where he'd last seen Penny. "What are you—"

He was interrupted by the sound of a diesel engine bursting into life and out of the double doors lurched a Bedford truck, resplendent in the green and gold Beddows livery with *Tom Beddows' Country Cider, Court Farm, Lower Kings Canon, Herefordshire* painted on the side in gold. Penny drove the vehicle slightly past him before stopping and jumping down. On the back doors it read, *Naturally the Best Cider*.

"Here are the keys," she said, "The truck was Daddy's idea. I think it was his way of trying to make amends for the sadness he caused you and your family when he had to evict you. He felt very bad about that, you know, so don't refuse him. I know you can't drive, but you'll soon learn, and I can drive it for you until you pass your driving test."

And so he moved into Court Farm and set up the cider production. The business grew and as the months passed he had to increase the volume of production to keep up with the popular demand. The product had a distinctive flavour; a dry fruity taste that was very much liked. His truck became a familiar sight in the Herefordshire lanes and, when he passed the driving test, he personally delivered to the black and white farms in the hidden corners of the county.

Farm workers would stop and lean on their hoes as the green and gold Bedford passed. Tom would honk the horn and give a cheery wave. It almost became a part of the landscape and it was difficult to imagine the countryside without the truck, which became known as Tom's Cider Wagon.

The Old Black Lion began to sell *Tom Beddows' Country Cider*, followed by other pubs and before long almost every inn and hotel in the county was selling it. The *Hereford Times* wrote an article on the enterprise; a big centrefold feature, putting the emphasis on the mystery of the recipe, and that gave a further boost to his sales.

Penny had an idea one day, as she watched Tom tasting a sample. "I've just had a brain wave," she announced, "Why don't we smarten up the old barn which we don't use. We could clean it and put a lick of paint about the place and then we could get some nice cider casks and make a bar at one end."

"What for?" interrupted Tom, putting down the sample.

"Well," she continued, "we could make it all nice and then put up some signs inviting people to taste the various sorts before they buy. It would encourage more customers and they might buy more of the different types. How many cider producers do you know who do that sort of thing?"

Tom smiled his agreement and the idea became a reality. A man from the Tourist Board came and put up smart signs directing people to the barn.

Before long, Tom began to feel the benefits of the profits and the hairy hermit who used to live in the woods gradually metamorphosed into a smart and successful business man. The transformation was astounding and Penny said, "I knew you'd make a go of it. I recognised you as the sort of man who'll go places if you put your mind to it. You have the right sort of qualities."

"I'm going to build one of the biggest cider plants in the country," said Tom, who by now had confidence in his product and his ability. In his previous life in the woods he'd had no ambition, being quite happy to continue as he was for ever, but now the flood gates had opened and he was bursting with enthusiasm and determination to succeed. "There'll be no stopping me now, thanks to Granddad, and you of course," and putting his arm round her he kissed her on the cheek.

Penny had moved into Court Farm and they were living together. One evening, the couple had slipped out to the Old Black Lion for a meal and were sitting at a table near the fire enjoying their snacks. "This is jolly good steak," said Tom and then lapsed into silence.

It was Penny who eventually broke the silence, "Well, Tom, you've come a long way in a short time."

"Aye."

They continued their meal in silence, listening to snatches of conversation from those around them.

"I can't get much conversation out of you tonight," said Penny, "Have you got something on your mind?" She cut into her steak and continued, "You are deep in thought."

"Yes, I've been thinking and there's something I want to ask you, Dear. I've been thinking about it for a long time." He put down his knife and fork and took her hand in his. "How would you feel about my young brother and sister living with us? I know it's not a big place, but we could convert the loft into two good-sized rooms for them. Jane could help you in the house and I'm sure Pete would be useful in the business."

He paused for a moment and then said, "Since Mum died and they were put in that Home, hardly a day has gone by when I haven't thought about them and I'm too busy to visit them as often as I should. Now that I have some money, I could give them a proper home, something I should have done a long time ago."

Penny didn't hesitate. "I think it's a wonderful idea," she replied.

Jane and Peter were installed in their new home with much hugging and tears. Pete was pleased to join the firm and proved to be an asset. He was a young man of imagination and determined to work hard. He recognised the opportunity he'd been offered and he made up his mind to take the utmost advantage of it.

Jane also worked in the business. When she was in the Home she had been sent to a secretarial college and so was able to make herself useful in the office.

Pete had grown into a good looking young man with a neat beard and when he was put into a suit looked every inch the business man. "What we need," he said one day, "is a caravan."

"Do we?" responded Tom, slightly amused.

"Yes, I'm serious, we need to get a big caravan. Most likely it'll have to be specially made and we'll tow it behind the truck to agricultural shows all over the country. We can sleep in it and then let the sides down and set up a cider bar. People are always thirsty at those shows and it'll get our name known further afield."

"We're doing well, but we're not known much outside Herefordshire and I think we need to spread our wings and think bigger. If we can create an interest outside the county, we can start to get really big. Just imagine how successful we could be if we achieved the same level of sales nation-wide as we do round here. We know it's a good product, so there's no reason why we can't do it."

"Okay, you've convinced me. If you'd like to get that set up, I'll let you get on with it."

Pete reached for the telephone and Tom continued, "See if you can have it ready for July and we'll give it a try at the Abergavenny Show. It'll be a nice day out and it will give us a chance to see how successful it's going to be. If at all," he added with a grin.

Chapter Sixteen

In July, Angela Sturgess skipped out of the house and got into Brian's Jaguar. They kissed and she looked at the sky saying, "It's a nice day for it."

He looked up, "Grand," he agreed. He paused to light a cigar and then the car moved down the lane and turned into the main road, heading south-west and over the mountains. He opened the sun roof and the breeze ruffled Angela's hair. It was a welcome breeze, as the day was warming up and the car's interior was stuffy. She put on the radio and leant her head back against the seat, inhaling the warm smell of leather.

Brian was in a good mood and hummed along to the music as the big car headed towards Abergavenny. His window was open and he rested his arm on the door, "It's good to be alive this weather, isn't it?" He could feel the sun on his bare forearm. It was a hot summer and the fields were parched. The freshly sheared sheep huddled in the shade of the trees, looking leggy and awkward without their woolly coats.

As the car drove through the small town of Crickhowell, the traffic began to build up and they slowed to a crawl. Angela looked over her shoulder and said, "It looks as if the whole world is going to the Abergavenny Show. I expect the good weather has brought everyone out."

Brian nodded and continued to drum his fingers, humming softly to himself.

They started queuing two miles before the Showground and were relieved when they were eventually directed into the car park and were able to get out of the hot car. They walked around the Showground and Brian remarked, "I think you were right about the whole world coming here today. I've never seen so many at the show."

The Abergavenny Show site is in the meadows outside the town, in the shadow of a flat topped mountain called the Blorenge. To the north east is another mountain, the Sugar Loaf, so called because of its conical shape.

The attractiveness of the site helps to ensure good attendances; it is usually well supported and a good day out for people from South Wales and the borders.

Brian and Angela licked their choc ices and threaded their way through the crowds. Every so often, she gripped his arm and led him off to look at trade stands which caught her attention. He was more interested in the vintage tractors and stood by the Show Ring as they paraded; throbbing, snorting, and pumping clouds of diesel smoke into the clear blue sky.

They had been the object of loving attention from their owners and their paintwork gleamed in the sun. The vintage machines, which now appear so quaint, represent much rural history, but at one time they were the last word in agricultural technology and the work horses of the farm.

"These old tractors have so much character," observed Brian, as he watched a red Massey Ferguson rumble past.

Angela pulled at his arm. "Come on," she said, "You've seen your tractors, now let's go and see the cattle lines."

They were on the edge of the Showground and the stockmen were grooming the animals, brushing their coats until they shone. Angela was particularly interested in the Herefords; massive creatures, standing quietly as they were brushed and combed. She patted the curly white head of a placid bull.

"He's a big boy, isn't he?" commented Brian, putting his head on one side and looking at the beast's testicles, hanging almost to the ground.

"Don't be horrible. My Dad looks after a herd of these on the estate, but they're not as popular as they were, not with all these foreign breeds coming in. Dad says these are still the best though. He says they'll fatten just on grass, without the need for expensive feed."

"You are a mine of information," grinned Brian.

The stirring sounds of a military band drew them back to the Ring and they stood for a while, watching the scarlet and gold bandsmen marching in the sunshine, the sun flashing and sparkling on their brass instruments.

"This is great," said Brian, taking a deep breath and looking around him.

"It's thirsty work."

"Let's go and see what we can find. I can see a big crowd over there all standing around drinking."

They worked their way through the crowds towards the marquee that was clearly the beer tent. Just past the marquee was a queue stretching for twenty yards in front of the trade stands. Brian stopped abruptly.

His eyes narrowed and he began to stride briskly to the head of the queue with Angela breaking into a run to keep up. There they found people standing in groups with glasses in their hands. He looked at the green and gold caravan surrounded by people clamouring for *Tom Beddows' Country Cider.*

"I knew it," he hissed, through clenched teeth, "I just knew it was him."

"Oh, it's Tom's caravan!" cried Angela, clapping her hands with delight, "Isn't he doing well?"

The cider stand was doing very well and causing a sensation on the showground. Brian kicked out at a terrier that was sniffing his shoe and it yelped and scuttled off with its tail between its legs. "Bloody Beddows cider. Come on, we're going home," and with Angela trailing behind, he elbowed his way through the crowds, knocking an ice cream out of a small boy's hand, without a backward glance.

"What's all this about?" asked the breathless Angela, when she caught up with him, "That was an extreme reaction wasn't it? And aren't you going to ask me if I want to go home?"

He got into the car without a word, started the engine and began reversing before Angela had settled in.

"Why this change of mood?" she asked, "And if you ask me, it was very childish."

"Well, nobody asked you."

Angela was still trying to close the door, "I can't understand it. You were happy enough until you saw Tom's caravan and then you changed like Dr Jekyll."

He engaged first gear and let out the clutch so violently that the wheels spun, showering turf and small stones in all directions. The car snaked across the grass with the wheels scrabbling to get a grip.

"Slow down before you kill someone!" she screamed. He changed gear and slowed down, breathing noisily through his nose and groping in his pocket for a cigar.

"I don't like that man," were the only words she could get out of him until they were almost home and even then he would only grunt one word answers.

At the show, Tom and Pete were delighted with the way things were going. By mid-morning they'd had to send someone out for more stocks and now they were running out again.

"The hot weather helps," said Pete to one of the girls, "It makes them thirsty and they drink more, but they obviously like the stuff anyway."

The girl was one of the staff on the trailer. Like the other girls, she wore the Tom Beddows' uniform; a green and gold costume designed by Jane, to look like a country wench of the last century. The men wore a costume in the same colours, with *Naturally the Best* on their straw boaters. Outside the trailer was a full size replica of a cider press with the Tom Beddows sign over it.

"A pint of your best cider, please, Sir," said an old man.

"Walter, you old devil! How are you, my old pal?" asked Tom, grabbing his hand and pumping it up and down, "This is on the house."

Tom served him the drink and then after pouring himself one stepped down from the trailer. "Come round here," he said, putting his arm round the old man's shoulders and leading him to the side. They sat on canvas chairs in the shade, "And what are you doing here, all dressed up like this?" he asked, pointing to Walter's nineteenth century costume.

"I'm part of the show," he replied. "I'm dressed up like this because I've got to drive Juno round the Ring pulling the yellow cart."

"That's the one we used to use for hay-making, isn't it?"

"That's right lad, the very one, but we use tractors now."

"So the Major has finally caught up with the twentieth century."

"Aye, lad," said the old man, putting his glass on the ground, "but I'm not so sure it's a good thing. Give me Juno and the yellow cart any day."

Tom sighed, "Those days have gone forever I suspect, but I'll never forget those hay-making days when I was a boy. They were magic. Tell me, do you still play the mouth organ?"

Walter picked up his glass and held it against the sun, "Oh, yes, I've always got it with me. It's in my pocket now." He squinted at the sparkling golden liquid with the sunlight shining through and said, "Your great-grandfather's cider is doing well by the looks of it."

"Yes," replied Tom, "Frank gave me the recipe one Christmas."

"The old bugger did something useful in his life then. Well, good luck to you lad. I'm glad to see you doing so well. Do you remember me telling you, that whoever made your great-grandfather's cider today, would make a fortune?"

Tom slapped him on the thigh, "I remember old man, I remember."

A few weeks later, the tyres of the new Daimler crunched on the gravel as Tom drove down to the banks of the river Wye and switched off the engine. He turned to Penny and said, "This looks like a good place for a picnic to me." He got out of the car and stretched, "I can see a lovely place on that pebble beach over there."

He pulled a picnic case from the boot and, when they were settled, Penny watched him pour the wine and said, "Well, this is all very nice Tom, but what's it in aid of?"

"Why not?" We deserve a break after all the hard work we've been doing."

"You know what I mean. You've brought me here for a reason. I know you well enough by now."

"I can't hide anything from you. Let's eat first and then I'll tell you what I have on my mind."

"I can hardly wait," she replied, and they had their lunch under the weeping willow tree, throwing morsels of bread to the ducks and laughing at their antics as they splashed and squabbled. "You see that duck there, the one with the tuft on its head. When I was at school, we had a teacher who looked just like that. She was called Miss Clufton and we used to call her Olive. It wasn't her proper name and I don't know why we called her that. I never liked her."

"She must have been an odd-looking woman," smiled Tom, "Did you like school?"

"Yes, I did. It was a nice school and they were happy days, but I know it cost Mummy and Daddy a lot to send me there."

"I didn't. I hated my school. At the Junior School, we had a head teacher called Miss Acton. I remember she wore a red blazer and carried a cane under her arm and we were all frightened of her. I got caned a few times and I still feel the pain when I think about it."

"Were you a naughty boy at school?" she asked, pointing at him with a chicken leg.

He thought for a moment before replying, "No, not really, but I was often in trouble, because there was a nasty boy called Brian Jones and he managed to make my life a misery, always doing wicked things and putting the blame onto me. I always seemed to get the cane for the things that he did, as I remember. I saw him yesterday, driving through the village and they tell me he's doing well in his haulage business and diversifying into other things."

"Jones Haulage Limited. I see his lorries all over the place." Then she looked at him intently and said, "Didn't you have a happy childhood?"

"Oh, yes. I didn't like school, but my childhood was happy. I used to spend a lot of time with my Granddad and I owe him a lot. It was what he taught me that helped me to survive in the woods when I had that breakdown and, come to think of it, his death was one of the reasons I fell apart and couldn't cope with life, until you came along, that is," he said, putting a hand on her knee. "He taught me how to catch game. He was a poacher, you know, in your Dad's woods —Hey, I bet you don't know how to catch a pheasant with a handful of corn and a spade."

"I don't know, but I expect you're going to tell me."

"Easy," he replied, "Granddad showed me how. You dig a trench about a foot deep and three feet long, but you taper the width from a foot at one end to nothing at the other, and then you sprinkle corn along the bottom and that's it."

"Well, what happens?" asked Penny, intrigued.

"Then you go away and leave it." He took a drink of wine and looked up the river and then he looked downstream.

"Is that it?"

"Not quite. You come back the next day and just pick him up; he'll be wedged in the narrow end. You see, the pheasant comes along and says, 'Oh, look at all this lovely corn,' and hops down to start eating. He pecks it up and moves along the trench which gets narrower and he won't go backwards because he doesn't like ruffling his feathers backwards, so he gets stuck."

"I don't believe it. You're teasing me," she laughed.

"No, it's true, because I've done it and perhaps one day I'll tell you how to catch drunken pheasants," he said, putting a finger to his nose and winking.

"I'd rather you told me why we've come here today. I know you're up to something."

"Well, do you remember when you took me to Court Farm to show me your surprise?" but before she could answer, he continued, "Well, I've got a similar surprise for you. Let's get cleared up and be on our way. It's not far."

The car came to a standstill by a high gate of chainlink fencing, topped by coils of rusting barbed wire. A faded sign hung from one corner and, although the paint was peeling, one could still read:

M.O.D. PROPERTY

KEEP OUT

"Here we are," said Tom, "This is what we've come to see."

"What is it?" asked the wide-eyed girl.

"It's a disused army camp and it's perfect for us. Three hundred acres of wasteland, seventy-nine rusty nissan huts, thirty-three miles of barbed wire, and a huge building with a leaky roof, and it's going for a song."

"Tom—" she said, after a stunned silence, "are you telling me that this is the site for a new cider production plant?"

"Yep, and here's the plan. We buy it and clear the site and then the offices will go there." He waved his arm in the direction of a vast concrete slab with weeds and small bushes growing through it. "The fermentation vats over there; twelve of the biggest vats you've ever seen. Just over there will go the bottling plant, and over there to the left will go the offices, and over to the right will be the warehouses, and —"

"Tom," she interrupted, " There's one thing bothering me about all this."

"What's that?"

"If you're going to realize your dream of building the biggest cider factory in Europe—"

"Yes?" said Tom expectantly.

"What's bothering me, is where are we going to get all the squirrels from?" she grinned.

"That's easy. I've thought of that. We'll modify the recipe and throw dead sheep in there instead." He put his tongue in his cheek and winked.

"But seriously though. Where will the money come from for plans as big as these?"

Tom replied, "We have some saved in the bank, but we'll build in stages and borrow the money for stage one. It'll be a complete and fully functioning unit and, when it's up and running and we have a bigger income, we'll borrow some more money for stage two to enable us to expand and so on. Pete has produced some figures which look good and I've had a word with the bank manager, who's been helpful. He seems to think it's a good idea."

They strolled arm in arm and Tom explained where buildings would go and how the different stages would develop. They drove back to Court Farm with their heads filled with ideas, excitedly discussing the possibilities.

Penny opened her window to allow the breeze to blow on her face and said, "Well, I wasn't expecting that when we set out on the picnic this morning. I knew you had something up your sleeve, but I had no idea of this. I thought your surprise was something to do with the river, though I didn't know what."

"And you are the one who's always telling me that I can't keep secrets. You'll have to change your tune now."

They sat in silence, each lost in their own thoughts, and then she said. "Well, it's very exciting. When are we going to start?"

"I was waiting for your blessing. I didn't want to start on anything this big without you being in on it. I had to find out if the whole thing was feasible and only then let you know all about it. You are part of the plans and now that you've given it the thumbs up, we'll get things rolling when we get into the office on Monday."

It was a busy summer. There were negotiations with the bank and planning officers, the Ministry of Defence and the County Council, and eventually everything began to fit together. The land was purchased by the end of the summer and Penny and Tom were driving to the site at weekends to watch the first stage grow. Before long, enough of the first stage had been completed to allow brewing to commence as the rest of the construction went on around them. In spite of the chaos, *Tom Beddows' Country Cider* got into production.

Impressive offices were built with landscaped gardens and ponds surrounding them and a sales team had been recruited, who built up new markets all over the country. The cider was produced on a large scale, but Tom personally supervised every stage. He even took sole responsibility for some of the more secret stages and, by keeping his personal interest in the processes, he retained the quality and character of the cider.

He said, "I want Great-Granddad's cider to be exactly the same as we made in the tin bath and exactly as he made it two generations ago. Even though we're growing, I think the secret of its success will be to keep it the same product, same taste, same colour, same cider."

The Home Farm cider orchards were not big enough to supply the apples for the increased production, so Tom did some research and found some alternative modern apples, which had the same qualities and were more readily available.

He discovered that a Lord Scudamore, who was Charles I's ambassador in France, had taken an interest in cider orchards and when he retired to Herefordshire he had specialized in the study and cultivation of cider apples.

Tom found that Redstreak was one of the apples that he developed and they were still growing in abundance all over the county. He also found some more modern varieties that were equally good. Like the old varieties, they had strange names, such as Chisel Jersey and Brown Snout. Hundreds of tonnes of them were brought into the new factory and, by strictly controlling the processes, Tom was able to ensure that the cider retained its distinctive characteristics.

Penny looked up at one of the vats, towering up into the sky above the bottling plant, and said, "Well, Tom Beddows' Country Cider Limited has come a long way since I wore Walter's overalls and bashed the apples in the tin bath outside your shack. I'm glad I brought you those sacks of apples now."

"So am I, and we have to thank Granddad for all this too, for giving me the recipe in my Christmas stocking. Who would've thought it would lead to this."

Tom came home from the factory one evening and said, "What's for supper, Love?"

"I haven't cooked anything, because I thought you might like to go along to the Village Hall as it's the Harvest Supper tonight. There'll be plenty of food and drink and the Hall committee have laid on entertainment. I thought it might be fun."

Tom, who had taken off one shoe and was unlacing the other, said, "What a good idea," and started to put his shoe back on. "It'll be nice to see some old friends. We've been so busy recently; we're out of touch with village life and we might hear some juicy gossip too."

The Harvest Supper was a big event in the village, as big as the School's Christmas play. Lower Kings Canon was still very much a rural community. It had expanded in recent years with the building of new bungalows, like the one to which the Gregorys had retired, but the Supper went on and had done so every year for as long as anyone could remember. It still goes on every year, right up to the present day.

The Hall is in the centre of the village close to the School and, although it does not look large from the outside, it seems to be elastic and have the magical power of seating unlimited numbers. Most of the village manages to squeeze itself in for the harvest supper.

Tom and Penny entered the doors to find themselves swallowed up in a seething mass of humanity, all talking noisily with an air of expectancy. Three rows of tables had been laid out from one end to the other and at the far end a stage had been erected, "For the entertainment," said Tom, nodding towards it. The stage curtains were closed and the tables were laden with food which had been prepared by the committee ladies.

There were not many people in the Old Black Lion that evening. Even the Young Farmers were at the supper. The landlord presided over a pub that was empty, except for a small group in the top bar who had driven out from Hereford. The log fire was burning and oak logs, which had just been put on, had caught alight and long, orange flames snaked up the chimney. Particles of soot on the fireback, ignited sporadically, sparkling like stars and then extinguishing, and the bar filled with the smoke's fragrance. The landlord gazed at it vacantly and muttered to no one in particular, "I hate Harvest Suppers. They're not good for trade. Haven't even got the Young Farmers in tonight."

In the Hall, the villagers settled themselves at the tables. The vicar stood up and gradually the tumult subsided as people realized that he was on his feet and they nudged their neighbours. The last few to realize found themselves talking loudly in a silent room and clapping their hands over their mouths, fell silent.

Tom tapped Penny on the arm, "Shush," he said, putting a finger to his lips, and she stopped chatting to the fat lady behind her. When all was silent, the vicar made a brief speech of welcome and then said Grace.

After the Amen, the silence exploded into noise again as the conversations were resumed. Tom and Penny were sitting with Angela's parents, Mike Sturgess and his wife, and on the other side were two strangers from the new houses. Opposite sat Bill Price, a tall bony man in a blue suit smelling of mothballs. He didn't talk to anyone but piled his plate with everything he could reach, slices of ham going on top of turkey, and on that went two chicken legs, followed by baked potatoes, crisps, pork pie, and salad. Mike looked at the plate and said, "It looks as if you haven't eaten since the last Harvest Supper."

Bill Price winked and took a bite from the chicken leg.

Tom leaned towards Penny and said, "I'm glad you suggested this. It's a banquet."

The committee ladies made sure that no one went hungry on these occasions and some food was left over as the tables were cleared in readiness for the entertainment. As they leaned back to allow the women to clear the plates, Mike Sturgess put his face close to Tom's ear and, lowering his voice, said, "I saw a friend of yours in the Black Lion, the other day."

"Who was that?"

"Brian Jones."

"Oh, him. I went to school with him, but I wouldn't say he was a friend."

"I know that," said Mike, beckoning for Tom to lean closer and lowering his voice still more, "I want to give you some advice. Watch that man. He's dangerous."

"Why's that?"

"I overheard him talking to some friends at the bar. I get the impression he hates you and would spoil things for you if he could. Your success seems to make him mad."

"He's always been jealous of me ever since our school days. I think his being little has something to do with it and we both liked the same girl."

"It's more than that. Some of the things he was saying were not the things a sane man comes out with. I think he has a screw loose and he really does hate you. Like I said. He's dangerous and I'm not happy that he's paying attention to my daughter, Angela. I keep hoping they'll split up, but I can't see any signs of it. I don't want her marrying that bastard. I've learned a lot about him recently and I don't like what I've been hearing. Anyway, I just wanted to warn you."

"It's funny, someone else said a similar thing to me recently."

"Well, you make sure you watch your back. I don't know what he could do, but watch him."

"Thanks Mike. I will. We never got on, but the more successful I become, the worse he gets. It's silly really, because it's not as if he isn't very successful himself."

"I don't know how his mind works, but watch him. Jealousy can be a terrible thing so they say."

An elbow in the ribs halted the conversation, "The vicar's talking again," hissed Penny.

He was on the stage asking for quiet once more to start the entertainment. The star turn was Walter and he made his contribution every year. This year he played the part of a country yokel in smock and straw hat, chewing a piece of straw. He grinned his gappy grin and bowed to hysterical applause, which took minutes to die down. His introduction was a medley of tunes played on the mouth organ and he followed that with some jokes.

"Ooh, Ahrr," he said frequently, believing that country yokels had to say Ooh, Ahrrr to be authentic. "Ooh, Ahrr," he said again, "There oy was, up in the top medder looking at moy cows, when up comes this city feller in his suit and bowler 'at. 'I say, my good man', sez eeh, 'would you be so kind as to tell me the time'."

"Ooh, ahrr, sez oy. Oy will tell eeh the toym, and oy ups and oy goes over to moy cow and oy lifts her udder. Ooh, ahrr, sez I. It be a quarter parst three,

"The city feller ups and sez. 'Well, that is truly astounding. I would never have guessed it was possible to tell the time by lifting a cow's udder'."

"No, sez Oy. Oy looked at the clock on yonder church tower, but moy cow was in the way, so oy lifts her udder to get a better view of the clock."

Then he burst into music on his mouth organ and bowed to the rapturous applause of the audience.

Bill Price, the thin man sitting opposite Tom, took the opportunity of consuming a bowl of salted peanuts during the ovation. The evening continued with David Pugh's monologue of *Albert and the Lion* and various contributors sang or read poems.

The Grand Finale was a Victorian melodrama performed by the Black Lion regulars to much hissing and cheering.

Every event in the hall finished with a raffle and Tom and Penny spread their tickets on the table. The vicar flamboyantly drew the tickets from a biscuit tin and called out the winning numbers.

"I never win anything," complained Tom, screwing up his tickets in disgust, but Bill Price won a box of chocolates and went onto the stage to collect his prize to whistles and cheers.

"I shouldn't think you've got room for those," shouted someone from near the front.

It was a successful evening, as everyone agreed, "One of the best ever," and the villagers left the Hall, to make their way home. A harvest moon shone down on the village.

"Just look at that moon," said Tom, as they walked arm in arm to the car. The huge moon was low in the sky over the School roof, with the weather vane silhouetted against it. They paused to look at the bright disc illuminating the village like daylight. Penny put her head on his shoulder and his arm went about her waist. "It's light enough to read a book," said Tom, "You know, I saw a film once, when Clark Gable, I think it was, proposed to his girl friend under a moon like that."

She turned her head to him as they stood outside the hall, jostled by the high-spirited exodus.

"Why don't you then?"

Tom looked surprised and then said, "Why not," and as the crowds pushed past he went down on one knee and, taking her hand, asked, "Will you please marry me, Darling?"

A passing elderly lady said, "Go on Love. Say yes."

Penny took both his hands and pulled him to his feet. "Yes, please," she said.

"Well done, Love," said the old lady, who had stopped to listen to the drama.

Chapter Seventeen

The wedding was a quiet affair and took place in the village church with only a few guests and the reception was held at the Manor House. For the honeymoon they drove to Salcombe in Devon.

"We have enough money to have gone anywhere," said Tom, "the Caribbean perhaps, or America? Anywhere you wanted."

"I know, but I came here when I was a little girl with Mummy and Daddy and thought it was a lovely place. I remember telling them that when I grew up and got married I was going to come here for my honeymoon, so that's what we've done."

The Ship Hotel overlooked the estuary and they had breakfast on the balcony.

"Well," said Penny, putting down her orange juice, "That was a whirlwind romance. You proposed to me under a harvest moon a few weeks ago, and here we are, married and on our honeymoon."

Tom leaned over the balcony and narrowed his eyes to look at the white boats, bobbing on their moorings in the autumn sunshine. He turned his back on the view and, putting his elbows on the balustrade, leaned back to look up at the hotel. "Look at that!" he exclaimed.

She followed his gaze to a sign, high on the wall, bearing the words: *We sell Tom Beddows' Country Cider*.

"You'll have to get used to that. Now that we're getting so big you'll see your name everywhere we go and, now that Pete has signed the agreement to export to Australia, your name will be seen everywhere on the other side of the world too."

"Yes, I know, but it takes a bit of getting used to. It's a strange experience."

The smell of cooking bacon drifted up to the balcony from the kitchens below. The smell on the morning air was exquisite and reminded Tom of a morning when he was a boy and went poaching with Frank.

The smell of the bacon triggered a flood of memories and he recalled his mother cooking the home-cured bacon as they came back along the lane on a perfect summer's morning.

He snapped back to reality when Penny said, "I wonder how they're getting on with phase three of the factory."

"At this moment I couldn't care a carrot. We're on honeymoon and I'm taking you sailing as soon as we've finished breakfast."

They ate watching the seagulls wheeling and diving into the water and the fishermen preparing their boats to catch the tide. The tall building of the hotel was perched on a rocky outcrop near the centre of Salcombe, and close to the jetty from where the ferry plied to the beaches on the other side of the estuary.

The summer was over but there were still visitors strolling around the narrow streets and pottering about on boats. From the balcony the honeymooners were able to watch the comings and goings in the small town.

Tom looked across the water to a three-masted schooner at anchor, rising and falling majestically on the swell, with flickering patterns of light reflecting on the white hull. "Now that we're rich," he said, "we ought to have a boat like that."

"You don't know anything about sailing."

"I can learn, but anyway with a boat that size we'd have a crew. We could have it moored in the south of France—Monte Carlo perhaps," he added, gazing dreamily at the yacht.

"There are lots of things you can have now that you have money," said Penny, refilling their coffee cups. "It's a big change for someone who used to be penniless and lived on berries in the woods."

"Yes, but some things haven't changed for the better."

"Like what?"

"Like these eggs for a start," he said, poking a fried egg with his fork. He lifted it to see underneath, "Look at the colour of this yolk, pale yellow, and it doesn't taste like the ones that my free range hens used to lay, or the ones that we had when I was a boy. The hens are kept in cages these days, you know, never seeing the sun, and you can see and taste the difference."

He pushed the egg to one side. "It's true I've got money, but I used to enjoy the meals I produced in my shack. They were more tasty than those I have now."

She put her hand on his arm, "You sound a bit sad, Darling. You wouldn't want to go back to all that again, would you?"

"Oh, no, that was another life in another world. I'm very happy, but I was just saying that in some ways life was better." He leaned across and kissed her, "No, I wouldn't want to put the clock back."

"I suppose it's only human nature to look back at things with nostalgia. Things often seem better in hindsight and we tend to forget the bad things. I bet there were some things you'd rather forget from those days."

"Oh, yes, you're right." He got to his feet, "Come on, Darling, finish your coffee. Get dressed in nice warm woollies because I've arranged for us to go sailing up to Kingsbridge and the wind might be a bit keen on the water."

At the cider factory, Pete was supervising the new development. The old MOD site was transformed. Modern buildings had gone up, as had several enormous vats. There was a bottling plant, office block, and ancillary buildings, and the site was attractively landscaped. The workers strolled round the gardens at lunchtime and some ate their lunch on benches by the fish ponds.

"It's a factory in a garden," observed Pete, looking down from his office.

There was an incessant stream of lorries bustling in and out, taking Tom's cider all over the country and beyond. The distinctive green and gold vehicles became a familiar sight on the roads of Britain. The factory and business were still expanding and Tom had handed over much of the responsibility for the day to day running to his brother. Pete was now managing director and he skilfully steered the firm through the tricky stages of expansion. He'd grown into a confident young man, always well groomed and smartly dressed.

He sat at his desk perusing a letter, but not concentrating on it as his mind was elsewhere. His attention was focused on Melanie, a vivacious girl, who was his secretary and had her desk on the other side of the office, opposite him. She was typing, her eyes darting from notebook to typewriter, and her fingers dancing over the keyboard. Her hair was short, making her look younger than her years, and she wore a tight black skirt. Her blouse was white and Pete found himself distracted by the form of her breasts in her lacy bra, clearly visible through the thin material.

He pretended to read the letter, but whenever he thought she was concentrating on her work, he took the opportunity of studying her. He thought she was a most attractive girl, with her big brown eyes and fresh complexion. She had grown up in Hereford and this was her second job since leaving school, her first being in a solicitor's office in Hereford. It had been Tom, Pete, and Penny, who had inter- viewed her for the post and, although Tom had certain reservations about her, it had been Pete who'd persuaded him that she was the girl for the job.

"Well, she'll be your secretary." Tom had said, "and you'll be the one who has to work with her, so I suppose it's only right that you should have the final say," and so Melanie had become an employee of the firm.

"She'll be good for us," said Pete, "smart, intelligent, and she comes with excellent references from her previous employer."

As the weeks passed and she settled into her job, Pete found himself becoming more and more distracted by her. She sat with her back to the window and he was fascinated by her silhouette against the light. He could see through her blouse and it was difficult to keep his mind on his work. Her new perfume filled the office and made her presence even more distracting. He finally made a decision and put his pen down so firmly that she looked up in surprise. His courage overcame his nervousness and he asked for a date.

"Nothing special," he said, "I just thought you might like to go for a drink in our local, the Old Black Lion. It's a good pub and they do nice food."

"That would be lovely," she replied.

A long low whistle came from the old men around the fireplace as the couple came in. Edward nudged his companion, "Young Pete's found himself a tidy wench," he grinned.

She ignored the whistle with great composure.

On their way to the pub, Pete had made a detour as they came into the village and parked outside the little red brick house where he grew up.

"That's where we used to live," he said, pointing at the house, "and this is the first time I've seen it since the day we had to leave. Granddad, Mum, Dad, and the three of us lived there. They were happy days."

He wound down the window and looked the house up and down. "It's funny," he said, "It seems much smaller than I remember it." He looked at the overgrown garden and continued, "My sister and I used to play hide and seek in those bushes and Dad built us a tree house in that Bramley. Look, there are still a couple of planks left up there. We used to keep chickens in that paddock. Tom looked after them, you know, feeding them and collecting the eggs, and all that. And that was my bedroom, up there above the door, and from there I could see across the fields to the church."

Melanie looked at the house and listened respectfully to his reminiscences, wondering what comment was appropriate when her boss was showing her scenes from his childhood, apparently overwhelmed by nostalgia.

She was spared the decision when Pete said, "I must be boring you to death on our first date. Let's get along to the pub. It's only round that bend and along a bit."

As Pete brought the drinks over to her in the lower bar, she looked around and observed, "I've been in here before. My Mum and Dad brought me out here, one summer's evening. It's a lovely old pub, typical Herefordshire with its beams and stone roof, and I love the wisteria climbing up the wall. It must be hundreds of years old, judging by the thickness of its trunk."

The conversation that evening was awkward. Both of the young people were anxious to create a good impression and both were keen not to 'talk shop' as they worked in the same office; polite small talk was interspersed with long silences. During the silences, they looked around the bar watching the other customers and whenever Pete could he studied her from all angles, becoming ever more fascinated by the beautiful young woman.

"She really is an attractive girl," he thought, and resolved to ask her out again and get to know her better.

A voice from behind them called out, "What's that straw in the road for, landlord? It smells of disinfectant or something."

The voice belonged to a man who was passing through the village and had called in for a quick drink.

The landlord replied, "We've had an outbreak of Foot and Mouth in the area and the straw is soaked in disinfectant to stop the disease from spreading from farm to farm." He shook his head and added,

"It's a terrible business. If a farm gets it, the Ministry make them slaughter their stock and burn the carcasses."

"That was the big fire outside the village on the Hereford road."

"That's right, Sir. It's heart-breaking for the farmer, because it means that his breeding stock which takes years to build up is gone. The disease spreads like wildfire once it starts, carried on people's feet or car tyres. I don't think they're quite sure. Some say that birds carry it."

"Same again, please," said Edward, standing at the bar with his empty tankard.

"Right you are, young man."

"I heard," said Edward, "that Major Hudson up at the Manor House has been hit with the disease and they're going to slaughter his herd of pedigree Herefords."

The landlord filled the tankard, "A terrible business," he muttered, "A terrible business."

"Aye, it must be true," said the old man, "because I heard it from Jean Evans."

"It must be true then," winked the landlord, "She knows everyone's business. That woman is better than the Hereford Times for local news."

Jean Evans was a short, round woman, who lived on a small-holding outside the village. She was married to Sam Evans, who worked as a driver for Jones Road Haulage. She kept her finger on the pulse of local affairs and nothing happened in the village that she did not get to hear about.

Pete whispered in Melanie's ear. "The woman they're talking about is our local busybody. If she confirms a rumour, you can be sure it's true. Foot and Mouth is a terrible problem for farmers and it can destroy herds that took a lifetime to build up."

"Who's losing his herd, Major somebody wasn't it?"

"Oh, he's our Lord of the Manor chappie. He owns the Manor House, a big estate that employs a lot of men from the village. Major Hudson's his name."

"The poor man—Major Hudson! That's Penelope Beddows' father isn't it?"

"That's right. Penny's father and Tom's father-in-law and ex-employer."

He took a long drink and went on, "My brother used to work for him on his farm and so did our father, and our grandfather worked on the estate too for the Major's Dad. He lives in a mansion with formal gardens and acres of parkland. Penny's their only child."

"I suppose you could say she's quite upper crust, then?"

"Yes, I suppose she is. She grew up with servants and expensive holidays abroad and went to a private school. She's had everything on a plate." After a pause, he added, "I wonder how the honeymoon's going."

"We'll find out tomorrow because they're due back. It's a romantic story isn't it?"

"What is?"

"Well, the story of Tom and Penny. I've been told that Tom had a breakdown of some sort and lived the life of a tramp when he met Penny, the daughter of the Lord of the Manor. Then, together they built a business and he became rich and they got married. It's a better love story than any I've ever read. In fact if the story was put into a book, no one would believe it."

"Well, they say that truth can be stranger than fiction but, yes, it's certainly an amazing story." He took a drink and continued, "Tom'll be back in the office tomorrow and he'll be wanting to see how the plant expansion is going. He won't rest until we have the most successful cider company in Europe and I don't think he'll be happy to stop there. We're the biggest in this country now and there's no reason why great Granddad Beddows' recipe shouldn't make us the biggest in the world. That's what he wants. He has something inside him, driving him on."

They relaxed as the evening went on and in due course were talking to each other naturally. They finished their bar snacks and the bar slowly filled with locals. The Young Farmers took their places by the fireplace and several villagers came in. Melanie frequently took out her handkerchief to wipe the tears of laughter as Eddy Morris and his pals entertained them with tales of the old days and of Nellie Partridge.

Pete drove her home and stole a kiss as they said goodnight.

"See you in the office tomorrow," she said, climbing out of the car.

The Manor House

Chapter Eighteen

A pall of smoke hung over the village. They were burning the carcasses of Major Hudson's herd. In the Black Lion, the landlord closed the windows to keep out the stench. A yellow digger was making a pit in which to bury the charred bodies of the animals, which had only yesterday been grazing on the last of the summer's grass.

A group of workers stood silently watching the operation as if they were at a funeral. They stood with solemn faces, not looking at each other, but gazing at the pall of smoke which rose into the sky and blotted out the sun.

The Major stood on the steps at the front of the house with his arm round his wife. They watched the smoke drifting over the barns towards the village and the pale autumn sunshine formed shafts of light as it percolated through the dense clouds.

They turned their heads at the sound of car tyres on the gravel. Penny swept down the drive in her new red sports car and she climbed out and kissed them both, "They told me at the factory," she said, looking at the sky, "So, it is true."

Her father looked grave and nodded, without answering.

"Well, cheer up," pleaded Penny, "It's not the end of the world."

"It's the end of our world," he said, sadly, "These animals will be compensated for but all of our breeding stock has gone. Ruler of Blaircorn has gone. The Duchess of Herefordshire is gone and so has Prince Barraclough."

He took her arm and said, "Come inside, Dear. We've seen enough and we don't want to stand on the doorstep all day."

He asked a maid to bring some tea and cakes and then continued, "We're going bankrupt. We've been in trouble for a year or so and this is the last straw. We'll have to sell up."

Penny was aghast, "Surely not?"

The maid entered and he did not answer until she left the room. She set the tray down on the coffee table and went out, closing the door behind her. When she had done so, he continued, "Our investments have gone down. We've lost out on the price of beef and even the forestry profits are down."

Mrs Hudson gave a little sob and the Major put his hand on hers. Penny stirred her tea and asked, "Isn't there any way out of this mess? I'm sure Tom will help if he can, especially as he's been looking for a way to thank you for helping him when he started with the cider."

He shook his head. "Anything Tom could do would be a drop in the ocean. We're in deep trouble; an ocean of debt. We'll struggle on for a while, but I'm sure that the time will soon come when we have to sell everything to get out of trouble and even then we won't have much left."

Penny stared at her father, her brain struggling to comprehend the idea. The estate had been in the family for generations and she had grown up with the secure feeling that it would go on for ever. It was difficult to accept the idea that it might all be coming to an end.

The Major had aged in the last few years and he was no longer the upright military figure Tom remembered from the Christmas morning many years ago. He was bent and walked with a stick.

It had recently been a struggle to keep the business viable and he was facing the prospect of selling the estate and laying off the staff. The once immaculate house was shabby. The window frames had not been painted for years and the old paint was cracked and peeling. Some of the rooms were now kept locked and not used, as the heating costs were too much. Penny kissed her father on the cheek and said, "Don't worry, Daddy. Maybe things will work out alright."

He shook his head sadly, and she noticed that his eyes were shining.

Life at the Manor went on apparently normally, though Jean Evans knew differently. She worked as a cleaner at the house and so had access to inside information. It was not long before the entire village got to hear about the Major's problems and his imminent bankruptcy.

At the factory, Penny walked into Tom's office and said, "Why don't you have tomorrow off? The Hunt is meeting at Daddy's and I thought we could see them meet and then go for a nice walk, as the weather is so lovely."

The Golden Valley Hunt was meeting at ten o'clock, just as it always had done. In spite of the cloud of gloom hanging over the house, nothing seemed different to the onlookers or to the scarlet clad riders. The horse boxes and trailers had been parked in the field at the end of the drive and the riders and horses were milling about in front of the house. Tom and Penny mingled with the group of followers. More people followed the Hunt on foot and in Land Rovers than actually participated on horses.

Bill Price was there. He went to all the meets just for the stirrup cup and the chance of a sausage roll. The stirrup cup was usually sherry, but on this occasion, as there was a nip in the air, a large bowl of hot punch had been made, and he was in luck this time because sausage rolls and cakes were also being served.

Penny had not ridden to hounds for some years. The fall which she had in the woods had un-nerved her and she was reluctant to get on a horse. She still had the old thrill though as the riders gathered. It was a picturesque sight and it would be difficult to imagine a more typically English scene.

The mellow stone of the house formed a back-drop to the picture. The gables, tall chimneys and mullioned windows of the Manor House were a perfect setting. The virginia creeper on the east wall was at its best; a splash of red against the beige stone. The thoroughbred hunters pawed the ground and tossed their heads and the riders drank from goblets, talking in groups. Three maids moved warily between the horses with trays of drinks and food. The hounds were kept together by the laurel bushes; cracks of the whip from the red coated master keeping them in a tight group.

"It makes a pretty picture, doesn't it?" said Tom.

A sequence of notes on the horn was the signal for them to move off in the direction of Cwm Woods and soon the courtyard was empty, except for a figure in a dark coat, who crouched down scraping horse muck into a bucket. "It's good for the roses," said the gardener, as Tom and Penny passed near him, arm in arm.

The gardens were a notable feature of the estate, laid out formally in a pattern of neatly trimmed box hedges. The focal point was a fountain made up of bronze female figures reaching upwards and from the centre issued jets of water. The gardens fell away in a series of terraces.

They sat on a stone bench looking towards the house and Penny pulled up her collar as it was a biting wind. Tom looked at her and asked, "Don't you wish you'd gone with them?"

"The Hunt, do you mean?"

"Yes,"

"No, not any more. I still get a thrill, but I lost my nerve the day I was thrown off in the woods and you came to my rescue. I like riding at my own pace, but it can get hectic during the chase and I get a bit frightened. No, I'd rather sit here with you and watch them moving off. It's just as exciting."

Tom nodded and smiled. He looked at the house and said, "It's a beautiful house isn't it? I've always liked it. When I was a boy it represented another world to me, one I couldn't aspire to. When I was small, it seemed like Buckingham Palace and you were a princess." He kissed her on the cheek and said, "And fair play, I still think you're a princess."

"Oh, Darling, what a lovely thing to say. You can say lovely things when you want to; a real silver tongue."

He smiled and said, "I never dreamt I'd end up married to you."

She kissed his cheek and then sighed and said, "I don't know how much longer it will stay in the family. Daddy didn't say anything about it when we arrived, but I could see that he was upset and Mummy had been crying, so I think it may be sold soon."

"It doesn't have to leave the family."

Penny looked stunned, "You mean—," she began, but did not complete the sentence, when he smiled and nodded.

"We can afford it," he said, "and we need a new house. Court

Farm has served us well but we've outgrown it now. This place would suit us better and the money would pay off your Dad's debts. He wouldn't have to dismiss any of the staff, which I know has been worrying him, and the estate will still be in your family."

She clapped her hands with glee and kissed him again, "What a wonderful idea. Mummy and Daddy have often said they'd like to live in The Lodge at the end of the drive when they retire. It would suit them perfectly. Let's go and tell them."

In the Old Black Lion some months later the landlord polished a glass and said, "I hear that young Tom and the Hudson girl have moved into the Big House."

"Aye," replied Edward, "They have, and it's funny when you think about it. The girl grew up there in the family home and then she marries a boy like Tom Beddows and then buys her own house off her Mum and Dad. Strange ain't it?"

"Funny old world," replied the landlord, "Who'd have thought it. That young lad, who used to tap on the window to call old Frank for his dinner, lived in the woods like an animal, and now owns that great big cider factory and lives in the Big House."

"It's a funny old world and no mistake. Another pint in there, please. He's got all that money and look at me. I'm ninety and I've got thirty-three quid in the Post Office."

"Yes, Eddy, but you've got your health and all your marbles and there's not many who can say that at your age. That's worth a lot of money in the bank, you know."

"Aye, I knows that lad," he sighed, "but there's a lot I've lost as well. I've lost old Frank for example. Remember him? He used to sit on that stool there." He jerked his thumb in the direction of the fireplace. We used to have some good times in here with Frank and the boys."

"Of course, I remember him. How could I forget an old boy like that? Like I told you, Tom used to come and collect him for his dinner. I miss him as well. When I was at school I had a teacher who used to say, 'There's nothing as constant as change' and I used to think, silly old biddy. What's she talking about? But now I'm older, I'm beginning to realize what she was getting at."

Edward took a drink from his cider and looked vacantly at the bottles behind the bar. "Do you know," he began slowly, "Sometimes I reckons I can see him sitting on his stool by the fireplace and going on about young Nellie Partridge and her dumplings. I miss that old bugger and now I'm ninety I reckons I'll be joining him up there soon. I hope he's keeping a place for me by the big fireplace in the sky."

"They don't have fires up there do they? That's the other place down there."

Edward chuckled, "Aye, you might be right. Frank was an old bugger but he won't be down there. He'll be up there with his trousers tied up with string sitting on a cloud playing a harp. You wait and see." He took another drink and added, "I hope he's saved a cloud for me, next to him."

"What a morbid conversation. Can't we talk about something more cheerful?"

"Yes, let's talk about Nellie Partridge's dumplings."

"Hey!" cried the landlord, looking about him wildly in mock fear, "Did you hear a ghostly chuckle when you said that?"

Edward grinned and raised his glass, "Well, anyway, I drink to him, and to young Tom too, and the best of luck to him at the Big House."

"To the both of them," said the landlord, raising his glass.

In the office at the factory, Pete put down the *Daily Telegraph* and announced, "There you are, Tom. It's official. Tom Beddows' Country Cider is the biggest and most successful cider company in the world. It says so here in black and white." He tapped the newspaper with the back of his hand. "We ought to mark the occasion with a celebration of some kind."

Tom went over to the drinks cupboard and poured two whiskies. "Here's a toast," he said holding up his glass, "to Granddad and Great-Granddad."

"To Granddad and Great-Granddad," they said, in unison.

Tom put down his glass and said, "What about a party at the Manor to celebrate and combining it with a belated house warming party. Nothing like killing two birds with one stone."

Terry Jones was leaning on a gate with his sheep dog at his feet watching the mist clearing from the far side of the valley. He was a farmer, a large man with receding hair and a loud resonant voice, and he owned Cwm Maerdy farm in the Dingle on the edge of the village. The farm was mainly a dairy enterprise but he also had a large flock of sheep. Cwm Maerdy nestled in a wooded valley and his south facing fields were lush and green.

He wasn't thinking about anything in particular, but he'd just finished a good lunch, the grass was growing well, and he was feeling content with his lot in life. The mist in the valley was receiving his full attention and the valley floor looked like the sea with the mist lying flat on the bottom. The hills appeared to be islands surrounded by the gently undulating water. He was so engrossed in the view that he didn't hear the arrival of a battered green Land Rover.

"Hello, Terry. How are you?" came a voice from behind the scratched windows.

He turned and said, "Oh, hello, Steve. I didn't hear you come. I was looking at that meadow and wondering if it was ready for cutting, but I don't think the weather's settled enough. There's some rain forecast and I don't want to risk it, as I lost a good crop last year when it turned black."

Steve Bufton was a neighbouring farmer who did not do much farming. Most of his income came from dealing in old tractors and spare parts. When his father died he took over, but did little farming, using the modern barn to house his tractors.

The inside was a remarkable sight. Down either side were rows of rusting tractors, some relatively modern, but most of them venerable old machines. Some had no engines and some had no wheels. Around them were scattered oily engine parts and gearboxes. There was an untidy pile of rusty wheels, hydraulic pumps, radiators, and cables.

Outside the building was a graveyard of old tractors stretching into the distance. Steve never seemed to sell any of his machines, or even a spare part for one, and the income from his farming was minimal, but he baffled the villagers by leading an expensive life-style with holidays abroad, and he had recently bought a new Mercedes.

The graveyard tractors had finished their working lives years ago and the hulks sagged and leaned against each other for support with nettles growing up through them and chickens' nests in their bowl shaped seats. Steve was frequently to be found in the pub or the cattle markets of the county. He never seemed to buy or sell livestock but considered the market to be a day out, passing the time with other farmers, leaning on the rails and watching the activity.

He climbed down from the Land Rover and joined Terry Jones leaning on the gate. "A grand day," he observed, looking towards the Brecon Beacons that were beginning to clear. He pulled his cap down lower over his eyes and asked, "Has young Tom Beddows invited you to that party at the Big House?"

"Aye. I'll be there. Never miss the chance of free food and drink."

"I expect they'll put on a good spread, so I won't have any dinner to leave room for it. They tell me he's celebrating his factory being the biggest in the world. They say there's even going to be television cameras there."

"In that case, I'd better put my best suit on."

Steve pushed back his cap and scratched his head. "It wasn't so long ago I chased him off my farm with a stick when I found him scavenging about my tractors. I don't know what he was after, some rubbish to make something for his shack, I expect. Now look at him!"

Terry said, "People complain about your place looking a mess but I reckons his place in the woods was a damned sight worse. Did you ever see it?"

Steve grinned and replied, "Yes. Perhaps that means I'll be rich like him one day. They say 'Where's there's muck there's brass', don't they?"

At the Manor House preparations for the party were well under way. Invitations had been sent out and Penny was supervising the decorations in the ballroom. When Tom bought the estate, the Major and his wife moved into The Lodge and all the furniture had been left just as it was.

Nothing had changed and the ballroom was exactly as he remembered it as a small boy. Even the ancestral portrait which had once caught his eye remained and the huntsman looked down from his gilt frame, as he had done every day since 1750. Penny and Tom had had the shabby house redecorated and it looked cared for once again.

Penny had made decorations from greenery and flowers and several of the estate workers had been pressed into service climbing ladders putting them up. The gardener and his young assistant had brought the foliage in by the wheelbarrow load and laid it on the table for Penny to make up into decorations. Jane was helping to tie ribbons and roses into the garlands. Outside, some men were up ladders wrapping yards of ribbon around the Ionic columns and under the cornice was a banner bearing the words, *Tom Beddows' Country Cider. Congratulations.*

Jack, the gardener, stood at the top of the steps shouting instructions to the apprentice, "Bring in another barrer of roses and another barrer of chrysanths as fast as you can!"

In the kitchens at the rear of the house there was similar activity and Mrs Taylor, the cook, was ordering everyone about. The maids busied themselves with the food preparation. Their ranks had been swollen by ladies from the village and they were making sand-wiches, sausage rolls, pies, and cakes.

Mrs Taylor wiped the flour from her hands and taking another tray from the oven said, "This is the biggest party I've ever had to do. We used to have big ones here, years ago, like the hunt balls but none of them were as big as this." She placed the tray on the table. "Good morning, Sir," she said as Tom entered the kitchen.

"Good morning, Mrs Taylor," he replied and popped a sausage roll into his mouth, "Phew, that's hot!" he exclaimed, moving it rapidly with his tongue and fanning his mouth with his hand.

Mrs Taylor wagged a finger at him, "That'll learn you," she said.

"It will," he replied, taking a drink of water from the tap. "I won't do that again in a hurry. I've burnt my mouth. Anyway I called in to see if you're making any cider cake."

"Yes, Sir, the Lady asked me to."

"Good, because old Walter's coming and it's his favourite. It's the only reason he ever comes to parties in this house and I promised him there'd be some just like the old days."

As he walked to the door, he hesitated and said, "It is made with

Tom Beddows' cider, isn't it?"

"What else?" she replied, waving the empty bottle in the air.

Penny was still in the ballroom supervising the arrangements and Tom went up to her and said, "I was talking to Mrs Taylor in the kitchen when I had a thought."

"You haven't been thinking again have you?" she teased.

"Yes, when she referred to you as the Lady, I realized that when we bought this house we also took over the Lordship."

"Yes, I know that. Because the house is the Manor House, the title, which has been handed down through the generations, now rests with you." She curtsied and said, "Congratulations, Darling. You are Lord of the Manor of Kings Canon."

"I suppose it was obvious, but I didn't give it a thought with all the excitement of moving. Well it's nice to have you curtsy to me, but don't forget, that if I'm the Lord, then you're the Lady."

They laughed and linking arms skipped across the ballroom.

The morning room had been prepared for a press conference while the last of the party arrangements were going on. Tom, Penny, Pete, and Jane, sat at a table and the room was filled with reporters and photographers and two television crews. Behind the table was a sign advertising the cider and they answered questions as the cameras flashed. It was Tom who was the centre of attention and the other three hardly spoke.

"Mr Beddows," asked a young reporter at the back, "I understand that these celebrations are to mark the completion of the factory expansion and the recognition of your firm's success in capturing foreign markets." Tom nodded, and the reporter continued, "In a few years it has grown from nothing to what we see today. It's now bigger than all the brands which have been household names for generations. The business world has never seen anything like it. Now, I understand that you started making your cider a few gallons at a time when you were a penniless hermit. Can you confirm that, Sir?"

"That's quite right," replied Tom, "and I have to thank my wife, Penelope, for helping me to get started. The two of us used to make it in the early days and without her none of this would have happened. We used to make it a few gallons at a time just for our own pleasure."

Another reporter asked, "Sir, there are hundreds of farms in Herefordshire making cider. A lot of it is very good and years ago almost every farm in the county used to make it. Can you explain why yours in particular has caught on so well?"

"I have a good management team and the work force is made up of local people who take a pride in the product."

The journalist persisted, "That's all very well, Sir, but your cider must have something special about it for it to stand head and shoulders above the others."

Tom put his hands behind his head and leant back in his chair, "Just natural ingredients, no chemicals, good Herefordshire apples, and a lot of know-how."

"I understand that you use a secret recipe handed down your family. Is that true?"

"Indeed it is. Tom Beddows' Country Cider is made from a recipe which was given to me by my grandfather and it was given to him by his father. My grandfather told me that many years ago people used to come from miles around to taste his cider and we try to make it just as good as it was then, real country cider; nothing more, nothing less."

He then paused and said with a grin, "I have to confess that it does contain a few special ingredients but I assure you they are quite natural and can be found anywhere." He caught Penny's eye and winked at her. "Are there any more questions gentlemen?"

At this stage, Pete, who had been silent up till then, joined in, "We have several hundred people working for us who are involved in various processes, but the recipe is so secret that Mr Beddows is the only one who knows it in its entirety. Even I don't, and he carries out some of the stages behind closed doors."

A reporter addressed his question to Tom, "Is your brother telling us that you, the Managing Director, actually roll up your sleeves and get involved in the process yourself?"

"That's right," replied Tom, "Perhaps that's one of the reasons for our success."

Chapter Nineteen

Brian Jones was in his office working late. He had a date with Angela later and he was catching up on some work before he went to meet her. He dictated letters into the hand-held recorder with one eye on the portable television which he had brought in. He was sitting in the high backed chair smoking a cigar and holding the Dictaphone. He was waiting for a programme to be screened, featuring Tom. When the programme began, he put down the machine and re-lit his cigar.

The presenter talked about the history of the business, starting with Tom's modest efforts in the woods, and then extracts from the press conference were shown with the producer putting much stress on the fairy-tale, rags-to-riches aspect of the story.

His face was expressionless as he drew on his cigar and blew smoke from tightly pursed lips and, when the programme finished, he violently stubbed out his cigar and stalked over to the window looking onto the haulage yard. His eyebrows were creased in a frown and his mouth set in a hard line. "The little bastard," he muttered. He put on his coat and switched out the lights, "The creepy little bastard!"

He went down the stairs two at a time and out to his car. It was parked amongst the lorries with *Jones Road Haulage Ltd.* painted on their sides. The transport side was flourishing, but nowadays represented only a small part of his business. His export and import concerns had grown to a point where he found himself at the head of a formidable group of companies, and he'd moved his head-quarters into Hereford with his registered office in London.

In spite of his success, he still nursed a profound and illogical hatred of Tom Beddows and his cider company. The childhood rivalry over Angela's affections had fermented inside him and Tom's spectacular rise had fuelled the fire. He now harboured a dangerous hatred and the more successful that Tom became, the more his festering hatred grew. He had been a small child and as a man he was still lacking in height. Tom was taller than he was and even that fact also fanned the flames.

When he left school he had gone straight into the business, helping his father with the office work. He had no qualifications but the work was simple enough for him and, when he became familiar with the routine, his father took early retirement leaving Brian with total responsibility.

Jones Road Haulage was well established, carrying mainly hay and straw. The firm also hauled timber from the forestry plantations over the border in Wales and he had built it up by winning lucrative contracts, which ensured the firm's continuing success as a major haulage company. He then diversified and developed other successful businesses.

As a child he had been arrogant and filled with a feeling of self importance. He knew that one day he would inherit the family firm and this gave him a sense of superiority over his fellow pupils. He was a bully and when he did become the managing director he became even less likeable, as he strutted and posed in his expensive suits, self–consciously smoking his cigars for effect. He had few friends, though he did spend some evenings with Matthew.

They were sometimes to be seen having a drink in the Old Black Lion and occasionally they went to the races together. Matthew Davies was a neat man with a thin, angular face, and was the Transport Manager. He was ambitious and, although he didn't like Brian, he pretended to be a good friend in the hope of further advancement in the company.

The party at the Manor House was big. Almost everyone whom Tom and Penny knew had been invited and most of them had turned up. The guests milled about in the ballroom talking noisily, while the waiters carried trays amongst them. On the patio through the open French windows, a jazz band played, resplendent in boaters and striped blazers.

Walter enjoyed the cake. He was now retired, looking frail and walking with a stick, but his eyes had not lost their twinkle and he still wore the same trilby.

"How's the cider cake, Walter?" asked Tom, as he edged his way through the guests towards him.

"Very good, Tom. Made with Tom Beddows cider, isn't it?"

"Of course."

"I'd know the taste anywheres." Taking another bite, he said with a full mouth, "I saw you on television."

"Did you?"

"Aye, and you came over well, fair play. Quite the gentleman now, aren't you? I hear people calling you Sir. Well, I suppose you're the Squire, now that the Major's left."

Tom put his hand on the old man's shoulder and said, "I'm the same loveable lad that used to help you with the horses and the hay-making. Are you still playing the mouth organ?"

"Aye," he replied, "I always has it in my pocket in case I feels like playing a tune. Are you going to ask me to join the band on the terrace?" he grinned.

Tom shook his head, smiling.

Walter reached for a sandwich, lifted a corner to see inside and said, "Egg. I know a joke about eggs. Do you want to hear it?"

Tom grinned, "I've heard it."

"No, you haven't."

"Yes, I have."

"Well, I'll tell you again, anyway." He pushed his trilby back and took a deep breath. "There were two eggs boiling in a pan," he began, "and one egg said to the other. 'Phew, it's getting bloody hot in here', and the other egg said, 'You think yourself lucky. When you get out, they'll bash your head in'."

He began to chuckle, going red in the face and showing his gappy teeth.

"You are an old fool, Walter, and your jokes don't get any funnier."

"Well, try this one for size then. A chap walked into a pub and got talking to the man at the bar. He took a box out of his pocket and put it on the bar. 'Guess what's in there', he said.

'Buggered if I know.'

'A centipede.'

'Really?'

'Yes, but it's special.'

'What's special about it?'

'It can do anything you ask it.'

'Anything?'

'Yes, ask it to do something, anything you like.'

So the man thought for a while and then tapped the box. 'Mister Centipede, can you hear me? Will you go round the Newsagents on the corner and get me a newspaper.'

Nothing happened, so the man tapped on the box again. 'Mister Centipede, will you go and get me a paper.'

Nothing happened again, so once more he tapped the box.

Then a little voice came from inside the box, 'Will you stop banging. I'm still putting my shoes on'."

Tom spluttered on his drink and walked away, shaking his head.

The party went on until late and after midnight many guests remained, dancing to the lively music of the jazz. The Wye Valley Stompers played on until the early hours, with the moonlight flooding in through the patio doors. Penny took Tom by the arm and kissing him on the cheek said, "Well done, Tom."

Life got back to normal after the party and in the office Pete had asked Melanie to go away for a weekend with him. They had been seeing each other for a few weeks, going out for dinners and to a dance in Hereford, and he was keen for the relationship to develop into something stronger.

He had grown increasingly fond of her each time he'd taken her out, but he felt that she was not warming to him as much as he would like.

He had been favoured with goodnight kisses and, on one occasion, they had cuddled at her bungalow, but that had been interrupted by the early return of her parents. How to get closer to her was occupying his thoughts and he'd resolved to try and take her away for a weekend.

"We don't need to go far," he thought, gazing through the window at the lorries coming and going in the yard. "Maybe the Welsh coast or the Cotswolds. Yes, that's it, the Cotswolds," he decided. "They'll be perfect. We could find a nice cosy pub to stay in and look around Lower Slaughter and Bibury and all those charming villages. She'd like that."

He continued to daydream, with visions of a picturesque country pub and Melanie in their bedroom, wearing flimsy lingerie.

He asked her in the coffee break and she thoughtfully stirred her coffee.

"Well, what do you think of the idea?" he asked again.

"Separate rooms?"

"Whatever you want."

"We don't know each other all that well yet, do we?"

Pete replied, "We've worked together for quite a while and we've been out a lot in the evenings."

"That doesn't mean we can share a bedroom."

"Of course not. I just thought it would be nice to have a weekend away together. I hadn't got as far as thinking about the sleeping arrangements," he said without conviction.

She smiled at him and snapping her chocolate biscuit in two said, "Alright, I'd love to. Thank you, Pete, and I'm sure it'll be a lovely weekend."

"Wonderful!"

"And about the sleeping arrangements—"

"Yes?" he replied, trying to conceal his excitement.

"I'll think about that."

In the office next door, Tom was drinking his coffee and reading the *Hereford Times*. He was leaning back in his chair with one foot on the desk. He put down his cup and shaking his head in exasperation looked up at the ceiling.

He blew through tight lips and looked at the paper once more. He had been perusing the readers' letters and under *Smells and Eyesores* there was a letter complaining about the cider plant. It began:

Dear Sir, I write to draw the attention of your readers to the ugly buildings and structures which are disfiguring our beautiful Herefordshire countryside.

I refer to the Tom Beddows' Country Cider factory, near Lower Kings Canon; a hideous collection of cider vats, spoiling our skyline with ugly modern buildings, which look totally out of place.

It went on to complain about the lorries rumbling through the countryside, and about the pollution of the air with the stench of fermenting apple juice. It ended with:

Do we really have to tolerate this spoiling of our heritage in the name of profits for the few? I call on all who hold dear the traditions of Herefordshire to oppose any further development of this hideous wound in our lovely landscape.

Mr Brian Jones, Jones Haulage Ltd.,Westwood Farm, Lower Kings Canon, Herefordshire

Tom looked up at the ceiling again, irritably drumming his fingers on the desk. Then he shrugged his shoulders and carried on with his work.

This was not the first letter of complaint that Brian had written. He wrote them regularly and they had succeeded in stirring up much ill-feeling. Letters appeared in the newspaper most weeks and, although Tom had worried about them at first, he'd learned to disregard them. Brian's activities had led to the formation of a local action group dedicated to the removal of the factory, and banners were often fastened to the perimeter fence carrying legends such as *Keep Herefordshire Green* and *Remove this Eyesore*.

Once, a group of irate ladies had sat in the road outside to prevent lorries moving in and out. They had been carried away by the police, screaming abuse in the direction of the factory, and Tom had suspected that Brian was behind it, but he had no proof.

"Brian Jones wrote another of his letters to the paper this week," said Pete as they drove towards the Cotswolds.

"Oh, did he?" replied Melanie, without any genuine interest.

They had decided to drive to the Cotswolds, spend the day exploring, and then look for a small hotel or pub to stay for two nights.

"Not a nice day so far," observed Pete, casting a glance through the side window. It was raining heavily and the windscreen wipers were barely coping as they thrashed from side to side. Flashes of lightning lit up the sky and every so often he changed course to avoid large pools lying in the road.

The wind drove the rain in grey curtains and as they passed through Evesham the sun came out briefly, illuminating the fields of grazing cattle with an evil orange light. The sunshine made the sky seem a deep navy blue behind the glowing trees whilst ahead of them was a rainbow.

Pete looked at the rainbow and said, "I think it's going to clear up. I listened to the weather forecast last night and it said the rain would clear away and we'd have a dry, bright weekend."

"I hope so. It'll make it all the more pleasant."

"You wait and see."

By the time they drew into Broadway, it had stopped raining and the sun was shining in a clear blue sky. "I told you it'd clear up didn't I?" said Pete and then began to sing, "'The sun has got his hat on, hip, hip, hip, hooray. The sun has got his hat on and he's coming out to play'."

They spent the day touring the honey-coloured villages nestling in the rolling countryside. It was the end of summer, almost autumn, so they were able to enjoy strolling about without being jostled by tourists, and Melanie commented that it was "Lovely to be able to visit the area without being overrun by all those objectionable Americans. This place is usually full of them and they are so arrogant and stupid," and then she did a good impression of an American accent, "Gee, Elmer, ain't these little cottages quaint? I must take a photo of that one to show the folks back home."

Pete laughed and responded with, "Sure thing, Honey."

They linked arms and slowly wandered along the bank of the stream running through Bourton-on-the-Water. The weather had warmed up and they licked their ice creams as they stood on a low stone bridge to watch the ducks. They could see rainbow trout in the clear water, darting about to catch pieces of bread that children were throwing in for the ducks. Every so often one leapt clear of the water and fell back with a sparkling splash.

In Stow-on-the-Wold, they were pleased to discover that they had arrived on the day of the Cotswold Horse Fair and the whole town had been taken over by gypsies. Everywhere they went, gypsies were riding their piebald horses bareback through the streets and on the edge of town many thousands were camped. Families sat outside the painted caravans and drank tea by their fires, while children played and the horses ate from their nose bags.

The blue smoke drifted across the stone roof tops of the town and, as the couple wandered aimlessly through its streets, she put her head on Pete's shoulder and said, "Time's getting on. We ought to be getting back to that nice hotel we saw in Bourton-on-the-Water to find a room for the night."

Pete stopped and said, "Did you say one room for the night?"

"Yes, we only need one room, don't we?"

At the hotel, Pete was as nervous as a young man on his first date. He had been so nervous that he'd sent a forkful of peas rolling over the tablecloth and after the meal he noticed that his hand was trembling as he raised his coffee cup. They had a drink in the bar before climbing the red carpeted stairs and Melanie could not resist provocatively swaying her hips as she led the way. The room was comfortably furnished and overlooked a courtyard garden; the stone walls and flagstones illuminated by troughs of scarlet geraniums.

He stood in the window looking out into the courtyard and over the stone tiled rooftops. The White Hart was in the centre of the town, close to one of the low bridges over the trout stream. He was standing on tip toes trying to get a better view when Melanie appeared from the bathroom, with her hair loose and wearing a thin, translucent night dress. Narrow shoulder straps held up the lacy top and the diaphanous material flowed to the floor.

He swallowed hard as she entered and stood in the door with the bathroom light showing her form in strong silhouette. He sat down on the bed, open-mouthed, looking her up and down. The thin material did not conceal her nipples and he could clearly see them through the lace.

"Stay where you are," he said, "That's what they say in the films, isn't it? Stand still. I want to savour this moment for ever. Now I know what they mean. You look so beautiful."

"I hoped you'd like it," she said, doing a twirl in the doorway to make the night dress swirl around her body, "I bought it specially for this weekend."

Pete got his feet saying, "So, you intending sharing a room all the time."

She nodded and looked shyly at the floor. He moved towards her and sliding his hands behind her back, pulled her towards him. The thinness of the material and the softness of her body stirred him and he lightly ran his hands up and down her back. His hands moved up to her shoulders and he slid his thumbs under the straps and pulled them down, allowing the night dress to slither slowly to the carpet. He kissed her neck and then, holding her close, began to kiss her shoulders. Melanie wrapped both of her arms around his head and pulled it tight against her.

Easing his head from her embrace, he moved down and covered her breasts in light fluttering kisses, lingering around her erect nipples and fondling her breasts with both hands. As he became aroused, she could feel him pressing hard against her thigh and she slowly ran her hands down to his waist. Then, agonizingly slowly, she moved her hand down until it rested on him and she gently ran her fingers up and down. He gave a low moan and, kissing her on the lips again, pulled her onto the bed.

Chapter Twenty

Tom Beddows' Country Cider continued to expand. The local environmental problems which Brian had stirred up were but a minor distraction and the firm went from strength to strength. They diversified into other areas and the pectin, a by-product of the fermentation process, was sold to jam making companies to make their jam set and became a lucrative part of the business. They also started importing French wine.

"If we're going to import French wine," announced Tom, "we should import French cheese to go with it," and so another division of the business was born, *Tom Beddows' French Country Wines and Cheeses*. They also marketed a range of soft drinks and mineral waters and won a contract to be the sole agents for a well-known Spanish sherry.

As the business snowballed, so did the family's wealth, and Tom and Penny had a villa built in Provence in the south of France.

"It'll be a good base for searching out new wines and cheeses," said Tom, "It's in a good area for them, all sorts of farmhouse cheeses and little known wines are produced around there and it'll be handy for holidays, too."

Since their honeymoon in Salcombe and their sailing lessons, Tom had nurtured a yearning for a yacht. He still held a vivid mental image of the schooner moored near their hotel with the reflections dappling her graceful hull. From the time he had seen the boat, he'd promised himself that one day he would own such a beautiful yacht. Now he did have one and it was kept in the St Tropez marina, along the coast from the villa which they were having built.

He and Penny lived on the boat for weeks at a time when they were over there checking on the villa's progress. She was an elegant, white, three masted yacht, named *Sweet Cider*. In the fitting out no expense had been spared and there was a wealth of varnished hardwood. When they sunbathed on deck, they lay on varnished mahogany planking. Tom had become a competent sailor, though the boat was too big for him to sail on his own. They employed a skipper and crew and Jane had designed them a uniform with *Sweet Cider* embroidered on their chests.

Since their weekend in the Cotswolds, Pete and Melanie had

decided to live together with a view to eventually marrying. They lived in a converted water mill south of Kings Canon and they also spent much time on *Sweet Cider* cruising the Mediterranean coast, calling into harbours such as Monte Carlo and Nice. Pete was able conveniently to combine business with pleasure on the yacht. He could moor in Nice and tour the vineyards of Provence seeking out wines that he could market in Britain. The yacht was ideal for entertaining and doing his deals. She was a great ambassador for the company, because of the dignified ambience which she created, and many a deal which might not otherwise have been concluded was clinched in her state room.

Monsieur le Brun was the foreman in charge of building the villa, five miles inland from Nice. The site was not only in open countryside but also close to Nice airport. It was on a hill which offered panoramic views over the Provencal countryside and the Mediterranean and, on a clear day, they could see the island of Corsica, a long hazy shape, shimmering in the blue sea.

Monsieur le Brun was in charge of the gang of workmen and he conducted the operations with unshakeable good humour. He was deeply tanned and, wearing only a pair of faded denim shorts, spent his days issuing orders with much waving of the arms and excited shouting. He smoked strong smelling *Gauloise* cigarettes and was rarely seen without one hanging from his lips.

The villa was clearly going to be an impressive building on an elevated site overlooking the red pantile roofs of the other villas clinging to the steep hillside. It had fifteen bedrooms and one feature, which Tom had designed, was a colonnaded patio around the swimming pool. On one of their visits, Monsieur le Brun showed them the almost completed patio.

"Voila!" he said, with an expansive gesture of his arms and then, walking over to the pool edge and looking over, called out, "Pauvre petit chat!"

Penny looked into the water and called, "Hey, Tom, do you want this dead cat for your cider?"

"No," was the reply, "It's a French cat and they don't taste the same. If it was a Herefordshire cat, I'd have it."

Monsieur le Brun pulled up some chairs, "Do 'ave some wine with me," he pleaded.

The workers had finished for the day, so the three of them had the villa to themselves. The foreman spoke some English and Tom had picked up a little French on his visits. Penny was fluent, as she had learned the language at school, so they were able to communicate satisfactorily.

"Moment, Monsieur," said the French man, walking to his battered Citroën van and returning with bottles and glasses. "It is the wine of my village," he proudly explained.

The sun was sinking low over the hills and the clouds were tinged with pink. Frogs were starting to croak all around them. They settled into their chairs and drank the wine and as the light faded they watched the dancing lights of fireflies. When it got darker and the fireflies became brighter, the distant lights began to twinkle. The red glow of the sky slowly changed to a deep velvet purple and the coastline became studded with a pattern of lights. The sweet smell of *Gauloises* hung on the still air and far out at sea the lights of a ship moved almost imperceptibly across the horizon.

Monsieur le Brun refilled their glasses and looked over the roof tops saying, "It is beautiful, n'est ce pas?"

Penny followed his gaze, and linking her arm in Tom's replied, "Oui, Monsieur, it is beautiful."

In Herefordshire, Sam Evans climbed into the cab of the lorry and started up the big diesel engine. As he settled into the seat and turned the key the engine groaned and then roared, discharging a cloud of black smoke from the exhaust. He leaned out of the window and adjusted his outside mirror.

He eased the vehicle into first gear and the lorry and trailer moved out of the Jones Road Haulage yard. Sam Evans was married to Jean, a cleaner at the Big House and source of all local gossip. He was a driver for Brian Jones and was setting out for Yorkshire.

He had worked in the same job since he was old enough to drive lorries and he enjoyed the work. He had fair hair and moustache and he wore jeans and a white tee shirt. When he was in his cab, he was his own master and he liked the sense of adventure as he set out on each trip. After all his years of driving, the excitement had not diminished, although the job had recently lost some of its satisfaction, as his mind was elsewhere.

The lorry headed north and he was lost in his thoughts. His wife Jean had been ill for several months and was deteriorating. She had a rare form of cancer and was having treatment five times a week. Only a few months ago, she had been a jolly, round lady, but he'd watched her get thinner. Now her eyes were hollow and staring and the drugs were causing her hair to fall out.

He stopped at the transport cafe, ordered his bacon and eggs, and became engrossed in the *Daily Mirror* as the bustle of activity went on around him. The cafe was a popular stopping place for lorry drivers and at this time of day it was busy as they came off the road, for their breakfasts.

"Double egg and chips," shouted the shrill woman from behind the counter, followed by "Two bacon sandwiches," and "Bacon, egg and double chips."

The juke box thumped out pop music so loudly that the base notes vibrated the tea in his cup, making concentric waves, and the pin ball machines pinged and chattered. But it all washed over Sam as he stared at his paper. His thoughts were in Hereford with Jean and he remembered how she used to enjoy working at the Big House and being the first to broadcast choice morsels of gossip.

He looked down at his breakfast and his eyes grew misty as he recalled how she loved cooking his favourite meals for him. As he wallowed in nostalgia, he thought back to the days when their daughter was born and Jean had had cried with joy. He ate his bacon and eggs without enjoyment and made his way back to the lorry.

He continued his journey deep in thought, but came back to reality when he arrived at his destination and had to find his way though the busy streets to the warehouse. He found the building and drove through the gates saying, "What's this?" as a piece of paper was thrust into his cab. It was a message from his brother-in-law.

Sam.
Return to Hereford immediately.
Jean very ill in hospital.
Dave.

He did not remember much about the return journey, as he had been wrestling to solve the problem that had been preoccupying him for several days. His problem was that Jean would not get better unless she had an operation that was not available in this country. It was only performed at a specialist hospital in California and it would cost a great deal of money to take her there; money which he did not have and, if she didn't have the operation, she would die.

He walked towards her bed filled with foreboding and an uncomfortable fluttering in his stomach. "What am I going to find?" he thought.

A nurse said, "She's having a little sleep. She's had a busy day."

He stood by the bed and remarked, "She's going downhill, isn't she Sister?"

She smiled sympathetically. Then she looked at him solemnly and said, "Never give up hope, Dear. While there's life, there's always hope, and in this job we do sometimes see miracles, but I have to say that she's dangerously ill. I'd be misleading you if I said otherwise."

He stayed with her and after two hours she opened her eyes and with a faint smile, fell asleep again.

By the time Sam left the hospital, he'd made a decision. He had decided what to do about the problem he'd been agonizing over and as soon as he got home he picked up the telephone, took a deep breath, and dialled. His brow creased in a frown and his finger trembled. "Hello, is that David Peters."

"It depends who's asking."

"This is Sam Evans and we met two weeks ago in the Kings Oak, remember? And you put a little business proposition to me."

"What sort of business?" was the cautious reply.

"The sort of business we discussed and I said I wasn't interested in."

"You'll have to tell me more. You could be anybody."

"I was in there on my own when you came in with your two mates and we talked about business."

"Would you be the fair haired bloke? A lorry driver?"

"That's right."

"Got you and I remember now, Sam Evans. Right, Sam, fire away."

"I've decided I can put some business your way, after all."

"Okay, I'm interested," and after a pause, Peters said, "Meet me in the King's Oak at eight tonight and we'll see how we can help each other. In the back room, okay?"

David Peters arrived first and sat with a whisky in the small room at the back, checking the racing results in the evening paper. He was a smartly dressed man of about thirty, who ran a garage in Leominster.

He dealt in second hand cars but that was just a front for his illegal activities. When he was a young man, he had served a jail sentence for burglary, but since then had managed to steer clear of any brushes with the law, in spite of being involved in some very shady deals.

He looked up when the door opened, "Hello, Sam," he said, getting to his feet, "Let me get you a drink."

"A pint of bitter please."

When he returned with the drink, Sam said, "Let's get down to business. We don't want to waste time on pleasantries."

"Suits me."

Sam took a long drink and with a glance at the door to make sure they were not being overheard, he lowered his voice and said, "I've been thinking over what you said and I'm ready to do it."

When the two men had last met, they had been the only customers in the pub and in their conversation had got on to the subject of making extra money on the side. Peters had hinted that he made a large amount of money trading in stolen goods. He didn't actually admit to it, but the inference was clear enough.

Sam had asked why he was telling him, a stranger, about his trade. "I could be a policeman for all you know," he had said.

Peters had lit a cigarette and winked, "I know you're not a policeman. In fact you'd be surprised what I do know about you. This is a small community and I make it my business to know things about people who might be useful, if you see what I mean. I know that you drive for Jones and I also know that you have reasons for wanting extra money at the moment. You can't do me any harm for telling you this, because I'm far too clever. How is your poor wife, by the way?"

That was how they had met some weeks previously and since then Jean's condition had worsened. At the time, he had no intention of taking Peters up on his offer, because he didn't trust him, and he had no wish to get himself caught up in the sort of activities that he was involved in.

It was different now, though, and he found himself being drawn into the web. That conversation had played on his mind and, now he had made the decision, found himself in the back room of The King's Oak, discussing how they could be of mutual assistance.

"Yes," said Peters, "I agree we cut out the pleasantries and get down to the nitty-gritty."

Sam trembled as he found himself on the slippery slope, but there was to be no going back now. He was an honest man, who had never stolen so much as a pencil in his life, but seeing Jean suffer had hardened him and his principles did not seem so important any more. He was desperate to get the money to take her to America and he resolved to worry about the consequences afterwards. At the moment nothing else mattered.

He had taken an instant dislike to Peters, who was asking him to cheat his employer, Brian Jones, but as he liked him even less, it made the decision easier.

Peters said, "You're in a position of trust at that firm and with some creative paper work you'll be able to cover your tracks and purloin goods for me. I'll pay you well and it's electrical goods I want, mainly televisions and the like."

"I can get you what you want. I might only be a lorry driver, but I've got a lot of responsibility for the paper work, and I won't get caught out."

"I'm pleased to hear it, Sam, because if you do, I've never even heard of you. Is that understood? You won't get any help from me."

Sam nodded and Peters raised his glass and said, "Here's to a mutually profitable business relationship. When can you start?"

"Tomorrow."

"Okay, I'll see you at the back door of my place at eleven o'clock tomorrow night."

In that manner a 'business' arrangement began between the two men. Sam was able to supply him with goods which he stole from Brian Jones' lorries, and a clever falsification of documents ensured that suspicion was not aroused. Goods were often damaged or missing after deliveries, and it was Sam's job to order replacements to balance the books. His thefts were recorded as loss or damage replacements. He was to make many trips to the back door of Peters' garage and he was paid in cash, which he hid under his mattress. He counted it every night before he went to bed and over the next weeks a handsome sum accumulated.

Chapter Twenty One

At the factory Tom was catching up with some office work. The sun was streaming in through the windows and dazzling him and as he was closing the Venetian blinds, the door burst open and Penny came in, flushed and breathless.

"Whatever's the matter?" he asked, anxiously.

"This has just come in the second post." She held a letter out to him.

He sat down at the desk to read it, with the bars of sunlight from the blinds curling over him and on to the desk. His face was in shadow against the light, so Penny put her head on one side and narrowed her eyes to try and judge his reaction.

"Well, this is good news," he said, lowering the letter.

"Good news!" she exclaimed. "It's brilliant news!"

"Yes, it's brilliant news."

He threw the letter in the air and hugged her and then she went over to the cupboard and poured two sherries. She handed one to him and said, "And you haven't heard it all yet. There's more."

In the Old Black Lion, the landlord wiped his moustache with the back of his hand and studied the *Hereford Times*. The newspaper was spread out on the bar, and he was leaning on both elbows scrutinising the front page. The main headline read 'TOM SCORES A DOUBLE.'

Bill Price was standing at the bar and he threw a salted peanut in the air which he caught in his mouth. "What's that about Tom Beddows?" he asked, twisting his head to read the headline.

"It says here that young Tom has been awarded the OBE for his outstanding contribution to British industry and at the end of the month the Queen is going to visit the factory."

"Well, I'll be buggered," said Bill, throwing another peanut in the air.

All of the Young Farmers, who used to sit by the fireplace with Frank, were now dead and they had been replaced with a younger group. The bar was no longer witness to their rural humour and tales of their youth. Old Frank and his friends lay in the churchyard, only a few cottages away, and no longer joked about

Nellie Partridge and her dumplings. Generations who used to laugh and joke the evenings away, were lying in the same place.

Tom stood in the churchyard with head bowed beside the grave of his parents. He rested his hand on the gravestone and then wiped away a tear that trickled down his cheek and into the corner of his mouth. He walked the few steps to his grandfather's grave. "Thanks for the Christmas present, Granddad. I kept it safe, like you asked me and you were right. It did come in useful after all."

They were hay-making in the meadow by the church and the sweet smell of new mown grass caught his nostrils. He stood in the shade of a yew tree and looked over the wall to watch the mowing. He remembered when fifteen men would have been employed to cut it with their scythes and he recalled how as a young boy he sat on the gate kicking his heels against the bars, watching the men working in the hot sun.

He remembered how he was sent running from this very spot to fetch his bike and tell the men that the grass was ready for cutting. He recollected the smell of the grass as he kicked it up and, as long as he lived, he would never forget taking the hay to the barn with Walter and his mouth organ. He looked across the field and watched the solitary red tractor, criss-crossing the grass, mowing a strip eight feet wide. The driver sat in the cab looking straight ahead and loud Beatles music came from the tractor's radio as it raced up and down.

Brian Jones sat in a deck chair on his lawn. He had taken a day off from the office to spend some time tidying the garden. The beautiful day had turned into a gloomy one as he read the *Hereford Times*. He had tired of weeding and had sat down for a break to read the paper. The main headlines were inescapable. "I'll get the bastard," he muttered to himself and he sat brooding in the deck chair for most of the morning; his hatred of Tom and his success boiling inside him.

He'd smoked several cigars before he said, "Right," and strode determinedly towards the house.

Later that day, Matthew Davies arrived. Brian had phoned him at the office and asked him to come over immediately.

"It must be important," he thought, as he turned into the drive, "I wonder why he wants to talk to me at his home."

Matthew was ambitious and had long ago decided that he disliked his boss, but his urge to better himself had sublimated his contempt for the man, and he did everything he could to gain favour and perhaps promotion.

"I wonder if that's it," he thought, "Promotion. I've had a few successes recently. That must be what he's called me for."

He was greeted by his boss as he locked the car and walked towards the front door.

"Come round to the back garden," said Brian, "It's far too nice to be indoors." He shook his hand and gestured for him to go to the back of the house.

"Make yourself at home on the lawn and I'll bring some drinks out for us."

Matthew found the deck chairs on the lawn and made himself comfortable while he took stock of his surroundings. The garden was large and well cared for, with an abundance of summer colour in the borders, and the lawn had been freshly mown.

Brian appeared with a tray, asking, "How are things at the office? No problems, I hope."

"Oh, no problems. Everything's going as smoothly as ever."

Brian sat down and slapping him on the shoulder said, "Thanks to you."

Matthew took off his jacket and hung it on the back of the deck chair.

Brian grinned and said, "This is better than being in that stuffy office, Eh, Matthew. Here you are, lots of ice in it." He handed him a drink.

"It certainly is better than being in the office."

"How's that pretty daughter of yours?"

"Oh, fine."

"I heard the cuckoo just before you arrived. I think he's in that tree over there."

"Really?"

And so the small talk continued.

Matthew looked round the garden and desperately searching for something else to say asked, "The garden is looking nice. Do you have a gardener or do you do it all yourself?"

"The wife does most of it. She's a keen gardener and we have a man in to do the heavy work."

Brian's wife was Angela, the object of his and Tom's affections at school. Since meeting in the Old Black Lion and the first date for dinner at Clunton Manor, they had become engaged and eventually married. Angela had gone ahead with the marriage, in spite of nagging doubts about him.

Ever since her experience at the Abergavenny Show, Angela had worried about certain aspects of his personality, but he had charm and he'd wooed her very skilfully. Although she did not realize it, his money and life-style had an influence on how she felt about him and it made up for his shortcomings. At the time of the marriage, she thought she loved him, but being married to him had become more and more difficult, as he was not an easy man to live with.

But Matthew was still wondering why he'd been summoned, "I expect he'll get round to it soon, in his own good time," he thought.

Brian refilled their glasses and inquired, "How long have you been with the firm Matthew?"

"Six or seven years, I think. Yes, seven years this October."

"Are you happy with us?"

"Yes, I think it's a good firm to be with."

"Well, with a young family growing up, I should think you could use some extra money."

Matthew hesitated and replied, "We could all do with some extra money."

Brian went on, "Maybe it's about time you had more responsibility in the organization —Sales Director perhaps. What do you think?"

"I don't know what to say. Are you offering me promotion?"

"Ah, I didn't say that. More like thinking aloud, you know."

"Oh, I thought—"

"No, Old Boy. If you want a job like that, you've got to earn it."

"I thought for a moment you were trying to say that I had earned it. Sorry, I misunderstood."

Brian smiled and slowly shook his head. "I think you're jumping the gun a little, but don't get me wrong. I think you've done well and a little extra effort in certain directions could reap dividends for you, not to mention your family."

Matthew scratched his head in bewilderment. "What do you mean?" he asked.

"There's the cuckoo, look, at the top of that tree." He pointed to the top of a beech tree. "There you are, I told you so."

Matthew was confused and said weakly, "Yes, I see it," although he didn't.

Brian jumped to his feet and said, "Let me get us some more drinks. Your glass is empty. Come on, pass it over."

The conversation had disturbed Matthew and, while his boss was in the house getting the drinks, he struggled to make sense of the situation. His initial excitement as promotion was mentioned had turned to bewilderment. He took out a handkerchief and mopped the sticky sweat from his neck. Dark patches had appeared under his arms and he shifted uneasily in his chair.

"Now, where were we?" asked Brian, returning from the kitchen, "I hear that Tom Beddows is still doing well. Did you read about him in the paper?"

"Yes, I read it in the office, this morning."

"I went to school with him, you know. We were in the same class and he was a trouble-maker even as a boy. He hasn't got where he is by ability, but by luck and dirty tricks. He doesn't care who he tramples on. No, he doesn't deserve his success."

"Didn't he used to live the life of a hermit in the woods?"

"That's him."

"They tell me he used to live on berries and snails."

"Yes, and that's where he ought to be now, the snotty little bastard." His voice rose as he became more angry. "That's where he belongs, living in the woods with the other animals."

"I can see you don't like him."

Brian bit his lip and lowered his voice, "I'll tell you something Matthew, just between you and me, I hate the bastard and it would give me great pleasure to see him brought back down to his knees." He paused, and looking intently at his companion he said, "and that's where you come in."

"Me?"

"Yes, I'd like to see you get promotion. I would like to see you able to afford expensive holidays for the wife and to give your kids a good start in life. I expect you could use a nice new car too." He took a drink and thoughtfully swirled the glass, allowing the ice cubes to chink against the sides. He studied the glass and said, "And with your family growing up as they are, becoming more expensive by the day, it would be a great pity if you lost your job and were out of work."

"Jobs like yours aren't easy to come by and your family would suffer real hardship and that would make me sad. We can't assume that we'll keep our jobs for ever these days, can we? We hear all the time about people losing them and the hardship it causes."

He lit a cigar without offering one and continued, "Now if you felt the same as I do about Tom Beddows —If you were anxious to see him brought down—now that would be a different story. There wouldn't be any risk to your job then, if you get my drift."

He looked at Matthew expectantly, but the wretched man could think of no response. He took a drink and loudly gulped it down.

"An intelligent man like you could be a big asset to me," continued Brian.

Matthew's thin face screwed up in frustration, "I have to confess that I'm confused and I don't really know what you're trying to say."

Brian blew smoke from pursed lips and said, "Then let me spell it out to you in words that you might understand. I want you to do everything in your power to ruin Beddows. Dig up the dirt on him and if you can't find any, then you can invent it. I want you to blacken his character. I want him ruined. Do you get my meaning?"

Without waiting for an answer he continued, the pitch of his voice rising as he became more excited. "To put it into terms even easier to understand. You ruin Beddows and I'll make you a director and give you a handsome cheque and I mean handsome—fail, and who knows?" He made a sign across his throat with a finger.

He then relaxed into his chair and re-lit the cigar. He lowered his voice and with a broad smile and chilling calmness asked, "Well, what do you say?"

Matthew shuffled uneasily and stared at his empty glass.

"Well, what do you say?" he demanded again, more forcefully this time.

He mumbled something unintelligible.

"Speak up man. What did you say?"

"I said okay, you have a deal."

"Good man. I knew I could trust you. Now don't forget, no holds barred. Play as dirty as you like. I want him back in that hovel where he belongs."

At the Manor House Penny put the last of the red roses into her arrangement and stood back with her head on one side, "What do you think of that Tom?"

"Lovely, Dear," he replied, standing behind her and sliding his arms round her waist. He nuzzled into her neck. "Mmm, I like your perfume. It reminds me of bluebells in the spring woods. Come here," he said, turning her round and beginning to unbutton her blouse.

"I must remember to wear this perfume more often."

He smiled and having undone the last button, untucked the blouse from her skirt. With some fumbling, he undid her bra and then began to cover her naked breasts with kisses.

"Oh, Tom," she sighed, "I love you so very much," and she sighed again as his mouth found her nipple. He kissed it and her hand slid down to his waist, unfastening his belt and slowly undoing his zip. She slid her hand inside and murmured, "Gosh this perfume has a wonderful effect on you, doesn't it?"

"It's not the perfume that does it. It's you. Let's go upstairs."

Later that afternoon, Penny threw back the sheets and went over to the window, "What a lovely way to spend an afternoon," she said, standing nude in front of the window. She stood looking out across the lawns and then went over to the bed and pulled the sheet off, saying, "Making love with Tom Beddows OBE, the biggest cider maker in the world, and the biggest lover, too."

He stretched out his arms and said, "Yes, it's one of the best afternoons I've spent for a long time."

She moved back to the bed and sat on the edge, "The afternoon isn't over yet, Tom. It's an exciting day because I've got some news for you. I've been saving it for the right moment and this may be it."

"Oh?"

"I went to see Dr Sherwood this morning and he told me something that might interest you."

"You're pregnant!"

"Yes."

He reached towards her with both arms and pulled her down onto the bed, saying, "That's the best news I've ever had, Darling. When's it due?"

"January."

He pulled her close to him and pressed her head against his chest. They stayed like that for several minutes and then he pulled away from her slightly and taking her face in both hands gave her a long lingering kiss.

The following Sunday, D.C. Pugh climbed the steps at the front of the Manor House and knocked on the heavy oak door. "Is Mr Beddows at home?" he enquired.

He was shown into the drawing room. "D.C. Pugh, Hereford Constabulary," he announced, holding up his warrant card. "May I have a few words with you, Sir?"

"Certainly, Officer. How can I help?" replied Tom, slightly puzzled.

"I have reason to believe, Sir, that you may be able to help us with our enquiries."

"If I can."

"Can you account for your movements on Wednesday morning, last week? At twelve midday to be exact, Sir."

"I was in my office. Why do you want to know?"

The Officer replied, "And can you give me the name of anyone who might be able to confirm what you have told me, Sir?"

"My brother Peter will be able to tell you—" He put his hands on his hips and said, "I wish you'd tell me what this is all about, Officer. I'm obviously suspected of something. Can you tell me what's going on?"

The policeman remained impassive and said, "I have already spoken to your brother, Sir, and he has told me that you were out of the office at that time. He said that you went out at about ten o'clock but he was not able to tell me where you went. I was hoping that you would be able to fill in the gaps for me."

Tom thought for a moment and said, "I remember now. I wasn't in the office. I went for a drive."

"Do you often do that, Sir?"

"Not often, but sometimes," he replied, with a note of irritation in his voice, "What's this all about?"

The police officer scratched his upper lip with his pencil and said, "We are conducting an enquiry into an incident which occurred near the village school on Wednesday. A small boy was going home for his lunch when a man approached him and he was sexually molested. It was a rather nasty case and the boy is very distressed."

Tom clutched his wife in horror, "And you think it was me. Why?" he demanded in amazement.

The Officer continued, "We had a phone call from someone who said that he saw a man answering your description loitering near the School and after the incident a car bearing your registration number was observed, speeding away from the scene."

"And did the boy himself describe me?"

"He is too distressed to be interviewed, Sir. We have a WPC with him now and she will ask him questions when they think he is ready."

After the Officer left, Tom recalled that he had gone for a walk in Cwm Woods and he met Terry Jones of Cwm Maerdy Farm. They'd spent an hour or more, leaning on a gate, talking about farming and forestry.

"Thank you for your help, Sir," said the Officer, when he returned, "Mr Jones has confirmed your alibi, so we will not need to trouble you any further. Our original information came from an anonymous source and they're often not reliable, but we have to follow these things up of course. We won't be troubling you further on this matter."

In the Old Black Lion that evening, the incident of the assault on the small boy was the main topic of conversation.

"I heard that it was Tom Beddows."

"Really?"

"He was questioned by the police."

"Someone saw him hanging around by the School, where it took place."

"Well, he must be a bit funny in the head. He lived in the woods, didn't he?"

"And he looks such an ordinary chap too. They let him off, but I say there's no smoke without fire, and I wouldn't trust him with my kids."

When mud is thrown, some of it sticks, even on the cleanest of people, and this mud had been thrown by Matthew, aided and abetted by Brian. The gossip in pub and post office, like Chinese Whispers, became more distorted with each telling. Matthew had gathered round him a small group of trusted friends, who were prepared to say anything in return for Brian's cash.

The assault on the boy had been genuine, but Matthew had seen an opportunity, and an anonymous call to the police station and some well-chosen words in the right ears were all that were needed. It was left for human nature to do the rest.

Before long, Penny noticed women whispering as she passed by and Tom even noticed his secretary shuddering slightly if he got near her.

In the Manor House, Tom found Penny wiping away a tear. He put his arm round her and asked, "What is it, Darling?"

She leaned her head against his chest and began to sob. "It's all going wrong. We were so happy and everything was going right for us and now I can sense that people don't like us."

"Oh, I think that's an exaggeration."

"No, it's not. We used to be respected and now I find people looking at us as if we've crawled out from under a stone." She reached into her pocket for a handkerchief and he held her tight against him.

"I know, I know," he murmured, "I can feel it too, everywhere I go, but you don't believe any of it, do you?"

Penny immediately stopped sobbing and sat upright, looking startled, "No," she cried, "No. The thought never entered my head, but it's still upsetting to see that people do believe it."

"I'm not sure that they do."

"But they do. I can see it in their faces. I know that you would never do anything like that, but the rumours are persistent, and people are beginning to believe them."

Tom took her handkerchief and dabbed her eyes, "Mike Sturgess and others warned me about Brian Jones. He told me at the harvest supper that he was dangerous and was out to ruin me and I'm sure he's behind all this. It's got to be him."

"There can be no other explanation. I don't know how he's managed it, but these rumours have got his stamp all over them. He was the same at school and he's just carried on. The only difference is that he's increased the stakes and now the consequences are more serious."

In Hereford hospital the condition of Jean Evans had improved slightly, but her only real hope was still the specialist operation in America. Sam visited her every day, becoming ever more convinced that he was doing the right thing; stealing goods from his employer and passing them on to Peters.

The money he received was only a small proportion of their value, but he was stealing regularly and his funds were building up. He still had a lot more to accumulate, but he was confident that he would be able to raise enough and was beginning to make enquiries about travel arrangements.

He came out of the travel agent's, putting brochures into his pockets and making mental calculations. "Another two months," he thought, "Hang on Love, I'll get you there."

"You're doing a good job," said Peters, when he made one of his deliveries.

"I'm not proud of myself."

"Hey, you can't afford to have scruples in this business."

"I'm only doing this because I'm desperate and I can't think of any other way of getting the money I need."

"How is your wife?"

"None of your business. You keep giving me the money and I'll keep bringing you the goods."

While these recent events had been unfolding, Pete and Melanie had continued to live together in the Mill House. They'd refurbished the building and it had become an attractive home. Dai Evans Restoration Ltd had been contracted to do the job and Chris Gregory did much work on the structure. He had lovingly restored the timbers and the old mill machinery, spending several months working on it.

On one occasion, Melanie had come home unexpectedly and found him asleep, smelling of whisky.

"What do you think we should do about it?" she asked Pete.

"I think we should do nothing. We have no complaints about his work and the job is nearly done. His drinking problem is nothing to do with us."

The Mill House nestled in a dingle just outside the village. It looked picturesque, reflected in the mill pond. The still water was like a mirror and a perfect image of the old building was reflected in it. The pond had water lilies at its edge and brilliant damsel flies hovered over them. It was approached from the lane by a flight of worn stone steps and the original workings had been preserved as a feature of the kitchen.

The building that used to be a working mill, ringing to the sounds of grinding machinery and the sounds of men hauling flour sacks, now rang to the sounds of two young children. The couple were still unmarried, but they had added twin girls to the Beddows family, and they had reached the age where they could crawl and explore their surroundings.

Pete and Melanie sat drinking coffee, watching the girls on the carpet. Melanie looked up and said, "You don't think there's any truth in these terrible rumours about Tom do you? Everyone's talking and I overheard someone in the Post Office saying that he's always been a bit odd and they thought he could easily be a child molester. It makes you shiver doesn't it?"

"Tittle-tattle. Don't believe a word of it. You know what people are like and well-known people like Tom often do come in for this sort of thing. It's like the Royal Family or show business people, anyone in the public eye falls victim to it. Perhaps it's the evil green-eyed monster coming out. You know, jealousy—I was talking to Tom this morning and he reckons that Brian Jones is at the back of it all in some way and I think he's right. That man has got a screw loose and we all know how he feels about Tom."

Tom and Penny spent an unpleasant summer. Matthew was doing his job well and unpleasant rumours surfaced regularly. Tom Beddows was the main topic of conversation in the pub on many evenings and the campaign inevitably took its toll on the couple. Penny was often in tears and they began to argue, which was a new experience for them as their marriage had been harmonious up to now.

They had frequent visits from the police. The child molester had made further attacks in the county and Matthew seized on every opportunity to implicate Tom by making calls to the police and eventually his campaign became self-perpetuating. Whenever there was a case of attacks on children or women, Tom was automatically suspected. He was also accused of shop-lifting and there were rumours that he was having an affair with his secretary.

Not only did Tom have to endure the humiliation of police enquiries, but other things went wrong. Sales of his cider began to fall off in the local pubs as people associated his name with the attacks. He also had problems in other areas, when there were enquiries into his planning applications and dark suggestions of fraud and bribery. The environmental bandwagon gathered momentum again and that also, became self-perpetuating as the ranks of protesters swelled. Tom Beddows' Country Cider became synonymous with all that was bad in the environment.

"Anyone would think we were blackening the sky and polluting rivers, instead of brewing cider from good Herefordshire apples and providing jobs," Tom complained in exasperation, as they drove through a group of protesters at the factory gates.

Chapter Twenty Two

The summer's gloom was lifted in September when Pete and Melanie got married. It had been the weekend that they spent in the Cotswolds that had been the catalyst in their relationship and after that they had decided to live together.

"Well, why not?" was Melanie's answer, when he had summoned the courage to ask her to live with him. "We'll be seeing a lot of each other now, so if we lived together it would make life easier."

"That's wonderful, brilliant, but are you sure?"

"Everybody's doing it these days."

"Maybe, but there are still a lot of people who feel that it's wrong and I want you to be sure that you're happy with the idea. I really had in mind your Mum and Dad. They're a bit old-fashioned, aren't they?"

"Oh, don't worry about them. I've already told them about it and persuaded them that it's a good idea."

Pete looked at her open-mouthed and then burst out laughing, "How did you know I was going to ask you?" he asked, in amazement, "I didn't know myself until this morning."

"You would never have heard the last of it if you hadn't—not after your performance that weekend we went away," she added, smiling broadly.

So they began to live together and that led in due course to the birth of the twins and their wedding.

The wedding took place in the village church and Tom was best man. A large number of guests had been invited and the church was full. After the ceremony, the couple walked back up the aisle, passing under the stony gaze of Miss Acton, high in the roof. Outside, the photographs were taken and as the couple walked between the topiary Penny and Jane threw confetti.

They were transported to the reception in a carriage drawn by two dappled greys. On the Manor House lawn a large marquee had been erected and Jane had gone to a great deal of trouble with the decorations. There were beautiful floral displays and swags and garlands on the tables.

Jane had liked art at school and was now developing into a

successful artist. She stood back to admire her work with obvious pride. "It looks lovely Jane," said Penny, as she walked around the marquee before the ceremony.

Brian Jones' activities had brought a blight on the lives of the Beddows family and they were determined that there would be no expense spared to lift their spirits. Penny sat on the top table, wearing a maternity dress as her baby was only two months away. Tom stood and tapped his glass with a spoon to attract attention and launched into his best man's speech.

"I'm delighted to see that my little brother has found himself such a beautiful wife. Little did Penny and I realize, when we interviewed Melanie for her job as secretary, that we were in fact choosing a wife for him. I'm sure you will all agree that we could not have chosen better."

After some anecdotes and jokes he went on to say, "I'm sure you'll all be aware that we've had a less than pleasant summer, because of the rumours that have been circulating, but this is not the time to dwell on them. I just wanted to say that this very happy occasion has taken our minds off them for a while and I want to thank Pete and Melanie for that. I wish them every happiness together."

Walter was one of the guests, more frail than ever, and needed someone on either side to help him to his seat. He'd been brought from an old people's home in Kington, where he now lived. He had been the victim of a stroke and was paralysed down his left side, speaking in an unintelligible mumble, and being helped with his eating. A helper from the home was spooning food into his mouth and wiping his face, as he dribbled from the corner of his mouth.

Tom had gone over to greet him with, "Hello, Walter, old chap. How are you keeping these days?" but the old man stared vacantly and showed no signs of recognising him.

Tom walked away with the tears welling up. The old man's mouth organ would now stay silent and no longer would he be the star turn at the village hall. The cloud of gloom, which he used to experience when the school holidays were coming to an end, had been closing in this summer, and the sunshine brought out by the wedding had turned back to darkness after seeing Walter so destroyed.

Matthew intently studied the document on his desk. He stood up and paced around with his hands behind his back. He had his eyes fixed on the floor as he paced and then he sat down again and reached for the telephone, dialling with one eye on the book. While he waited for the call to be answered, he thumbed back through the pages, slowly shaking his head. "Hello, Mr Jones. It's Matthew —Very well thanks—No, but I've got some information on a different matter, which I think you ought to know about—Yes, I know you're very busy, but this is important."

He took a deep breath and said, "Well, Mr Jones, I've suspected for a long time now that Sam Evans has been stealing from the firm and our associates, so I set a trap for him and now I have proof, and it's big. He's been systematically milking us—Yes, more than five thousand pounds so far, and I may find more. He's been clever and it takes a lot of sorting out. I'm getting there, now that I know how he's done it—No, there's no doubt." He held the phone away from his ear until the angry response subsided, "Yes, I'm absolutely sure. I waited until I was certain before phoning you."

Brian arrived at the office, took off his coat and shaking off the rain hung it on the door. Lighting a cigar, he sat down at the desk and tapped the open book. "Show me," he demanded.

Matthew turned a page and said, "Look at those figures in that column and then compare them with the ones in that column."

There was silence while he studied the figures. His cigar went out and he re-lit it before continuing with his reading. Eventually he pushed the book away and said, "I can't see anything wrong with them. What's all the fuss about? I was watching a good programme before you dragged me away."

"Those are the figures based on Evans' dockets and delivery notes. Now compare them with these."

Again there was silence, while he compared the two sets of figures, and once again his concentration allowed his cigar to go out and he re-lit it before going back to the figures. "The sneaky bastard," He eventually muttered, "He's been very clever."

"I'm sorry to drag you back into the office on your day off, but you can see why I thought it was important. If we hadn't spotted it, he could've gone on for years and just imagine how much he would have got away with."

Brian nodded, his brow furrowed with deep thought.

Matthew stood to one side of the desk waiting for his response.

Brian took his cigar from his mouth, studying the end with a puzzled expression, and Matthew shuffled paper on the desk while he waited.

"Well, Matt, do you remember the little talk we had in my garden? You know, about your career in the firm and the possibility of advancement or other less pleasant possibilities?" He continued quickly, without giving him chance to answer the question. "Now that you've found this out, you have another stick with which to beat Beddows."

Matthew looked perplexed and asked, "How do you mean?"

"Use your imagination man. I'm talking about blackmail. It's not for me to tell you what to do, but I'm sure that an intelligent chap like you can turn this to your advantage. Isn't it said that every cloud has a silver lining? Now if you really use your imagination, you can make this information work for you—but I can see that you don't know what I'm talking about."

"Think about it. You've got a hold over Evans. Blackmail him man. Let him know that you've found him out and press him into service in your campaign to nail Beddows. I don't want to know how you do it, just do it and while we're on the subject of Beddows, it seems to have gone quiet recently, I haven't seen evidence of your efforts."

"Oh, I'm still working on it."

"Well, you're not working on it well enough for my liking. It's about time we had some action. I want to see him finished and for good and your efforts haven't done that yet. Let's see if you can use Sam Evans to good advantage."

At the maternity hospital, Tom held the door open for Penny and then struggled through with her suitcase. "You need wide doors these days," he joked as she went through.

"It won't be long now," said the nurse, ushering her through a door into a small side room.

Penny climbed into bed and said, "Are you sure you won't change your mind about being with me at the birth. You know how I'd like it."

"I know, Dear, but like I explained, I'm a bit squeamish about that sort of thing and I think it's women's work. You'll have enough on your plate, without worrying about me passing out. I nearly fainted when I cut my finger on that sardine tin last week. No, I'll wait outside, until I'm called."

He was told to wait outside while she was examined and he sat on a bench in the corridor, thumbing through some magazines. He was excited, as the moment had arrived at last, but he hated hospitals, and he had still not got over his childhood fear of them. He had gone weak at the knees as soon as they drove into the car park and now he sat with uncomfortable butterflies in the stomach, lifting his feet as a cleaner passed down the corridor with an electric floor polisher.

"Thank you, Love," said the West Indian lady, "Don't look so worried, Love. Everything will be alright."

He looked up at the heavy woman in the blue uniform, who smiled down at him as she pushed her machine.

"Is it your first?" she asked.

Tom nodded. "Yes, I'm new to this game."

"Ah, lovely." She did some more polishing and asked, "And will you be there with her?"

"No, I don't think so."

"What a shame. She needs you at a time like this and the doctors encourage it these days, don't they?"

"Yes, I understand they do."

"My husband was present when I had my little Henry and I don't know what I'd have done without him. He was such a support and he wasn't looking forward to it, because I had to beg him to be there, but do you know when it was all over, he told me he wouldn't have missed it for all the tea in China. I think a man feels more involved if he's there at the birth, don't you? Well, I must get on," and she moved off down the corridor.

Before she had got as far as the next bench, she was kissed on the cheek. "Thank you, Dear," said Tom, "I'm just off to be with my wife when our child is born."

"Ah, lovely," she responded and continued with her polishing.

A nurse called, "Mr Beddows, you can join your wife now if you wish. It won't be long, so I think you'll have a Monday's child—fair of face," she smiled.

Sarah was born before Monday came to an end while Tom held Penny's hand and mopped her brow.

"One more push, Love, we can see the head now," he said, "That's the way. Here it comes. That's the way. Soon be all over."

The baby cried and when the midwife announced that it was a girl, Penny squeezed his hand and sobbed, "It's a girl, It's a girl. It's Sarah."

When the baby had been cleaned and wrapped in a little blanket, Penny cuddled her and cried, and so did Tom.

"The nurse was right," he said, "She told me we'd have a Monday's child—Fair of face, so the rhyme says. Fair of face, just like her Mum."

"She's so tiny," said the tearful Penny, "Just look at her tiny little hands, so perfect."

Tom held out a little finger and Sarah's tiny hand wrapped round it and held it tightly. "I think she likes me," he croaked, struggling to keep back the tears.

"Another little Beddows," she whispered, "Sarah Beddows."

Next morning, Tom arrived at the hospital clutching flowers and carrier bags. He strode along the corridors whistling his way towards the ward and found Penny, sitting up in bed, reading a letter which she hurriedly hid under the sheets when she saw him. She lifted her tear-stained face and he kissed her. He put his bags down and went to look at his new daughter sleeping in her cot.

"She'll be waking up for a feed soon, so you'll be able to have a little cuddle," said Penny.

"She's so beautiful and so tiny." He pulled up a chair and sat down. He asked, "What were you reading when I came in?"

"What do you mean?"

He held her hand and said, "You were reading something that looked like a letter and you put it under the sheets when you saw me coming."

She sobbed and flinging both arms around him, burst into tears.

"Shh, shh," he said softly, holding her head against his neck.

The woman in the next bed looked embarrassed and a nurse drew the curtain around them. Penny pulled the crumpled letter from under the sheets and making an effort to regain her composure, said calmly, "This was delivered this morning and I thought it would be another letter of congratulations, but when I opened it—" Her voice failed her and she handed him the letter.

He looked puzzled and smoothed the crumpled paper with the back of his hand. It read:

Dear Mrs Beddows

You ought to know that your husband is mentally unbalanced. He is a child molester and has a particular taste for little boys and very young girls. Ask him about the little boy outside the village school and the one in Eardisley last month.

Years ago, he lived a weird life in Cwm Woods and he used to entice children into his shack. I have heard of several children who had unpleasant experiences when they were playing in the woods.

How can you live with such a monster?

If you will take my advice, you'll make sure he does not get too close to your child when it is born. He is not to be trusted with children.

You have been warned. The letter was unsigned.

Tom stared at in disbelief and then looked at his wife. Her face was tear-stained and mascara was running down her cheeks in dark streaks. "Oh, Tom, it's spoiled it," she sobbed, but he did not answer. He threw back the curtains and ran down the corridor, but he was sick before he got as far as the toilets.

Wednesday is market day in Hereford and farmers from all over the county go into the city to buy and sell livestock. Terry Jones had been up before it got light and herded his cattle into the stock lorry, as he was selling twelve of his finished beasts. They had been in the lush bottom meadow and had fattened well, so he was hoping for a good price. Dawn was breaking as he eased the lorry into the lane. In the east was an orange slash of light low in the sky and, as he headed towards the city, the grey fields began to take on some of the colour.

He switched on the radio and turned it up high, so that he could hear it above the engine's roar. It was playing a Rolling Stones hit and he drummed his fingers to the rhythm. The market was busy and he had some difficulty negotiating obstacles and reversing into a position where he could unload his livestock.

After the paperwork was completed, he got himself a cup of tea and leaned on the rails of the sale ring, watching the cattle being auctioned. He stood next to Steve Bufton and the two men drank their tea and exchanged views on the price of sheep and cattle.

"A good turn out today," observed Steve, glancing round the saleroom.

"Aye, it is Steve. Let's hope I get a good price for my beef."

The sale proceeded and the man in a white coat prodded the cattle with his stick to keep them moving, while the auctioneer accepted bids for the animals.

To the uninitiated, the scene was one of utter chaos. The ring was surrounded by a mass of farmers, nearly all of whom wore tweed caps and dark green coats. The cattle bellowed and the auctioneer shouted out a continuous stream of apparent gibberish. No one appeared to be bidding, but most of the farmers were known to the auctioneer and he knew which ones to watch. Just a wink or a raised eyebrow was sufficient to register a bid.

Terry was satisfied with the price that he obtained. "Good," he said, turning away from the ring, and he leaned back against the rails. "Well, how's the second hand tractor trade these days, Steve?"

"Oh, up and down, you know."

"And how are the family?"

"Okay, but I've had a bit of bother recently. My brother's little boy was assaulted by that sex attacker and it's caused a bit of upset in the family."

"Oh dear. I'm sorry to hear that. I think it's about time the police caught that bloke, as it's been going on for so long."

Steve looked about him and leaning closer said, "There's still a lot of talk about Tom Beddows being the one who's doing it."

"I know. I don't believe it though. Do you?"

"I'm not so sure. The police have been round to see him a few times and a while ago, I'd have said no way could it be true, but I'm not so sure now. The rumours don't go away and they say he used to entice youngsters into his shack. I've heard a lot of people say that."

"Aye, I think a lot of people are thinking the same way now."

Tom's sister held baby Sarah in her arms at the Manor House and gently swayed her backwards and forwards. "She's absolutely beautiful, so perfect," she sighed. She stood in the big bay window with the sun streaming in through the stained glass panels, casting patches of coloured light over her and the baby. The patches of light flowed over them as she swayed, red, yellow, and blue.

"I'm trying to decide which one of you she looks like. I can see Penny in her eyes and I can see Tom around the mouth, but she's so beautiful." She sat down in an arm chair, still holding her, swaying backwards and forwards humming a lullaby and kissing her on the forehead.

Jane was part of the cider business but she had taken a back seat. She helped with the public relations, but her real interest was in art, and she was a keen landscape painter. She had recently opened an art gallery in a converted barn at her cottage; a typical Herefordshire barn, which she had refurbished to create an attractive gallery in which to display her pictures.

The paintings were landscapes of the Herefordshire and Welsh countryside in oils and painted with sensitivity. They often had a background of misty blue hills and a patchwork pattern of fields and hedgerows with black and white houses in the foreground. The trees were silhouetted against the sky and she populated the pictures with sheep and cattle. "I'm interested in the seasons," she would say, "and different qualities of light."

She nuzzled the baby's head and said, "When I'm a famous artist, you'll be able to tell your school friends that I'm your Aunty."

At Westwood Farm, Brian was playing cards with three colleagues from the office. The air was thick with cigar smoke and Angela was sitting in the kitchen, watching a portable television. Snatches of raucous laughter, cheers and groans came from the lounge. She was watching a game show with little interest and she absent-mindedly groped in a purple box and popped chocolates in her mouth.

One of the contestants had won a washing machine and the smooth game show host was exploiting the excitement which it generated, but it didn't excite Angela. She merely stared vacantly at the screen and popped another Turkish Delight into her mouth.

She had drifted into marriage with Brian and, although she'd been happy for the first few months, the marriage had deteriorated. Soon after the wedding, Brian had seemed to lose interest in her. He still bought expensive presents but they often sat through entire mealtimes without speaking, each lost in their own thoughts. It was rare for them to be seen out together and her life had become set in a routine which did not please her.

She was a girl who needed the affection which she was not getting from her husband and it seemed to her that she was just like the washing machine that the television contestant had won. As soon as Brian had won his prize, he was no longer interested in it. His obsession with Tom also frightened her and she worried whether he was becoming unbalanced, as he talked about little else. It upset her, because she still had a soft spot for Tom and had followed his success with interest.

"Where's the coffee, Angela?" he shouted from the lounge, "I asked you half an hour ago and there's no sign of it yet."

She took in the tray and put it on the card table.

"Thank you, Mrs Jones," said Jack.

She smiled and moved towards the door. As she put her hand on the door handle, another wave of guffaws boomed from the table, interspersed with the name Beddows. That had a big impact on her and all the frustration and anger boiled to the surface.

She swung round and shouted, "I'm sick and tired of your nasty sly comments on poor Tom Beddows! You never stop and it goes on day after day, week after week! Will there never be an end to it? That poor man!" Her voice rose to a screech as she became angrier and all that had been building up exploded in one venomous out-pouring. "And the same applies to you, Jack. You're no better. Get out—all of you!"

Her outburst was out of character and the men were stunned into silence. The guests looked at each other in amazement and Brian muttered his apologies.

"These people are our guests," he protested.

"Go on, get out, and never come back!" she shrieked, throwing Jack's coat at him.

Brian nodded at his guests and with an embarrassed smile, gestured for them to leave.

When he'd shown them to the door, offering profuse apologies for his wife's behaviour, he returned to find Angela on her hands and knees, picking up the cups which had been knocked off the table.

"Do you have an explanation for your appalling behaviour tonight?" he demanded, standing over her, "I've never been so embarrassed. What are they going to think of me now?"

"I don't care."

"You don't care?" He raised his hand as if to hit her and she flinched, covering her face with both hands, but when no blow came, she slowly took them away and rose to her feet. He was standing close to the table, with his face half turned away, glaring at her from the corner of his narrowed eyes. He breathed noisily through his nose and clenched and unclenched his fists, struggling to control his rage.

She spoke in an almost inaudible whisper, "You were going to hit me!" she said incredulously. "You nearly hit me!" She had suffered a lot in her marriage, but it had never occurred to her that he was capable of assault. Her voice rose in volume and became more shrill. She looked at him with contempt. He was still trying to control himself and glaring at her with furrowed brow and narrowed eyes. She was confused and her mind was spinning wildly as her emotions unified into an inexorable wave of hatred.

"You bastard!" she shrilled, prodding him painfully in the chest.

He shrugged his shoulders and moved towards the door, but the emotional wave engulfed her in a maelstrom of boiling surf and she lost all self control. She picked up a broken cup and hurled it at the back of his head but it bounced harmlessly from his shoulder as she cried, "You nasty little worm. Poor Tom is twice the man you are, and twice the man you'll ever be!"

Her face, stained with running mascara, froze as he turned and raised his fist above his shoulder. For a few seconds, time seemed to stand still and then the silence was broken as he moved towards her, emitting a guttural noise from the back of his throat and smashed his fist into her face. She staggered back and fell heavily to the floor, where she lay unconscious for a few seconds, before becoming aware that she was lying face down, bleeding into the rug surrounded by broken crockery.

The pain from her face was as nothing to the pain she felt inside. The loathing she felt for the man, blotted out any other thoughts. His feet were inches from her face as his menacing form stood over her. She rolled onto her back and looked up at him, but his features were obscured, as his head was in silhouette against the electric light; a dark shape, surrounded by a halo of light.

It seemed to her that she lay there for several minutes, while the waves of revulsion turned to waves of anger and, as she reached to the table and pulled herself up to her knees, a second blow thudded into her cheek, splattering blood which mingled with her tears and stained her white blouse. One side of her face was covered with blood, tasting salty as it ran into her mouth, and she was dimly aware of Brian picking up debris and a broken chair as she struggled to her feet once more.

By the time Brian had picked up the pieces and tidied the room, Angela was knocking at the door of her parents' house. Mike Sturgess opened it and found her standing on the doorstep, bloodstained and torn, but free of Brian Jones. The door opened and she said, "I've left him Dad. Can I come in please?"

Chapter Twenty Three

Tom kissed his wife as he came in and said, "I've arranged for Mrs Edmunds' daughter to look after little Sarah and we're going wassailing tonight. You've never done it and I think you'll find it good fun."

Later that evening, a high-spirited crowd carrying sticks and shotguns assembled outside the leaning porch of the Old Black Lion and made their noisy way by torchlight through the village. At the church, they turned into Ford Lane and on through the gate into the orchards.

It was a winter evening and the temperature had dropped to below freezing. Frost sparkled in the light from the flaming torches as the procession passed through the orchard. The flames cast dancing shadows and with a wild flapping a flock of roosting wood pigeons took to the air, startled as the noisy crowd passed below them.

The leader of the group, the farmer who owned the orchard, held up his hand and the procession halted, standing with breath condensing in the torchlight and drifting up through the skeletal branches. With great ceremony, a bowl of cider with a slice of toast floating in it was put down on the grass and he then went up to an old apple tree and started beating the trunk with his stick.

That was the signal for everyone to join in and the tree was soundly beaten with sticks, while others shouted and crashed kettles and tin trays together.

The cacophony carried on the still night air through the trees and over the fields as far as the village; the hubbub being augmented by the deafening sound of shotguns fired into the tree.

One after another the guns were discharged with an awesome noise which vibrated the air and made the ground throb underfoot. Tom could feel the noise in his stomach and, when it ceased, his ears were whistling and the air was heavy with the smell of cordite.

A cheer rang out when the guns stopped and then cider was poured over the tree's roots. As the gun smoke slowly cleared and everyone drank copious amounts of cider, Tom put his face to his wife's ear and explained that it was to improve the orchard's yield for the following year.

"The tradition goes back for centuries," he explained, "I read in a book of old customs that wassailing comes from the old Norse 'waes heil', meaning to be of good health, and the idea is that the greeting is transferred from the drinker to the tree."

He took a long drink from his glass and said that they now had to eat a morsel of the cider–soaked toast, and that when they'd all had some, they must leave a tiny piece for the robins.

Penny asked, "Do you think that's the origin of the expression 'drinking a toast'?"

"I don't know. I hadn't thought of that. I'll have to have another look at the book."

The dancing and drinking went on into the night and Tom and Penny meandered off through the trees, with Tom holding the flaming torch high in front to light the way. Back at the pub, they could hear the sounds of merry–making drifting across the meadows in the darkness and in the frosty air they occasionally caught a glimpse of a dancing light surrounded with a halo.

Sam continued to cheat the company by taking goods to Peters and his funds were augmenting with each trip that he made. It hurt his conscience, but he muttered to himself, "I don't care if they lock me up and throw away the key, as long as I can get Jean to America before it's too late." Her illness was the driving–force which kept him going in his criminal activities.

He reversed the lorry into the garage after a long trip to Hull and jumped down from the cab. It had been a long day since setting out before daylight and he was keen to have a bath and get along to the hospital. He slammed the door, just as a message came over the public address system, "Sam Evans to the office please. Sam Evans to the office'. The voice echoed round the empty building.

"Damn!" he thought, "I wonder what that's all about, not another trip I hope. I've had enough for today," and putting on his jacket, he climbed the steel stairs to the offices.

The office girl smiled, "Hello, Sam. It's Matthew Davies who wants to speak to you before you go home."

He tapped on the door marked *Transport Manager* and put his ear against it to listen for a response. "Come in," was the muffled answer.

Matthew was seated at his desk behind an untidy pile of papers. He had his back to Sam and was holding his glasses up to the light. As he entered, Matthew turned and put his handkerchief in his pocket. He put on his glasses and peered at him over the rims, gesturing for him to take a seat. "Mr Evans," he began, "Let's not beat about the bush, I've asked you to come up here to tell you that I know."

"Know what?" replied Sam with genuine innocence.

"Know what, indeed," replied the transport manager, mimicking Sam's response.

"I don't know what you mean."

Matthew put both elbows on the desk and leaned forward towards him, "Tell me, Mr Evans, how do you fancy a nice refreshing change of job? You've been driving for many years according to my records."

"What, in the warehouse or something like that?"

"I mean at Tom Beddows' Country Cider, but let me explain what I'm driving at, because I can see that you're puzzled. The fact is, Mr Evans, I know all about your thieving from this company. I know what you've been up to, down to the last penny, and I have done for a long time. I know exactly how much you've stolen. You must have known that you couldn't go on for ever without being caught. It was only a matter of time before someone saw through your amateur attempts to cover it up." He stood and moved round the desk, standing above him, so that he was against the light from the window and Sam could not see his face.

Sam gulped in surprise and then was silent, before asking in a trembling voice, "Are you going to report me to the police?"

Matthew threw back his head and laughed, "Oh, dear me, no, I'm going to give you a new job, a new beginning."

"What do—"

Matthew interrupted, "Let me explain. I think we can help each other here. I want to strike a bargain with you. The deal is that I do not report you and we forget all about your little transgressions and, in return, you will help me by taking a job which I've arranged for you at the cider factory."

"Now don't ask me how I arranged it. Let's just say that an old school friend owed me a favour. As from first thing tomorrow morning, you will be working as a caretaker's assistant in the factory and, when you've settled in, I want to see you again and we'll discuss how you can be of assistance to me."

Sam walked to his bicycle with his mind in torment. He was struggling to make sense of the situation into which he was drawn. Unknown to him, Brian had decided to act, because Matthew's campaign to destroy Tom was faltering and, although he had been successful in blackening Tom's character, it was not destroying him and Brian would settle for nothing less.

He had decided to use the power he had over Matthew and Sam to gain access to the factory. He had an evil plan; a chess game in which both Sam and Matthew were to be pawns. Sam was to be put in the front line and Brian was using Matthew to place him there, in order to put distance between himself and the deed, in case things went wrong.

At the Manor House, the family were sitting down to dinner and Pete and Melanie were there with their daughters. The now frail Major and Mrs Hudson were also guests and they sat with their backs to the fireplace. Jane had a boyfriend, Paul, a shy bespectacled young man, who glanced around him, overawed by his surroundings.

Tom had decided that the occasion justified the use of the dining room, which was not often used. It was an impressive room sparkling with chandeliers and the walls were hung with dark landscape paintings in heavy gilt frames.

"It was carved by Grinling Gibbons," said Pete, noticing Paul studying the ornately carved fireplace.

"Pardon?"

"I said it's carved by Grinling Gibbons. The fireplace, I'm talking about."

Tom looked across the table at Jane and asked, "How is your art gallery coming along?"

"I'm quite pleased," she replied, "but it's a bit out of the way to attract many visitors. I had a few tourists in the summer but now that it's winter hardly anyone comes, so I'm looking for new premises in the centre of Hereford."

"You should have more customers there," commented Melanie.

"Yes," said Pete, "I suppose that the more people who see your work, the better; if you want to become famous, that is."

Tom said, "I think your work has improved out of all recognition in the last year."

"That's because I've been taking it more seriously and putting much effort into it."

Paul had hardly spoken since he arrived, so Tom tried to involve him in the conversation and said, "Paul we're having a shoot on the estate tomorrow and you're welcome to join us. I'll find a spare gun for you if you like."

"I have never ttttried and I—"

Jane interrupted, "Paul doesn't believe in killing for sport."

"I dddon't believe in kkilling anything for any reason, not for ffffood, and certainly not for sport," stuttered the boy, not looking anyone in the eye, but keeping his gaze fixed on his plate.

Tom looked at the beef which he was just about to eat and put down the fork. "Does that mean that you're a vegetarian?" he asked.

The boy blushed and mumbled, "Yes."

"Oh, Paul, I do wish you'd told us, so that we could have prepared something else for you and, Jane, you never said anything," said Penny, in consternation.

Jane responded, "He didn't want to make a fuss and put you to any trouble."

Pete had never been one to miss out on the opportunity of a controversial discussion and he tried to provoke the hapless boy, "We've never had a vegetarian here before. Do you never eat beef, Paul? Because this is particularly good beef and it came from Buttercup, a lovely brown cow with long eyelashes. She used to lick my hand and when I went in her pen she followed me like a puppy. I saw her killed and she—"

"Pete!" cried Melanie, with raised voice, "That's enough of that," and turning to the boy, who was squirming with embarrassment, she said, "Take no notice, Paul. He's only trying to tease you."

Paul was too overwhelmed to speak and he looked shyly at his girlfriend, who smiled back at him reassuringly.

She glared at her brother and said, "You really must learn to be more tolerant of those who hold different views to yourself. There's a big world outside Lower Kings Canon, full of people with different backgrounds and attitudes to yours, and they're not all potty, just different, that's all."

Paul coughed nervously and nibbled a finger nail.

Tom tried to put the boy at his ease by saying, "Perhaps we'll be able to find a few clays for you to practise on, if you don't want to kill anything," but that only increased his discomfort and he knocked over a wine glass in his confusion.

"Never mind, Paul, no harm done," said Penny, dabbing at the stain with a napkin.

Pete got back to the subject of the shoot, which he found infinitely more interesting than a boy with cranky vegetarian ideas. "About this shoot, Tom," he began, "How many guns are there going to be?"

"Ten."

"And are we allowed to shoot at ground game?"

"No, not unless you see a fox. You can have a go at them as we're getting overrun with 'em this year. I think they're being caught in the big towns and the silly so and so's aren't killing them, but bringing them out into the country for release. You can tell that a lot of them are urban foxes just by looking at them, and it's very misguided, because they're not doing the foxes any favours. There are too many of them for the available food supplies and they're only used to scavenging in dust bins, so they can't look after themselves in the wild for long. Poor old Jack, down the lane, is trying to make a go of free-range chicken farming and the foxes are causing havoc amongst his flock. They're getting them in the daytime, so the bloke doesn't stand a chance."

Tom was warming to one of his favourite topics, one on which he held strong views, and he continued, "These blasted people in the towns have no idea what life in the countryside is all about. They don't live in the real world but in an unnatural urban environment, and it breeds strange views."

"They see the country as one big playground for them at weekends; damned armchair conservationists with their stupid ideas. They want to ban fox hunting, you know. Have you ever heard anything like it? They bleat about not wanting eggs produced in factory farms, because it's unkind to chickens, and then they protect the foxes and try to ban hunting because they don't want the dear furry creatures harmed, making it impossible to produce eggs any other way."

Penny attempted to interrupt him, but it was too late now that he was in full flow.

"No one loves the countryside more than I do," he continued, "I used to be part of it, but these conservation people get on my nerves. They don't think the issues through, but just react emotionally like the rest of the flock, and then there are those who complain about the flails on the backs of tractors, which keep the hedgerows trimmed."

"'Oh, you mustn't do that.' they say, 'You must treat the hedgerows more sensitively'. Well, how do the stupid people think we ought to deal with the hedges? Pleach them every year? They seem to think that flails are sinful. What Tommyrot! If we didn't cut them back, they'd soon grow into a row of trees and then they'd complain about them overhanging the roads and where would all their hedgerow creatures live then?"

There was silence and he picked up his knife and fork and continued with his dinner.

"Phew, I'm glad you got all that off your chest," said Jane, "I bet you feel better now."

"Yes, well let's change the subject now," said Penny, passing more vegetables to Paul.

"Do you know what a woman at the factory said to me the other day," asked Pete, continuing on the same theme. He mimicked the woman's high-pitched voice, "She said, 'I never bring a real Christmas tree into the house because I'm a conservationist and I can't bear the thought of cutting down the world's trees'."

"Well, there's another example of woolly thinking for you; emotional thinking by the green brigade. Don't they realize that Christmas trees are grown like a horticultural crop? If it wasn't for the Christmas tree trade they wouldn't exist and, as soon as one is cut, another's planted to take its place. They take carbon dioxide from the air and provide a habitat for wild life. These woolly thinkers confuse the issue with cutting down the rain forests. It's the same thing in their book. They don't make a fuss about cutting cabbages, do they? And it's just the same."

He took a drink and continued, "The stupid woman said that she uses a plastic one, because it's better for the environment—plastic." He spat out the word with contempt, "A plastic Christmas tree made from precious oil resources and producing toxic fumes when it's burnt. It's upside-down thinking." He took a deep breath and shook his fist at the ceiling.

"I think there'll be a sharp frost tonight," said Penny, trying to move the conversation onto less controversial tracks.

After dinner, they all moved into the lounge for coffee and the main topic of the evening was the following morning's shoot.

The morning dawned bright and crisp and the guns assembled on the lawn at the front of the house. Tom addressed his guests, "It's a grand morning for it, gentlemen, couldn't be better, and I hope you all have a good shoot. The beaters are in position and when I give the signal the first drive will begin. Safe shooting, please."

He had a whistle round his neck and wore knee breeches, tweed jacket, and cap. The guns were standing in a group, passing round a flask of whisky, and some of them had black Labradors for retrieving the game. It was a cold morning and the men stamped their feet and rubbed their hands together.

In the meantime, the beaters had walked to the other side of the copse and lined up with a space of ten yards between them. Several had a spaniel on a cord. The beaters were also stamping their feet and blowing on their hands, their breath condensing in clouds in the sharp air. They waited for the signal to move off.

Tom asked the guns to move to their pegs. Pete had been allocated a peg below the big oak next to Alwyn, who had two black Labradors, Sue and Bramble, sitting at his side, nostrils a-quiver and trembling all over.

Pete opened his gun and holding it up looked through the barrels to check that they were clear. He put two cartridges in and closed it with a clunk, squinting over the trees from where the first pheasant would appear. Alwyn had a practice swing of his gun, wriggled his shoulder, and swung again.

The beaters were feeling the cold, "I wish that bloody whistle would blow," grumbled one, "before I freeze to the spot. I can't feel my feet."

The sound of the whistle reverberated round the chill woods and the beaters moved off in a line, tapping trees with their sticks and making as much noise as they could. The spaniels ran on ahead, burrowing into clumps of bracken, tails wagging vigorously.

The guns heard the muffled noise and concentrated their attention on the strip of sky above the trees. The first bird went up from the bracken; a cock bird, which rose, zig-zagging through the branches into the open sky, clattering in alarm. The beaters shouted "Forward," and then stood still as it rose and within seconds two shots rang out, and then there was silence, whereupon the men resumed their noisy progress through the undergrowth, thrashing their sticks and struggling to lift their legging clad legs through the ensnaring briars.

The first pheasant had flown nowhere near Pete. It had gone far over to the left but soon three birds came over at the same time. He raised his gun and, pulling it tight into his shoulder, swung through the bird's line of flight. His shoulder kicked back from the recoil and then he fired the second barrel almost instantaneously.

"Good shot, Pete!" called Alwyn, "A left and a right!" as the birds' flight stopped in two bursts of feathers and they fell to the ground with a thud. One lay still and the other flapped momentarily and then it too was quiet. Pete turned to look, flinched as Alwyn fired, and then the guns all along the line blasted into life.

The birds were coming over in quick succession and the air all around them was filled with loud bangs and the thud of falling bodies. The men were firing and reloading as fast as they could then, suddenly, the tumult stopped when the whistle signalled the end of the first drive. Wispy feathers floated to the ground like snow flakes and thirty-nine pheasants lay on the bracken.

"About thirty-nine or forty I reckon. That's not bad for one drive and no runners," remarked Alwyn, as he opened his gun and took out the cartridges.

The Labradors were slipped from their leashes and sent off to retrieve the game for the beaters to collect and put in the Land Rovers.

"No foxes came out from there," observed Pete, "just a few rabbits and a hare."

After the fourth drive, the guests were given lunch in the Manor House and the beaters had theirs at a trestle table in the barn. The table was put out down the centre and stew was ladled from a large tureen, which it had taken two men to carry from the kitchen. Conversation died away as they ate their lunch and for a while it was eaten in silence. They sat on wooden benches and the spaniels lay curled up on the floor with one eye on the table in case morsels came their way.

Austin Thomas broke a piece of bread and threw it to his spaniel, which was curled up at his feet. The dog's fur was wet and matted with burrs and bits of twig. She was weary after a busy morning's burrowing in the undergrowth and putting pheasants into the air. She snapped up the bread and then sat with her chin resting against Austin's thigh.

"She's worn out already, before the afternoon's drives," he said between mouthfuls.

"This stew's going down well," commented another of the beaters, "I was ready for it, I don't mind telling you. That last drive through the spinny was bloody hard work. I don't know why they don't clear some of those briars. It would be easier on the beaters."

He belched loudly, "Pardon me," he said, "and there's another thing that would improve these shoots; a few more bloody stiles. I reckons I left my balls on the barbed wire up on the hill."

"I didn't see them," said Mark, "I think I would have noticed them." He stood up and said, "Hey, boys, did anyone notice Dai's balls hanging on the barbed wire? Sorry, Dai, nobody saw them. You'll have to more careful where you leave them hanging in future."

The stew was followed by a hunk of Wensleydale cheese which was more than enough for the group.

Dai belched again and cutting himself a generous portion of the cheese said, "I'll tell you something boys. You'll notice that the shooting won't be so hot this afternoon after they've been on the brandy. They'll see two pheasants when they go up and it's fifty fifty which one they hit, so it'll halve the bag this afternoon," He belched again, "Pardon me."

The afternoon's shooting took place in falling temperatures. It became even colder and there were flakes of snow in the wind. The beaters continued shouting and thrashing their way through the woods and the shotguns blasted all afternoon. As the bitter wind increased in strength and the bare branches waved against the leaden skies, the pheasants became more difficult to hit as they accelerated across the sky. The shooters' hands were numb and blue on the cold steel of the gun barrels and several hip flasks of brandy were handed round.

At the end of the day's shooting, there was a bag of one hundred and twenty pheasants and two foxes. The beaters took off their mud caked leggings, tied the pheasants at the neck and hung them in pairs. Tom produced port and glasses and they stood in the barn, sipping the port and warming their hands on the electric heater.

Brian Jones heard the guns as he drove past the estate and pulled into a gateway for a while to watch the shoot. He smoked a cigar and watched the Labradors covering the ground to pick up the game. He was on his way to Mike Sturgess's house to see Angela. Since she had left, he found that acquaintances were asking awkward questions of her whereabouts and he'd decided to go and get her back.

She was in the kitchen, preparing a meal for when her father got home from work. The aroma of garlic drifted through the house and as she closed the oven she heard the knock on the front door.

"Oh, it's you," she said, finding him on the doorstep. She was drying her hands on a tea towel and pushing stray hair from her eyes with the back of a wrist.

"Hello, Love, I've missed you and your cooking," he said, sniffing the air and moving to kiss her. She pulled away to avoid the kiss and said, "What do you want?" blowing from the corner of her mouth at the stray hair that her wrist had failed to control.

"I don't want to talk on the doorstep. Aren't you going to ask me in?"

"No," she replied, "the doorstep will do for you."

Brian stretched out two hands to her shoulders, but she winced and pushed his hands away.

"I want you to come back to me," he said.

"You've got a nerve," she snapped, "My face has hardly healed from when you hit me. How do I know it won't happen again? I had a job to stop my father from coming round to get you and he wanted me to go to the police and have you charged with assault."

He put on a dejected expression and pleaded, "Please, Angey."

"There's no way I will ever come back and share your roof because I wouldn't feel safe, and I detest the way you try to bring poor Tom down. I know that all those wicked rumours are something to do with you?"

She stepped back and started to close the door.

"Just a moment, what about a deal?"

"What sort of a deal?"

Brian took out a cigar and lit it before speaking, "I'll tell you what I'll do. If you come back, I promise that I'll forget all about Tom Beddows. I'll never say anything about him again and if there are any further rumours about him, they'll be nothing to do with me."

Angela looked at him intently and asked, "Is that a promise?"

He nodded solemnly.

"And how do I know you won't hit me again?"

"I won't. I'm ashamed of that and very sorry."

"And will you do all you can to undo the harm you've done Tom?"

"I promise," he replied, licking his finger and making a sign across his throat.

When Mike Sturgess arrived home, the house was filled with the smell of cooking and in the kitchen was a note,

> *Dear Dad,*
> *Your dinner is in the oven, Mum has*
> *gone shopping in Hereford, and I have*
> *gone back to Brian.*
> *Thanks for having me.*
> *Love, Angela.*

Sam Evans left the hospital with a heavy heart. The slight improvement had dissolved away and now Jean was worse than ever.

He did not yet have enough money to send her to California and since Matthew had discovered the thefts his source of extra income had disappeared. The job that had been found for him at the cider factory paid very little and he was feeling low. He was heading for the office at Jones' Road Haulage because he'd received a message to go and see Matthew Davies as soon as possible.

"How's the new job going Sam?" asked Matthew, as he entered the office.

Sam was still perplexed by the turn of events and mumbled lamely, "Alright."

Matthew smiled and said, "Now we come to it," sliding without comment a small cardboard box across the desk to him.

Sam took it up automatically and asked, "What's this?"

"Just a little present, Sam. No don't open it yet, not until I've explained."

He placed the box on the desk and folded his arms.

"This is where you can start to repay the firm for your little transgressions. If my old school friend has done his job properly, he should have installed you in the warehouse where the bottles are stored before they go out. Is that right?"

Sam nodded.

"So if I'm right, you have access whenever you want. Now you can open your little present."

In the box was a hypodermic syringe and a bottle of liquid. Sam took out the bottle and turned it over in his hand, looking at it quizzically.

"You're looking very puzzled, but let me explain what you are to do with it. You will go to warehouse A1 and at the end away from the doors, you'll find cases of plastic bottles marked *Still Vintage Cider*. Make absolutely sure that you are alone and inject a small amount of the liquid into some of the bottles near the top."

"The needle will go through the plastic easily, but you must be certain it's 'still' cider, otherwise it'll fizz out through the hole. Make sure that you've wiped this little bottle first and you must wear gloves. We don't want any fingerprints on it.

Sam stared in amazement, his mouth hanging open, "No way," he responded, pushing the box away from him.

Matthew smiled and firmly pushed the box back to him, "I don't think you have a choice. You'll be no help to your wife in jail and that's exactly where you'll be if I spill the beans, as they say. Also when you've done this, you may qualify for a golden handshake from your old firm," he said, tapping the side of his nose and winking. "It would pay for a trip to California."

Sam thought for a moment and said, "What's in it?"

"Nothing for you to worry about. It'll just make a nasty taste and spoil Mr Beddows' sales figures a little. It's very strong stuff, so you won't lick your fingers will you? Of course, if anyone else got to hear about it, things could go badly for you, if you get my drift. Mr Plod, the policeman, might be making notes about you in his little black book."

Sam's face was expressionless as he put the box into his pocket and stood up to leave. Matthew hurriedly moved to the door and put himself between it and Sam.

"There's something else before you go," he said, "When you've done the deed, I want you to top up the bottle with apple juice and then sneak up to the offices with your broom in your hand —in case you're spotted and that'll give you a reason for being there—and put the bottle and this note on Tom Beddows' desk, okay?"

Sam bit his lip and began to shake his head, but Matthew wagged his finger at him, lifted his hands to his lapels and, sagging at the knees said, "Evening all, 'ello 'ello what's going on 'ere then?"

Sam frowned and turning on his heel pulled open the door.

Matthew had been given the bottle by his boss, Brian, "It's something that'll make his cider taste very nasty indeed and give a few people the tummy–ache. It will be so unpleasant that it'll put them off drinking it for ever," he had said, rubbing his hands together, gleefully.

Both Sam and Matthew believed that they were involved in a plan to damage the cider business by making people ill, so that the publicity would have an adverse effect on the sales figures. They were blissfully unaware that they were the unwitting agents of a much more sinister plot. The hatred which festered within Brian was now out of control and he was driven to make evil decisions without the slightest pang of conscience.

This force was making him a pawn in the game, just as much as Sam and Matthew, and was driving him to kill people in order to gratify his lust for Tom's destruction. The bottle which he'd given to Matthew was in fact a very potent poison and he was quite happy to allow people to die and for his two agents to be involved in their murders.

The poison, which he had obtained from who knows where, was strong enough to kill with one tiny drop and he had put enough in the bottle to kill scores of people.

It was a foggy day when Sam set out to perform his task. A dense freezing fog enveloped the factory; so thick that he could not see the warehouses as he cycled through the gates, but as he crossed the car park the featureless grey mass of the building slowly took form and he went into warehouse A1 as instructed.

The steel doors screeched when he opened them and he could hear the echo of his footsteps in the silent building. He felt his heart pounding against his ribs and he went weak at the knees. The cases of vintage cider awaiting transport to supermarkets in London were what he was looking for, and he found them stacked on a palette, with Tesco, London, written on the top.

He began to take the bottle and syringe from his pocket when, with heart-stopping suddenness, the steel door screeched again and he dived behind the cases and crouched down. The doors screeched shut and, looking through a gap between the cases, he saw a man in a brown smock carrying a clipboard. He was whistling and making notes as he moved around the warehouse, studying the palettes of cider.

Sam crouched lower as the man came nearer. The cases were not high enough to conceal him properly and with panic in his eyes he looked around for a better hiding-place, but there was none. As the man got closer, he was convinced that he would be caught and desperately searched the recesses of his mind for a reason to give why he was hiding there.

He was wishing he'd never agreed to be part of the plan. "I should have said 'no'," he thought, "and hang the consequences," but he was here now, trapped in a nightmare from which there was no escape.

The man continued to whistle and was now only a few feet from him. Two more piles of cases to inspect and Sam would be looking him in the eyes from his hiding-place and he could think of no convincing excuse why he should be there. The man was now at the next pile, turning one of the cases round to read what had been written on the side. He wrote on his board and moved towards Sam, who was preparing to stand up and say something, though he still didn't know what.

There seemed to be no point in waiting and being caught furtively crouching down. He hesitated, when the man stopped to take out a handkerchief and blow his nose, a loud blow which echoed round the building and, as the echo died and the man put his handkerchief away, another noise disturbed the silence. "Here is a staff announcement. Will Mr Jackson please go to the main office on the ground floor. Mr Jackson to the main office please."

The message was difficult to understand because it was distorted and the steel walls made it echo, but it was Sam's salvation. The man in the brown smock turned on his heel and Sam listened to his reverberating footsteps and the screech of the door, and then all was silent again. He drew a deep breath, exhaled noisily, and with pounding heart accomplished his mission and left without being detected.

Sam had played his part and within hours the lethal cargo was loaded onto a lorry and the vehicle inched its way out of the yard to join the slow-moving traffic on the main road. It was still foggy and the lorry was moving at crawling speed, stopping and starting, until it left the city and got into open country.

The driver had instructions to take his load to a Tesco's distribution centre in north London and he was impatient. It had taken him an hour to get out of the city and he was behind schedule. He opened his lunch box and, turning the radio up high, he ate his sandwiches. He drove with narrowed eyes, leaning forward to see through the blanket of fog. The engine throbbed and he made as rapid progress as he dared under the atrocious driving conditions.

In a London supermarket, an under-manager had been called into the Store Director's office. "Come in, Mr Roberts. Sit down. I wanted to have a word with you about the BWS. I've just been doing my rounds and I couldn't help noticing that it's looking a bit thin, quite a few gaps on the shelves, you might say. What are you doing about it?"

The young under-manager was nervous. He'd had a bad week; one of those when everything seemed to go wrong. It wasn't his fault that some of the shelves in the beers, wines and spirits section were under-stocked. He was having problems with the distribution system and had spent much of the week on the phone trying to obtain fresh stock. Beer and cider was very low and he was annoyed that he was having to endure a ticking off from his superior, when no one could have tried harder to solve a problem which was not of his making.

"Yes," he said, "It's a bit thin, to say the least, and I haven't been able to get any satisfactory answers out of the distribution people, but I've been promised that there are new supplies of cider and beer coming today, so I'm hoping that I'll have the problem solved this afternoon, at the latest."

"I'm pleased to hear it," said the director. "Don't let it happen again."

"Certainly not, Sir," said Mr Roberts, as he left the room. He closed the door behind him and vented his pent-up frustration by putting up two fingers at the closed door and sticking his tongue out.

By mid-day, the outstanding beers had arrived and the shelves were filled without delay, but Mr Roberts found himself on the phone again, chasing up his cider. He leaned back in his chair, lit a cigarette and loosened his tie while he waited for the phone to be answered. "Hello, put me through to dispatch please—David, you're getting me into a bit of bother here. I've been chasing cider all week and now my shelves are almost empty and I'm catching the flack from all angles; the customers, the boss—What? Alright I'm listening."

The Dispatch Manager explained that he had been expecting a delivery from Tom Beddows' Country Cider in Herefordshire. "I've been waiting for it for a couple of days, but now I've got it," he said, "It came in an hour ago."

"Good man. Get it off to me then. That'll save my skin," he grinned.

"Ah, it's not as simple as that. You've probably been too busy to hear the news, but there's been terrible pile up in fog on the A40."

"And?"

"Well, unfortunately, the Beddows lorry was involved in it; a nasty business, people killed. Going too fast in the fog, I expect. The news has been full of it and there have been pictures on TV. It was a terrible multiple pileup. One vehicle stopped and then everyone kept piling into him. The fog was so thick they didn't have time to brake and just slammed into the others."

"Anyway, to cut a long story short, the driver's in hospital, not seriously hurt fortunately, but the lorry turned over and you can imagine what's happened to the cider, all that glass, what a mess. Running down the road in rivers it was, by all accounts."

"Oh, no, I don't believe it!" replied Roberts, "and here was I thinking my week was taking a turn for the better. Is it all a write off?"

"Yes, it is really. The lorry was towed off to a garage and one of our trucks went out to salvage what it could. We've got it in the yard, but I don't think that what we've retrieved can be sold, what with the labels being scratched and cut and all that."

Roberts returned to his shelves to find the Store Director talking to another manager. "Roberts," he called, "What's going on? These shelves are still looking very sorry. It's the cider we need and double-quick too if you want a career in Tescos."

Roberts explained what had ocurred, but the director was not sympathetic. "I don't care what happened. I don't care if a flying saucer landed and loads of little green men got out and drank it all. It's your responsibility and I want to see cider on these shelves within the hour. Do you understand? I don't care how you do it, but do it."

Roberts went back to his office and lit another cigarette while he struggled with his problem.

Within ten minutes, he was behind the wheel of a Tesco's van heading for the distribution centre. Scavenging amongst the bottles salvaged from the crash, he was able to find some that looked presentable. Most of them had scratched and stained labels, but with some help from two warehouse men, he was able to find enough to get him out of trouble until he had a new delivery in the morning. They picked out the most presentable and loaded it into the van.

"Thanks for your help lads," he said, as he closed the van doors. I'm indebted to you."

Penny sat in the drawing room reading another poison-pen letter. She received them on a regular basis and the content was usually vicious criticism of Tom. At first, they had upset her and then she treated them with contempt, but in recent months she'd undergone a change of attitude. She re-read every letter, over and over again, analysing the contents and found herself beginning to wonder if there was truth in them.

Did he have a perverted interest in children? Had he cheated over planning permission for the factory? Was he unbalanced? Because he did have an extreme reaction to his grandfather's death and he'd slipped into what the doctors call clinical depression. Had he been shoplifting in Hereford? Had he had an affair with Mrs Taylor, who worked in the office? He'd had the opportunities.

All these and other questions kept going through her mind. She watched him over the breakfast table and she eyed him when he was looking at television. Her mind was in torment because up to now she'd had had complete faith in her husband, but the poison in the letters was beginning to fester.

Was there some truth in them after all? Surely not. She knew him too well, but the nagging doubts grew with every letter that she received.

It seemed to her that she was drifting away from her husband, who had been her lover and best friend. Sometimes she felt that she didn't know him. She occasionally noticed a look in his eyes that had not been there before. Or perhaps it had been and she had never noticed it.

She became aware of a curl to the corner of his lip which she hadn't seen before. Did she really know him as well as she thought? After all, when they had met, he was a strange, ragged creature, living like an animal, so he must have had something weird about him to live like that. Normal people didn't do it. And what about all the talk of children being approached by him when they were playing in the woods? Could it be true? She put down her sewing and stared at the ceiling, heaving a sigh which shook her whole body.

"It's time we revived the tradition of Christmas morning parties in the ballroom," announced Tom, a few weeks before Christmas. "It's a tradition going back generations and it's a shame that we let it stop when we took over the Manor. When I was a boy, Christmas without them was unimaginable."

"Alright," replied Penny, "Let's do it."

And so the tradition was revived and preparations were made. Pete and Melanie were not planning to be there, because they had already decided to spend Christmas in the Provencal villa.

They were going over with the twins. "It would be fun to go for a sail in *Sweet Cider* on Christmas Day," Pete had said, "We could open the presents, have lunch, and then go on board. I've already had a word with the skipper and crew and they're quite happy. They jumped at the idea of a Christmas Day sail. I must say, I thought they'd be a bit grumpy about having to turn out, but they weren't."

"That's a lovely idea. We could sail down the coast to Monte Carlo, have supper in Frederick's, and spend Christmas night on board. What a novel way of spending Christmas," she said, eyes sparkling, "We could have a Christmas tree on board and tinsel in the rigging."

"Hey, let's not get carried away."

And so it was decided and the plans at the Manor went ahead without them.

On Christmas morning, Tom and Penny stood in the doorway of the ballroom greeting the guests as they arrived.

"This is just like the old days," grinned Bill Price, filling up his plate.

The old house was alive once again with laughter and the excitement of Christmas morning. The fragrance of wood smoke and cigars was in the air and, as in the past, all the estate workers and their families were invited, but their ranks had been augmented by an additional guest list of colleagues from the factory.

Jean Evans could not be there, but her husband, Sam had been invited and, after struggling with his conscience, he had decided to go along. He was due at the hospital later and he thought it would be nice if he could tell Jean all about the party.

"A Happy Christmas, Sam," said Penny, shaking his hand, "I'm so glad you could make it."

"A Happy Christmas, Sam," said Tom, "How is Jean? We've sent her some flowers at the hospital. We thought they might cheer her up for Christmas."

"Thank you very much, Sir, I'm sure they will," he replied, not looking him in the eye. He had great admiration for Tom and his arrangement with Matthew filled him with self-disgust.

Tom continued, "Let's hope that the New Year will bring good news and happier times for you both."

A log fire was burning and four of the lads who worked on the farm stood smoking their Christmas cigars, warming their backs on the fire. One of them looked up at the paintings and chandeliers and said, "Posh in here, ain't it?"

"Aye, it's a fine old house," replied his companion.

"Yes," said Bill, "I used to come here on Christmas mornings when I was no bigger than a bucket. I remember I couldn't see over the table there. The old Major was the Squire in those days. He was a real gentleman—not that I'm saying Tom Beddows isn't mind," he added hastily, looking over his shoulder.

"He was a gentleman, that's true," said another in the group, "but he was a bit behind the times when it came to farming. He lived in the past and didn't invest in new machinery and ideas. That's why he went bankrupt, the poor old sod."

"Aye, we could see it coming. All the other farms had tractors and combines when he was still using horses and the whole place got run down. It would have been cheaper for him to buy the new machinery than to pay the wages of all the workers he had to have, but he couldn't see it."

A small boy in a Donald Duck mask ran through the middle of the group with both arms outstretched, "Eeeeagh rat tat tat tat," he went, as his aeroplane banked and headed for the Christmas tree in the corner.

"Come here, you little monster," called his mother, grabbing his arm, "You stand next to me and don't move until I tell you to or I'll tan your hide, Christmas or not."

"Don't worry, Mrs Lloyd," said Tom, "When I was his age, I used to hate coming here because my mother made me stand still, just over there, and I can still hear her saying, 'Don't move until I tell you to'. It's Christmas morning; a special day for kids, and I don't mind if he wants to be an aeroplane."

Mrs Lloyd was just about to answer him when Tom cupped a hand to his ear and said, "What's that noise? Can you hear it?" He stood on a chair and shouted to attract attention.

"Children, can you hear that noise?" he asked again. As the excited chattering and laughter died down, he put a finger in the air and said, "I think I can hear the sound of sleigh bells, can you?" No one answered and a few cynical children shook their heads.

"There it goes again". He put both hands up and looked surprised. "Could it be Father Christmas, do you think?" The small children looked excitedly about them and the older ones looked at each other with a knowing, worldly look.

"It is. Everybody say 'Good Morning, Father Christmas'."

"Good morning, Father Christmas," rang out as the red coated figure entered the ballroom, bent by his sack of presents. He had one for every child in the room and called out their names, one by one, as he took the parcels from his sack.

The guests drifted out of the Manor and made their way home to their Christmas dinners, the children clutching their presents.

The Beddows family left the clutter of the ballroom and went into the drawing room. Major Hudson was helped by Jane and Paul.

They led him to the fireplace and sat him in the big, leather armchair. The family settled around the fire, wearing paper hats and drinking sherry, until the bell summoned them to the dining room.

"Here we go," said Tom, getting to his feet. He linked arms with Penny, saying, "Shall we lead the way Dear?"

They moved towards the door, "Come on, Dad, time for lunch," he said, looking at the Major, who had his head back and his paper hat at a jaunty angle. His mouth was open and his eyes closed.

Jane went over to help him up. "Tom!" she shouted in horror, putting both hands over her mouth, "Oh, God, no!"

✖

Pete and Melanie were sitting down to their dinner in France when the phone call came, dampening the festive mood and causing the cancellation of their sailing trip.

"The poor old boy," murmured Pete, as he disconsolately poured the gravy on his turkey.

The funeral took place on a chill December morning a few days after Christmas and, standing with his head bowed in the church yard, Tom's mind went back to his father's funeral, and his mother's, and then there was Frank's, and soon there would be Walter's.

The churchyard, which had been baking in the hot sun on the day of the hay-making all those years ago, was now a cold, grey place. The only sounds were of slow footsteps and their muffled echo in the damp air. The dripping yew trees were dark, brooding, presences, as the black procession moved silently between them.

After the holidays, Tom arrived at the office and took off his coat. On his desk was a bottle of apple juice and a note, which read:

MEMORANDUM
Mr Beddows.
I would like a word sometime about
the enclosed sample, but it is not urgent
so just hang on to it until I have another
sample to compare with it in a few days.
Mr Edwards, Quality Control

Tom read the note, put the bottle in a desk drawer, and began the day's work.

Chapter Twenty Four

In the Old Black Lion the grandfather clock ticked and the domino players rattled their pieces on the table. The game continued while the landlord read the evening paper, supporting his head on the bar with both hands.

It was early in the evening and it would be another hour before the pub began to fill, so he was catching up with the news before the rush started. He pulled himself a pint and returned to his paper. The front headlines were of an outbreak of food poisoning in the London area. Twelve people had been taken to hospital with severe stomach pains and the authorities were holding an investigation to track down the source. The landlord tut-tutted and turned the paper over to the sports page.

Little Sarah had been put to bed and Tom and Penny settled down in front of the television for the evening. There was not much to interest them and Tom pressed the buttons to avoid the poor quality American programmes.

"Just look at that," he complained, "nothing but American soaps, disgraceful. The only thing worth watching tonight is the news."

Four of the people who were said to have contracted food poisoning had died and another twelve were seriously ill. The source had been traced to a London supermarket and the police suspected that a group of animal rights activists had contaminated food. The presenter said:

> Police believe that the food has been contaminated by animal rights activists; the same group who last month set fire to lorries used for transporting livestock to market. The outrage bears all the hallmarks of their work but as yet no group has claimed responsibility for the attack.

The news report then went on to interview the supermarket manager and relatives of the victims.

Penny got up to make the cocoa and said, "I'm always amazed how some people can feel that strongly about the welfare of animals. There would be more sense in it if they were concerned about the welfare of human beings, with all the problems that there are today. Some of these idiots seem to think that animals are more important than people."

Tom needed to be at his desk early the next morning, so he made an early start. The car had been left out all night and he had to scrape ice off the windows before he set off. It took much effort as it had been a hard frost; a hoar frost that had spangled the cobwebs and the delicate tracery of the bare twigs. As he drove, he switched on the radio and hummed along with the music.

He drove through freezing fog, so he had his headlights on. He made slow progress as it was dense and he kept the rear lights of the car in front at a safe distance, glad to be following someone as it made the driving easier.

Bare trees loomed up out of the mist and passed, ghost-like, by his side windows. As he slowed down to negotiate a roundabout, his attention was caught by the main news item. Another thirteen people had died and the police had tracked down the source of the problem. He sighed and shook his head.

The cider plant was not far ahead and he turned off the main road, screwing up his eyes to see through the fog. It was not so easy now that he was no longer following someone. He wiped the windscreen with his sleeve and noticed headlights in his rear view mirror. He frowned as they got close to his rear bumper.

"Fancy driving that close in these conditions," he thought, "If I stopped suddenly, he'd go right into me." Up ahead, he saw some red rear lights. He glanced in his mirror again and the headlights had changed to flashing blue lights; more blue lights were also in front of him, intermittently illuminating the car's interior.

He pulled into the car park and stopped. The whole place seemed to be filled with police cars, with their flashing lights turning the grey fog into a pulsating blue mist. The legs of police officers, standing in front of their cars, cast long dancing shadows from the headlights.

He switched off the engine and surveyed the scene with bewilderment but, before he could open the door, it flew open of its own volition and he found himself dragged out by many pairs of hands. There was much shouting and running about and he found himself face down with his wrists handcuffed behind him. His nose was pressed tight against the tarmac, which was cold, smelling of diesel oil, and he felt his suit rip at the shoulder.

At the police station in Leominster, he was put into an interview room and three officers sat on the other side of the table. The room was bare, save for a filing cabinet in the corner. He shook his head when he was offered a cigarette and his brain struggled to understand what was happening.

Before he had been bundled into the police car, someone had told him he was under arrest. He didn't have to say anything, but if he did, it could be used against him. He'd not caught why he had been arrested, because the policeman spoke too quickly and he'd been confused. The pain from a kick in the ribs also blurred his perception.

"Will someone tell me what's going on? Why am I here? And do you know that one of the officers kicked me when I was on the ground?"

No one replied, but a policeman pointed at a plastic bag on the table and asked if he had seen it before. It contained a bottle, the one which had been found in his desk.

"Yes," he nodded, "but what's this all about?"

"Yes!" replied the Officer, ignoring his question, "Would you like to tell us where you have seen it before?"

"Well, if it's not that one, I've seen several just like it, because it's one of the bottles we use for samples at the factory. We collect samples of the apple juice for analysis."

"Apple juice, heh. It's jolly strong stuff isn't it?"

Tom folded his arms and said, "Isn't it about time you told me why I've been arrested? What am I supposed to have done? Surely I have a right to know?" He could feel the tears of frustration coming and his mind was cast back to his school days, when he found himself in Miss Acton's room because of situations that Brian had engineered.

He was experiencing just the same sensations. It was the feeling of injustice which really hurt. He knew he was innocent of whatever he was accused of, but the feelings were all the more intense because he had not yet worked out why he was there.

The Officer stared at Tom; a withering stare that he was determined to return without giving way.

"Mr Beddows," he began, "or may I call you Tom?"

Tom remained expressionless and did not reply.

"You were told why you have been arrested, but I will tell you again. You have been arrested because twenty-four people in London have died of poisoning and several more are seriously ill. Our investigations have led us to you. The common link was your cider; all the victims having drunk it in the last few hours. The cider was purchased in a supermarket and it was all from one batch. We have closed down your factory until further notice, but it gets worse."

"We had some information from an anonymous source which led us to look in your desk where we found this." He pointed at the plastic bag. "We've had it analysed and found that it contained a very nasty poison, the same one that killed those unfortunate people in London. A bit of a coincidence, don't you think?"

Tom sighed and looked up at the polystyrene tiles on the ceiling.

The Officer leaned towards him, "You won't find any help up there. You're in big trouble Tom. The finger prints on the bottle are yours. They match the ones we took from you when you were brought into the station. Take off your belt please and your tie and shoe laces."

The cell door slammed shut and he was alone.

Chapter Twenty Five

The factory had been closed as soon as the police realized that the cider was the source of the poisoning. Production had stopped and the green and gold lorries stood in rows in the yard. The gates of the factory were locked and guarded and none of the workers or management were allowed in. Inside, men in plastic suits and head visors carried instruments which they used for doing tests on juice and equipment.

"They look like spacemen," said one of the workers waiting at the gate, as a team of investigators went into the bottling plant.

A policeman at the gate tried to answer questions put to him by irate workers.

"When'll we be allowed to carry on with our work? The processes need constant attention and, if we don't get in soon, thousands of gallons will be wasted."

"Are we going to get paid?"

He explained, calmly and patiently, that he didn't know the answers and there would be an official statement before long. Occasionally the gates were opened to let police vehicles in and out, but none of the employees was allowed in. Reporters and television crews stood in groups and whenever a vehicle arrived there would be a rush to surround it and a flurry of camera flashes.

A young television reporter stood with her back to the factory, facing a camera. She positioned herself so that the sign *Tom Beddows' Country Cider Ltd.* could be seen over her shoulder. The camera was adjusted and below it a man crouched on one knee, holding a microphone covered in grey fur. The girl pushed some hair out of her eyes, put up one side of her collar to shield herself from the biting wind, and began:

I am standing outside Tom Beddows' Country Cider and as you can see the gates are locked and no one is being allowed inside the plant. We have seen men clad in plastic suits and respiratory apparatus going into the buildings and we are told that they are carrying out tests. It is assumed that they are looking for signs of poison, because it was a particularly potent poison that claimed the lives of victims in London and the police have told us that they have traced it to this cider plant.

One batch was distributed to a supermarket in the London

area and all the cider from that batch was found to be contaminated. The supermarket concerned has cleared its shelves of the drink, but such is the seriousness of this incident that all Tesco stores have been closed. The poison which claimed twenty lives is Methanol, a poison so toxic that only thirty millilitres could be fatal to human beings.

It is not yet known what the motive is, but a man has been arrested. Police have found evidence to link the founder and owner of the company, Thomas Beddows OBE, to the crime and as I speak he is helping them with their enquiries in Leominster police station. He was arrested this morning at eight forty-five as he arrived at his office. The police are not saying what evidence has come to light to link Mr Beddows with the crime, but we are told by sources within the complex that they have found a bottle containing traces of the poison with his finger prints on it.

Groups of workers stood behind the reporter and listened, whilst hoping to be seen on television. She finished her report with:

I have spoken to several employees outside the gates and all are saying that they are stunned by the news. Mr Beddows is well-liked and people cannot believe it. One lady I spoke to was in tears and said that there must be a mistake as Mr Beddows is incapable of such a thing. Lower Kings Canon in Herefordshire is in shock today, as it tries to come to terms with the disaster that has directed the eyes of the world to this sleepy village.

Penny did not move far from the radio that morning. There had been a steady stream of well-wishers to her door, running the gauntlet of the press encamped at the front of the house, but she was too distressed to see them and would not allow them in.

"Are you going to the police station to see him?" asked her mother, as she poured the coffee.

Penny dabbed at her eyes with a soggy tissue and shook her head.

"I think you ought to, Dear. He'll be needing your support at the moment." She handed her daughter some more tissues.

"I'm not going to see him and I don't want to see him ever again!"

Mrs Hudson stiffened in amazement and could only manage, "Oh, aren't you?" and then, "Why? Do you think he's guilty?"

"I don't know. I'm all mixed up."

"Surely you don't think so?"

"I don't know—No, I don't think he could do a thing like that, but this is the last straw. For a long time now my life has been a misery, one thing after another, and living with Tom is destroying me. There's always a nasty feeling; suspicions that he might be something he doesn't appear to be—letters, visits by the police, gossip, and I've had enough. I can't cope any more."

She sobbed convulsively and her mother put an arm around her shoulders, "I know, Dear, I know. You've had a terrible time recently and I can understand how it's all getting on top of you." She stroked her hair and made soft murmuring sounds to calm her.

They stayed like that for a while and then Mrs Hudson broke the silence with, "It's terrible. It said that a lot of those who died were young people, at a twenty-first birthday party. Brothers and sisters died and they said it was a horrible death."

She continued to stroke Penny's hair and then said,

"I think you ought to go and see him and explain, Dear. He'll be wondering where you are and you can't just leave it like this. It'll be hard, but you owe it to him to explain how you feel and how you can't cope any more. Tell him about the treatment you've been having at the hospital. Don't keep that a secret any more."

Penny nodded and blew her nose. She had received another letter that morning. It had not been delivered by the postman but pushed through the letter box later. It spoke of the poisoning and the anonymous writer claimed that he knew that Tom was planning the crime and that the responsibility for any deaths would lie with her, because she was harbouring and supporting a psychopath. The letter ended with:

I have been warning you about him for a long time and now it is too late. It is all your fault and I hope you can sleep at night."

The inexorable stream of letters had planted the seeds of doubt and this was the last straw, as Penny put it. The day's events had been so disturbing that she could not think straight and she was getting through the day in a confused haze, but she knew that she had to go to the police station and explain why she couldn't cope any more, and why she was leaving him. She felt better when the decision was made; as if she'd cast off a crippling burden.

It was the day that Jane opened her art gallery in Hereford; an exciting event for her, as she had been working towards the opening for months, producing enough pictures to hang on the walls and some extras to go into the store room. The gallery had been decorated and furnished and she had decided on cream walls and a dark green carpet. Outside, she had a sign *The Jane Beddows' Gallery* and a banner with the message OPENING TODAY. Tom had promised to come along later in the morning to have a sherry and wish the venture success.

He had said, "I have to go into the office to catch up on some work and I'll see you later in the morning."

She opened the doors and greeted several friends and potential customers. They had been given a sherry as they entered and they looked around the gallery, which smelled of fresh paint and coffee. The pictures were hanging with ample space around them to do justice to the subtle colours and she had fitted a system of spot lights, which lit up the paintings and brought them to life.

The gallery was in the centre of the city, near the cathedral, and she was anticipating a lively trade when it became well-known. She had spent some time over the last few days arranging for some publicity, but she was staggered to find that an army of reporters and photographers had turned up, jostling each other as the cameras flashed.

"I never expected this much interest from the press," she said to one of the customers.

She posed in front of her biggest painting. It was of the Black Mountains, with a field of buttercups in the foreground, and the photographer asked her to stand at the side holding a glass of sherry. She sipped her sherry and a reporter asked,

"When did you last see you brother, Tom?"

"At the weekend, but I'm expecting him soon. He's going to put in an appearance later on," she smiled.

"How did he look? Did he seem normal?" asked another.

Jane hesitated, "Normal? What a funny question. What's all this about, and why the interest in my brother? I thought you were here to cover the opening of the gallery."

"You obviously haven't heard. Your brother won't be coming here this morning."

"Haven't heard what? What's going on?"

The answer she got stunned her and she had to sit down as the strength drained away from her legs.

As soon as Pete had heard the news, he made arrangements for the firm's lawyers to represent Tom, and their solicitor immediately drove to Leominster police station. He elbowed his way through the crowd of pressmen clamouring around the door. A group of young men with shaven heads were shaking their fists at the windows and chanting, "Pois-on-er Pois-on-er." Their faces were twisted with hatred, as they spat out the words.

He arrived in the interview room just as D.C. Pugh had begun further questioning. He looked across the table, "I will ask you again," he was saying. "How did you get hold of Methanol?"

"I've never even heard of it," replied the unshaven Tom.

"It's a very noxious poison and thirty millilitres can kill, but I think you know that very well. There was a lot of it in the cider that went to London and we want to know how it got in there."

Tom shrugged and blew from pursed lips.

D.C.Pugh said, "We found a bottle in your desk with enough of the stuff left in it to do a lot of damage, and it had your prints on it. How do you account for that then? We are also told that your cider is made to your own secret recipe and at some stages in the production you're the only one who's allowed to be involved in it. That's a very convenient arrangement for someone who might be planning to poison it, don't you think?" He lit a cigarette while waiting for the answer.

"Pois-on-er. Pois-on-er," arose from the crowd outside and the chanting increased in volume.

Tom answered. "I went into my office a few days ago and the bottle was on my desk with a note from Mr Edwards in Quality Control saying that this was a sample of the juice he wanted to have a word about. There was no urgency and he wanted me to hang onto it until he came up with another sample to compare with it. Ask him."

"Oh, we will have a word with the gentleman in due course, but tell me, is it usual just to put samples aside like that? What if there'd been something wrong with it? In fact there was something very wrong with it, wasn't there? Wouldn't you say so?"

"It would have been tested already before it was given to me and I'm sure that if it had been contaminated, it would've shown up in the tests. There's no way that contaminated juice could get through the system. It's checked at every stage and, as for my finger prints being on it, that happened when I handled it and put it in the desk."

"So where's the note from Mr Edwards?"

"I threw it away, but if you look you should find it in the rubbish bin."

"We already have and we didn't."

"Tom," said the other detective, "We've been looking back at your history and it's very interesting. On the face of it, you appear to be a very successful business man, owning the biggest cider plant in the world; OBE, well respected, and all the rest of it, but it hasn't always been like this, has it, Tom?"

He smiled and offered him a cigarette before he lit his, "Now tell me, Tom; you don't mind me calling you Tom, do you?"

He stared blankly at the Officer and asked, "What are you getting at?"

"I mean that many people we have spoken to remember you from years back. You live in a small community and we had no trouble finding people who know you very well. We've learned that at one time you didn't have two half-pennies to rub together and you lived in an earthen hovel in the woods. One lady said you have always been a bit peculiar and, when you lived as a hermit, you looked like a wild animal and lived on snails. The village children were frightened of you and their parents wouldn't let them play in the woods in case you attacked them."

He glanced over his shoulder at the window as the chanting rose to a crescendo and there was the sound of breaking glass.

Tom sat with arms folded, looking unflinchingly at the policeman.

D.C.Pugh then continued with the interrogation, "Now it's starting to look like a whole new ball game. You are clearly not the man you appear to be. You've had a very colourful past. I wonder if you could be a cold, calculating killer. We were wondering why you lived on your own, shunning the rest of the human race. Could it be that you detest the rest of us? Normal people don't become hermits do they? Could it be that you hate the human race enough to try and destroy some of it—uh? What do you say?"

The Officer blew smoke from his nose and continued without waiting for a response to his question, "We have also had a word with some of the staff at Hereford General Hospital. Their records make interesting reading. They tell us that you were admitted suffering from clinical depression, but you discharged yourself before you could be given any treatment, and your school record doesn't make nice reading either; a bit of a naughty boy weren't you? A trouble-maker."

The Officer frowned and tilting his head back looked down his nose at Tom. "Did you know, Mr Beddows, that several young people died at a twenty-first birthday party?"

He banged his fist on the table, startling everyone in the room. "They died in agony, young people with a bright future at a party celebrating a friend's birthday and you crushed their young lives. You did it didn't you? Admit it!" he shouted and took another cigarette, lighting it from the stub of the first.

"I did not do it. How many times do I have to tell you?" shouted Tom. He was shaking and took deep breaths to calm himself.

Mr Cargill, the solicitor intervened for the first time, "Officer, my client has told you that he's innocent of this crime and I don't think it serves any useful purpose to shout and bully him into admitting to it. You should know that a man is presumed innocent until he is proved guilty."

"We say he is guilty!" said D.C.Pugh.

"Well, I am telling you I'm not!" shouted Tom, still shaking with rage.

"Admit it! shouted Pugh, "We know you did it and we've got your finger prints on the bottle. Any jury would convict you on that evidence. Admit it."

Mr Cargill said. "I really must protest at the way you—"

"You are supposed to be detectives," interrupted Tom, "You go out and find out who really did it, because it wasn't me." His voice trembled with rage. "And another thing, if you want to know where to start looking for the real poisoner, I suspect that—"

Suddenly, the window shattered with a loud crash. A building brick hit the wall behind them and dropped to the floor as glass fragments showered everywhere.

The cell door slammed shut and the echo reverberated around the small room, shaking the plastic water jug on the table. A police woman put a plaster on a cut over Tom's left eye and when she left Mr Cargill drew up a chair and said, "Well, Mr Beddows, your brother called me this morning and I came straight over. I am so sorry to find you in this predicament. I have to ask you this question. Are you guilty or innocent of this?"

Tom looked at him aghast, "Even you!"

"No, no. That's a question I have to ask, you understand. We've got that out of the way and I want you to know I believe you. Now let's see what we can do to get you out of this mess."

Reaching down to the briefcase at his feet he produced a black file and put it on the table, "Now, Mr Beddows, take some deep breaths and tell me everything you can think of and I mean everything; every detail, whether you think it important or not. Then we'll see what we can do for you."

The two men sat either side of the table, looking at each other in silence, and then Tom looked up at the ceiling and sighed with frustration. "There really is nothing to tell. I'm innocent. What motive could I possibly have? Why would I want to do a terrible thing like that?"

"I can't think of a reason, but we have to think about how the prosecution will present the case and, from what I have gathered so far, they'll make it look bad for you. They've dug up a lot of character witnesses who will talk about you in the old days when you had a breakdown and got away from everything in the woods. It won't look good that you lived the life you did in that shack; a recluse, shunning human company. It'll appear as if you hate the human race, maybe enough to do this. That's what we're up against, I'm afraid to say."

Tom stood up, knocking over his chair, and stared at his solicitor in amazement. "I hadn't thought of all this. It's not going to look good is it?"

Mr Cargill was stony-faced, "Sit down and listen, because I want you to know what you've got against you. Maybe it will concentrate the mind and help you to think of something that might help us to put your case together. Don't forget they've got the poison bottle with your finger prints on it. How do you think that happened?"

Tom sighed again, "I have explained all that to the police, over and over again."

"I know, but I want to hear about it."

He glanced at Tom's exasperated face and quickly said, "Let's leave that for the moment. We'll come back to it when we've talked about other things. I think the police may not have told you this, because it's only just been discovered, but they've found a book in the boot of your car. It was hidden under the spare wheel; a book on poisons. It lists all the known substances which are poisonous to human beings and describes their effect and potency."

He took off his glasses and leaned back in his chair, "It's looking worse than ever isn't it?"

Tom buried his head in his hands. They sat in silence, with shafts of sunlight and shadows from the window bars on the table between them.

Tom broke the silence first, with a barely audible whisper.

Cargill leaned forward and said, "I'm sorry, I didn't catch that."

"It was Brian—Brian Jones."

"Who's he?"

"A very nasty, vindictive person, who's held an insane grudge against me from childhood." He paused and then went on. "But it's difficult to believe that even he, with his deep hatred of me, could do a thing like that." He shook his head in disbelief.

The solicitor took the top off his pen and began taking notes as Tom told the story, going right back to childhood days when Brian stole a spinning top and planted it in Tom's desk to get him into trouble with Miss Acton. He went on to explain how he believed that he was also responsible for involving him in the police enquiries into attacks on children and all the other enquiries.

"And then there were the poison-pen letters to my wife."

The solicitor interrupted him with, "This is all very well, but it won't stand up in court. It's only your word against his and, even if we could prove some of the things and show him to be a vicious character, it's a big jump to accusing him of this poisoning." He held his arms wide saying, "And where's the evidence? I'll have a word with the police though about our friend Mr Jones. They might be able to come up with something, but we've got to do better than this. I'll go now and give us time to do some serious thinking."

He put his hand on Tom's shoulder in a fatherly fashion and said, "Try not to worry, old boy. You're in a pickle, that's true enough, but I'll do my very best to get you out of it."

The tears flowed the moment the cell door slammed shut. Tom sank down to his knees, head in hands. He stayed like that for several minutes; a tragic figure, caught up in a dreadful situation over which he had no control. He could see no hope of getting out of the nightmare. Would he spend the rest of his life in prison? What would it be like? How would he cope?

He was a man who loved the open air, bird song, and the perfumes of the countryside. The thought of being imprisoned filled him with terror. He thought back to his school days and the claustrophobic feelings he had after the summer holidays on the first days back in the Victorian school house with high windows. What would happen to the business he had built up and to all the people who relied on it for their living? And what about Penny and his daughter Sarah?

He gradually became aware that he was no longer alone in the cell. While he knelt head in hands, the door had creaked open and someone had entered.

"Hello, Tom."

He raised his tear-stained face and framed in the doorway was Penny. She looked pale and her hair was untidy. He slowly rose to his feet. It was Penny. He knew that, but she looked different, with a vacant expression, and she looked at him through eyes that did not seem to be hers. She was a stranger.

"Hello, Tom," she repeated, a little louder this time.

"Penny!"

He went to kiss her and she winced and recoiled from him. It was an awkward moment and they stood in silence before Tom motioned for her to take a chair.

"I'm so sorry that you should see me in a place like this." He attempted a joke to relieve the tension. "Miss Acton, my old Head-mistress, always said I'd end up like this."

There was no response.

He continued, "How are you? How are you coping with it all?"

Again she did not answer, but gave an involuntary sob. She took a handkerchief from her handbag and dabbed her eyes. Tom went to put his arm around her shoulder but, when she winced, he pulled away again. He withdrew and sat down in the other chair.

He repeated, "I'm so sorry."

"It's awful," she said, at last, "Awful."

"I know and it all looks hopeless. I don't know what's going to happen. How is Sarah and how are things at home?"

"Terrible. Sarah is very unhappy at school, shunned by all her friends. Their parents have told them to have nothing to do with her. Even her best friend, Emily, taunts her and says her Daddy is a murderer, and you should see the press camped outside the Manor. There are bus–loads of police controlling the crowds and I even have a policeman outside our bedroom in case anyone gets in and attacks me."

Once Penny had broken her silence, everything came pouring out, and Tom listened with mounting horror as she went on, hardly pausing to draw breath.

"We've had enough," she continued, "We're moving out. It's no good for Sarah. It's having a terrible effect on the poor child and I'm having treatment for my nerves. We're going away."

"Away! Away where?"

"I'm not telling anyone, not even you."

She began to cry again, "I just can't cope with it all. Everything was wonderful between us in the old days. We were a good team, good for each other and I was so happy, but it's all gone wrong. The love has gone. No, listen to me," she said, as he opened his mouth to reply, "I've come to tell you something important. I've not been happy for some time and you must have noticed."

Tom shook his head and opened his mouth to speak again but she continued. "Everything has been going wrong over the last year or so. There was all that business about your shoplifting in Hereford and then there was the molesting of the children, and those letters, and everything."

She dabbed her reddened eyes, "I can't cope any more and neither can Sarah. Living with you is bringing nothing but un-happiness and now all this."

"Do you think I am guilty of this, then?"

She hesitated and then said, "No, I mean I don't know. Oh, I don't know what I think any more. There's no smoke without fire, so they say, and perhaps Daddy was right when he told me to keep away from the madman living in the woods. Every one is saying that you have a grudge against humanity and there was a time when I would have said it was nonsense, but now I'm all mixed up and don't know what to think."

"No, Tom I can't believe you did this or any of the other things really. I know you said it's all to do with Jones, but I just can't cope with it any more. Wherever you go, trouble follows, and I've had enough. There's nothing you can say that'll make any difference. I know that perhaps none of this is your fault, but nothing can ever be the same between us again. I've made up my mind that I'm leaving you and that's that."

Tom could think of nothing to say, as he struggled to understand the new bombshell.

She put her handkerchief to her face and sobbed while Tom paced around the cell looking at the floor.

"I don't want you to go," he said, "I can't face life without you. Even if I go to jail, I would like to know that you were still with me and supported me. If you go, everything will be a thousand times worse. I love you Penny." His eyes filled with tears and he repeated, "I love you, please don't leave me, please."

Penny shrugged and said nothing.

He sat down again, resigned to the fact that he could not make her change her mind. He asked weakly, "Tell me where you're going. I must know where you and Sarah are. Even if I end up in jail for the rest of my life, I must know how you both are."

She shook her head.

"Please, Penny, it's bad enough you leaving me, but you can't cut me off from my daughter. Please tell me where you're going."

"Alright, you've persuaded me, but you won't like it. I wasn't going to tell you this as I've already kicked you below the belt."

"Tell me!"

She took a deep breath, "I've met another man and we're going to live with him."

Tom slapped his forehead with the palm of his hand, "Oh, no! I never dreamt—"

"Yes, he's been very supportive through all this and I love him."

"Do I know him?"

"No—well, yes, I owe it to you to tell the truth. Yes, you have met him."

"Who?"

Penny blew her nose and carefully put the handkerchief back in her bag.

"Tell me!"

Very slowly, she lifted her head and looked him in the eye, "It's Pierre le Brun."

"Le Brun, the builder in Provence? My God! I would never have guessed."

"Yes, I've been seeing a lot of him when he was working with a French firm on a building project in Hereford and we're going to live in France. When we're settled I'll give you our address so that you can keep in touch with Sarah. I don't want to stop you contacting her but I don't want you getting in touch with me. It's over and I'll ignore any letters. Do you understand?"

Tom nodded and once again buried his head in his hands.

"Good-bye, Tom," she said, as she tapped on the cell door. "God Bless."

Chapter Twenty Six

Pete and Melanie sat in the Mill House kitchen. Pete watched the twins playing in their Wendy House as he absent-mindedly stirred his coffee. He had one elbow on the table, supporting his head, and gazed at the slowly turning liquid. He looked out of the window at the police car parked at the end of the drive.

The poisoning had sparked off demonstrations against the Beddows family and people had taken to the streets to vent their anger. The factory was the main focus and several demonstrators had been dragged off by the police when they became abusive and threw missiles at the officers. 'Poisoning Scum' had been daubed on the factory walls. A group had also collected at the gates of the Manor House but, as yet, there had been no violence there.

Pete returned his gaze to his coffee and sighed, "It's the end you know," he said, without taking his eyes from the cup.

"What do you mean?"

"It's the end of the road; his business; everything he's built from nothing over the years; all his dreams; his livelihood, all gone."

"You don't believe he did it, do you?"

"I don't know—I mean no, of course I don't, but it doesn't matter if he did or not. The cider isn't selling and the factory is closed."

Melanie's eyes opened wide and she said, "But surely, if he's found to be innocent, which I am sure he will, it'll reopen and people will start drinking it again."

Pete shook his head sadly, "It won't work like that. No one is going to trust it again. Well, would you risk drinking it after all this? It's stirred up such strong feelings that I will be amazed if another drop is ever drunk anywhere in the world again.

Even if we changed the name, they'd find out. The name used to be synonymous with everything that's good and natural about the countryside and now it stands for poison and death. The best advertising man who ever lived couldn't overcome that obstacle. Can you imagine the slogan? 'Drink Tom Beddows' Cider And Die' perhaps, or 'The Taste To Die For'. It's the end I tell you and I don't know what'll happen to us now. I suppose I'll have to try and get a job of some sort."

He sighed and stirred his coffee again.

At the police station, the mob had been dispersed by the riot squad but the press remained; a group of journalists, photographers and television people. One journalist blew on his hands and said, "That was 'rentamob'; yobbos bussed in from London to cause trouble. It's what they thrive on. They don't care what the issue is; animal rights, ban the bomb—It doesn't matter as long as they have a nice conflict with the police and do a bit of shouting."

Inside the police station, Tom was being interrogated again and he had Mr Cargill with him. D.C.Pugh began with, "We've had a word with your Quality Controller, Mr Edwards, and he tells us he knows nothing about the bottle on your desk or of any note, yet you've told us that's how you came by the bottle. Have you been telling us little pork pies?"

Again Tom had to endure a session of interrogation. He constantly denied the charge and he was determined not to give in and admit it. He'd heard of cases where innocent people had admitted to crimes under police pressure and he now understood how easily it could happen. All he wanted was for the nightmare to end and confessing was beginning to seem an easy option, but he kept denying it, in spite of the intense psychological pressure.

That evening, there was a specially extended television news bulletin to cover the events. The news reader solemnly reported that another two of the victims had died during the day and the Queen had sent a message of sympathy to the bereaved relatives. The report continued:

Mr Thomas Beddows, OBE, is this evening still in police custody helping them with their enquiries. As yet, no charges have been brought but a police spokesman said tonight that there was overwhelming evidence pointing to him as being the poisoner, but they are still keeping open minds. It's now known that the cider was contaminated with Methanol, administered with a hypodermic syringe.

Tests have revealed minute holes in the plastic bottles, so it is assumed that it was tampered with after the bottling stage and some time before it went onto the shelves; not during the manufacturing process, as was previously thought. It is believed that the involvement of animal-rights activists has now been ruled out.

All sales of Tom Beddows' cider have been banned world-wide, as have the other products marketed by the firm, such as wines and cheeses. Anyone who has any of their products is advised to put on gloves before touching them, place them in a plastic bag and take them to the nearest police station without delay. The gloves should be burned. Tonight the biggest cider plant in the world is at a standstill and the gates are locked against employees and management alike, while tests and enquiries are carried out.

The normally sleepy village of Lower Kings Canon, near the border town of Hay-on-Wye, has been besieged by newsmen, who have made the village pub the Old Black Lion their base. The cider factory has seen violent demonstrations by mobs of youths, shouting slogans and throwing stones at the police. A mob also attacked the police station in Leominster where Mr Beddows is being held. Police in riot gear broke up the demonstration and the town is peaceful tonight.

Mystery surrounds the whereabouts of Mrs Penelope Beddows and her daughter Sarah. Our correspondent outside the Manor House, the seventeenth century home of the Beddows family, tells us that they have fled to an unknown destination, and none of the staff has any idea where they have gone.

And so the tumultuous day in the life of the village draws to a close as the villagers and the rest of the world try to come to terms with the disaster. Thirty-two people lie dead tonight, victims of a psychopathic mass-killer, and everyone whom we have spoken to in the village has expressed sadness and shock."

The report then went on to interview some of the factory workers and a studio discussion took place on what motivates individuals to commit such crimes.

Later that evening, Jane had a phone call from the police asking her to go into Hereford to see her new gallery. She stood, hands on hips in the pouring rain looking at her shop front. A group of sightseers gathered around the gallery and the police moved them on.

"Come on, move along, please, everybody. The show's over.

Nothing more to see," said the police officer, walking towards them with arms outstretched.

"Why do this to me?" she asked, "I've only just opened my gallery and look at it," she sobbed, standing in the road.

"I don't know, Love," replied the policeman, "I see a lot in my job that I don't understand, but I just get on with it and try and help as best I can. "Come on, Love, we can't do anything out here. Let's go inside out of this filthy weather."

Tears and rain ran down her face as she looked up at the sign of which she had been so proud that morning. It had been daubed with 'Poisoning Bastard' and the plate glass window was smashed, allowing the wind-driven rain to soak her display. Her dried flower arrangement of mauves and white was a soggy pulp on the floor covered in glass fragments.

She carefully stepped over the glass and saw that the pictures on which she had lavished so many hours of attention had also been daubed. An aerosol can had been used to spray 'Poisoner' on them.

Tom was charged with causing the deaths of thirty-two persons and was taken to Strangeways prison to await his trial. In the meantime, Pete and Melanie did everything they could to try and restart the cider plant.

Nothing had been heard of Penny and Sarah, although there were rumours in the pub from time to time. They had been seen in Devon, Ludlow, Scotland, and London, according to the locals.

Sam Evans was alone in the house, as he had been for months since Jean was taken to hospital, and he was watching television to catch up with the news. He'd been devastated when the storm broke. Thirty-two people had died because of something he had done. He'd been instrumental in their deaths and Mr Beddows had been charged with the crime.

Sam was having a huge struggle with his conscience. When he had been blackmailed into doing it, he had no idea that it was poison which he was injecting, as he thought that it was just something which gave an unpleasant taste. Tampering with the bottles had seemed wrong but not a great crime and he had no choice. He could not believe it when he heard the news and he kept reading the newspapers over and over again, hoping he would wake up from a nightmare.

The news stunned and frightened him. His body shook all over and he had to sit down before he fainted. His first response had been to give himself up and implicate Matthew Davies, but would he be believed? He might be held wholly responsible and he knew that if he did, he would be signing Jean's death warrant. California was her only hope and if he confessed there would be no chance of taking her.

He sat in front of the television and watched the news. He could not tear himself away and, long after it had finished, he sat staring at the screen, oblivious to the following programmes. He was finding it difficult to come to terms with the new desolation and horror that had come into his life. Should he go to the police? Did Matthew Davies know what was in the bottle he gave it to him?

He did not sleep all night, but tossed and turned, suffering agonies of indecision. Just before dawn he made a decision. A grey light was creeping through a gap in the curtains and a bird sang in the apple tree outside the window.

He was uncomfortable after the restless night and his pyjamas were damp with sweat. He shivered and pulled the bedclothes over his head in an attempt to shut out the world, but it kept encroaching into the womb he had made for himself. He was curled up in a ball, like an unborn baby, but as the grey light slowly illuminated the room, he realized that the real world was still there, as harsh and cruel as ever.

The horror of what he had done weighed down on him, as if he were trapped in the ruins of a collapsed building. He could feel the concrete beams pinning him down and he knew that he was not going to be rescued.

He made his decision. He was going to keep quiet for Jean's sake. The police had already questioned him and he felt that he was not under suspicion. He was sure that Matthew would not implicate him for fear of dragging himself into it. "And if I do confess, it won't bring those poor people back," he thought, in a despairing attempt to justify his decision.

The factory had reopened and got back into production now that the tests had been completed, but there were no orders for the cider. In the vast warehouse, the bottles stood on palettes stacked up to the ceiling and the lorries remained parked in the yard, side by side in rows of green and gold.

Pete walked around the factory with his clipboard trying to present a confident image, but he knew that they would have to close again, probably for ever.

None of their customers were stocking their cider or any of their other products and, without any orders, there was little point in going on. Wage bills and overheads were enormous and income was nil. He knew it was only a matter of time before it all came crashing down and he could see no hope at all.

In his office, he was in conversation with the chief accountant, who studied pages of figures while Pete watched the rain running down the window. The lines of water, like the bars of a prison cell, distorted the view and he could not see the grey world outside. He watched the drops chasing each other in sudden rushes down the window pane.

When the accountant took off his glasses and said, "Well, Mr Beddows—" Pete interrupted him and said,

"I know what you're going to tell me. We can't carry on like this and we'll have to go into liquidation—Yes?"

"I'm afraid I can see no alternative, Mr Beddows. The day to day out-goings in a business of this size are inexorable and awe-some—frightening, and with virtually no income the debts are increasing at an unbelievable rate. Why, since we've been sitting here, they must have increased by a hundred thousand pounds, and the rate is going up all the time. In truth, Mr Beddows, the business is failing in spectacular fashion. I can think of no precedent for such a spectacular collapse."

Pete replied, "I know, but we can't let it go without a fight. There must be something we can do, surely? I'm going to see the bank manager in an hour. Let's hope he can help."

The accountant gave a weak smile and shrugged his shoulders.

"I know," said Pete, "I know."

He crossed Broad Street in Hereford and headed for the double doors of the bank. He gripped his collar tightly closed and held his umbrella almost horizontally to stop the sleet from stinging his face. A fierce wind roared down the street and he caught its full force in the centre of the road, so he closed his umbrella to avoid it being blown inside out and with head lowered pressed on into the gale.

Inside, the quiet warmth enveloped him and he rubbed his stinging ears.

"It's a bit wild out there," said an elderly lady, wiping her steamed up glasses on her handkerchief.

"It is a bit," said Pete, combing his hair, which was immediately ruffled by a gust of wind when the door burst open and another customer entered, negotiating the door with her shopping trolley.

The old lady put her glasses back on and said, "I don't like coming in here if I can help it but I've got to ask if I can borrow some money for my granddaughter's twenty-first present. I hope he lends it to me—more than thirty pounds I want, so he might say 'no', I suppose. It's a lot of money."

Pete smiled, "It is a lot of money and I hope he lends it to you, Dear. I'm going to ask him to lend me a few pounds more than that, so we'll keep our fingers crossed for each other."

He said in a trembling voice to the young girl behind the glass, "I have an appointment to see Mr Davies."

He was directed to wait in an armchair outside the Manager's door. Looking around at the oak-panelled walls with their brass wall lights, he picked up a copy of *Farmers' Weekly* and idly thumbed through the pages. He was too nervous to absorb the contents and, after glancing at pictures of tractors and cattle, he put it back on the coffee table. He looked at his watch and decided he had time to visit the room marked *Gents*.

The face that stared at him from the mirror was hollow-eyed and frightened. He splashed some water on his face and dabbed it with a paper towel. He felt sick, so he had a drink of water, which made him feel better. Then he combed his hair again and, standing on one foot, he polished his shoes on the back of his trousers. After taking a deep breath, he went back to wait in the green chair.

The Manager, a fat man in a dark suit, smiled and vigorously shook his hand, "Please sit down, Mr Beddows."

He was given a warm welcome and a cup of coffee, but when he turned up his collar against the driving sleet again, he became more despondent than ever. The Manager had been sympathetic, "I am so sorry to hear of your problems, Mr Beddows," but he made it clear that there was no chance of borrowing a penny from his bank.

"We are talking about a level of borrowing that I cannot authorize. I will pass on your observations to my superiors, but please don't hold your breath while you're waiting for the answer. The situation is so unprecedented that—well, to put it bluntly, Mr Beddows, you have no more chance than a snowflake in hell. No bank in the world would lend in these circumstances. It would be financial suicide for us."

Pete crossed the road again, not risking his umbrella in the gale. "I am very sorry, Mr Beddows," he muttered, mimicking the Manager's gravelly voice.

The next few days were a whirlwind of journeys to different parts of the country. He went to see managers of supermarkets, hotels and country clubs. He coaxed radio stations into allowing him to be interviewed to defend the cider. He appeared on television and did everything he could think of to resurrect the company's fortunes, but all to no avail. Tom Beddows' Country Cider continued to build up debts and the public steadfastly refused to have any confidence in the company's products.

At the Mill House, the twins were having their fifth birthday party. Pete and Melanie had been concerned that their special day should not be spoiled by the tempestuous events. The twins had started at the village school in September and had made friends who'd been invited to their party.

Miss Acton was no longer the Headmistress. She had retired several years ago and was replaced with Miss Henworth, a young teacher, much better liked by the children. Little Rachel had the same desk where Tom had sat when he started under the beady eye of the fearsome red-coated Miss Acton.

Pete sat in the kitchen, deep in thought while the excitement went on around him. The children ran happily from the kitchen to the lounge, squealing with delight, "Let's play Pin the Tail on the Donkey now, Mummy," called Rachel, clutching her new doll.

Melanie organized the games, while Pete sat with furrowed brow, taking no interest in the party.

Chapter Twenty Seven

At the prison Tom had been put into isolation, as it was considered that feelings were running so high that it would be dangerous to allow any contact with other prisoners. "It's for your own protection," said the prison officer, gesturing for him to go through the door. He sat on the bed, looking at the walls, which seemed to be closing in on him, and he experienced a momentary spasm of claustrophobia. They were of bare brick, which had been painted with cream gloss paint, and the room was sparsely furnished.

He'd been put into prison uniform; a blue and white striped shirt and a short, navy blue jacket, and he had been given his first taste of prison food. It was unappetising, but he had morosely eaten it all, even the beetroot-stained, mashed potato and the soggy sprouts, which had been cooked to a pulp. They no longer had their firmness and lay on the plate in flat blobs, exuding water.

He pushed them around the plate with his fork, but decided that he was not going to get anything better and swallowed them with his eyes closed. He had heard about prison overcrowding, but was relieved to find that he had a cell to himself. "The bed's a bit hard," he thought, as he bounced on it.

He stretched out on his back, with his hands behind his head looking at the ceiling. A spider crawled across and as he watched its progress for fifteen minutes, his thoughts drifted back over the years. As he lay, he fancied he caught the smell of new-mown hay. He remembered lying in the hay when he discharged himself from hospital and went back to the little red house where he grew up.

He'd hitched a lift in the pouring rain, put on dry clothes and settled into the soft hay. He recalled its fragrance and was transported back still further, to the day when he was sent off on his bicycle to tell the men that hay-making was starting. He'd been so proud to think that Angela watched him go on his important mission and had felt like a hero.

He recollected a picture of his father, Ken, swinging his scythe in the hot sun, when he had had his first taste of cider and fallen asleep under the oak tree as the buzzards wheeled in the clear, blue sky.

The smell of the drying hay and memories of Walter came back to him. He looked at the ceiling of his prison and remembered lying back on the load of hay, with the sun flickering through the branches as they passed under the trees. He recalled the creaking and jingling harness, the soporific clip clop of the hooves, and the melancholy mouth organ music played by the unforgettable Walter.

He turned onto his side and, closing his eyes, was transported into a life a whole world away. People and events he'd known mingled together into a strange dream, becoming ever more bizarre, as he drifted away from the confines of his cell.

"Come on, Tom, we need some more wood getting in for the range," called Mrs Beddows, and the young Tom struggled in with an armful of split logs to stack by the fire.

"Move your legs for the boy," said Ken, so old Frank took his feet down to let him through. Frank was rolling himself a cigarette from his battered tin box and as he moved he lit the cigarette and the paper flared up.

Ken and Frank were sitting either side of the fire as they always did. There was a smell of apple wood smoke in the air and little Jane and Peter played with a clockwork train on the kitchen floor.

Mrs Beddows, wiping her hands on her apron said, "Isn't it about time you had a shave, Frank? The Queen's coming to visit the cider factory this afternoon and she won't want to see you looking like that and, while you're about it, you can have your annual wash."

"Alright, woman. I've got a nice brace of pheasant for her in the shed, which I caught in Cwm Woods."

Tom winced with pain as the cane came down on his hand and he looked up at the flaming red jacket. "You wicked little boy!" Miss Acton shrieked, "I will not have nasty little poisoners in my school. You killed thirty-two people and I will not have it. Do you understand?"

The cane swished again and he pressed his hand against his chest to relieve the pain. "I didn't, Miss," he cried, "It wasn't me, honest. I didn't kill them."

Walter pushed his trilby back on his head and said. "It wasn't the lad. Fair play. It was Keith Jones's boy that did it. He's the one you should be caning."

Tom blew on his throbbing hands and saw Brian Jones suppressing his giggles with a hand over his mouth.

He turned the spit and basted the hare that was roasting nicely. It was a warm summer's evening and the sun was low in the sky, casting long shadows as it radiated through the trees. The hare sizzled when he poured the fat and the fire flared as juices dripped onto the glowing embers. Smoke drifted through the trees and the sunlight filtered through the branches in radiating beams.

"That smells good Tom," came a voice from behind him and, as the smoke slowly cleared, he saw Frank standing in the clearing with a cigarette hanging from his lips.

"I taught you well, lad," he said, nodding towards the roasting hare.

He gave the spit another turn and pulled his hand back sharply, as the pain seared his hand once more. "It wasn't me, Miss. I didn't kill them."

"No lad," said Frank. "It was Brian Jones. He killed all those people just to get you into trouble, and he took the spinning top and hid it in your desk."

"Here, Tom," said Mrs Beddows, "put some of your Dad's Brylcreem on your hair because we're going to a party at the Big House."

"Oh, Mum, I want to stop at home and play with my presents."

"Let's not go, Mum," pleaded Jane, pulling at her skirt.

Tom pressed his hair with the cream, combed it smooth, and put on his scratchy Sunday suit.

The ballroom was bright and noisy, full of chatter and cigar smoke. Tom leaned against the big table and looked around the walls at the ancestral portraits; large dark pictures of people who lived long ago. Walter and Frank were in their best clothes, eating cider cake by the marble fireplace, and Major Hudson's daughter, Penelope, was a waitress carrying trays of drinks. Walter put his plate on the mantle piece and looked down at Tom, who was clutching his precious clockwork train, his best Christmas present.

Walter said, "I don't think you killed the people, because I know it was Brian Jones, but it looks as if he's got away with it again. Miss Acton thinks it was you, and nothing'll make her change her mind. Brian's over there, look, laughing at you, the little bugger."

Mike Sturgess came over and said, "I told you at the harvest supper to watch out for him. I warned you he was dangerous didn't I? He's jealous, mad with jealously, and it's a dangerous emotion is jealousy. Oh, yes, it's a dangerous emotion to be sure."

Frank and Walter started talking about Nellie Partridge while Tom sat on a chair in the window, kicking his feet, which did not reach the floor, and Monsieur le Brun went over to him, 'Allo little boy,' he said, "What do you 'ave there?"

"It's a clockwork engine, my best Christmas present. Watch." He slid down from the chair and getting onto his hands and knees demonstrated how the train worked. He proudly wound the key and put the engine on the carpet. With a whirring noise it went round in a circle under the chair.

Monsieur le Brun smiled and said, "It is very 'andsome. Give it to me. I will 'ave it for me."

Tom made a grab for the toy, but le Brun beat him to it, "Now I 'ave it and it will live with me in France." He ran out of the room, leaving poor Tom sobbing on the carpet.

Terry Jones put the new lamb to its mother and stood back to watch him searching for the teat while he wiped his hands on some dry straw. He put on his jacket and said, "I've been farming all my life, but I never gets tired of seeing lambs come into the world. Just look at that, Tom."

The lamb was only a few minutes old and still wet, but he was standing on wobbly legs and nuzzling into his mother. He found the teat and furiously wagged his tail as he sucked his first milk. Young Tom picked up another of the lambs, a white one with a black head, and lifted it up to his face.

The lamb nibbled his ear and Terry said, "He's hungry. Here you are son, he's a tiddler; no Mum." He passed him a wine bottle with a rubber teat and the lamb sucked eagerly while Tom stroked the tight curls. When he put it down, it skipped sideways across the straw and leapt high in the air.

Tom felt a hand pulling at his arm, "Come on, Darling," said Penny, "There's a gypsy caravan behind our cider stand and she's telling fortunes, so let's go and see what she has to say about our future."

She led him around the *Tom Beddows' Country Cider* stand, past *Abergavenny Produce* to the caravan. It was a lovingly restored carved and painted Romany caravan and gypsy Megan was inside, telling fortunes. They climbed the ornate steps and entered the dimly lit interior.

"I see a long and prosperous life for you," she began, "but it will be a bumpy ride before you reach the smooth waters. Ups and downs are in store and I see a small man who will blight your life. His name begins with B, and he has something to do with lorries. That's as much as I can see, but I know that he will introduce darkness into your life, but it will pass, and you will emerge from the dark tunnel into a brighter life than you ever knew."

"What a load of rubbish," commented Tom as they descended the steps, "Come on, Love, I've arranged for us to go sailing after breakfast."

They put on life jackets and climbed into the sailing dinghy. "I've never sailed before," said Penny.

The red-bearded teacher smiled and said, "We'll have you sailing like Sir Francis Drake by the time we get back from Kingsbridge. Tom pulled on the jib sheet as he was instructed.

"That's right old boy, a bit tighter until the jib goes to sleep." As if a huge hand was pushing it, the white boat headed across the estuary. The sails filled with wind and the water at the stern hissed and foamed as the salt spray stung their faces.

"Wheeh!" shouted Penny above the noise, "This is wonderful."

Tom headed the boat into the wind until the sails flapped madly and dropped the anchor. "Everybody into the dinghy," he cried, "We're going ashore for lunch at La Brebis. They do great Fruits de Mer in there."

He winced again as the cane descended onto his outstretched hand, "It wasn't me, Miss, I didn't kill 'em. It was Brian. Why won't you listen to me? I'm telling you it was Brian Jones. He did it."

He threw back the blankets and sat upright. "It wasn't me, Miss, honest."

The prison officer said, "It looks as if you were having a nightmare, Beddows, and so you should."

He wiped the sweat from his brow and sat on the bed, heart pounding. He looked at the warder and at the walls, and with a sigh lay back again, staring at the ceiling.

Tom was tried at the Old Bailey, where he was charged with causing the deaths by poisoning of thirty-two persons. Pete had arranged for a change of clothing to be sent to him and he arrived in court wearing a dark suit. In spite of his prison ordeal, he was looking fresh and well groomed. Pete, Melanie, and Jane were there, but there was no sign of Penny. She had not been seen since the day she left with Sarah.

Tom had been driven to court in a police van with darkened windows and taken in through a side door. A mob chanted, "Pois-on-er, Pois-on-er," as the van drove rapidly into the yard, and one man ran forward as it passed, banging on the sides shouting "Murderer."

The strong feelings of revulsion which the murders had stirred up, had not subsided since the news first broke. The press were there in force; reporters, photographers, and television crews, all clamouring for a glimpse of him.

He stood in the dock, feeling sick, and he looked around the court room. He could not see Penny, but his brother and sister gave him an encouraging thumbs-up when he caught their eye. There were men and women dressed in intimidating black robes and white wigs.

It was the first time he had been inside a court room and he was frightened. The judge looked down at him over his half moon glasses and said in a loud voice, "Will the Defendant please rise."

The day before the case came to court, Matthew Davies sat head in hands, fighting with his conscience. On the day of the poisoning, his life had changed and it seemed to him that his whole world had fallen apart. He was stunned by the news and could hardly believe the horror. He'd been in torment and sat morosely in the conservatory, unaware of his wife and children.

"What's the matter with you?" asked his wife in frustration. He was a changed man and she couldn't understand why. "We can hardly get a word out of you. There must be something wrong. Have I said something?"

"Nothing," he replied, staring at the apple tree in the garden.

"Well, have I done something to upset you?"

He shook his head and, taking a deep breath, got up from the wicker chair and stalked out of the house without kissing his wife, or saying good-bye.

"Where are you going?" she demanded as he slammed the car door and started the engine. He had decided that he was going to find Brian, though he wasn't sure what he was going to say. He wasn't even sure why he was going, but he thought he had to do something.

He was frightened and seething with anger that Brian should get him to do his dirty work, but he was terrified that if he went to the police to give evidence against him, he wouldn't be believed. He had no proof, so perhaps it was better to let sleeping dogs lie.

Sam Evans was keeping very quiet and maybe he should do the same. It seemed to be a solid case against Tom Beddows, so he could let things stay as they were, but he wasn't sure as he headed towards Westwood Farm.

Angela opened the door and said that he was away on business for a few days and she didn't know when he would return. She thought he'd gone to Amsterdam, but wasn't sure. He thanked her and got back into the car and the tyres spun on the gravel as he swept out of the drive, heading for the Kings Arms.

The Kings Arms is a white stone building a few miles from Lower Kings Canon. It was early in the evening and Roger Meddows, a manager at the Farm Supplies Centre, settled down in the window seat. He was looking forward to a pint before he went home after a frustrating day. Customers had wanted goods which he didn't have and everyone had brought their problems to him.

"Thank goodness," he sighed, stretching out his legs. He took a drink from his pint and began reading the evening paper. He was engrossed in the sport pages and only vaguely aware of someone entering the bar and ordering a drink.

The newcomer sat at a table near the other window and undid the buttons of his gabardine raincoat. Roger looked over the top of his paper at him and said, "Hello, Matthew, I've not seen you for a long time. How are you?"

He had not seen him for over a year, but they used to be friends many years ago, when they were both in their first job, working together in the shop at the Farm Centre, selling fertiliser and dried lamb's milk to the farmers of the surrounding area.

The Farm Centre is a large building where one can buy almost anything for the farm. Matthew had moved on to a job at Jones Road Haulage, but Roger had stayed and risen to the post of manager. Matthew was staring at his drink, not really conscious of his surroundings and, when he heard the voice, he looked up and said, "Oh, hello," without any warmth, and with expressionless eyes.

"Come and join me. Don't sit over there on your own."

"Okay, I'll be over in a minute." He threw back his head, downed the whisky, and bought another before pulling up a chair at Roger's table.

Roger shook his hand and said, "I'm still at the same place, still trying to earn an honest crust, you know, selling things to farmers. Are you still working at the Haulage firm, er—Jones' isn't it?"

Roger folded his paper and they talked about their youth, though he found it difficult at times, because his companion seemed to be preoccupied with his own thoughts and frequently lapsed into silence. Occasionally he would say, "Oh, pardon, what did you say?" and Roger would have to repeat himself.

Matthew made numerous visits to the bar, "No, not for me," protested Roger, with his hand over his glass, "I'll make this one last me for a while. It's early yet."

As the evening wore on, the whisky loosened Matthew's tongue and the conversation flowed more easily, but after more drinks his speech slurred and he became gloomy. His shoulders hunched over his glass and his eyes became bloodshot. He exclaimed a loud "Shit!" when his elbow knocked over his glass.

Roger looked around in embarrassment. It had gone quiet and eyes were everywhere, like a flock of sheep caught in a car's headlights. Then they turned away and the buzz of conversation filled the silence once more. He was relieved that he could not see anyone he knew and said, "Do you think you ought to drink any more old chap? You're looking as if you've had enough for one evening."

"No, I'm alright; jusht going to get another," and staggering to the bar he returned with another double whisky.

Roger had lost count of the drinks Matthew had had and, feeling uncomfortable, glanced at his watch. He'd been pleased to see his old colleague but now he was regretting calling into the pub. He wanted to make an excuse and leave, but he felt responsible for him and thought he ought to stay and see that he came to no harm, now that he was so drunk.

"Why do you keep looking at your bloody watch? Shick of my company already?"

He put an elbow on the table and supported his head on a clenched fist, pushing up his face, so that his eye closed and one side of his mouth was pulled up. "Lishen," he said, waving a finger at Roger, "I've got a terrible shecret—so terrible that I can't tell you what it is; musht keep it to myself." His head slipped off his fist and he snatched it back up with a start.

"Look, Matthew, old chap, I can see that you've got a problem of some sort, which you're trying to drown with whisky, but take it from me, it doesn't work. I've seen a lot of folks try, and a lot of folks come to grief. It never solves problems; just makes more."

Matthew looked at him vacantly and belched.

Roger continued, "I suppose you must have come here by car. It's too far to walk. Do you have it in the car park?" He leaned back in his seat to get a better view of the cars parked outside the window.

Matthew nodded and tried to stand, but Roger put a restraining hand on his shoulder saying, "No more. I'm making it my business to insist you have no more and I'm going to drive you home."

It was with some difficulty that Matthew was manhandled into the car. "Do you still live in the same house beyond the Dingle?"

He nodded and said, "You're a good friend Roger. Everyone needs a good friend."

"You certainly need one at the moment. I hope your wife's an understanding woman." He looked in his mirror and turned onto the Kings Canon road.

Matthew twisted in his seat and said, "Because you're my friend I want to ashk you a kes—k—question. If someone said do something and you did it would that make you a bad person?"

"You're not making sense, old chap," grinned Roger.

"I mean if shomeone said, do that, and it was bad, and I did it, would it be my fault?"

"I still don't know what you're getting at." He pulled off the road and said, "Yew Tree Cottage. Here we are, now let's get you out and back to your wife. I don't know what sort of reception you're going to get, being brought home in this state."

"Don't care what she says—Now wait a minute. You're my friend aren't you?"

"Yes, I'm your friend, now let's—"

"No, jusht a minute. Friends should share shecrets so I'm going to tell you my secret."

Roger sighed and resting his forearms on the steering wheel said, "Go on then, I'm listening."

He drove the short journey home with a broad grin on his face. He shook his head and thought, "The things people say when they're drunk. He's got a good imagination. I'll say that."

At the Old Bailey, the trial was under way and it did not look good for Tom. The evidence that the prosecution presented seemed insurmountable. The poison bottle with his finger prints was shown and it was pointed out that he had a history of instability.

Expert witnesses were produced to talk about the effects that depression can have and much was made of his apparent hatred of the human race, when he shunned human contact and lived a life of isolation in the woods.

The rumours that Brian had engineered were used as part of the character assassination and Tom's spirits sank even lower as he listened to the evidence. His finger prints on the poison bottle were the most damning evidence and the poisons' reference book found in his car boot was also produced.

He looked around the room, desperately studying faces in the hope of finding a flicker of sympathy to give him encouragement, but all the faces in the jury were impassive. They listened to the evidence with stony faces. He looked from the jury to those sitting in the gallery and from them to the white wigs and thought, "It's hopeless. If I were sitting on that jury listening to all this, I'd say 'Guilty. Lock him up'."

So resigned was he to the inevitability of his fate, that he lost interest in the proceedings and intently studied a fly that crawled over the wall to his right. Would it go over the light switch or would it go round? It changed course and went round and Tom's interest in the fly dissolved, and he looked across at his solicitor, Mr Cargill.

He was leaning to one side speaking to a man in a black gown, who had entered the court room and quietly gone up to him. Tom was puzzled when Mr Cargill wrote something down and then stood and announced that fresh evidence had come to light. He requested an adjournment to give him time to consider it.

The Judge agreed and Tom found himself alone in a cell. The cell must have been at the front of the building, because he could now hear the crowd outside his window chanting, "Pois–on–er, Pois–on–er." He was kept in there for an hour wondering what was happening. It was clear that something dramatic had unfolded and it must have been important to merit an adjournment. His spirits began to rise slightly as he considered the possibilities.

Could it be that Brian's conscience had made him confess? During his interrogation he'd repeatedly told them that it might have been Brian and they had interviewed him but nothing had come of it. They clearly thought it was nothing to do with him, but had he confessed? Tom could think of no other reason for the adjournment. Or perhaps it wasn't Brian at all. Surely, even he wasn't capable of such an atrocity?

Perhaps he was completely innocent and somebody else had been caught. Perhaps it had been a group of terrorists, trying to draw attention to their cause. Yes, that was it. He sat on the bed, listening to the chanting, his mind in turmoil.

The key turned in the door and a beaming Mr Cargill entered. "I do believe you're off the hook," he said, pumping his hand up and down. "Something quite unexpected has occurred, which will I'm sure cause the collapse of the prosecution's case."

The unexpected occurrence to which Mr Cargill had referred had been the discovery of Matthew's body, hanging from a branch of the apple tree outside his conservatory. It was obviously suicide, but there had been no note and there was nothing to connect the event with the case at the Old Bailey, but news of the suicide had spread like the proverbial wildfire.

Roger Meddows had been having a pint in the Old Black Lion and, as if fate had taken a hand, he overheard a conversation. He was sitting under the case containing the stuffed pike, talking to a colleague from the Farm Centre. They didn't usually go in there during the day but had decided to slip out for a quick drink in their lunch break, something they'd rarely done before.

"Did you hear that?" asked his colleague.

"Hear what?"

"That woman in the tweed coat said that someone in the village has committed suicide."

"Really? I wonder who."

"Only one way to find out," said his companion and leaning back in his seat said, "Excuse me, I couldn't help overhearing you just now. Did you say that someone's committed suicide?"

The lady and her husband sat down at their table. "Yes," she began, "We were passing Yew Tree Cottage and—"

"You mean the cottage below the Dingle?" interrupted Roger.

"Yes, that's right, and there was an ambulance outside and a police car, and the people who were standing there told us that a man had been found hanged in the garden; hanging from a tree he was."

The husband added, "We're not sure who he was but someone said he worked at Jones Haulage, some sort of manager there, by all accounts."

Roger put down his glass and looked at the pair open-mouthed. "Oh—my—God!" he said slowly. "Oh, my God!"

At Leominster police station, Roger recounted his evening spent with Matthew Davies, and his confession. "I didn't believe him and didn't give it another thought until I heard he'd killed himself, and then it hit me. He must've been telling the truth. He said it was his fault that all those people died, and he kept muttering about a bottle, and getting someone else's finger prints on it with a trick to make it look as if they'd done it, but now he couldn't live with himself, and how sorry he was." He paused for breath and the Officer asked,

"Did he mention any names?"

"No. None."

"And did he talk about killing himself?"

"Yes, he did, and I didn't take that seriously either. He was very drunk you see, and I had to take him home because he was unfit to drive. He was coming out with all sorts of stuff and I thought it was the drink talking. It seemed too ridiculous for words."

"And did he give any indication why he should do such a thing?"

"No, not really. He just kept going on about what scum he was and how he was a mass-murderer and didn't have the right to live—and I just laughed at him," he added.

"Thank you. You've been very helpful, but before we finish this interview, just try and think of every last detail he told you, Sir, even things that seem trivial."

"I think I've told you everything," he said, but thought a little longer and added, "He did say something about a note."

"A note?"

"Yes, a note from a Mr Edwards, I think he said. It was part of the trick to get someone else's finger prints on a bottle. He said that was the cleverest part of the plan, and he kept going on about starting rumours, and getting someone into terrible trouble. He must have been talking about Tom Beddows. Oh, and he also told me he'd planted a book about poisons in someone's car, to make it look good, he said. "

It had never been made public that Tom claimed he had had a note from the Quality Controller. The police did not believe it ever existed and no mention was made of it in public until Mr Cargill talked about it at the trial, so Roger Meddows could not have known about it. The finding of the poisons' book had also not been publicised, so credibility was given to his statement and it was instrumental in the prosecution's collapse.

Tom was found not guilty and outside the Old Bailey a television presenter stood in front of a camera and said:

Mr Thomas Beddows, OBE, the founder and owner of Tom Beddows' Country Cider Limited, has been found not guilty of causing the deaths of thirty-two persons by poisoning. When the verdict was announced, there was an audible gasp in the court room and cheers from his family. Mr Beddows, wearing a dark suit, looked relieved and was clearly struggling to hold back the tears. An unexpected turn of events has occurred which has shed new light on the case.

In a highly dramatic twist, a Mr Matthew Davies was found hanging in his garden in Lower Kings Canon. He was discovered by his wife and it is believed that he committed suicide after confessing the crime to a friend. He told him that he could not live with his conscience and intended taking his own life. It seems that he contaminated the cider and used a subterfuge to ensure that Mr Beddows' finger prints were found on the poison bottle.

There does not appear to be any motive for his action and, if there was a motive, the secret has died with him. Mr Matthew Davies was Transport Manager at Jones Road Haulage Limited and there seems to be nothing to connect him with Mr Beddows. This dramatic turn of events brings a bizarre conclusion to an extraordinary case; one of the worst cases of mass-murder in criminal history.

No doubt this mysterious case will be written into the folklore of the sleepy village of Lower Kings Canon in the Welsh Marches for generations to come. There will be celebrations in the Beddows' family home tonight, as Mr Thomas Beddows OBE walks from the court a free man.

At the Mill House, Pete opened a bottle of champagne and filled the glasses, "To Tom," he said. They drank the toast and Jane called out "Speech, speech."

Tom got to his feet, coughed and said, "I just want to thank you all for having faith in me when the rest of the world seemed to be turning against me and believed I had killed those poor people. It's been a terrible experience and now I want to put it behind me."

"My one regret is that Penny has gone and taken our little daughter. She couldn't cope with the awful pressure and I don't hold it against her. Who could have coped? I thought about her a lot in prison and I realize that it was the end of the line for us. Now that she's with another man, I don't want to cause more unhappiness if she is settled and happy. But time will help me to get over it and, once again, thank you all very much for your support."

After the celebrations, Tom leaned on the kitchen table and said to Pete, "This is all very well, celebrating my freedom, but it's only the start of our problems isn't it?"

Pete nodded, "I've been trying to keep everything afloat, but we're going down like the Titanic. Even though you've been cleared, there's no way that anyone is going to drink our cider again and, quite honestly, the only thing we can do is go into liquidation and sell up. The way our debts are increasing we'll have to sell everything, and I mean everything, just to clear them."

🎐

Chapter Twenty Eight

Chris Gregory had been drinking all day. He had not gone to work but had sat around the house drinking whisky and left before Susan came home, walking unsteadily down the road to The Rising Sun. He went in through the front door and pushed open the bar door. Behind the bar, the landlord looked up and saw him trying to disentangle his jacket from the door handle.

Chris pulled at his jacket and said, "What a stupid place for someone to leave a door handle. It's obvious it's going to catch on someone's coat putting it there. Why couldn't you put it higher up out of harm's way?"

"You must be joking," said the landlord.

"What? I'm not joking."

"I meant you must be joking if you think I'm going to serve you any more drink when you're in that state."

He glared at the landlord through an alcoholic mist and lurched towards him with his fist held high, "I might only have one hand, but I can make you see stars." He fell over before he reached the bar and hit his head on a table.

As he lay on the floor, clutching at the chair to pull himself up, the landlord called, "John—David, come here and throw this drunk out. He belongs down at Dr Sherwood's place in the village. Take him home before he gets himself into trouble, will you."

Susan was at home when he was delivered to her like a parcel. The men rang the door bell. "Does this belong to you, Love?" said David as they leaned him against the wall. His wet hair was falling over his face and a trickle of blood ran down his forehead.

A pool of water collected at his feet as the rain ran off his coat and, when they let him go, he slowly slid puppet-like down the wall and collapsed in a rubbery heap on the carpet. She snorted with disgust and went into the kitchen, returning with a jug of cold water which she threw in his face.

"Just look at the state of you!" she shouted. I'm ashamed and I've had enough. Either you pull yourself together or I divorce you. Daddy was right when he said you were good for nothing. We can't go on like this."

He turned his head to one side and was sick over the Chinese rug. It was obvious that he was not going to pull himself together.

After apologizing and promising that he was going to give up the drink, he continued to have binges and they got worse.

Dr Sherwood put an arm around his daughter and said, "You've given it a good try, Dear. No wife could have tried harder to make a marriage work, but I think the time has come to let him go. I really do."

She put her head against his shoulder and replied, "Yes, Daddy, I think you're right, and I know you tried to warn me and I didn't listen. He keeps promising he'll stop, but he never does and seems to get worse. I've taken all that I can bear. None of my friends will come to the house and if I meet them outside I'm ashamed to look them in the eye. I feel like a social outcast."

Her father stroked her hair and she burst into tears.

Whenever she tackled her husband over the matter of his drinking, he lost his temper, "I can cope with it and I don't have a problem. I just drink because I like it and it makes my problems go away. The world seems a better place when I've had a drink or two. I feel as if I've got two hands like everyone else, but I could stop tomorrow if I wanted to, so stop making such a fuss. You and your Dad keep saying I'm an alcoholic, but you're wrong, and if you don't like me the way I am, perhaps I ought to go."

"Then perhaps you should because I can't stand any more of it."

He packed his bags and moved back into the bungalow with his parents; an event which effectively marked the end of his marriage to Susan.

The factory inevitably closed and a large number of Kings Canon residents lost their jobs. Tom Beddows was the main employer in the area and in some cases whole families worked there, so it was a major blow to the local economy when it closed.

Some of them went to work at Bulmers Cider in Hereford and there were other smaller cider producers in the area, like Westons Cider and Symonds Cider, who took some, but for most it was a tragedy. The liquidators made every effort to sell the company as a going concern, but because of lost confidence no buyer could be found.

An auction was held to sell off the equipment before the buildings were sold. An estate agent in Hereford was employed to conduct the auction and they set up a marquee outside the main building to sell refreshments.

Large numbers of people turned up on the appointed day; some genuine buyers, and some driven by curiosity; the same morbid attraction that makes people stand and stare at the scene of road accidents.

The crowds gathered for the ten o'clock start. "Look at the vultures gathering," said Tom, gloomily. "I never realized that there were so many cider producers in the country, but then I suppose a lot aren't cider makers. They'll be interested in the office equipment and the vehicles." People had come from far and wide in the hope of picking up a bargain.

Some of them represented the big producers and others were farmers who produced only a few gallons a year and were looking to improve the standard of their equipment. The firm had extensive offices and all the equipment was up for sale; typewriters, photo-copiers, desks, filing cabinets, and coffee machines. There was also a large fleet of cars, lorries and vans.

The auctioneer walked along the rows of neatly laid out items followed by a large crowd, and a helper pushed a wheeled platform on which he stood to speak with the aid of a loud hailer. He sold item after item in quick succession.

"He's giving it away," said Pete in consternation. "He's not making much effort to up the price before he moves on. Look, he could have got more for that machine. As soon as there was a lull in the bidding, he brought the hammer down and moved on."

"Three thousand pounds for that lorry," muttered Tom, "and it was new last year too. It's heart breaking."

At the end of the day when the crowds had dispersed, the brothers stood in the empty warehouse looking around the litter-strewn building. Plastic coffee cups lay on the ground and the wind lifted discarded sale catalogues into the air. Tom kicked at one of the cups and said, "Well, Pete, it's all gone. Tom Beddows' Country Cider will soon be but a memory, something to tell our grand-children about."

It was too early to have the final figures, but it was obvious that the sale had realized only a small proportion of the stock's value.

They looked sadly around and Tom put an arm around his brother and said, "Come on. Let's leave all this behind us, like a bad dream."

They walked towards the car park and Pete stopped and grinned. He nodded towards the car park and said, "What're we doing? We haven't got cars to go home in. They were sold, along with the lorries and everything else."

The Manor House was auctioned only a few days later and Tom was sitting on one of the benches laid out for the occasion, browsing through the catalogue. The ballroom was chosen as the venue and he lifted his eyes from the catalogue for a nostalgic last look at the room before it left his life forever.

By chance, the bench on which he sat was near the marble fire place and under the painting of one of Major Hudson's ancestors which had impressed him so much that Christmas morning when he was a boy. His mind went back to that day and he recalled the young Penny, home from boarding school, carrying trays of drinks amongst the guests. He smiled sadly and looked over to his left to see Penny standing by the wall.

She had arrived too late to find a seat and had joined those who were standing at the side. She was on her own; no sign of Sarah or of Monsieur le Brun. It had not been long since he last saw her, but she seemed different; older and care-worn. She looked steadfastly to the front, in spite of Tom's waving of his catalogue. He got the impression that she knew he was there and refused to look at him.

Most people were looking round the room with interest, but she was the only one who looked unflinchingly ahead. She presented Tom with her profile view but it was sufficient to see the haunted look in her eyes; the look of someone carrying a heavy burden.

The auction's start was imminent, so Tom abandoned his attempts to attract her attention. He listened to the auctioneer's introduction with one eye constantly on her but she never once looked in his direction, even when the bidding got under way and those standing at the side eagerly scanned the crowd to see who was making the bids. She continued to stare at the auctioneer.

After the auction, Tom tried to elbow his way through the crowds towards her, ignoring everyone else, but she disappeared from his life again like a ghost, as if she had never been there.

The auctioneer made his introduction. He put his heavy framed glasses on the end of his nose and looked at his audience over the rims. "Ladies and Gentlemen, we are pleased to offer for auction today a splendid estate, comprising seven hundred acres of arable farmland, including woodlands, seventeen cottages, double bank salmon fishing on the Wye, and a period Manor House."

"The house has been extensively refurbished and the land is in good heart. Who will start us off with a bid?" He looked over his glasses and there was silence. "Who will give me three million pounds, just to start us off? Two million pounds? One million? Come on, ladies and gentlemen, estates of this quality come onto the market very rarely, and don't forget that the purchaser will be able to assume the title of Lord of the Manor of Kings Canon. Do I hear a bid of seven hundred thousand?"

Tom put his face close to Pete's ear and whispered, "Good God, they're not going to give this away too are they?"

"Five hundred thousand," shouted someone at the rear. Tom swung round, but was not quick enough to see who had made the bid. It was quickly followed by five hundred and fifty thousand by a man in the front row. The price rose steadily and, as far as Tom could tell, there were three people bidding, all strangers. It rose in increments of fifty thousand and passed the million mark, and then the two million, before the bidding stopped at two million eight hundred thousand.

"It's with you, Sir," said the auctioneer to the grey suited man on the front row. There was silence in the ball room and he continued. "Going for the first time. I have a bid which I am going to take. Going for the second time, and going for the—" He lifted the hammer.

"Two million eight hundred and fifty thousand," came a shout from behind Tom. The auctioneer looked at the man on the front row, who shook his head and looked away.

"Any advance on two million, eight hundred and fifty thousand?—Going for the first time. Going for the second time. Going—"

Tom felt weak and had a sick feeling in the pit of his stomach. His heart raced

"Sold to Mr Jones of Jones Road Haulage. Congratulations, Sir."

At the Mill House, Pete and Tom studied a sheet of figures on the kitchen table.

"Well, it's looking better," said Tom, "but we're not there yet. We still have a lot of debt."

Pete scratched his beard with his pen and said, "I'm afraid it's looking obvious that we'll have to sell the other bits and pieces, the yacht, the villa and—"

"Yes, the Mill House too."

Sam Evans wiped his hands on the tea towel and answered the knock on his door. It was Penny, with a scarf over her head, shaking the rain from her umbrella. "Hello, Sam, I'm Penelope Hudson from the Manor House."

He stood to one side to allow her to enter. How is Jean?" she asked, as she went in. He showed her into the front room, sadly shaking his head. She leaned the umbrella against the side board and looked round the room. It was clear that there had not been a woman in the house for some time, as the surfaces were thick with dust and she noticed cobwebs on the ceiling. There was a musty smell, as Sam had not bothered to heat the house since Jean was taken away.

"I'll put the kettle on," he said, disappearing into the kitchen.

When he returned, he put down the tray, and Penny asked him again if Jean was any better. He bit his lip and shook his head, "She's not good."

Penny said, "I've been talking to someone who used to work at the Manor and knew Jean well and she's told me all about your problems. I am so sorry to hear about them. She told me about the only hope for her being an operation in a Californian hospital. I understand it can't be done in this country."

Sam nodded and bit his lip again.

"Jean was part of our household for as long as I can remember and she was a good friend to me. We used to talk in the kitchen for hours, laughing and joking. I can remember the tears rolling down our cheeks sometimes and I miss her. She used to keep me in touch with the gossip," she smiled, and then her countenance saddened again. "By the way, I suppose you heard that we've lost the house and the estate. It went at auction to Brian Jones and—"

"Brian Jones!" Sam was startled by the information. He'd heard about the sale, but had not heard that Brian had been the successful bidder.

"Yes, and I'm told that he's been over to France and bought our yacht and the villa."

"Really?" He shook his head, and sighed.

Penny continued, "Tom and I are no longer together. We're not a team any more and I'm living in France. I couldn't—but enough of that. You've got problems of your own and you won't want to hear about mine." She continued, "I've come here because I think I might be able to help, Sam," she put a hand on his arm, "Can I ask you a personal question?" and without waiting for an answer went on, "How much money do you need to pay for the operation?"

"Five thousand pounds."

"Well, the money from the auction sales won't cover the firm's debts and as a partner I'm liable so they'll be coming to me and they'll want everything I've got. Now if I was to give some of it away to you, they couldn't get their hands on it and I'd be helping Jean." She smiled, and asked, "Well, what do you say? If you say yes, at least some good will have come out of this whole sorry mess, and you'll be helping me to feel a bit better. Well?"

He stared incredulously, not knowing what to say. He scratched his head and leaned back in his chair.

"Well," she asked again. "Is it a good idea? I could give you the money now on the table here and you could be on your way as soon as you can get a plane." She reached into her handbag and withdrew a bulky brown envelope. "There's more than the five thousand pounds there, but you'll need some money for a hotel and you'll need to eat. Take it please."

Brian Jones moved into the Manor House and he stood in the ball room with his arm around Angela. "It's all ours now," he said, puffing on a large cigar. He walked up and down looking up at the chandeliers —the house had been sold complete with all of the furnishings—"Well, you're looking at the Squire now, the Lord of the Manor of Kings Canon. Exciting isn't it?"

He looked at his wife, who was standing in the middle of the room watching him closely. "You don't look very excited," he observed, "Just think. We've got all this and his villa and yacht too; a beautiful villa in Provence, and a beautiful yacht moored in the Med, though we'll have to change its name. I don't like *Sweet Cider*. We'll have to think of another more suitable name. Why aren't you looking pleased?"

"But all of this belonged to Tom Beddows and it doesn't seem right, profiting from his downfall. I don't feel at home here and it doesn't feel like ours, not like Westwood Farm did."

He frowned, "Don't be so stupid, woman. Of course it's ours. We bought it fair and square at auction and Beddows crashed because he was incompetent. That's nothing to do with us. We've got everything now and that's the way of the world. Stupid woman. Anyone would think we stole it from him. And another thing, I don't want to hear you talking about him in my house. Do you understand?"

They settled into the Manor and tried to make it their home, but Angela was never happy there. She didn't love her husband and felt that they should not be living in a house which by rights should belong to Tom. She had only agreed to go back to her husband because he'd promised to no longer make life difficult for Tom and to undo all the harm he'd done. It was part of the deal.

The new Squire proved to be unpopular with his staff and with the village as a whole. He did not command the respect that Major Hudson and Tom had done and many of the staff left to work elsewhere, even the faithful ones who had always worked there, following in the footsteps of their parents and grandparents. Brian Jones was Lord of the Manor and he did his best to ensure that everyone knew it. It is said that few people can comfortably wear the mantle of leadership and high esteem and it certainly did not fit Brian Jones.

Chapter Twenty Nine

As soon as he could Sam Evans took Jean to America. They were booked into a hospital in California and he stayed at the Hotel Europa only a walking distance away.

The specialist told him that there was a fifty–fifty chance of success, but if he'd brought her sooner the odds would have been better.

"I know that," said Sam, "but please do your best for her."

"We'll certainly do that, Sir, but the tests show that we mustn't be too optimistic."

She lay unconscious and Sam held her hand and kissed her before she went for the operation. The doctors left him alone with her for a few minutes and he sat by the bed, holding her hand to his lips, talking quietly. He'd been told that she might be able to hear him, but he didn't believe it, "They're just telling me that to give me some comfort," he thought, but even so he chatted to her.

He had the gloomy premonition that it may be the last time he would be able to talk to her or even see her alive. "See you later, Love," he whispered, fighting back the tears, "Everything'll be alright. I've got you here at last and these are the best doctors in the world for your problem. They'll soon have you up and about again and we'll be having a drink in the Old Black Lion to celebrate with our friends. Penelope Hudson gave us a lot of money to get you here, so it's her we have to thank."

She lay without moving and not showing a flicker of response. He sat in silence for several minutes, studying her thin face. His eyes widened with horror and he put his ear to her lips to check if she was still breathing, but with relief he detected very shallow breaths. He'd never prayed before, but he prayed as hard as he knew how and then, giving her one last kiss, he said, "See you later, Love," and left the room.

He went out into the bright sunlight, but for him the sun was not shining. He sat on a bench beneath a palm tree, feet outstretched and arms behind his head, looking across the lawns striped with long shadows cast by the palms. He closed his eyes tightly and hoped that when he opened them again the nightmare would be over and Jean would be well.

He listened to the whirring of roller skaters passing his bench. A shadow passed over him and, slightly opening one eye and squinting in the bright light, he made out the silhouette of a man. Sam pulled in one arm and shuffled along the bench to give the newcomer room to sit. The man mumbled a thank you and took a sandwich box from his briefcase. He offered one to Sam, "Salami and salad. Would you like one?"

He shook his head and turned away but, realizing that he was being discourteous, hastily added, "No, thank you very much."

They sat in silence watching the skaters and Sam nodded towards the sky and said, "Nice day."

The man studied him for a moment, chewing on his sandwich, and then said, "I guess you're English."

"Yes, I suppose my accent gave me away."

"Well, sorta—You English are always preoccupied with the weather. We can tell an English person by the way they comment on the weather when they meet and we laugh about it over here."

"Oh."

"The weather is like this most days at this time of the year, so there's no point in making the observation that it's a nice day. Only the English do that."

"Oh, really," replied Sam, only half interested in the conversation and wishing he would go away and leave him with his thoughts. "I suppose so."

The man continued to eat his sandwiches, "Are you over here on holiday?" he asked.

"No, I'm here because, well—no, I'm not on holiday."

"Pardon me, didn't mean to pry."

After a long silence, the American spoke again, "Damned woman!"

"Pardon?"

"I said damned woman; my wife. She's forgotten to put mustard in this one and she knows I like it. She's useless." He turned to Sam and asked, "Are you married?"

He nodded in reply and once again directed his gaze across the shadow striped grass to the roller skaters beyond the palms.

The man continued, "I often think all us guys would be better off not being married. Mine causes me a lot of aggravation. She's useless. If I had my way I'd swap her for a hot-dog tomorrow and consider it a good deal. She knows I must have mustard on my salami." He put down the sandwich and went on, "I guess she's so useless that—" but, before he could finish the sentence, Sam was walking between the palms, head bowed and hands thrust deep into pockets.

At the hospital, he winced and put down the cup of bitter coffee. White uniformed nurses hurried past him as he drummed his fingers on the chair. Once again he looked at the clock on the wall and then at his watch and continued to tap his fingers.

He'd been waiting for this day for months. Against his principles, he'd stolen and become involved with unscrupulous men like the detested Peters. That had led to his involvement with Matthew Davies and the nightmare of the poisoning and, after all the planning, he was here. He couldn't bear the thought of losing her and, now that his hopes had become a reality, he felt numb, as if he was being carried along in a dream with no control over events.

He'd gone through so much to get the woman he loved to the only hospital which gave her a chance. He'd expected to feel happy when he got her here, but it wasn't like that. The doctor had not given him much hope when he told him that it might be too late. "Where there's life, there's hope," he kept repeating to himself, "Where there's life, there's hope."

When he had been sitting on the bench outside, his spirits had risen a little. At first he'd been depressed, but the sunshine and the vitality of the youngsters on their roller skates fanned a spark of hope. The innocent remarks of the man on the bench had plunged him back into darkness.

The hands of the clock had not moved since he'd last looked but once again he checked with his watch to make sure that the clock had not stopped. He'd leaned his head back and closed his eyes when a nurse said, "Mr Evans, could you step this way please," and he was shown into an office at the end of a corridor. The sign on the door read *Mr Goldthorn Jnr* and inside a doctor in a white coat put down his pen and stood up to shake his hand.

Sam sat once more on the seat under the clock, trying to recall the interview with Mr Goldthorn Junior. He'd been in the office for twenty minutes but his mind had been spinning so wildly that much of the information had gone over his head.

He did remember the important parts though. The operation had been long and complicated but she had survived, in spite of their worries that she might have been too weak to stand it. He couldn't see her yet and it would be at least twenty-four hours before they'd know if there was any chance of success.

A nurse came up to him and suggested that he went back to his hotel as there was nothing he could do at the hospital. "Later on you could be spending a lot of time here, so if I were you I'd go and freshen up and we'll call you if you're needed."

It was another twenty-four hours before a message came through to his hotel. He had not dared leave the building in case they phoned and had spent most of the time in his room or the lounge, thinking of nothing else but Jean; remembering the way she used to return from the Manor House full of gossip and how it used to irritate him. He used to ask if she had nothing better to do than gossip about other folk's private business, but now he would love to hear her talking about Mrs Pugh's wayward daughter.

He was on his way almost before the receptionist had finished speaking. He ran the short distance across the park arriving breathless to be greeted by a smiling nurse. "She's conscious and talking," she announced.

Jean still looked very ill, but her eyes were open and she recognized him. "Hello, Sam," she said, weakly, "I hope you've got enough clean shirts. I'd better do some washing when I'm out of here."

He sat at the side of the bed and held her hand, but he could not speak. He had been longing for the moment when he could talk to her again, but now that it was here he could utter no sounds as his throat knotted up and he looked at her through a mist of tears.

The doctors allowed him to stay with her for half an hour and then said he must go and allow her to rest. "See you later, Love, and we'll be going home soon."

The sun shone more brightly outside and he went back to the hotel and treated himself to a large dinner; the first meal he'd enjoyed since arriving in America.

He returned to the hospital with a spring in his step and flowers in his arms but when he was met at the door by the grave-faced doctor, he knew it was all over.

"I'm sorry, Sir. We did all we could and we thought we'd succeeded, but she suddenly took a turn for the worse and there was nothing we could do. The problem was that it had been left too long, but we had to give it a whirl didn't we?"

Sam sat on the same park bench again. The sun was still hot and the youngsters still roller-skated between the palm trees while he sat all alone. On the next bench a couple sat holding hands and it seemed to him that everywhere he looked there were men and women together.

"Well, we had to give it a whirl," he said out loud. "We had to give it a whirl. He had my Jean's life in his hands. The minutes he spent cutting into her were the most important in our lives and he said he was giving it a whirl. He even got her name wrong. She was Jean, not Janet, and he spoke as if he'd failed to mend a pair of spectacles, not the most precious thing in my life."

The couple on the next bench kissed and Sam stood up and went to the hotel to pack. He crossed the wide expanse of grass in front of the hotel; the only person on the grass, a solitary figure, head bowed, and alone.

Chapter Thirty

The Mill House had been sold but the proceeds went to pay the firm's debts and Pete and Melanie found themselves almost penniless. They had taken the precaution of putting some money aside when they saw the crash coming, but it was not enough to keep them going for long. They were distressed by their change of circumstances, because they had become used to a good standard of living and they sat in the kitchen discussing their next move.

"Well, said Melanie, we have to be out of here in a few weeks so we've got to make a decision. If I could find someone to look after the twins when they're on holiday, I could find a secretarial job somewhere. I could try and find a job that fits their school hours. It would be the holidays that cause the problems, but I'm sure we could overcome that."

Pete put his feet up on a chair and said, "Now that this has happened, it could be an opportunity to do something completely different. It could be the start of a new adventure."

"Like what?"

"Well, I've always fancied the idea of having a bit of a small-holding. When I was a boy, we used to have chickens and pigs and I used to help Dad on the farm so I know a bit about it. What do you think?"

Melanie thought for a moment and said, "If you think that's what you'd like to do, why not? Life has changed so dramatically, we might as well try something different, but I don't think we'll get rich doing that."

"No, I know that, but it's a satisfying way of life, producing one's own food, I mean. Perhaps we could have some goats and sell the milk, and we could have some chickens, and sell the eggs, and we could—"

"Now, just hang on a minute before we get carried away, we have to find this small-holding first."

Pete winked and said, "I think I can solve that little problem, as long as you agree in principle with the idea."

"Yes, I think it might be fun."

"That's settled then. I'll see what I can do."

When the company car was sold, Pete bought an elderly Volkswagen Beetle. It was bright yellow and dented and rattled and squeaked its way along the lanes. The previous owner had been a young girl, who'd covered it in stickers announcing to the world that she loved dogs and horses.

She apparently wanted to save the whales and get rid of nuclear bombs, too. "It's not like the Jag, but it'll get us around and one day our fortunes might change. You never know."

"You never know," echoed Melanie.

Jane continued to paint and still had her gallery in Hereford, which was becoming well-known, and she had built up a following of loyal customers, who regularly visited her to buy pictures from the walls or commission paintings.

The company's collapse did not affect her as badly as the rest of the family, but Tom was devastated and began to slide back into depression, just as he did when he was a young man and Frank and Ken had died in quick succession. He sat around, looking dejected, and his enthusiasm for life seemed to have ebbed away.

Jane had special exhibitions on a regular basis and she had sent out invitations to what she called her Spring Collection. On these occasions she provided wine and the customers thronged around the pictures. When one was sold, her assistant would put a red star on the corner of the frame.

"I can't see many red stickers yet," complained Jane, "Put two or three on the cheapest pictures to encourage them. It's good psychology."

While the assistant was doing that, Jane felt a hand on her shoulder, "Hello, Jane. Nice to see you again."

It was Paul, the shy vegetarian, who had been her boyfriend briefly a few years ago. "I didn't have an invitation," he explained, "but I was told that you wouldn't mind if I turned up."

"No, not all. I'm pleased to see you again," she said, kissing his cheek.

Paul beckoned to a man who was engrossed in studying one of the pictures, "I also took the liberty of bringing someone else. He said he was interested in art, so I suggested he came along with me—This is Chris Gregory. This is Jane Beddows, the owner of the gallery, and the artist who did all these."

They shook hands and exchanged pleasantries and Paul explained, "Chris is doing some work on my cottage for me and we got talking about art."

Jane handed him another glass of wine and said, "So you're interested in art."

"Yes, I've liked art since I was at school and I particularly like the ones you've done of old Herefordshire buildings, because that's a special interest of mine."

"Oh?"

"Yes, it's my job. I'm foreman of a firm specializing in the restoration of historic buildings, especially timber ones. We use the same techniques that craftsmen used when they were built and we work on buildings like that one."

He pointed at a painting with a black and white house in the middle distance and misty blue hills in the background. "That's Orchard House, Weobley isn't it? I thought so," he said when she nodded, "I did some work on it, so I know it pretty well. We replaced that big tie beam there." He paused and looking round the walls said, "I think they're beautiful paintings and you deserve to do well."

"Thank you, Josh."

"Chris."

"Pardon?"

"The name is Chris."

"Oh, I'm sorry," she replied, clapping her hand over her mouth, overcome with confusion and blushing.

"That's alright. Look," he said, "I mustn't keep you to myself. Please go and talk to other guests. I'm stopping you selling pictures."

They drifted apart while she circulated amongst her clients and he systematically studied every picture, making a determined effort not to drink too much wine. He was drawn to a small picture which was in his price range of a brick bridge over a stream. It had some trees on one side and in the middle distance a patchwork pattern of fields, fading into the blue hills.

When he had the opportunity, he caught Jane's eye and asked, "Can I buy this one please?"

"Certainly you can," she replied, signalling to the young girl, who stuck a red star on the frame. "I'm glad you like it."

"Can I ask you to sign the back and put 'To Chris' please?"

"It'll be my pleasure," she replied with a smile, and took the picture from the wall to sign on the back.

He watched her and said wistfully, "I wish I could paint like you."

She smiled at him again and said, "We all have our talents. There are lots of things I wish I could do. I would love to play the piano for instance, but I'm useless. I bet if you tried hard enough, you'd be able to paint. The techniques can be taught, you know. Maybe we have to have something special to be a great artist, but we can all achieve a reasonable standard if we're taught properly. Can you play a musical instrument?"

He shook his head sadly, "No," he said, "I used to have piano lessons at school, but I know I'll never play again."

"Why's that?"

He held up his arm and said, "That's why."

Again she blushed, "Oh, I'm sorry," she gasped, "That's twice in one evening I've put my foot in it. You must think me very clumsy."

He took a sip of wine and shrugged his shoulders, "No matter," he replied.

They stood in silence and searching for something to say to break the awkward silence she said, "I wonder why you chose that particular picture."

He looked at it for a moment and replied, "I think I like it because when I was a small boy I used to play near a canal. It wasn't around here, but a place called Gorston, and my favourite place was a bridge which looked like that one. The background was different though, sooty walls and derelict factories, but the bridge itself was very similar, so I suppose that's why. It reminds me of a favourite place when I was a boy."

Most of the other guests had left and they found they were almost alone in the gallery. Jane looked over her shoulder, "Oh, it looks as if the viewing is over. Would you like a coffee?"

The coffee was the first of many over the following weeks as they saw a great deal each other. Jane was attracted to him because he was good-looking and she liked his sense of humour; mischievous and dry. They became good friends and in due course, lovers.

❧

Tom was invited to move into the small-holding that Pete and Melanie were renting. It was called Pant-y-gelli near the river at Hay-on-Wye. Pete said, "You helped Jane and me years ago by providing a home for us, so it's my way of repaying you. You've got nowhere to live and Melanie and I have, so why not join us?"

Melanie found a part-time job as a secretary for a small building firm in Hay. It was only for three afternoons a week and did not pay well, but they eked out a living by selling eggs from their free-range chickens and milk from their goats. It was hard work and Pete found that he was working harder than he ever did at Tom Beddows' Country Cider for a small fraction of the remuneration.

Pant-y-gelli was a stone farm house with a range of run-down out-buildings round a cobbled yard. From the upstairs windows they could see the silvery river Wye and the Black Mountains soaring up like a stage backcloth. Many of the farm buildings were lacking a roof and the one over the house leaked. Buckets were placed at strategic points all over the first floor and had to be emptied regularly in wet weather.

When it snowed, it would drive in through gaps between the stone tiles and if Pete did not climb into the roof and clear the drifts it poured through the ceilings when it melted. Every time it snowed, he spent hours passing buckets of snow through the hatch for Melanie to tip into the bath.

Not only did water come through the ceilings, but it came up through the floor. When it was very wet, they had 'gushers' coming up between the flagstones; little fountains of brown water which they had to walk around when crossing the room.

Melanie sat at the kitchen table with her feet on the chair to avoid a new gusher and asked, "Pete, what does Pant-y-gelli mean in English?"

He moved his foot to avoid another brown fountain and with a wink replied, "I think it must be Welsh for The Watery House Under the Waterfall."

Tom moped about the house and spent most daylight hours sitting in the window seat, vacantly looking out at the misty hill behind Clyro, while Pete bustled about in his overalls, mucking out the goats and tending the poultry. One day he came in from the yard, soaked to the skin, his hands blue with the cold, and he sank into an armchair saying, "Oh, my back."

Tom half turned from the window to look at him and turned away again. Pete pulled off his wet jumper and said, "Tom, when we invited you to come and live here, we did expect you to do a little bit to help about the place, but all you do is sit in that bloody window seat staring out of the damned window.

We all know you're upset about what's happened. Who wouldn't be? Everything you worked for has gone, but we've lost a lot as well, you know, but you don't see us sitting about the place. We're getting off our backsides and getting on with life. I've seen you like this before and it frightens me. You ended up in hospital," and, with his voice rising as he became more angry, he added, "and it was your fault that Mum committed suicide and we had to leave the house."

Tom winced, but then continued to stare impassively out of the window.

Pete grimaced when he stood up and stretched his back, "I'm going to make myself a nice cup of tea and I'm damned if I'm going to make you one. If you want one you can make your own."

Later that evening when Tom had gone to bed, Pete and Melanie sat at the kitchen table cleaning eggs. Pete put an egg in the bowl, took it out again to clean off a mark that he'd missed, and said, "I think we should ask Dr Sherwood to look at him. I'm worried that he's sinking into depression and it had a terrible effect on him last time. He went downhill and had a breakdown. I can see the same thing happening again if he doesn't get help."

She nodded in agreement, "I think so. He obviously needs it."

Next morning Melanie shouted up the stairs, "Tom, if you think I'm going to bring you up a cup of tea you've got another think coming. Get up you lazy sod!"

She made a pot of tea and sat at the table with Pete. He looked up at the ceiling and said, "He's very quiet. I can't hear any movements."

"He'll be down when he gets hungry."

"Yes, but he's usually—"

They both looked startled, stood up and went upstairs.

They looked at the empty bed and in unison they exclaimed, "He's gone!"

Tom's Shack

Chapter Thirty One

The battered Land Rover rattled along the Cwm Maerdy lane belching dark clouds of diesel fumes. They hung in the air before dispersing among the hedgerows and a pheasant took to the air, wings whirring, clattering in alarm. Terry Jones, with his arm out of the window, drummed his fingers on the roof in time to the music on the radio. He rumbled over the stone bridge and slowed to avoid a hunched figure in the verge. As he passed, Terry turned to his wife and said, "Hey, wasn't that Tom Beddows?"

"Was it?" she replied, "I thought it was a tramp, someone down on his luck."

Terry bent his head slightly to look in the rear view mirror and recognizing Tom said. "You were right. It was someone down on their luck."

It was a hard winter, one of the coldest on record. The weather forecast talked of temperatures of minus thirty degrees and there were some of the heaviest snowfalls in living memory, cutting off towns and villages. Sometimes the roads came to a standstill because of the blizzards and on January the twentieth the main news item was the weather. The presenter said:

Most of the country has been reeling from the worst winter conditions since records began. Some motorists in South Wales are spending their third night sleeping on the floor of a village

274

hall after their vehicles became trapped in deep snow drifts. Several people had to be dug from their cars and rescue services are still digging for others who are believed to be trapped.

A police spokesman said that they had found other vehicles buried in the snow and rescuers were furiously digging to reach them. It was feared that there was a risk of many deaths from hypothermia as temperatures were expected to plummet again that night. In Cardiff, the roofs of some houses had collapsed under the weight of the snow and, in Herefordshire and Shropshire where some of the lowest temperatures had been recorded, there had been explosions as the freezing temperatures fractured gas mains.

Throughout that harsh winter, Tom was living rough in his beloved woods. Once again the world seemed to be an alien environment and he had gone back to his bolt-hole; his refuge from the world and its problems. Life was less complicated in the woods and he could cope with it.

It was a small world, which he understood and in which he felt comfortable. He found the remains of his old shack and dug himself in, but he was finding it hard, not only because of the harsh weather but because he was several years older than when he last led this life. The shack had deteriorated. Children had been playing and taking pieces away and because of the snow it was difficult to find materials for repair. It was also not easy to find game and he'd not had the opportunity to plant any vegetables.

He survived on snails, but even they were hard to find in the atrocious conditions, and for most of the day he sat huddled in his shack under a sheet of polythene. That was how life was for him during the worst of the winter.

One morning at the end of January, Tom emerged from the shack to a white world. A deep layer of snow had enveloped the woods and the only sound he could hear was the occasional crack of a branch giving way under the weight of the snow and a distant barking dog.

Otherwise there was silence; a heavy silence that he felt he could touch. The sky was clear and the branches formed white linear patterns against the blue. A solitary wood pigeon sat in the tree above him with feathers fluffed out and its head under its wing.

Tom pulled his duffel coat up to his chin and trudged through the snow to check his snares. He found a rabbit in one, but not a very fat one, as they too were finding it a struggle to survive the extreme conditions. There was a dry stone wall on one boundary of the woods and on the sheltered side he found some stones that were not covered in a deep blanket of snow.

Lifting a large stone he found some snails which he gathered and put in his pocket. In the oak tree behind the wall was a squirrel, scampering up the trunk making his way through the trees, jumping from branch to branch and showering loose snow as he went. Tom stealthily followed, keeping out of sight behind the tree trunks.

The wind was picking up and the snow was stinging his face and going down his neck as it blew off the branches. He put up his hood, tied it tightly under his chin, and continued through the deep drifts. It was hard work lifting his feet, but he kept the squirrel in sight and eventually his patience was rewarded as it led him to a store of nuts.

They were hidden in a hole under a tree and he was able to reach in to find a hoard of hazel nuts, which the squirrel had hidden as his larder for the winter. They, too, were put into his pocket and he retraced his steps through the snow back to his shack.

He'd been living there for several weeks and was beginning to get organized. He raked the embers of his fire to bring them to life and put on some dry wood. It quickly flared up, giving some warmth into the tiny room, and he held his hands close to the flames to bring some feeling back to his numb fingers.

He stamped his feet and hung his wet coat by the fire and, when the cold had gone from his bones, he prepared a rabbit and snail stew, which simmered on the fire and filled the shack with a delicious aroma. When he had finished his dandelion coffee he felt better and set about splitting some dry oak for his fire.

Such was the pattern of life for him over the next few months. He lived through snow and frost and through some gales which almost destroyed his shack. On a number of occasions he was up in the night doing repairs to his dwelling in total blackness, with the wind wailing like a banshee in the wildly thrashing trees.

As the winter wore on, it became a little warmer but he had to contend with heavy rain, which caused flooding. Because of the poor roof he lived for weeks with wet clothes and bedding. He was reluctant to leave his dwelling because everywhere he went was a quagmire of sticky clay, which stuck to his boots and made walking difficult.

The wet weather seemed to be going on forever and, even when the rain did stop for brief periods, water continued to drip from the branches, so Tom lived with a polythene sheet tied around him with twine. He was raking the embers once more and glancing up at the dark threatening sky, when his attention was caught by a movement on the other side of the clearing and he saw a figure coming towards him.

Having visitors was an unusual experience and he got to his feet as the figure drew closer. He did not recognize the visitor, as he wore a dark coat and the hood was pulled over his head so that none of his face was visible.

He could tell by its movements that it was a man, who was making slow progress through the sticky mud. He saw that he was wearing light shoes, which had collected a mass of clay, and the figure kept pausing to try and rid his feet of their burden.

Even when the figure reached him, he was unable to see his face. The man stopped and pulled back his hood. Holding out his hand, he greeted Tom with, "Bonjour, Monsieur."

Tom was surprised and scratched his chin for a moment. The man said, "Allo, Monsieur Tom. I am Pierre—Pierre le Brun and I 'ave pleasure in meeting you again."

"Monsieur le Brun!"

"They told me in the pub that I would find you 'ere."

"But what—why?" spluttered Tom.

The last time the two men had met had been in the hot Provencal sun, when le Brun was the foreman in charge of building the villa. They had spent a pleasant evening drinking wine on the patio, watching the fireflies and distant lights brighten as the evening light faded.

Tom was stunned. "You—Penny went to you—and Sarah—How are they? Why are you here?"

Le Brun raised his hand and said, "Moment, Monsieur. Many questions, but I will explain."

Tom did not invite him to sit or enter his shack and they stood in

the sticky mud with rain dripping from the branches running down
their necks.

Le Brun pulled his hood up again and said, "You must listen to
me. I 'ave some bad news for you and I 'ad to come to tell you
myself. I am a man of honour and it was my duty."

"What bad news? What's happened?"

"Monsieur, please allow me to tell my story. It is Penny, and I am
'ere to tell you that she is dead. I am sorry."

"Dead? What do—"

Please allow me to finish, Monsieur. I 'ave come a long way to
give you this news. I am sorry she is dead. She drowned in the
'arbour; fell off the 'arbour wall."

"Dead. Penny dead? I can't believe it. Are you sure?"

"Oui. I am sure. She died on Wednesday and she is to be buried in
your church tomorrow morning."

Tom went into the shack and sat heavily on the wicker chair,
gesturing weakly for le Brun to take the other. He put his head in
his hands and sat for a full minute. There was silence in the woods
now that the wind had dropped and all that could be heard was the
dripping from the trees. Le Brun went to put a comforting hand on
Tom's shoulder, but he hesitated and withdrew. When Tom lifted
his head he was calm and asked, "How did it happen?"

"We are not sure, but we think she may have slipped on the wet
stones and hit 'er head. She was on 'er own, you comprehend?"

"And what about Sarah? Where is she and how has she taken it?"

Le Brun did not answer but looked uncomfortable.

"What is it? What's the matter?"

"Monsieur," he began, "I 'ave to explain it all to you, but it is sad."

Le Brun went on to explain in great detail that Penny had not
been happy living with him in France. She constantly talked about
home, about Tom and the Manor House where she grew up. She
cried a lot and was having medical treatment for a nervous
breakdown. On several occasions she had threatened to take her
own life and, on the morning of her death, she had repeated her
threat. She had argued with le Brun and gone out for a walk along
the harbour wall.

Le Brun said, "I do not believe she killed 'erself. It was 'ow you
say? A coincidence that she died that morning. Please, believe me, I

do not think she did it."

"So, she wasn't happy with you?"

"No, Monsieur. I 'ave to tell you she was not. At first she was 'appy but not later."

"And what about Sarah? Where's she?"

"I am not allowed to say."

"What do you mean you're not allowed to say? Where is she?" He got to his feet.

"Please sit down, Tom. I 'ave more news which is not good. Sarah blames you for the poor 'ealth of 'er mother. The doctors say she was not right in the 'ead." He made circular motions with his finger while pointing at his head. Everything was too much for 'er. She could not manage with life."

"But tell me more about Sarah."

"Like I said, Monsieur. Sarah blames you and she believes that 'er mother killed herself, and she blames you for that also. She told me to say that she will never forgive you." He hesitated and said, "But try not to worry about her, Monsieur. She will be looked after by a very nice French family. They treat 'er like a daughter and she will be 'appy and 'ave a good start in life. Do not worry about 'er."

Tom put his head in his hands once more and le Brun put a hand on his shoulder. Tom pulled away, "Don't touch me!" he shouted, putting his head in his hands again.

When he looked up after a few minutes, le Brun was squelching through the mud again and had reached the other side of the clearing.

"Monsieur!" shouted Tom. "Did you say the funeral is tomorrow? In the morning?"

Le Brun turned and pulling his hood down said, "You must not go, Monsieur. It will cause un 'appiness. It may cause a scene and it would be 'ow you say? undignified. Please do not go. You will not be welcome."

Next morning, Tom stood behind a yew tree on the edge of the churchyard, watching the cortege move slowly and silently from the lych gate to the church. He kept well out of sight and saw Sarah at the head of the procession, all in black, supported by a woman he did not know. While the service took place inside the church, he sank to his knees and prayed.

It had started to rain again and the wind was rising, sweeping wet curtains across the churchyard. He was bare-headed and the water ran down inside his clothes. The rain was torrential and cold and he could feel it collecting at his waist, where his tight belt restricted the downward flow. His hair was plastered on his face.

When the coffin was brought out through the porch, he shivered and pulled back behind the topiary. The procession moved towards the grave that had been dug at the edge of the church yard. She was to be buried near her parents in an area designated for members of the Hudson family.

Tom recognized many of the mourners but he could not take his eyes off Sarah. Remembering what le Brun had said, he restrained himself from rushing over and putting his arms round her when she sobbed at the grave side. The sounds of her sobbing were taken away on the wind as the coffin was lowered into the ground.

When the burial was over and the mourners silently drifted through the lych gate, Tom moved from tree to tree to gain a closer look at his daughter and le Brun caught a glimpse of him as he moved between two trees. He stopped and whispered something to Sarah, pointing at Tom. She too stopped and looked in his direction. The two figures looked at each other across the gravestones.

It was a pregnant moment and the last of the mourners, who were making their way from the grave, sensed the drama and froze, standing like statues with water pouring from their black umbrellas. Then the tension snapped. Sarah put a handkerchief to her face and ran towards the waiting cars. Le Brun looked at Tom and shrugging his shoulders smiled sadly and followed her to the car.

After a particularly bad night struggling with gale force winds and rain, Tom made a decision and pulling on his duffel coat and putting some polythene over his shoulders, he trudged off through the dripping trees across the ploughed fields. He stepped over the furrows, his feet becoming heavier as the wet clay stuck to his boots.

There had been a dusting of snow in the night and it lay in the bottom of the furrows, making a delicate pattern of undulating white lines, clear in the foreground and fading into the mist as they curved into the distance. The faint outline of the church made a focal point and a flock of rooks chattered noisily in the sky above the gaunt elm trees.

He arrived at the other side panting for breath and sat on a stile to recover, crouching with the polythene pulled over his head and held tightly across his chest. It flapped noisily about his ears as he tried to control it in the wind.

The rain had stopped by the time he reached Cwm Maerdy Farm but the wind was still blowing in violent gusts. A barn door banged and some loose hay blew out and spiralled up into the sky as he made his way across the courtyard.

"On your way!" shouted the figure in the porch. He pointed a shotgun at the ground between them, "Go on, keep walking, there's nothing for you here. Don't think I'm afraid to use this gun."

Tom pulled the polythene sheet from his head saying, "Terry, it's me, Tom Beddows."

They sat in the farmhouse kitchen drinking hot Bovril. Wet clothes steamed by the fire and Tom sat in a dressing gown with a towel wrapped round his head. Mrs Jones was knitting by the fire.

"Thank you," said Tom, "I was all in, but I feel better now. I'm getting too old for that sort of life. I could cope with it when I was younger but not these days. I used to enjoy the challenge but now I'm getting on a bit, it really is a struggle."

"It's the least I can do. Where were you off to?"

Tom blew on his Bovril, took another sip, and said, "I wasn't on my way anywhere. I was coming here."

Terry looked at him over his mug and raised a quizzical eyebrow, "Oh," he said.

"Yes, I remember talking to you some time ago in the Old Black Lion. I was in very different circumstances then and you were saying how the farm work was difficult for you on your own and how you couldn't find anyone to help."

Terry scratched his stubbly chin, saying, "Yes, that's right."

"Do you still need someone?"

"I suppose I do really. I had stopped looking for someone, but are you trying to tell me that you're offering?"

Tom pushed his straggly hair from his face and nodded, "I think you also said that you had a cottage which could go with the job."

"That's right, not much, but it's dry and clean." He stood up and said, "What do you think, Ethel? Do you think Tom will be useful about the place?"

She put down her knitting and said, "We could certainly do with some help, especially at lambing, and Tom knows what he's doing when it comes to farming. He knows one end of a ewe from the other."

"That's settled then," said Terry, offering his hand, "The job's yours if you want it."

Tom smiled broadly, "Thank you," he said and they shook hands.

Chapter Thirty Two

Since the poisoning, Brian Jones had been a happy man. He was delighted to have implicated Tom by using Sam and Matthew. It had not quite gone as planned, because Matthew's suicide had changed the course of events.

He had really wanted Tom to go to prison for the rest of his life but, now his business had collapsed and he was a broken man, Brian felt that his plan had succeeded. To cap it all, he now owned the Manor House, the French villa, and the yacht, so he was content. He had also received reports of Tom living in his woods.

"Perfect," he thought, "That's the best bit. He's where I wanted to see him, back in his hovel where he belongs. Back with the animals." He smiled broadly as he leaned forward stubbing out the last of his cigar.

Brian was now the Squire, but he was not popular and was greeted in the street with grudging tolerance by the villagers. Angela was still with him, though they were not happily married.

As far as she could see, he'd kept his promise to leave Tom alone and she had no reason to suspect that he was in any way involved with his downfall. She lived in the Manor House with him but they led separate lives and she was now working as a vet, based in Hay-on-Wye, travelling to farms to tend sick animals.

They never went out together and they even had separate circles of friends. The staff on the estate had a greater respect for her than Brian and, while he was despised, she was known affectionately as Lady Angela, and had come to be responsible for the day-to-day running of things, because she had a better response from the staff.

"They seem to like you better than me," complained Brian, "so you might as well keep things going. I have enough worries with all the businesses."

And so they drifted along, man and wife under the same roof, but man and wife in name only. They no longer shared a bed or even the same bedroom.

At Pant-y-gelli, Pete and Melanie were finding things difficult. No eggs were produced in the winter and they didn't make much money from the goats. One Sunday, Melanie had just got out of the bath and was in the bedroom, wrapped in a towel, when she heard a rumbling coming from the yard. Looking out of the window, she saw Pete sitting on a rusty tractor, shaking and quivering, while black clouds emanated from the exhaust and drifted up to her.

He gave her a cheery wave and when he pulled the stop button the machine shuddered and wheezed and then was silent. He sat in the bucket seat grinning up at her as the smoke drifted into the sky. It was very rusty, but it was possible to detect that it had once been grey. There was little tread left on the tyres and most the machine seemed to be held together with wire and baler twine.

She opened the window and, fanning the fumes away from her face, she asked "What is it?"

"It's a tractor."

"I can see that. I mean what are you doing with it?"

"It's ours. I bought it cheap from Bert Stokes's farm sale. Good isn't it?"

She opened the window for a better view. He'd jumped down from the seat and was lovingly polishing the bonnet with his sleeve.

"What do we need a rusty old tractor for?"

"We don't, but I'm going to do it up to sell again and make us a nice profit."

She looked down at him incredulously, saying, "But you don't know the first thing about tractors. You couldn't even mend the twins' pedal car."

"I know a bit, but there's nothing wrong with this beauty. It only needs a few screws and a tin of paint. It's a Fergie, so I'll get some grey paint, and she'll be in showroom condition before I've finished with her."

Melanie shook her fist at him and uttering a guttural growling noise slammed the window.

For the next few weeks Pete had tractor parts on the kitchen table. He took off the panels and rubbed them down before painting them Ferguson Grey, and he oiled and greased everything that seemed to need oiling and greasing.

"There you are, I told you so!" he shouted, waving a cheque in the air. He had put an advert in the *Hereford Times*,

'Ferguson Tractor in immaculate condition. £750.'

The telephone had started ringing on the Thursday morning as soon as the paper came out and he'd sold it to a farmer from Llanigon by lunch time. "That's more than we make in the whole of the summer selling eggs." He held the cheque in the air and danced round the kitchen table, "Let's go for a drink in the Black Lion tonight, to celebrate."

And so they did. They sat by the fire and he smoked a cigar. He blew a luxurious cloud into the air and studied the cigar. "Do you know, this is the first one I've smoked since the crash and I do enjoy them."

"Well, I shouldn't get a taste for them again on the strength of selling one tractor."

But from the sale of one tractor grew a relatively lucrative side-line. Pete frequented the local farm sales buying up old tractors. He bought them cheap and without spending much money on them managed to make a profit by smartening them up and selling them.

Farmers think of their tractors as workhorses, rather than elegant transport, and do not treat them with respect. They stand out in all weathers and become caked in mud and grease. They are knocked about but with a little attention with cloth, screwdriver, and paint brush, they can be made to look more respectable. The older diesel tractors were simple and rugged, so they rarely went wrong and were easy to work on and even with his limited engineering experience, Pete was able to make a profitable business.

"Well, it won't make us rich, but it doesn't half help," he said to his wife over the bacon and egg one morning, "and it helps having Steve Bufton in the village."

Steve Bufton was the farmer who no longer farmed but had turned his yard into a tractor graveyard. Pete was a frequent visitor, buying spare parts and asking for technical advice, which was freely given. He wandered about amongst the rusting hulks, pulling aside shoulder-high nettles and purple willow herb to find the parts he needed.

He often disturbed laying hens in the bowl shaped seats in his search for hydraulic pumps, radiators, and power take-off shafts, and the rickety building at Pant-y-gelli which had once been a goat shed, became a tractor restoration shed.

Tom settled into the cottage at Cwm Maerdy farm. He had running water and electricity and a roof that did not leak. He worked on the farm doing routine jobs with the sheep and cattle. He was paid very little but it was enough to buy food and clothes.

He now had a grey beard and, as he had lost much of his hair, he looked older. He was also having trouble with arthritis in his hip and was a frequent visitor to Dr Sherwood's surgery. When the pain got bad, he walked with the aid of a stick, but most of the time he managed without it.

It was lambing time now that spring had arrived. Cwm Maerdy had a large flock and it was the busiest time of the year. "How did you manage before I came along?" asked Tom, as he put a new-born lamb to his mother and stood back to watch the result.

"Buggered if I know," replied Terry, "I can carry on here for a while, if you can go and check the ones in the top medder."

Tom put his jacket back on and opened the gate leading to the fields. The weather was warming up and he could feel the sun on his back as he walked towards the top meadow. Growth was getting under way and the meadow, which was being kept for hay, had not been grazed and was colourful with spring flowers.

The sound of church bells drifted over the fields from the village,and a light aircraft droned overhead in the clear sky. When he climbed the gate to the top meadow, he saw several dead lambs lying on the grass and he went over to study the lifeless bodies.

"Foxes!" said Terry, when Tom returned with the news.

"Yep, I would say so. They had their throats torn out, and one of them was chewed in half."

"It sounds like it. The trouble is, the poor old ewe finds it hard to protect more than one. She'll stamp her feet and butt the bloody thing to protect her young but he keeps circling and biding his time. She can't look after two lively youngsters, so if he waits long enough he gets his grub, and he isn't satisfied with one. He'll go on killing for the fun of it. Sometimes it's like a battlefield out there. I lost about twenty-five last season and that's a big dent in my income."

"It certainly is. I know where his earth is, just inside the dingle under the rock. Lend me your shotgun and I'll take Timmy and solve your problem for you."

Under the big rock Tom could smell the fox and there were

pieces of bloodstained wool near the hole. A chewed off lamb's head had rolled down the bank and lay staring up at the trees. Timmy, the Jack Russell terrier, began to whine and yelp and, when Tom took the twine from the dog's neck, it darted down the hole. Tom slipped two cartridges into the side by side and shut the barrels.

He heard a muffled yelping from underground and a big dog fox flew out of the hole in a shower of soil. Instinctively, the gun went up and the fox somersaulted and lay still. A flurry of wood pigeon rose from the ash trees and a startled pheasant took to the air as the bang echoed round the valley.

Tom walked over to the dead animal and turned it over with his boot. It had died instantly when the shot hit and it had blood coming from its mouth. Tom slipped the twine back on the terrier's neck, "Come on Timmy," he said, kicking the dead fox into the hedge.

When he got back to the farm, he found Terry leaning on the rails looking at a sick cow in the straw. She was a black and white Friesian and she lay with dull eyes, not moving when he called to her.

Tom glanced at the beast and said, "She's thin isn't she. What's the matter with her?"

"Don't know. I thought she was going to be alright but she's going downhill again. I'd better get the Vet to have a look at her. You have to think twice about calling the buggers out these days, the way vet's fees are going, but she's a valuable animal so I'd better get on the phone."

The Vet's Land Rover rattled into the yard and a woman climbed down from the cab. She had her back to Tom as she reached inside for her kit. Her hair was tied back under a headscarf and she wore rubber waders that flopped about the tops of her legs as she moved. She gathered up her bag and walked across the cobbled yard saying, "I've come to have a look at your sick cow. Where is she?"

Tom opened a gate and said, "In here, Love."

She went into the pen taking off her headscarf and, shaking her hair loose, she turned to look at him.

"Angela Sturgess!" he blurted out.

"Is it Tom?" she asked, squinting and putting a hand to her eyes to see him clearly as he stood against the light from the barn door. Dust had been disturbed and the light coming through the door reflected from it, so that Tom appeared as a silhouette in the grey haze.

"Yes, Tom Beddows," he replied, beaming. He moved closer and she could see him more clearly.

"Oh, Tom, it is nice to see you again, and I was so sorry to hear of your misfortune after you were doing so well," she hesitated and said, "Actually it's Angela Jones these days, not Sturgess."

"Yes, I know. I heard that you'd married Brian."

She opened her bag and said, "Let me attend to this lady and then I want to show you something that might interest you."

She checked the cow and gave her an injection in the loose skin of the neck saying, "This should do the trick and I'll come back at the same time tomorrow to see if she's any better. Just keep her dry and warm and give her plenty of water."

Tom opened the gate for her and said, "What have you got to show me? I'm intrigued."

She smiled and said, "Oh, I haven't got it here. It's at home at the Manor, but this is my last call of the day so I'll be back in about fifteen minutes."

He waited in the courtyard leaning on the gate. In the top of the silver birch, a song thrush's melody wafted over the fields on the balmy evening air and, from somewhere in the distance came the sound of a chainsaw, rising and falling like a bee flying amongst flowers. He concentrated on the bend in the lane, his ears straining to catch the sound of the Land Rover.

The distant chainsaw stopped and all he could hear was the thrush, the bleating of lambs calling to their mothers, and the answering calls of the ewes. The sounds echoed from the surrounding hills and then he stood on tip-toe to see over a holly bush as he heard the Land Rover bouncing up the rutted lane. It was in a low gear and slowly came into view, jolting and weaving to avoid the pot holes.

"I've got it," she said climbing from the cab clutching a brown paper bag. She had changed into a loose white summer dress with red poppies printed on it. She held the bag out to him and a broad smile spread over his face as he opened it and saw what was inside.

He turned it over in his hand. "It's my love-spoon!" He looked at her and then back to the piece of wood which had been hacked by his penknife, "And you've kept it all these years." He kept turning it over, fascinated by it.

"Do you remember carving it for me when we were at school? You told me that your Granddad had suggested you did it to give to the one you wanted to marry."

"I remember carving it in my Dad's woodshed and it took me hours. I cut my finger, so you could say I suffered for my art. I also remember when I gave it to you that you promised to marry me," he smiled.

"And I ended up marrying your rival, Brian."

Tom continued to study the wood, "It's not very good is it? But at the time I thought it was a fine piece of carving."

"You were very young and it's the thought that counts."

"Fancy your keeping it all these years," he said again.

"I've often looked at it and smiled to myself. Nobody else has seen it since the day you gave it to me. It's been our little secret."

Tom grinned, shaking his head in disbelief.

They sat on the low wall, side by side, talking until the evening shadows lengthened and the bright evening turned to twilight.

Tom said, "I never thought you'd marry Brian."

Her countenance saddened and she replied, "I made the wrong choice. I often ask myself why I married him." She thought for a moment and said, "I think it was because I was young and impressionable and he was rich and confident. He dazzled me and swept me off my feet, but I got older and wiser and began to see him for what he really is."

"I never liked him," said Tom.

"Never liked him? Is that all? I hate and loathe him. He's evil."

"But you're still with him."

"Let's say we have a bargain. We made an arrangement but there's no love there. He's hit me more than once and I've left him too, but I went back."

Tom put his hand on her shoulder and said, "I don't understand how you can stay with him. If you're not happy and he doesn't treat you properly, why don't you leave him?"

She didn't answer but looked down at her feet, bringing back memories to Tom. He caught the same look in her eye which he had last seen outside the church on that hot hay-making day. She had been embarrassed and looked down at her feet. The expression in her eyes was the same after all these years.

"You haven't changed a bit," he said, tenderly putting a knuckle under her chin and lifting her face to see it better in the fading light.

"Neither have you," she replied.

"Oh, I have, I have some lines on my face. I've lost some hair and sometimes I have to walk with a stick."

"No, you haven't changed. You're still the same Tom Beddows underneath; the same Tom Beddows who spent hours carving this love-spoon to show how you felt about me," she paused, and then said, "What happened to your marriage to Penelope Hudson?"

He scratched his head and said, "That's a very good question and I don't know the answer. We were happy. Very happy, and I have a little girl called Sarah somewhere in France I think, but it all went sour when she started getting poison-pen letters about me. She treated them with contempt at first, but they got to her in the end, and she turned against me when I got caught up in that terrible poisoning business."

"There was a lot of other trouble before that and I think she began to believe it all in the end. She said she didn't, but I'm not so sure, but whether she did or not doesn't matter. She couldn't cope with the pressure and she's dead now."

"Yes, I know. My Dad was at the funeral. I'm very sorry. Do you know who wrote all those letters and caused all the trouble?"

He nodded and said, "I've got a very good idea—Yes, I know who wrote them. They had his style stamped all over them."

"Brian?"

"Yes, Brian. It couldn't have been anyone else. He just never stopped his capers from school days."

"And he promised me," she murmured, "He promised me."

"Pardon?"

"Oh, nothing."

They sat in silence in the fading dusk. Mrs Jones put on lights in the farmhouse; the yellow glow spilling out onto the cobbles. Lights began to twinkle on the other side of the valley and bats flitted about. "I must be going. I didn't expect to stay here this long."

"Yes, Brian will be wondering where you've got to."

She sighed and said, "You must be joking. We go our own ways and he couldn't care less what I'm doing. He has a mistress in Hereford and I expect he's with her at the moment. He thinks I don't know about her but I've known for months. She's the manageress of a clothes shop but she doesn't worry me because I don't care. Anyway I must be off."

"Does that mean it'll be another forty years before I see you again?"

"I hope not. It's strange, we've lived in the same village all these years and this is the first time we've met since we left the Junior School. I've seen you a few times driving past in your car and I've seen you on television, but our paths have never really crossed."

He stood up and said, "Look, I've been thinking and I've got an idea. Are you working tomorrow?"

"I don't have to, why?"

"Tomorrow's my day off and I thought maybe we could go down to the river for a picnic as it's going to be a nice day. I'd like to get to know you better and it would be a shame to let you drift away from me again."

"That's a lovely idea, Tom. I did say I'd come back and see how Terry's cow's getting on. I must do that, but otherwise I can be free."

Next morning was bright and sunny. Angela called for him in the Land Rover and they went down to the Wye. They sat on the bank in the shade of a willow, dangling their bare feet in the water.

The sun was rising higher in the east, sparkling on the surface of the river in a myriad of spots of light with brilliant green damsel flies flitting over the surface. The Black Mountains were illuminated in the distance and the rooftops of Hay shimmered in the heat.

Angela pointed and said, "Did you see that kingfisher. It was like a flash of light. There he goes again look," and the bird flashed in front of them, the sun catching his fluorescent plumage.

They could hear a tractor working in the distance and through the trees they could see it going back and forth, harrowing the brown soil. It was red against the sienna earth and the scene was flecked with the white of seagulls, following the tractor and diving and wheeling around it.

The couple splashed the surface of the water with their feet and Angela produced a bottle of wine from her bag. Lying back on the grass, they drank the wine and talked about their lives since leaving school.

There was much to catch up on and Tom's life had been extraordinary. They lay on their backs watching the white clouds drifting across the sky and as the sun rose higher, they became lovers. It happened naturally, as if fate had decreed that it should happen, and afterwards they lay naked under the willow. Angela clung tightly to him. "I am never going to let you go again," she declared, nuzzling into him.

Her tears dampened his neck and he stroked her hair, gently pulling her head against him, "And I'm never going to let you go again now that I've found you. I feel so sad when I think of all the years we've wasted."

"Yes, we've got a lot of time to make up, so let's not waste a second of it." She pulled him on top of her and they made love again on the edge of the river, unaware of the swan and her cygnets dabbling in the water close to the bank.

The couple were alone but if anyone had been on the river that morning they would have seen two nude figures clasping each other in the grass, with the dappled sunlight flickering on their bodies; clinging so tightly, as if they never wanted to be separated again.

Chapter Thirty Three

Jane had soon discovered that her new boyfriend was an alcoholic. It was something he couldn't hide from her and after one of his binges he was brought back and dumped on the settee by two men, "He's been disgracing himself again. This is getting to be a habit and I'd keep him on a lead if I were you," said one of the men. When they had gone she made him a black coffee and said, "You've got a problem haven't you?"

"What sort of a problem?"

She blew from her tight lips and said in exasperation, "Now come on, you know exactly what I'm talking about. You're an alcoholic and you need help if you're going to make anything of your life. Just look at the state of you. I can see now why your wife left. I expect she couldn't take any more and I know just how she felt."

He blew on his coffee and took a drink, "I can handle it and I can stop drinking whenever I want to."

"Why don't you then?"

"I enjoy a drink from time to time and I can cope with it. It would be a dull old world if we couldn't go out and have a drink every so often."

Jane sighed and said, "I think you ought to talk to Alcoholics Anonymous. I was watching a television programme about them and they're very good. They've helped a lot of hopeless cases and their number's in the directory, so let me find it for you."

Chris grabbed her wrist and held it so tightly that it hurt, "Don't bother, I've told you I don't need any help. I can cope." He put his head back and fell asleep, snoring loudly with his coffee spilt down his trousers.

"Hello, is that Alcoholics Anonymous?—Yes—No, I don't need help but I'm phoning on behalf of someone who I think, does—No—I see. Alright I'll see what I can do. Thank you."

The gentle voice on the other end of the line explained that until Chris admitted that he needed help and went along for counselling there was nothing they could do. Jane was disappointed but determined not to give in and she resolved that she was going to help him with his drinking problem whether he wanted her to or not. She would embark on a campaign to get him to admit he needed help.

For the next few weeks he continued to drink heavily, starting early in the morning, and he lost his job with the restoration firm. His employer had been aware of his drinking for a long time and had turned a blind eye to it, but when he tripped and dropped a hammer from the scaffolding, he decided that it was no longer safe to have him working for the firm.

"I'm sorry," said Dai Evans to Jane, "I've been as patient as I can but he's unreliable. He often doesn't turn up for work and when he does he falls asleep on the job. There are a lot of hazards in this business and I can't afford the risk of having a drunk running up and down ladders and carrying heavy objects on the scaffolding above my lads. He's a danger to himself and everyone else. If you want my advice, Love, I'd get his problem sorted out, because he'll never hold a job down while he's like this."

Losing his job gave him the jolt that was needed and he agreed to go to Alcoholics Anonymous. They strolled through the church-yard, arm in arm. "Yes, alright," he said, "I'll go along with you. I can see that the drink isn't doing me any good and if you want I'll go and see them."

They walked between the topiary where two men were up step ladders clipping the yews into smooth round shapes and they stopped to watch them for a while.

They carefully snipped at the yew with their shears and made them into round shapes that looked as if they had been modelled from green clay. Chris watched them and said, "Now they're craftsmen in their way, carrying on traditions that've been handed down the generations. That's what I want to do, but I can see that unless I control my drinking, I'm never going to be a craftsman."

Jane breathed deeply and said, "Thank Heavens you've seen sense at last."

Brian lit a cigar and put his feet up on the office desk, "So, what news have you got for me?" he asked the fat man in a grey suit.

"Err, well Mr Jones," he replied, scratching his moustache with his biro. "Err, I am sorry to tell you that your instincts were right. Your wife is certainly having an affair. Err, I have kept her under observation for several weeks and during that time she has, errm, been seeing a man, always the same man, and I have all the meetings fully documented here with dates, times and, err, venues of the meetings. I have followed them to various places and I have plenty of evidence. Yesterday they went to a hay loft at Cwm Maerdy Farm and I kept watch and witnessed them, err, well, they were, err—"

"Come on, man, spit it out. I'm paying you a lot of money for this."

"They were making love in the hay."

Brian grinned and said, "I knew it, I knew it. Thank you, Mr Castle. If you send me your invoice I'll make sure that your fee is paid without delay." He looked out of the office window and over the roof tops, "The sneaky little cow. I just knew she was two-timing me. What sort of a man is he, tall, short, young, good-looking, rich?"

"He's about forty-eight, I suppose, thinning on top wth a grey beard. He works as a farm labourer at Cwm Maerdy and lives in one of the cottages."

Brian grinned again, "I thought she would have found someone better than that. Not the sort of lover the Lady of the Manor should be taking, but then I suppose Lady Chatterley had her gamekeeper. So her lover doesn't have a lot of prospects would you say?"

The detective shook his head.

"I wonder what she sees in him, what he has to offer that I haven't. He must have some special qualities to attract her. Do you know his name?"

The private detective rustled through the pages of his notebook, "Yes, here we are, err —I have ascertained that his name is—err, where are we? Ah, yes, it's Mr Thomas Beddows."

After the detective had left, Brian sat in his chair looking through the window and over the chimneys. He crushed out his cigar and immediately lit another. The cigar was half-smoked before he stirred from his chair. He drove out of the gates and turned onto the main road with his tyres squealing. He drove along scowling, deep in thought, with tight lips and breathing noisily through his nose.

Sam answered the knock on his door to find Brian standing on the doorstep with outstretched hand. "Hello, Mr Evans, do you remember me?"

"Yes," he replied without any warmth and with expressionless face.

"Can I come in? I have a proposition to put to you." Sam stood aside and they went into the front room. They sat down and Brian offered him a cigar which was refused with a shake of the head. "May I?" he asked and Sam nodded.

Sam stared at him and asked, "What's all this about? It must be something important that brings you to my door."

"Oh, I just wanted a little chat with you. Are you sure you won't have a cigar? I have them sent to me from an exclusive shop in St James's. No? Alright, so we'll get down to business. I know that you've been a bit of a naughty boy when you were working for me."

He wagged the unlit cigar at him, "My attention was drawn to certain discrepancies in the figures and when I put two and two together I realized that you'd been channelling some of the goods into other areas—but what's a few tape recorders and things between friends. I'm sure we're not going to fall out over it."

"I could quite easily forget it ever happened —water under the proverbial bridge—but I need a little favour in return. Now, I know that you need the money to take your poor wife to America for a life-saving operation. I expect that's why you borrowed things from me to raise money for it. I can understand that. I might have done the same myself if I was in the same situation."

He paused to light his cigar while Sam gazed at him open-mouthed. It was clear that he didn't know he'd already been to America and the operation had been too late. The news of her death had obviously not reached him.

Brian continued, "Now, if I was a nasty person and I reported the matter to the police, you would surely go to prison and then what would happen to your wife? I couldn't have that on my conscience, so I'll overlook the matter but, like I said, I need a little favour doing in return. I have an acquaintance, someone you also know, and I need your help in teaching him a lesson."

"Now, this might come as shock to you because I know I don't look like the sort of person who could say this, but I need him teaching a permanent lesson. Not to put too fine a point on it. We won't beat about the bush, as they say. I want you to kill him for me and in return I don't tell the police about your little indiscretion and

I give you a handsome lump sum to take your wife to America to be made better. I don't think you're in a position to do anything other than agree, do you? Not if you love your wife. I'm sure she's in a lot of pain and you now have the opportunity to relieve it and help her to lead a normal life again. Just think of that. There's no other way you'll raise the money and if you go to prison that'll be the end of her."

Sam stared vacantly, unable to absorb what he was hearing, and Brian seemed to be emboldened as he warmed to his theme.

"There's something else you don't know about me Sam. I am the holder of some very interesting information about you. I know that you put the poison in the cider which killed those unfortunate people. Don't ask me how I know, but I do. Now, I could also tell the police about that, if I had a mind to, but I know that you're far too sensible to let that happen, because you know that your wife would die. So what do you say? Will you do this little job for me? It can be done in such a way that everyone will think it an accident and you won't be implicated and, as soon as the job's done, off you go to America clutching a nice fat envelope of money and come back with a healthy wife, free from all that pain. Can you refuse?"

Again Sam didn't answer but stared vacantly at him.

Brian looked at his dead cigar and re-lit it. He viewed Sam through narrowed eyes, blew out the match and said, "The ball's in your court Sam."

"Give me a while to think about it. I'll call you as soon as I've decided."

Brian rose from his chair and said, "Fair enough, but don't take too long, because I might get tired of waiting and toddle along to the police station."

As he heard the car move off, Sam made himself a cup of tea and sat down at the kitchen table to make sense of what he'd heard. He was convinced that Brian had been responsible for the poisoning. He knew that he used to spend a lot of time with Matthew Davies and he had long ago worked out that Brian had his hand in it somewhere.

He was angry to think that Brian Jones had caused so many deaths and so much misery without a twinge of conscience. He was angry because he had blackmailed both Matthew Davies and himself and now he was trying to harm Tom Beddows again. "It's unbelievable," he thought.

He sat deep in cogitation long after his untouched cup of tea had cooled. Occasionally he stood and paced around the room and then sat hunched in the chair again. Eventually a broad smile spread over his face and he reached for the telephone.

Miss Acton

Chapter Thirty Four

"Right Sam, I'm glad we're going to do business together," said Brian, shaking his hand. He'd received the call soon after getting home and he immediately got into the car and driven back to Sam's house. "Here's the plan. I've made some enquiries and I know that he goes fishing in the Wye most Sundays. He fishes the Crawford pool, just upstream from Court Farm."

"Sometimes he has a girlfriend with him, but I can arrange things so that he'll be fishing alone this Sunday. It's no good trying to creep up on him, because it's too open, so you must pretend you're out for a Sunday morning walk. Go up to him as bold as brass and start talking. Sit down behind him and watch him fish for a while and when he's really engrossed hit him hard on the head with a stone."

"Don't pussy-foot about, but give him a good bang to knock him out and then push him in the river to drown, rod and all, so that it looks as if he slipped and hit his head. There's quite a drop to the water from where he fishes, so it'll look good, and it will be bye bye, Tommy, and for God's Sake throw the stone in the water afterwards. Don't leave it lying on the bank as it'll have your finger prints on it and maybe some blood."

Sam listened attentively and then said, "And what about my payment, you know, the money to take Jean to America, when do I get that?"

Brian drew deeply on his cigar and said, "As soon as I hear the news I want to hear, I'll be on your doorstep with a big fat envelope and off you go to America and your worries will be over."

"How much?"

"Five thousand pounds."

Sam noisily sucked air through his teeth and shook his head.

"Six thousand then."

"I was thinking that for this sort of job, fifteen thousand would be more like it."

"Okay," said Brian, "fifteen thousand it is."

"Or maybe twenty-five thousand."

"Okay."

"In cash of course."

"Of course."

Jane had made some progress in drying Chris out. He had not taken a drink for weeks and, now that he'd admitted that he had a problem and wanted to be helped, things were getting easier and he felt that he was making good progress. He sat in the railway carriage with Jane, looking out at the fields flashing past the windows. The rhythmic clacketty clack of the wheels and the gentle swaying had a soporific effect and he put his head back and closed his eyes while Jane read the *Hereford Times*.

They were on their way to set up an exhibition of paintings in a London gallery. She'd been enjoying increasing success and now it was culminating in a one-man exhibition in the City Gallery in Regent Street. The pictures had gone on ahead by lorry and Chris and Jane were due at the gallery by two o'clock to supervise the hanging. "Gosh, I am nervous," she said, "I have lots of little butterflies flitting around in my tummy."

"Don't be nervous. It'll be a huge success and it'll lead to much greater things. Who knows where it might lead, a major exhibition like this in a leading gallery? I'm proud of you."

He leaned towards her and said, "The thing is, with these London galleries you never know who might come in and notice them."

"I can't help being nervous. It's because it's so important to me. It's not a hobby. I want this to be a big success and I want to be a famous artist, like Graham Sutherland."

"Graham Sutherland. Who's he? He can't be very famous because I've never heard of him. I've heard of Picasso though."

Jane looked at him and smiled, "Oh, I'll settle for being as famous as Graham Sutherland."

The exhibition was set up with much head–scratching and soul-searching. She spent a lot of time arranging the pictures so that they would be seen to their best advantage. One of the gallery workers who was helping stood back and said, "Lovely, they are; Lovely. You have no idea what a breath of fresh air it is to have pictures like this in the gallery."

"The clients of this place usually see these modern paintings. I can't make head nor tail of them and if the truth were told, neither can they. It's like the Emperor with no clothes on. All these so-called art connoisseurs only think what they think they ought to think, if you see what I'm getting at."

He wiped his hands on his overalls and putting his head on one side went on, "They're frightened of not being thought trendy and if one of the fashion gurus says that the Emperor is wearing nice clothes then they all say 'Oh, yes, aren't they lovely, look at the material and the line.' I get sick of them. Now these pictures; they're real art."

Jane smiled and said, "So you're the little boy who said, 'Why is the Emperor wearing no clothes?'"

"That's me," he grinned.

When he'd left the room Chris said, "Well, there you are, he liked them. Maybe that's a good omen."

Jane screwed up her face and said, "I'm not so sure. The clients of this sort of gallery have been conditioned to like a different sort of art. I can see them now looking down their noses at these and saying, 'Oh, this is just chocolate box art—pot boilers,' A lot of these people don't look at art in the same way I do. They've been conditioned by fashion and snobbery so I haven't got a lot of confidence that this exhibition is going to do well."

Chris put his arm round her waist and said, "Oh, let's wait and see. You might be surprised."

The private viewing took place that evening and by the time the last person had left every picture in the exhibition was sold.

"There you are," said Chris, kissing her on the cheek, "I told you it'd go well. You can't do better than sell every one before the exhibition opens to the public. I think you're on the first rung of the ladder of success and I'll hang on to the picture I bought from your gallery. It might be worth a lot of money soon."

They had booked into a hotel in Russell Square and Chris went back ahead of Jane while she stayed at the gallery to complete some paper work with the gallery owners. After it was completed, the owner and his wife invited her out to dinner to celebrate the exhibition's success.

"Oh, that's very kind of you," she replied, "Thank you."

"What about your friend Chris?" asked her host, "He's invited as well."

She replied that he'd gone back to the hotel and, as he'd already waited longer than he expected, he was probably in the dining room ordering dinner. "I told him to start without me if I was delayed," she explained.

So she was taken to dinner at a restaurant near the gallery and didn't get back to the hotel until late. She'd had an enjoyable evening. Her host had been generous and after a splendid meal he'd taken her to his club, so she didn't get back to the hotel until the early hours. There was no sign of Chris in their room, so she went down to reception to ask if he'd left a message for her.

"Just a moment, Madam," said the Receptionist, "I'll only be a minute or two," and she went through a door behind the desk.

Jane leaned against the desk while she was waiting and looked around at the opulent surroundings. As it was so late, she was the only one in the foyer. The Receptionist was a long time, so she sat down in one of the leather armchairs. She'd been on her feet all day and they were aching. She was reaching for a magazine when the Receptionist returned with a man in a dark suit. "Good evening, Miss Beddows. My name is Mr Grant, the Manager of this hotel and I'd like to have a word with you if I may."

What the Manager told her marked the end of her relationship with Chris Gregory. He explained that earlier in the evening the police had been called because Chris had been drinking heavily in the hotel bar. He'd become violent, damaged a lot of the fittings, and injured a barman.

He'd been taken off to a police station and was being kept in a cell. After enduring this humiliating interview with the Manager, she decided that she had come to the end of the road with Chris. She never saw him again.

It was Sunday morning and Tom went fishing as usual. He walked across the field with his rods and shoulder bag and arriving at the river bank he settled down to a good day's fishing. The weather looked to be set fair and the water was in excellent condition, so he was hoping for some good sport.

He looked up at the blue sky and thought, "It's good to be alive on a morning like this."

Sam was also up and about early. His first visit was to his friend Trevor's garage in the village. Trevor did servicing and repairs from an untidy garage in the main street. It looked more like a scrapyard than a garage and some of the steel advertising hoardings were pre-war. Rusty hulks of cars stood on the oily concrete and pieces of machinery littered the whole area.

Although it was early on Sunday morning, Trevor was at work and Sam found his old friend's feet sticking out from under a Land Rover. He gave the feet a gentle kick and said, "Good morning Trevor. I'd know those feet anywhere. How are you?"

Trevor emerged from under the vehicle wearing grease-stained overalls and smiling a grease-stained smile.

"Hi yah, Sam," he said, "I haven't seen you for a while. What brings you round here?"

"I was going for a Sunday morning stroll around the village and I thought I'd call in and ask for some professional advice, please."

Trevor had not shaved and his stubble was streaked with grease. His spectacles were held together with dirty sticking plaster. "Fire away," he said, wiping his hands on a rag and throwing it on the ground.

"Well, I've got a job as a chauffeur," he lied, "driving a posh chap from Leominster around the place and I think I'm losing a drop of hydraulic fluid from the brakes."

"Oh, dear," said Trevor, wiping his hands on his overalls and taking a cigarette from a packet on the Land Rover bonnet, "That could be dangerous."

"That's what I thought. It's a Jag and I was wondering if you could tell me how to fix it, because I'm taking him out for a drive this afternoon."

"Well, it's a difficult thing to explain just like that. Can't you bring it in for me to see?"

"Yes, I suppose I'd better, but could the brakes fail if they lost their fluid?"

"Oh, yes, they could go completely."

"I'd better bring it in then, rather than try and do it myself. Better to be safe than sorry." He paused and said, "How are the wife and kids?"

Trevor replied that they were fine and while he leaned against the wing of the Land Rover they talked about gardening; a mutual interest.

"But going back to this business of the brakes," said Sam, "Losing all the fluid causing failure, I mean. When you think of it that would be a good way of doing someone in, wouldn't it?"

"What do you mean?"

"Well, if I were writing a crime novel and I wanted to create the perfect murder I could get the bad guy to saw through the brake pipes with a hacksaw and then when the victim tried to brake on a hill —bingo—he'd go over the edge. The perfect crime."

Trevor grinned, "Good idea," he said, "but the problem is that when the police examined the car they'd see the sawn pipe, so it wouldn't be such a perfect murder."

"Oh," said Sam, sounding disappointed.

"No, what I'd do is just loosen a nut on the pipe and then he'd lose the fluid and it really would look like an accident. I'll show you what I mean if you like."

"Oh, it doesn't matter," said Sam, trying to sound as if he'd lost interest in the idea, "It was only a thought that struck me," then he crouched by the Land Rover and said, "Alright. Go on then."

Trevor pointed out the nut that could be slackened and Sam asked, "Would it be the same on a Jag?"

"Similar, but you'd need to loosen two nuts, one on the pipe crossing the groove just there and you'd have to loosen another one beside it on another pipe. They've got a dual system."

Sam left the garage grinning to himself and rubbing his hands together, "Couldn't be better," he thought.

His next visit was the Manor House and he approached from one of the side entrances, keeping in the shadow of the beech trees, and went into the house through the green door at the back.

"Hello, Edith," he said, as he entered the kitchen.

"Hello, Sam, it's been a while since I saw you."

Edith was a maid at the Big House and had been a close friend of Jean's when she worked there as a cleaner, "I was so sorry to hear about Jean."

"It was a shock, even though I was half expecting it, I was still knocked sideways. Is the kettle on?"

Edith was an elderly woman with frizzy white hair. She had spent a lifetime in service and the constant bending over sinks and ovens had taken its toll on her physique, so she had a pronounced stoop. While she made him a cup of tea he asked, "The house is quiet this morning. Is the Squire in?"

"Oh, you mean Jones. I don't know how that poor wife of his puts up with him, I really don't. She's such a nice lady too. Yes, he's in, and we're getting his lunch ready." She looked up as two more of the staff came into the kitchen. Edith handed him the tea cup.

"Oh, thank you, Edith, I need this tea because I've had a very nasty shock this morning."

"Oh?"

"Yes, it was terrible," He took a sip and put the cup down. Taking a deep breath he said, "I came here through the Dingle and walked along the river bank and I saw something awful."

The women gathered round expectantly and he continued, "There was an ambulance and people standing on the bank and there were policemen everywhere."

He shuddered and continued with his story, "They were pulling a body out of the water. He had a bad cut on his head; pouring blood it was, all over the policeman. I couldn't swear to it because he looked so horrible, but I reckons it was Tom Beddows." He closed his eyes and shuddered again.

There was a collective intake of breath from the women as he paused to take a drink. "Yes, he was in his fishing gear and he must've slipped into the water and hit his head on a rock. His eyes were all staring and wild-looking, but I'm pretty sure it was him. Terrible isn't it?"

"It's awful," replied Edith.

One of the women said, "It must have been him, because he goes fishing nearly every Sunday morning. Was it at Crawford's pool?"

"That's right."

"It was him then," she cried, "Oh, my God, the poor man."

"A terrible business," he mumbled, "Look, I'm still shaking," and he rattled his cup and saucer for dramatic effect.

Later, Sam was back at his house sitting in his kitchen and putting a new battery in a bicycle lamp. He snapped it shut and switched it on to check that it worked. Then the knock came. Brian was smiling broadly on the doorstep and holding a bulky envelope.

"Here you are, your money as promised. You've done a good job but now we forget all about it, okay? You and I will never meet again and neither of us will ever talk about these events again. Is that understood?"

Sam nodded and took the package.

"Now," said Brian, "get your wife and your envelope off to America," and he turned to go. Sam dropped the packet inside the door and walked with him to the gate.

"Nice car," he said, gesturing to the gleaming black Jaguar parked in the lane.

"Oh, it gets me around. Now don't forget what I said, we never talk about this to anyone okay?"

"Okay, it's a deal—hang on," said Sam, walking round the car with his head on one side, "Have you heard any rumblings coming from underneath?"

"No. It seems fine."

Sam got down on his knees and banged the exhaust with his fist, "I thought so," he said, groping under the car, "Your exhaust is almost off. I reckons the next bump you go over, it'll be lying in the road. I thought it looked loose when I was standing there."

"Damn!" said Brian, tapping the exhaust pipe with his foot.

"Don't worry, it's only a loose bracket. I can fix it for you in a jiffy if you hang on a minute," and he went round the side of the house, returning with some tools. "Only a couple of nuts to tighten."

He crawled under the car and after a few minutes he re-emerged and shaking the exhaust said, "There you are, as good as new."

Brian grunted his thanks and got into the car.

"Are you going straight home now?" asked Sam.

"Yes, why do you ask?"

Sam picked up his tools and said, "Oh, it's just that Bill Price is moving his herd down the Cwm road about now, so you might be better off taking the top road. You could be held up for ages with those lumbering great beasts. He's never in a hurry to get them out of the way."

"Okay," he said, winding up the window and starting the engine.

In the Old Black Lion that evening all the talk was about the car crash on the top road. The landlord was leaning on the bar talking to two of the men from the estate.

"It was the Squire," said Ben Holloway. They say the brakes failed on his Jag and you never saw such a mess. It left the road on the sharp bend by the old quarry and ended up on the rocks. He didn't stand a chance because the car was flattened.

They had to use cutting equipment to get the body out. Killed instantly, so they say."

The landlord wiped his moustache with the back of his hand and said, "I don't think there'll many tears shed for that man, but I wonder what will happen to the estate now he's gone."

The funeral took place in the village church and Miss Acton's narrow eyes glared down her nose from high up in the roof. The coffin stood directly under her and a stony stare was directed at her former pupil throughout the service. He was laid to rest near a yew tree and the mourners stood in a group round the grave. The sun shone brightly and a skylark was singing in the clear sky.

On the day that Brian met his end, Tom finished fishing early as he and Angela had arranged to go out for a drive. Not having a vehicle, he didn't have the opportunity to get out and about and he was looking forward to it. When she arrived at the river bank in the Land Rover, she lurched and bumped over the rough field and came to a standstill near the bank.

"I thought I'd never get here, Brian was in a funny mood and kept insisting that I stayed in. I kept telling him that I had an appointment with a sick cow, but he got furious and said it was about time I spent a Sunday with him. He's gone off somewhere himself now. In a great hurry he was, so I expect he's gone to see his bit of stuff in Hereford."

"Anyway here I am. I've been able to get away after all. There's been a strange atmosphere in the house, a lot of whispering and shaking of heads. I don't know what it was all about." She jumped from the vehicle and they kissed. "Did you catch anything?"

Tom tapped his bag and grinned broadly, "I've had a good day," he said, "The sun was shining, the birds were singing, and the fish were biting. What could be better?"

He loaded his tackle into the Land Rover and the vehicle bumped across the field towards the gate. Angela asked, "Where do you want to go?"

"I'd like to go and see the old factory site, please," and he dropped down from the cab to open the gate.

She leaned out of the window as the gate opened and asked, "Is that a good idea?"

"Why?"

"Well, won't it be upsetting for you, seeing the site which represents the shattering of all your dreams? You built up the biggest cider business in the world and now it's all gone and you're almost destitute. If I was in your position I'd burst into tears to see the ruins of it all."

He climbed back into the cab after closing the gate and said, "I might cry, but I'd like to go and see it, just the same."

The big vats had gone and the offices and warehouses were derelict. Most of the windows were smashed and boarded up. They went through the gates and she slowly drove round the site, steering carefully round debris lying on the concrete. Weeds were growing through the cracks and here and there a gorse bush had gained a foothold. She stopped and they opened the side windows to get a better view.

"The delivery lorries stood here," he said, "rows and rows of them, all green and gold. It was a lovely sight." Now it was an empty expanse of cracked concrete with sheep wandering across in search of better grass. "That was my office up there and I used to look down on the gardens, but they don't look much like gardens now. They've been plundered and they're just a rubbish tip."

He jumped out of the vehicle and walked around, kicking at stones. Then he picked one up and threw it at one of the remaining windows, which smashed and the sound echoed from the walls of the derelict warehouse. As the tinkling died away, he stood looking at the dereliction for a few minutes and then with a shrug climbed back into the Land Rover.

"You aren't going to cry are you?" asked Angela anxiously.

"No, men don't cry do they?" Then he buried his head in her neck, sobbing like a child.

After their day out, she dropped him off at the farm and drove back to the Manor House to find a police car parked at the front of the house as she swept down the drive.

"I'm very sorry, Mrs Jones," said the police officer, "I'm afraid I have some bad news for you."

The next few days were hectic. There was the funeral to be arranged and many other things to be done, but when it was over she was in the Old Black Lion having a drink with Tom.

He stretched his arms and said, " Ooh, I've had a hard day today and I must say it's nice to relax. How did you get on?"

"Well, we got him buried; the vicar said the words and the mourners gathered round the grave, just like all the other funerals, but I didn't feel anything. There were only a few people there as he didn't have much family. His parents are both dead and there was a distant cousin and an aunt, who wept some tears for him, but I couldn't find any to shed. They lowered the box into the ground and I just thought, 'Well that's the end of him, now I can get on with my real life at last'."

She reached for his hand and held it tight, "You're my real life and my future. I'm free now so there's nothing stopping us getting married."

"But he's hardly cold yet and I expect the gravedigger is covering him as we speak."

"I can't wait. We've got a lot of time to make up ánd I want to get started. I don't care what people might say. In fact most people who knew him would have every sympathy with us if we got together so soon after he's gone."

He lifted her hand and kissed it, "I can't wait either."

Tom left the tiny cottage and moved into the Manor House and standing in the Ballroom with his arm round Angela's waist he looked up at the painting of Major Hudson's ancestor in the gilt frame and said, "It's funny, I feel as if I've come back home."

She snuggled into him and said, "And now that you're here with me I feel as if it's home and I never did before."

When the legal matters had been concluded, Angela and Tom sat at the dining table reading a letter from the solicitor. Angela read it and then read it again. She slid it across the table to him and as he finished it she said, "You know what this means don't you? Everything he owned has come to me; the house and estate, your villa and yacht—as I still call them—and his businesses; the road haulage, the estate agency, the import concerns, everything. I own all the farms and the Scottish estates. It's all mine and he was a very rich man."

Tom read the letter again, "Yes, that's what it says," he smiled, "Everything has come to you, every penny of it. You're a rich woman now. A very rich woman."

She took his hand and squeezed it, "Now, this causes a problem doesn't it?"

"How does it?"

"As I'm so fabulously rich I can't see your asking me to marry you, because it'll look as if you're a fortune hunter."

Tom grinned.

She continued, "But I know a way round the problem, I'll do the asking," She took his hand again and said, "Tom will you do me the great honour of becoming my husband?"

Chapter Thirty Five

And so at the age of forty-nine, a new era in Tom and Angela's lives began. They married as soon as it could be arranged and once again he was Lord of the Manor of Kings Canon. He stood on the steps looking across the parkland and the gardener walked past, pushing his wheelbarrow, and said, "Welcome home, Sir."

Pete and Melanie were brought into the group as directors and they bought a black and white house in the village.

"No more lifting our feet to avoid the gushers," said Pete.

"And no more nasty oily tractor parts all over my kitchen," responded Melanie.

When they were all at the Manor for lunch one Sunday, Tom announced that they were going to have a party to celebrate the reversal in their fortunes.

"We'll invite everybody, but we'll wait until Christmas and have it on Christmas morning like Major Hudson used to do in the old days. It'll be the biggest party the old house has ever seen."

On Christmas morning, Tom went to the bedroom window and drew open the curtains, "It's a white Christmas. I've been dreaming of a morning like this for the big party."

It was a crisp sunny morning with a blue sky and there had been an overnight fall of snow. The big trees in the parkland were covered and looked magnificent against the sky with ragged winged crows circling above the white branches.

A large gathering of villagers, friends, and relatives, had assembled and once again the ballroom was full of light and noise and the scent of apple wood smoke and cigars. Tom mingled with the guests, shaking hands and exchanging Christmas greetings.

He was standing by the fireplace looking at the happy scene when an elderly couple moved towards him, "Congratulations," said the rosy-cheeked man, "It's good to see you back in the Big House. You belong here and I hope you and Lady Angela will be very happy."

Tom shook his hand and said, "Thank you Mr—?"

"Partridge, John Partridge. I'm a retired butcher. I used to be Angela's butcher and she invited us today," and turning to the woman at his side he said, "And this is my wife Nellie."

The woman shook his hand.

"So you are Nellie Partridge!" he exclaimed, trying not to look at her ample bosom, "My Granddad used to talk about you a lot and he said he liked your dumplings."

"What do you—?"

"So you're not a figment of old Frank's imag—Well, well, well. Nice to meet you." She looked perplexed as he walked away, mumbling, "You old rascal, Frank."

Pete stood on a chair and banged the table with a spoon to gain attention.

"Ladies and gentleman," he began, "and boys and girls, a Happy Christmas to you all and thank you for coming to our gathering this morning. Once again the Beddows family is in the Big House and we are delighted to see so many of you coming along to help us celebrate on this beautiful Christmas morning."

"I know that Tom was keen to have this party because he remembers, as I remember, coming on Christmas mornings to this room. We used to stand just here on this very spot, afraid to move, because our mother had threatened us to stand still and not let her down. I wasn't big enough to see what was on the table and Old Frank stood there, Walter there, and our father, Ken, over there by the fire."

"I know that many of you will remember them with affection. Tom came from very humble beginnings and he first met his childhood sweetheart, the beautiful Angela, while they were at school. They lost touch with each other and went their separate ways until their paths came together again just a few months ago."

"Ladies and Gentlemen, I'm a great believer in fate and I think that this couple were destined to be together against all the odds. Both Tom and Angela have been no strangers to unhappiness and Tom has had the most remarkable ups and downs and suffered real tragedy. In the story of these two people, we have witnessed a real-life drama and a real-life love story. They grew up in a beautiful part of the world and in their Herefordshire Garden of Eden there have been many influences shaping their lives. I'm sure you'll all know what I mean, when I say, that of all the influences the greatest two have been apples and serpents." There was laughter and applause and when the applause had died down, he concluded, "I do like a story with a happy ending, don't you? Please join me in a toast—to Tom and Angela—Tom and Angela."

When the party was over, Tom stood in the big window with his arm around Angela and she asked, "What are you looking at so intently out there?" He was looking with narrowed eyes across the snow. The light was fading and a tinge of red was appearing in the sky, reflecting from the snow and giving it a rosy hue. The laden branches were turning into a criss–cross, linear pattern of pink against the red sky. "I was looking at that hunched figure in the snow collecting firewood. Do you know who it is?"

Angela looked across the snow and replied, "Yes, I know who it is. It's someone who's down on his luck. They tell me it's a man who's living in your old shack in the woods. He's had a hard time, an accident maimed him and he turned to drink. Everything's gone wrong for the poor chap and his life's in ruins," she sadly shook her head. "He's taken to the woods and he's struggling to survive, just as you did. What a way to spend Christmas, gathering wood in the snow."

"What's his name?"

"Oh, someone said he's called Chris, er, Chris Gregory, I think they said. Something like that anyway."

Tom was expressionless for a moment and then his eyes widened and his mouth opened. "Chris Gregory. I know who he is. He got together with my sister for a while and I remember now how his life came crashing down around his ears and he lost everything. The poor chap. He turned to drink because his life wasn't going right and it ruined him. I know exactly how he feels. I never had a drink problem, but I can sympathize with him, and he never had any opportunities for pulling himself out of the mess. Not like I did."

Tom stood deep in thought and then said, "Just a moment," and went upstairs, leaving Angela looking across the pink snow.

When he returned, he kissed her on the cheek and, wrapping himself against the icy wind, left the house and trudged through the snow. Angela watched him moving towards the huddled figure, dark against the pink. She saw the tracks of the two figures converge as they came together. It began to snow again and Tom handed something to the man.

"A Happy Christmas to you," said Tom, "The name is Chris isn't it?"

The ragged figure looked startled to hear his name and dropped his bundle of firewood. Tom continued, "I have something for you, a little Christmas present."

He handed him a small box wrapped in festive paper with a bow on the top and then, saying, "A Very Happy Christmas to you," he turned and retraced his steps to the house where Angela was still standing in the window.

It was snowing heavily now and as he neared the house he could see her silhouetted against the coloured lights of the Christmas tree. The sound of Christmas carols drifted across the snow from the house and light radiated from the window; the stained glass making coloured shapes on the snow.

Chris Gregory pulled off one of his woollen gloves and, blowing on the stump of his lost hand which pained him in the cold weather, opened the box. The fingers on his good hand were cold and stiff and he fumbled with the wrappings, eventually opening it with his teeth. Inside he found a note,

> *Dear Chris*
> *My Granddad gave me this for a Christmas*
> *present many years ago, and I found it very useful.*
> *I hope you find it useful too. Keep it somewhere safe.*
> *A Happy Christmas from Tom Beddows*

Underneath the note he found a piece of crumpled paper, yellowing and torn. He looked at it for a moment with furrowed brow and then with a smile put it inside his coat, picked up his bundle, and shuffled off towards the wood. He paused and, looking over his shoulder at the lights radiating from the house onto the snow, whispered "Thank you," and then more loudly "Thank you, Granddad". His weary shuffle changed to a more lively motion as he disappeared from view into the frozen Cwm Woods.

Epilogue

The old man in The Black Lion lifted his tankard and finished the last of his cider. He lowered it to the table with a flourish and looked at the young holiday makers.

The couple sat in silence, staring at him expressionlessly as he leaned back in his chair, stretching his arms and yawning.

It was the young man who broke the silence, "What an incredible story; amazing." He shook his head in disbelief. "So the man who was leaving in that big car as we arrived was Chris Gregory, the owner of Gregory's Country Cider?"

The old man smiled and slowly nodded his head. He opened his mouth to reply, but was distracted by the arrival of a large woman. "Ah!" he said, "Got to go now. The wife's come to collect me."

He rose to his feet, "Hello, Dear, I've just been telling these young people a story; all about what goes on in this sleepy village of ours." And turning to them said, "By the way, let me introduce my wife Nellie—Nellie Partridge."

Cappella Archive
Limited Editions

Cappella Archive provides a similar mastering service for the written word that a recording studio does for music. The typeset book file is stored in a digitized Archive and copies are printed on request as they are ordered; the Archive behaving as the printing equivalent of audio or video dubbing.

Cwm Maerdy Farm

Lower

H

Church

Westwood Farm

Village Hall

Court Farm